"To Pokolbin Prison, please," requested a woman in a very weak, barely audible low voice I could well relate to. A vision came to me of a gaunt, sickly, very depressed lady.

I worked out her travel plan. She had to catch a bus, two trains, and a bus again, for a three-hour journey. Then she asked, "How much would it cost for a pensioner and a three-year old?"

Tears gathered in my eyes. A poor young mother with a young child trying to visit her worthless husband at Christmas!

And she was not alone. "To John Moroney Prison, please," said a miserable mother.

To Silverwater Correction Centre, please." A sad girlfriend.

"To Long Bay Jail, please." A wretched daughter.

Long-suffering souls requested travel plans for Lithgow Jail, Parklea Jail, Goulburn Jail—you name it.

Come to think of it, there was hardly a male caller wanting to visit a female prisoner. Either the men did not use public transport or they didn't bother to visit. What did this tell you?

PRAISE FOR SYDNEY'S SONG

'This is a beguiling story which offers a new slant to the genre of "chick-lit" in that its heroine Sydney steadfastly holds principles that put her out of step with her generation of youth, with their partying ways and easy sex.

The voice of the central character Sydney is good and reads authentically on the page. SYDNEY'S SONG is intelligent, touching, interesting and funny.

This well-told, humorous, moving and heart-warming story is based on the author's own experiences but she has never deviated from the golden rule of fiction, and that is to tell her story well. Weaving the story around deftly drawn fictional characters, the author relives her own teenage traumas and her husband's accident. She visits his sufferings and shows the world that living with disabilities does not prevent a person from attaining happiness.'—*IRINA DUNN, director of Australian Writers Network, Sydney*

'SYDNEY'S SONG by Ia Uaro is an autobiographical novel of romance and struggle, a heart-warming tale of devotion and endurance… The early part of the story is the best part, featuring as it does Sydney's work on the city's 1-300-500 transit information telephone line. Long digressions to describe her experiences with callers give the book its primary source of intriguing detail. Watching Sydney's relationship with Pete in its early stages provides a good grounding for the drama that occupies the latter part of the book.

Sydney's Song demonstrates the way in which human beings can thrive under adversity using the power of their hearts and wills.'—*MATT POSNER, novelist, speaker, teacher, http://schooloftheages.webs.com, Queens, New York*

'A fantastic love story grounded quite firmly in a suburban setting with real characters. An honest and emotional story of incredible passion and emotion, SYDNEY'S SONG captures you from the off. Its serious story of love and heartbreak is expertly juxtaposed against the humour of the call centre.'—*JACOB COATES, Jaffa Books, Brisbane*

'…The twists and turns inside this book make the reading fairly easy. I found myself turning pages as fast as I could.

There is SO much more to this story, but I believe that you the reader should experience it for yourself. The morale is to listen to your heart and not always to those around you. Believe in something, anything, and then make it happen.

... The writing was superb, the story kept me interested and the ending touched me in ways most books don't. God works in mysterious ways sometimes, and this book proves it. I recommend this book to anyone, male or female, who is trying to find their way in this world.'—*PHIL NORK, author of real-life fiction, www.philipnork.com, Henderson, Nevada*

'This book is riveting in its context and in the author's expressions of a set time in her life. It has the honest and open opinions of a young woman who is very keenly perceptive in all people and situations about her.

I have also learned many things as it pertains to the Australian way. Many pieces of language and terminologies are apparently privy to that corner of the world. I found them to still be comprehensible; sometimes light and airy, sometimes comical.

The ultimate thrust of the story; the love, honor and valor of a very young woman placed in a very difficult situation, was vividly seen throughout the story! I applaud the author for her compassion in sharing this story and conveying the important issues of brain injuries which could happen to anybody at any time. Great story!'—*NORMA FOWLER, author of The False Prophet and several other novels, Northern Kentucky*

'Wow, what a beautiful story! Not just a look at life through the eyes of another, this story takes you on a journey as a girl travels from childhood to become a strong woman who can deal with whatever life throws at her. Tears fill your eyes as she struggles with disaster only to be replaced with pride as she triumphs over each obstacle. You will also find a good balance of laughter…'—*MERLENE M. ALLISON, author of A Whisper of Secrets, Jasper, Georgia*

'This book is a wonderful and compelling love story. Sydney and Pete brought me to tears thanks to my own related real experience. I highly recommend this to anyone who understood the power of love before they reached adulthood. The exploration of the dynamic of the broken family was deeply moving. I consider myself a happy bystander who had the honor to read about Pete and Sydney living their lives.'—*J. LENNI DORNER, author, what-are-they.com*

'It's amazing and emotional love story that pulls you in at the first page. If you can get past reading the first page you better make time in your day because you'll be hooked unable to put it down. SYDNEY'S SONG is written with such honest passion that's practically oozing off the pages. When Sydney isn't happy it makes you want to cheer her up, when her heart is racing you just want to check your own pulse, and when love is in the air you have to make sure to breath.

It's one of those stories that touches more than just the surface of love, but travels deep within the structure testing it every so often and battles all odds to come out on top.

…I feel very blessed to have been given the opportunity to read SYDNEY'S SONG. Thank you for creating such a masterpiece and for reminding me of the miracles of love even in the hardest of times.'—*BRENDA FRANKLIN, author of fantasy fiction, Louisiana*

'I have to say when I first started reading this book; it started off a bit slow, interesting but slow. However, the interesting part kept me reading and reading until to my sadness I was at the end. I felt as though I was walking along beside Sydney on her adventures, misadventures, ups and downs. I truly began to feel for her and what she was going through.

… I loved the banter and the frequent uses of the various Australian dialects; it really made me feel as though I was right there in Australia! Oh and the ending; I LOVED the epilogue! A perfect ending to such a great read… OMG wonderful. Aplaud, applaud!'—*REYNA HAWK, author of the Valentine/Petrilo Series, Alabama*

'… Haunting.'—*MARY METCALFE, author of Winds of Change, Canada*

'…I was too busy laughing and crying at every twist and turn of this story… This book is a love song; a song of songs to her beloved, to whom with amazing devotion she dedicates her life. What better quote for her transformation than the one at the opening: "You'll know who I am by the song that I sing." The soul and the voice are one.

It is hard, if not impossible, to fit this work into a literary genre, because the first half reads like an adorable girl-meets-boy story, only to take a sharp turn when… This is where the real fight, the fight for his survival begins; this is where you will get completely hooked with the Sydney's character.

The author of Sydney's Song is an artist as well... Inspired by real events in her life, this story is a tribute to her spirit, her voice, and her song.

Five stars.' — *UVI POZNANSKY, Author of Apart From Love, California*

'It is certainly a fact that many artists use their own knowledge and experience to focus on the meaning of life. However, and in spite of most writers' artistic skills, not all of them can touch people's hearts. Sydney's Song is one of these emotional stories that readers won't easily forget. Ia Uaro's beautiful, poetic words and splendid drawings accompany the avid reader on an emotional journey to the characters' minds and yearning desires. The author takes an in-depth look to the mental anguish caused by physical disabilities but, at the same time, gives a glimmer of hope that shines throughout the pages.'—*SADIE DUARTE, scriptwriter and author of Alas para Soñar, Spain*

'A Song to Remember. I related to Sydney the moment I met her. She was a teen product of divorce… But Pete took her into his heart and under his wing. Their relationship was beyond love and adoration. Their capacity to know, to sense and to FEEL each other shone throughout the story. Sydney's tenacity during tragedy was remarkably well described and…I wanted to stand up and cheer for her. Throughout the story, I cried, I laughed and I swelled with pride when young Sydney grew from shy teenager to a take-charge woman...I recommend "Sydney's Song" for young adults, parents, teachers, music lovers and anyone who does not believe that love exists beyond the physical plane. Five Stars!'—*BRIANNA LEE MCKENZIE, author of Enchanted Heart, Chesapeake Bay*

Ia Uaro

Sydney's song

This edition published in September 2012
First published in September 2012

Illustrations:
Vignettes by Ia Uaro
Portraits by Alexandra Davidoff
"Make Way For Ducklings" by Abbir and Will Belacqua

Ia Uaro
Sydney

Email: info@sydneyssong.net
Web: sydnessong.net

ISBN-13: 978-1478157458
and
ISBN-10: 1478157453

Internal design by Hope Welsh (www.ninjameldesigns.com)
Cover design by Ideantity (www.ideantity-sg.com)
Web design by FANU Solutions (www.fanusolutions.com)

Acknowledgements

My special thanks to Irina Dunn, critic and editor extraordinaire whose vision and sharp eye finally brought me to the finish line. You are Sydney's Treasure.

To Fanu Solutions and Ideantity, many thanks for a fantastic job on my website sydneyssong.net.

A lot of love and a lot of help from my families and friends have also accompanied the journey of this story. My deepest gratitude to:

Hubby. For everything.

My late father-in-law. For never giving up on hubby.

All hospital staff who looked after hubby for over 9 months. You are never forgotten, "*surprisingly*".

Uni *"band"* who sang by the lake. For posting up inspiring good-old-time pictures.

Charlie and Nidamus Prime. For naming the characters. You rock!

Dear darling daughter. IT support extraordinaire. Horrid taskmaster, even when falling asleep. Also for pulling me off my laptop to run around the oval. Nobody can be more beautiful than D.

Leonardo Dreoni for his input on Borgo San Lorenzo. Grazie.

My in-laws, Shaun, Jacqui, and Cynthia. For much appreciated feedback.

Fiona KW. *There are friends who pretend to be friends, but there is a friend who sticks closer than...*

Hamda K for checking the medical facts and always being there.

Aristina, Véronique, Guido, Isw, Mark, Clive, Siobhan, Bruno and Geoff, and the stars of a constellation. Just because.

Allan Wilford Howerton. For his friendship and support, tips, and for making me laugh.

Sean Huxter, for going through my manuscript even when crunching at work.

Will Belacqua, Abbir, and Alexandra Davidoff. For donating portrait and duck illustrations.

My opinionated, supportive friends of Amazon writers' boards. I will always treasure our writerly camaraderie and learning experience with fondness.

Jacob Coates, Sarah Lane, Mary W. Walters, Faith Mortimer, Brianna Lee McKenzie, Ben Winegarner, Gary Jones, Al Boudreau, Thomas A. Knight, Hope Welsh, and Gypsy Madden. For various assistance.

And Bronson. Of course.

Author's Notes

This is a work of fiction based on true stories and real events, woven using fictional characters.

The 1300500 calls have all been true. Every single one, unfortunately.

Names, times, locations have been altered (except names of the hospital staff, although I've changed the hospital's). Any resemblance is purely coincidental or used fictitiously.

The spelling used is Australian English, except when an American is speaking. God is referred to as "he" when the speaker is an atheist, as "He" when the speaker is a theist.

I did not set out to write tortuous vernaculars. The choice of words and phrases flowed naturally. For non-Aussie readers, in case needed here are some regional terms:

arvo – afternoon,
barbie – barbeque
bloke – man
bogan – low-cultured person
brekkie – breakfast
bush – forest
coldie – beer
grog – alcohol
gum tree – eucalyptus tree
HSC – High School Certificate
idiot box – TV
journo – journalist
Pom – British
pressies – presents
schoolies – a week-long Australian school-leavers' party
slower than a wet week – boring
uni – university
woop-woop – far-flung

FEEDBACK ON AUSSIE SLANG

My very best friend, author Allan Wilford Howerton, 89-year-old American WW2 veteran, retired federal civil servant, has proven Aussie slang isn't that difficult to digest. I showed him my Author's Notes and asked for his feedback. Allan, who had never heard of the above Aussie slang, promptly wrote:

"This non-journo bloke having read your Author's Notes this arvo without benefit of an idiot box or consultation with a brogan and sans the influence of neither coldie nor grog, do herewith pronounce it acceptable for perusal 'neath gum tree or wherever no matter how woop-woop the setting whether a slower than a wet week uni or lively schoolie."

For all my friends of a million yesterdays
*You'll know who I am by the song that I sing**

*) This line from John Denver's "Today"

This Is How You Cheat Using an Orange Travelpass

Early November 1999

"This is how you cheat using an Orange Travelpass," an Irish voice penetrated my gloomy thoughts.

I was standing against the wall outside the Asquith League Club at Waitara, where my training sessions for Sydney's public-transport inbound call centre were held. This was the second Monday of my training at work. I can hardly tell you about the first week. I don't remember much. My parents had abandoned me. The shock made me unaware of my surroundings. I had not noticed things.

Looking back, I would label this period "Life as a Zombie". The walking dead. When my best friends Lucy and Brenna were in Queensland's Surfers Paradise for schoolies burning the floor dancing to "Walk Like An Egyptian", I Walked Like A Zombie.

My dog Dimity was the love of my life. But she was at home. And I was stuck here, training. I couldn't form any opinion about this job yet. My mind was not here most of the time.

The company I signed with was a branch of an American call centre. They had just landed their first big contract in Australia. A government one. Our job would be to handle integrated transport-information systems within Greater Sydney—area bordered by Lithgow, Port Stephens, Goulburn and Nowra—which had two-million public-transport trips a day. We would feed requests into our computer and it would spit out the answers.

So far I had been rather oblivious of my colleagues. Vaguely I knew they were a bunch of boisterous young people. And numerous nice oldies. Those were my first impressions of them. I was totally unsuspecting of how great a role they would play in my life very soon after.

Today before the training some of us chatted outside. I stood silent, dark sunnies on, trying to hide my eyes just in case tears welled up, which after my recent issues was a common occurrence. But the backpacker kids were disgustingly cheerful on this bright, beautiful Australian morning.

Several male voices with Pommy accents responded to the Irish girl. About a third of the new recruits had non-Australian accents, many of them backpackers. I turned to look at them. Before today, I had barely noticed these kids. For whatever reason, perhaps because of that imposing Irish girl, I watched them now. The red-haired girl was in the middle of delivering a dissertation on how to cheat using an Orange Travelpass.

"You must make sure you board the bus *only* when there are other passengers with you," she lectured. "You must hold your ticket up when you step onto the bus, so the driver will see it in your hand. Then you let other people put their tickets in the machine, while you continue to the back of the bus still holding your ticket up. The driver won't notice whether you put your ticket into the machine or not."

They all hung on to her every word with mesmerized looks on their faces. Perhaps they were interested in what she was saying, trying to save a few cents of their hard-earned money, or perhaps they were interested in her.

"So one ticket gets you from Lane Cove to the City to Bondi Beach to Manly to Narrabeen," she concluded. "By bus and ferry unlimited."

"But an inspector may show up," piped a Pom. "He'll check

the trip prints at the back!"

"That's a Travelten," the girl told him breezily. "With a Travelpass bought from a newsagent, you won't get into trouble because it doesn't print the date of first use."

"Are you that desperate?" An American accent. Handsome black-haired guy. "Are you really using the same ticket week after week?"

"Sheesh," the girl bristled. "I hate it when you're being goody-goody. Haven't you ever, ever been so broke? Now I also have to buy a weekly train ticket from St Leonards to Hornsby!" She turned to the other boys, "There are times we can't even afford grog, and that's worse, isn't it?"

There was a chorus of agreement.

I wondered what it felt like to be this girl. To be that confident and at ease. To have an interesting life that she apparently enjoyed. Travelling. Drinking. Cheating. Not a care in the world. Perhaps I should get a life. Save some money and join Alex, one of my best friends, backpacking wherever he might be. No one would miss me anyway.

This thought depressed me again. Absentminded, I followed my co-workers into the training room.

"You smell very nice," commented a girl to my left.

I turned to her with a start. It was the Irish girl. "Sorry? What did you say?"

"Woolgathering, are you?" she grinned. "So early in the morning?"

"Sorry. Yes. I guess. I was lost."

Her smile broadened—an engaging smile that reached her eyes and produced a very deep dimple on her right cheek. She had very neat, not very white teeth. She had curly bright red hair tamed with a twist and a chopstick-like hair ornament at the back, and cute little freckles on her prettily-shaped uptilted nose. Blue eyes.

"I'm Sinead," she introduced herself. "From Dooblin."

"Yes. I noticed the accent."

"I saw you outside. Dark sunglasses on. Trying your best to look aloof and unapproachable."

I choked. If only she knew why! "Nothing like that. I—I'm Sydney."

"Hi Sydney. You smell very nice." She inhaled. "Very subtle. You're good at choosing a perfume."

"Not me," I became flustered. "Mum. She knows things like that."

"Oh blessed!"

"So, you travelling? How do you find Australia?"

"Grand! I loov Australia," she kissed her fingers, blowing a kiss. "Quite an education. We work and we travel." She gestured towards her backpacking buddies, some of whom sat nearby. "That's Pete. He's from Boston. I met him while working at Mt Buller. We were ski instructors last winter. And that's Lindsay from London. I met him while Pete and I were planting baby pine trees for the Forestry Department around Tumut. Do you know where that is?"

I shook my head.

"Do you know Batlow's apples? Tumut is a small place near Batlow. Well, your Forestry people planted new pine trees in the mountains there near the end of winter. Gosh, it was so cold! But very good money. Shame about that job, the team moved to work on Kangaroo Island. Too remote for me to go along..." She sounded wistful. "Then we headed north. Hard to get a job though. We've been spending and spending. Until this job."

"So you'll do 1300500 for the Sydney Olympics?"

"No no no. We backpackers are temps. *Casuals*. They took us on to support the opening of 1300500's Hornsby centre. They guesstimate we'll assist for the first three months. The plan is, when permanent employees get some experience and speed, we temps will be dismissed."

"You'll have to find another job?"

"Not here. It'll be getting cold here. What's the use of being in Australia if we don't feel warm? I've had enough cold at Mt Buller and Tumut. And hell, I'm from Ireland! I'll go to the sunshine. Queensland."

Next we had to be quiet because the trainer, humorous Matt, started speaking.

"Most inner streets of a suburb are designed to get a bus every half an hour. So that when they hit the main corridor on their way to the City their combined frequency is every five minutes. Think of it like small creeks flowing into a river."

I had lunch with Sinead in the League Club café. I had a turkey sandwich. She had hot chips—and nothing else.

"When you travel you have to be really careful with your spending," she explained. Right. Seemed like if she bought something to go with her chips, she would have less funds for booze. "Are you from around here?"

"Yes. Beecroft. Been there all my life."

"Where's that?"

"Northern Line. Eight minutes' train-trip away."

Our location was confidential, perhaps out of fear callers would bomb us for giving out wrong information. But since it was more than eleven years ago and they have since moved away, I guess it wouldn't matter anymore if you knew where we were, right? The training did take place at the Asquith League Club, but my office was going to be on George Street, next door to Hornsby Library, several minutes' walk from Hornsby Mall's water clock—our emergency meeting point in case of fire.

The suburbs Waitara and Hornsby belong to the green and leafy Hornsby Shire, Sydney's northern gateway if you are travelling north to the Central Coast or Newcastle. Vast and sprawling with residential suburbs and eucalyptus forests, Hornsby Shire is located 25km from Sydney's city centre and 130km from Newcastle. It has a population of 160,000, roughly 22,000 among them in the suburb Hornsby and 11,000 in my suburb Beecroft.

"I'm staying at Lane Cove," Sinead volunteered. "That's by bus from St Leonards. With the English boys. Lindsay and Mark and Gareth. Pete—you know, tall, black hair, green eyes? He used to travel with us, but he's so lucky he has relatives here in Roseville. He's staying with them rent-free. So he can afford to pay proper fares. Did you hear him this morning? He's the only

American. I hate it when he starts to moralise. '*Pay proper fares. Drink only when you can afford it'*," she did a poor imitation of his accent, "Where's the fun in that?"

"Maybe he's concerned you'll get into trouble."

"He always is. But then he's old. He's 22, you know. All the others are under 20. Come on, follow me, I'll introduce you to them." She dabbed her mouth delicately with a paper napkin. "They've been curious about you. The very pretty, very silent girl."

Oh? Had my silence made me stand out? How embarrassing.

Before long I found myself in front of a group of boys. A tall and very handsome blond hunk stood next to the tall and handsome American. There was also a scruffy dude with brown, curly hair. Another one with very short blond hair looked stern. They gave me inquisitive stares. I did not know what to say.

"This is Sydney, guys," Sinead cheerfully introduced us. "Kevin. Pete. Gareth. Lindsay. Kevin's an Aussie."

I nodded to their "Hi", "Hey", "Hello", and "How do you do?"

"I've seen you at the station," short-haired Lindsay told me. This guy was of medium height, gym-honed, with piercing silver eyes. I was to find out later that he never, ever smiled, although at times he would laugh. Shiny blond hair covered his muscled arms. "But you catch the train from the wrong platform."

"Wrong for you," Sinead interjected. "She has to go to the Northern Line."

"Join us for drinks after work," Lindsay moved in. "Then it'll be the right platform."

I looked at them warily.

"After work?" Sinead pressed.

"Um—I can't. I'm not 18 yet."

"Ahh, a baby... But that's no problem," Kevin said with a devastating killer smile. Later I was to find out that he was 19, a student of Pure Physics at Macquarie Uni, partied hard and changed girlfriends on a regular basis. "We adults will get the drinks." He winked.

"Then we'll all go somewhere to get foxed," Lindsay added.

I contemplated them. Perhaps they could see my apprehension, because Pete—the spunk with blue-black hair—came closer. This guy exuded calm. He was not as athletic as Lindsay, but with his height and magnificent broad shoulders he radiated strength. And there was grace in his movements. It was in the way he walked and in the way he tilted his head. I felt the hair rise on the back of my neck.

"Have you ever been totally drunk?" he asked in a very pleasant voice. Questioning eyes. Very, very alluring eyes. Deep-set. Exquisitely shaped. Beautiful brows. Long thick lashes. I felt entranced, lost in his eyes.

I shook my head.

"Wanna try it?" he asked slyly.

I shook my head, feeling really, really worried.

"Then stay away from this bunch!"

Ohh... he only meant to scare me away? For a moment he had given me a bad impression of him. Whew!

"Confound it Pete!" Sinead punched him. "You're such a wet blanket!"

He stepped back but looked unfazed.

"Ignore him. Pete's a killjoy, a goody-goody prude," Sinead told me. Really? What was he doing, hanging out with this lot himself? "We'll convert you yet. We'll have you hitting the pubs and cutting loose with us soon."

"Just look at her," Pete warned Sinead. "You've frightened her."

"You did," Sinead retorted.

"Did not."

"Did too. No need to force your stitched-up wowser values on the rest of us. Now sod off!" Sinead glared at him before whirling back to me. "Sydney? Come with us? It'll be mighty fun!"

"I—," I took a deep breath. "I don't think I'll try it. Yet. Um— I'm not ready."

During the next training session my eyes kept darting towards the gorgeous American. At one point he looked straight at me and made eye contact. I shivered but refused to look away. He nodded imperceptibly.

That afternoon I saw Sinead and Kevin laughing aloud together, arms around each other, as they climbed the steps of Waitara Station. When we reached the platform Pete was already up there, loosening his tie.

"Too hot for you, mate?" Kevin asked him.

"This is the first job I've had to wear a tie for outside the States," Pete grumbled. "Today sure is hot."

"You'll get cooked next month!" Kevin informed him cheerfully, before continuing his outrageous flirting with Sinead.

I took the train home from the *wrong* platform, from Waitara to Hornsby and changed to a Beecroft train. I thought about Sinead's invitation. Was I a coward? How was I going to get a life if I was a coward? But was life about drinking for the sake of drinking? How essential was getting totalled for its own sake? Could a person have fun without alcohol?

If they were prepared to get completely hammered and have sex too, would they also take drugs? Was being high on drugs the only way to achieve true liberation? How lasting would that be? If I went out with them to drown my sorrow, what guarantee was there that I would not wake up in anguish as I had been doing lately?

Remember The Traffic Jam At Olympic Park?

Late October 1999

My parents broke my heart right after I completed high school.

It was a Friday. It had started as an ordinary, beautiful spring day. One when you woke up to the fresh air, a cloudless blue sky, and rosellas squealing on the green branches outside your bedroom window, you felt grateful for your own lovely piece of heaven. There was no sign at all it was going to turn ugly that the painful memories of the day would remain with me forever.

In the morning, the HR manager who interviewed me a few days earlier called to offer me the job. I was ecstatic. I ran to the backyard, scooping up my grey, long-haired dog.

"Dimity!" I shrieked. "My first job! Wish I could tell Mum and Dad!" My strict parents would be driving at the moment. It was *so* unfair that they had asked the phone company to block calls from our landline to mobiles. "You know what Dimity? I'm going to buy my very own mobile phone with my first pay!"

Sensing my happiness, Dimity responded with a few celebratory yips. But she was not the exuberant puppy she once was. Old Dimity had been my companion since I was a toddler.

I danced and sang. When I let her go, I did a bit of gardening, still singing. While my best friends usually told me to shut up, poor Dimity put up with my off-key singing. She was a very understanding and considerate bearded collie.

My backyard bloomed with colour. Yeah, I was one of the many Aussies with a green thumb. Although our gardener mowed the lawn and did general cleaning, most of the flowers had been my work. I grew various types of plants to bloom at different months of the year. Lavender and hydrangeas adorned the back fence which bordered natural bushland, while roses blossomed along the walkway. I was passionate about roses and had planted many varieties. The wind had blown lots of petals off the flowers, turning the walkway pink. It was my favourite time when this happened. I called it "My Garden of Love".

When I cleaned up, a car with a P-plate pulled into the driveway. My best friends Lucy, Brenna and Alex came to take me ice skating at the nearby Macquarie Centre. As we were having lunch at the food court by the ice rink, we chatted about our plans. Alex was about to travel the world and defer uni for a year. Brenna and Lucy were going to the schoolies in Queensland. I told them about my upcoming call-centre job.

Now, Lucy's first job was dancing as a ballerina with a Pennant Hills ballet company. Brenna's first job was busking, playing her cello by the water clock at Hornsby Northgate shopping centre. Once she even climbed up the gigantic clock and played its chimes. Meanwhile, Alex taught little kids swimming at Hornsby Aquatic Centre. And they all burst out laughing to hear that my first job would be a supposedly very easy call-centre job.

"That won't need any skills or talent, will it?" Alex asked unnecessarily.

"Just you wait!" I wasn't offended, "In February I'll start uni and study animation. Someday, your kids will be watching the movies I make!"

"But how can you be happy now?" Lucy questioned. "When I dance, I love it! When Brenna plays cello, she's ecstatic. Alex teaches little kids swimming knowing he'll save lots of lives in the future."

Brenna's first job was busking, playing her cello,
by the water-clock at Hornsby shopping centre

"And when I tell people how to catch public transport to work, they'll earn their rent or mortgage. When they go to watch a game, they won't have to drive through the congested roads around the stadium. Remember the traffic jam at Olympic Park when Dad dropped us off? We ended up walking to the concert 'cause it was faster."

"I've heard that call-centre pay isn't good, though," Brenna chirped in.

"Probably. But as long as we pay tax, we contribute to the economy. Right?"

My friends continued to tease me and became annoyed when they could not make me angry. I had always been placid. Basked in my family's love, I felt very secure of my place in the world.

"So you wanna prove you aren't the average lazy, snooty rich girl?" Alex asked.

"Alex. We aren't wealthy," I told him distractedly as I watched a little girl in the ice rink flailing about. Her attentive big brother quickly caught her arm. Nice.

"You're comfortably well off," Alex stated. "Never had to work during high school."

"That's because my parents have been pushing me to concentrate on my studies, so paranoid about me not getting a place at uni after the HSC. Besides, I have no skills to earn money. Can't dance. Can't play any instrument. Can't teach."

"How was it your parents sent you to a public school instead of a private school? They could've afforded it."

"To be in touch with the real world." I rolled my eyes. "My parents had to work hard during their studies. They often tell me that kids should sweat through their education. But I enjoyed our school heaps."

"She's your down-to-earth Aussie girl," Brenna commented. "Jeans and all."

"We all know that," Alex told me, knowing he could annoy a close friend and still be forgiven, "The boys at school always say your only saving grace from being labelled a tomboy is the way you walk! It's so graceful and elegant like your mum's."

"Why, thank you!"

"Speaking of clothes," he went on unperturbed, "it's almost Christmas and there are lots of vacancies as shop assistants. If you don't have any skills, why didn't you apply to be one?"

"'Cause I dread meeting people. I can only laugh and be noisy with my parents and close friends. The notion of talking to strangers face to face makes my tummy churn."

"Why this job?" Blond and tall Lucy asked. She was analytical and the smartest girl in our class.

"My contribution to the Olympics." Olympic fever was running high in Sydney and thousands of Australians had offered to volunteer for free. "Never mind the low pay—I'm thrilled to be part of it! Besides, the HR manager said I could switch to weekend part-timer when uni starts. And the office isn't far."

It was going to be a time of my life, I thought, foolishly feeling secure that face-to-face conversations with my customers weren't required. Little did I know I would have to meet hundreds of co-workers. Little did I know my customers were going to be very angry commuters disillusioned by the government's inept handling of Sydney's prehistoric public transport. Or that, for me, this episode was going to be life altering.

I told them when my training would start, while in the ice rink a young mother helped her little boy with his first steps on the ice. He fell. He had a hug and a kiss. What a wonderful world.

"So soon? No chance you'll join us for schoolies?" Brenna asked me. "You'll miss the fun."

"What fun?" Alex scoffed at her. "It's just a waste of money!"

"Alex, don't be a smart ass," Lucy objected. "It's once in a lifetime fun. You only get to graduate from high school once. Then it'll be responsibilities after responsibilities. Or so I was told."

"It may be fun, but useless!"

"Who cares?"

"Well—," he sputtered. We girls had all finished our food, but poor Alex still had a full plate. More proof that boys were lousy at multitasking. "Good on you, then. I don't have that kind of money to throw away. If I could save even a dollar more for my world trip, I would."

"But Alex," mischievous, black-haired Brenna teased. "Someday we'll go around the world too. But we won't be miserable like you. We'll have made money first. Travel first class. Five-star accommodation. Chocolate, champagne and fresh fruit to welcome us. No sorry excuse for a shack to crash in."

They bantered happily, defending their choices. That afternoon we waved our goodbyes wearing broad grins, looking forward to our future and freedom.

Back at home, I was dreaming of buying a mobile phone when a car pulled up in the driveway. Whose car? Didn't sound like Mum's or Dad's. I peered down.

Holy moley... a sleek hot rod! Low, showy... and open-topped.

Mum was in the passenger seat saying goodbye to a brown-haired young man who had given her a lift home. Hang on, where was *her* car? And wait, wait a minute, they were now smooching. Did mere colleagues kiss like that? What was going on? This could not be happening.

No!

That was my mother. And that definitely was not Dad!

I sat down, trembling and feeling stupid. What on earth was happening?

Their laughter drifted up through my window. The car door slammed gently. Mum was coming into the house. I wanted to close my bedroom door, but my energy seemed to have drained. My hands shook. I felt ill.

"Hi honey," Mum greeted me in her sing-song voice.

"Mum, that wasn't Dad!" I blurted out.

"That was Ettoré." Mum pronounced both 'e's as in "Echo". She leaned on my door frame, but she wasn't looking at me. She smiled with dreamy eyes, looking distantly at some very pleasant memory. Ettoré. As if this name explained their kiss. "Your father will always be a good friend of mine. But honey, our relationship has run its course. Time to move on."

"Which relationship?" This was so beyond me. My parents

were devoted to each other. They had stuck together for years, not contributing to the statistics of Australia's high divorce rate. When Auntie Kate—Mum's best friend—separated from her first husband ten years back, my parents continued to be the epitome of a perfect couple. "You have a relationship with that guy Ettoré? What about Dad? He's your husband!"

"Not anymore," she announced in a sing-song voice. As if she was not imparting a bombshell. Her face was positively radiant as she pulled away from the door. "Honey, we'll talk about all this at dinner. Your Dad wants us together when we break the news to you."

"You're joking!" I jumped up and chased her to her door, but she closed it in my face. "Tell me it isn't true!"

"Calm down honey," she called from inside. "I'll see you at dinner."

"You can't do this to Dad! He loves you! Don't be cruel!"

Mum relented and opened her door, her smile replaced by a sigh.

"Sorry that you saw me and Ettoré, darling. That was insensitive, very lousy of me. We forgot ourselves because we were so happy. Sorry. But your father and I are being kind to each other. He needs to marry his girlfriend. When people are in love, as you'll be one day, they need to be together."

"Girlfriend?" I stood in total incomprehension. "*Dad*?"

She nodded. "Geraldine. That English geologist we met at the conference of the Society of Exploration Geophysicists in Houston. A few years back."

"But we were there with him," I reasoned, bewildered.

"*We* were busy enjoying all those tours. And the other spouse activities. *They* were at the conference." Her speech was slow as if addressing a simpleton, which I currently was. "He'll explain to you soon enough. At dinner. Let me ring restaurant delivery."

"This can't be true," I insisted. "*Dad* has a girlfriend?"

"Of course. Harry is only 42, you know. A year younger than me. He's a very successful man and he's very handsome."

"Then why don't you stay married to him?"

"Honey... We didn't tell you before, precisely because you'd nag us and try to change our minds. But you should know one more thing, to prepare you for tonight's conversation." She took a breath. "Your dad needs money to start a new family now. Geraldine is young. They want children. So they're moving overseas to an oil company in Indonesia. A petroleum geophysicist makes way over half a million dollars there as an expat. He plans to be there for a few years."

"Are you serious?" She couldn't be talking about Dad. "He's my best friend!" He couldn't cast me aside. "That can't be right. Mum?"

"We'll explain later. I just want you to be prepared."

I was stunned. As I gaped, she went into her room again but this time she did not close the door. She picked up her phone and ordered dinner from a nearby restaurant. And I ran out of the house and ran and ran.

So many thoughts crowded my head. My parents, who looked very beautiful together, must not separate. I would not have it! I would fight for them to stay together. Tonight I would confront them. Tonight we were going to have one hell of a rational dialogue and contrive a plan to resolve their conflicts.

After some time I registered that Dimity was running silently beside me and I slowed down. I thought very, very hard, trying to remember anything wrong, any sign or hint, about my parents' rift. It must be a trifle, because try as I might, nothing came up.

If you had seen our family albums, you would've known Mum and Dad had always been there with me.

On the day I was born, Dad looked positively ill. You would think it was him who had given birth to me—so traumatic was his expression.

On the second day of my life, he looked so happy and proud, as if no one could be more beautiful than his darling daughter, and that he had accomplished this feat all on his own.

There was a picture of him pushing the swing in a park, with one-year-old me big-eyed with wonder. I could not walk or talk yet, but they had me safely secured in the special baby swing.

This photo had always been one of my parents' favourites because of my 'precious' expression.

Also there was him looking indulgently at two-year-old me, when I was playing with a bubbler in the park that wet my frilly dress.

You could only conclude that if Dad was in the pictures, it must be Mum who had taken them. Although she did not join us on most of our outings, Mum had been a constant at home. She would not cheer or jeer along with us when cricket was on TV. But she did at tennis. She had not participated when Dad helped me gardening. But she would be sitting nearby, doing crosswords or manicuring her nails to perfection.

How was I to save their marriage when I could not even speculate on their issues? They sure had never advertised them. Did they discuss them behind closed doors? If so, I was completely ignorant of them.

It was a mild October evening. The leafy streets of my suburb Beecroft were as tranquil as ever. There was no indication that the world was coming to an end. A few people jogged. A few people walked their dogs. A few people were getting divorced. Just another day huh? Another day in the life of Australians.

That evening, I ate my very last dinner with both my parents. Or perhaps I didn't. I remember them gently telling me that their divorce had been approved. It had come through. They received the papers today. And when, just when, had they submitted them? No slim chance I could fight to save their marriage? What kind of parents broke sickening news like this? It made me run to the toilet and throw up, but I only spewed water.

My parents followed me to my room. Mum stood by the window, Dad sat at my desk. I was on my bed now, hugging a pillow. Trying to suppress the bile. What was I going to do now?

Fight!

My mind scrambled for what to say. Nothing was too late. Hang the papers. They could remarry. I would make them. Squaring my shoulders to bolster my courage, I said my piece.

"You're highly sensible adults. You're supposed to figure out your problems and work out the solutions. You shouldn't just give up. Have a rational dialogue. Think of all the good times. You've had a wonderful life for two decades. People have been impressed by how close you are to each other. By how compatible you are. You have a million reasons not to throw it away."

"Honey... we've seen a marriage counsellor. He said the problems would still be there ten years from now, so we should opt out while we were both still young and able to find happiness somewhere else."

"That marriage counsellor should be shot!"

"On the contrary. He gave us very sound advice. Which we considered for two long years. Yes. This is no sudden whim, honey. We started talking about it when I turned 40. But we love you. We've always kept your happiness foremost in our mind. For a long time now we've been waiting for you to grow up before we went our separate ways. Now that you've completed the HSC and will turn 18 next February, you are old enough to understand. Adults have their own life too. We also need to be happy."

Mum delivered all that in a very kind tone. The tone of someone delicately calling for understanding. Completely the opposite of her flighty mode when she had just arrived home. The way she talked made me feel like an inconsiderate, ill-behaved, spoiled little girl.

I turned to Dad looking for help. But there was no help there.

"Your eyes. The look in your eyes... We love you so much, darling," Dad, who had been silent, now spoke. He always waited for Mum to tackle difficult situations first. "Don't worry. Nothing will change. You will continue to live here. As usual. We're both moving out immediately, yes. You must understand that we can no longer live here."

In those kind, gentle tones I found infuriating my parents said they each loved me very deeply. This love for me would never change. They said I was an adult now, not a helpless kid. They said I should not begrudge them their happiness because their love for me would remain the same.

"I'm good to leave tonight," Mum announced later. "I've packed what I need now." You bet. Couldn't wait to jump the bones of her young boyfriend, seemed to me.

Dad kissed Mum's cheek with a loud smack, ruffled her hair, closed her car door and gave her a jovial wave. She waved back cheerily. And out she went. Out of the house. Out of my life. And into Ettoré's penthouse at McMahons Point.

"How could you let her go?" I cried. Fear had roiled in my stomach as I watched them. If they had shown grief and longing, there might have been some hope, perhaps? But their cheerful indifference struck me with its finality. Everything was simply beyond my grasp. It was all very hard to understand. My perfect family was no more. "Dad, how could you?"

"The flames dimmed." He lifted his broad shoulders. "Then went out. We've become simply good friends, sweetheart. So we've decided by mutual agreement to go our separate ways."

"That's it?"

Dad dragged me to the kitchen and took some yoghurt, cajoling me to eat something. He seemed to consider what to say next. I could see him turning it over in his mind.

"We're only in our early forties, sweetheart. Very young. We still have forty or fifty more years to live. A very long time. Shouldn't we be happy? Should we be condemned with 'make do', when life could be better?"

"But yours was my model of a happy marriage. I planned to grow up to be like you guys. To have just one—one!—love for my whole life. Now it looks like I had stupidly believed that was possible."

"Why not? Some other people are luckier, perhaps you'll be too. Just don't put up with crap, change your partner if you must... If you missed one train, another one will turn up shortly. Now, would you like to meet Geraldine?"

"Never!" I was ashamed of my sudden waspish attitude. I never knew my placid self could be so mad with anyone, let alone my parents. But I was very distraught. All this time they had waited for me to grow up... "Why don't you fix whatever is wrong, Dad... Why didn't you tell me?"

"Because you'd insist we stay together when we'd rather not." He shoved a generous slice of chocolate dessert in front of me, still trying to get me to eat something.

"But you say we have to fight to make things better."

"Honey," he took my hands solemnly. "Sometimes it's not worth it. Don't fight too hard."

"Dad... I can't believe you've been my model of happiness. Of fidelity"

"I'm human. I'm not perfect."

"Oh? I saw you and Mum staying faithful. Because of this, I've been saving myself for the love of my life, whoever that will be. And now you're telling me it has all been a farce? No such thing as fidelity? I better go party and throw my virginity to the wind now."

"No!" he protested. "Don't you dare!"

"Why not? Trial and error. Just like the grownups."

"Sydney," he chided with a warning tone. "Don't be sarcastic. You'll get over this. Let's talk about something else... Wanna come with me to Indo-land for a few months? Before uni starts? We'll be in Balikpapan. That's far, far away from messy Jakarta or Bali."

"Oops!" this brought me back to my own plan. "I've totally forgotten! I get the call-centre job. One-three-hundred five-hundred. I said yes."

"Sure you wanna do it? Work instead of holiday?"

"No. Yes. It's just that I've said yes, so... I'll keep my word... For now."

"Well, think about it. Give me a shout if you change your mind, okay? Join us any time."

Dad stayed several more days. When I returned from walking Dimity one morning, my stomach dropped to see him putting suitcases into his car. I had known about this and thought I was prepared. But I was wrong. With leaden steps I went to the backyard, unwound the watering hose, and watered my many, many plants.

Dad came out to the backyard and set down a brekkie tray. He had put cut-up mango in a bowl. Toasted bread. And cooked non-shiny uninteresting eggs. Yeah, Dad definitely had to stick to cereal.

He looked at me in helpless apology. His gaze imploring.

"Thank you," my lips wobbled. I loved Dad. Hated him. And life would never be the same again.

Before Dad left for the airport, he said he would love me forever and always. He said he cared for me and would always be there for me. He said I would always be number one to him.

And so many other lies.

That evening I opened the fridge and stood there dejectedly. Staring. Tears and chocolate for dinner?

But I did not even have the will to indulge myself like many broken-hearted females do. Being alone felt very unnatural to me. I had a strong need for companionship. After that day, when alone, I never bothered to expend my energy on feeding myself.

At night I woke up with a jerk of anguish in my chest. For a moment I could not recall anything. I gazed around, searching... trying to understand the pain. A slither of light came in from the partly open drape of my window. Full moon outside. And I remembered.

The divorce!

A horde of tumultuous feelings assaulted me. I felt insignificant. They had not cared about my opinion or feelings. I felt defeated. Not even given any chance to fight. I felt rejected. My parents were too deliriously happy with their new lovers to want me.

With a sob I flew downstairs and out to the backyard. Dimity whined and walked out of her doggy house to meet me. I threw myself down and hugged her for all I was worth.

"Dimity. I'll never ever fall in love. Because when you fall in love, you'll end up married. Have a child. And when you're not around anymore, your child will wish she'd never been born. I would never do that to anyone."

Dimity wasn't leaving. Gosh, she was very old now. No, she was not leaving...

Welcome to The UK

The Hornsby 1300500 call centre went live at 6am on a November day in 1999.

When I was stepping into the lift that morning, I saw Pete rushing into the foyer. I held the lift for him.

"Thanks." Tie in hand, he flashed me a white smile as he swept in with a faint whiff of citrusy aftershave. His hair was still a bit damp from the shower. "And good morning."

He dropped his small backpack and, facing the steel-wall mirror, he put his collar up and deftly knotted his tie to perfection, the quick, precise actions showing that he was used to this tie-tying routine. How good he looked.

His beautiful eyes caught mine in the mirror and he turned to face me with a smile. I smiled back. His grin broadened. He tilted his head and said, "You know, if you press number four, we'll get to our destination. You have a six o'clock start too, don't you?"

Bummer! In embarrassment I punched the lift button behind me. Pete's eyes were laughing with a teasing glint.

It was a beehive upstairs. We had so many visitors. All the big bosses from Sydney's trains, ferries, buses, and other clients were here—before 6am.

Briskly I set up to work.

"Welcome to the Transport Infoline," I responded to a very faint sound creeping through my headset. "This is Sydney."

"Sydney... Is that really your name? Or is it because we're in Sydney?"

"Both," I blurted, suddenly nervous. "I meant, my first name *is* Sydney. How can I help you?"

"Rightio Sydney, Charlie here from Chatswood. I'm going to the Saturday game at Olympic Park. But this morning I saw a trackwork notice up at the station. So how will I get there by six?"

"I'll work it out, could you please hold the line?"

I punched the MUTE button. The MUTE button was there so callers would not hear if an agent—that was what we were called—sneezed or coughed. Or would not hear when I called my manager. "JUSTIIIN!"

I was frantic. Much later they would develop a sophisticated system when the entire trackwork information would be loaded. But on that first day of my working life they gave me a big bundle of STN, or Special Train Notices. This was the train schedule used by train drivers. They also gave me a thick printout of various trackwork buses.

Hands trembling in trepidation, whatever eloquence and organisational skills I possessed evaporated. Even with the-also-panicking Justin's help, it took me 20 minutes to match the working numbers of two trains from the STN and the much-hated replacement bus. That's correct, 20 minutes! This immediately boosted my respect for train drivers' intelligence.

I had to say, Charlie was a most patient and polite customer. For the whole time I was fumbling with the fat STN, he only prompted me once, with a questioning tone, "Well? One-three-hundred five-hundred?"

The call centre was housed in a huge, open, squarish floor. Later an interior expert would bring in designer colours and comforting green plants, but originally it was a plain sunny room. Five or six workstations were joined in a flower-like pod. With spacious distance between the curvy pods, there wasn't the slightest sense of claustrophobia.

Instead of cubicles or high partitions, curvy low dividers of about 20cm rose between us—enough to make sure our stationery did not go on vacation into another agent's territory. In this very friendly setting we could easily see each other and chat between calls.

Sinead of the curly red hair and Irish accent happened to sit next to me that first morning.

As a backpacker, she hardly knew Sydney (except how to cheat using an Orange Travelpass, of course.) Therefore it was natural that I helped her to spell the Aboriginal names of the callers' origin or destination.

"Woolooware," I would answer her question while pressing my MUTE button in the middle of a call. "Double-U double-O L double-O double-U a-r-e. Woollahra. Double-U double-O double-L a-h-r-a. Woolloomooloo..."

After that she dubbed me her best friend.

As 1300500 was a full house of agents, we had hot seating. You sat wherever a workstation was available. Lindsay came to me late morning, peeved, "Sydney, you should've saved a seat for me. I wanted to sit near you. But now this pod is full."

Since our training Lindsay had been hounding me out for a drink *every day*. His piercing silver eyes conveyed he had more than drinks on his mind though. My hunch said he was okayish. He looked cool in his own way. He oozed strength, giving you a sense that he was dependable. But there was no spark there. And even fireworks as colossal as Sydney Harbour Bridge on a New Year's Eve wouldn't have moved me at this time of heartache.

I was saved from having to answer him by an incoming call. Lindsay, who never smiled, glared at friends around me as if blaming them for occupying the seats. His eyes paused on Pete. Pete looked back at him unperturbed. These two *measured* each other.

"Hot seating," Aussie Kevin told Lindsay.

"Does Sydney even want to sit next to you?" Sinead taunted.

"Wasn't our fault you asked for a later shift, mate," Aussie Jack topped. "I just had a customer *screaming* abuse at me because *he* left an important item on the train. Tough. Don't blame others for your own mistakes."

Pete did not say anything. I was soon to find out that he did not really talk. He had the most wonderful voice, but he preferred silence.

Lindsay threw me a wistful look before going somewhere else.

In the following days, whenever Sinead arrived she would look around, spot me, and a broad grin would alight on her lips and eyes. She would then glide confidently towards me to claim the nearest available seat.

"My saviour," she would tease, eyes glittering with humour.

Many mornings I noticed several very cool boys near me. Not attracted by me of course. They were only waiting for lovely Sinead's arrival. Except perhaps for Lindsay who kept doing his best to get friendly. Many British boys tried to pick up Aussie girls. Successful too. As it turned out, in their social lives the backpackers weren't any different from many of my Aussie co-workers.

My pod became a gathering of young people. I stayed quiet, contributing to conversation only in response to the others. Treading with care, I tried hard to conceal my depression. But our pod was noisy, happy, and vibrant. Some agents tended to talk louder on the phone when boorish customers had blaring TV or music in the backgrounds. My pod was loud because of laughter.

One morning a nice oldie called.

"Darling, next few buses from the first stop on Samuel Street in Warriewood to Spit Junction, please."

I told her it would be the L85 at 10:20, arriving at 11:19. "After that every half an hour."

"What's after 10:20 dear?"

"The L85 again at 10:50.

"What time will it arrive at Spit Junction?"

"11:49."

"What's after that?"

"Every half an hour"

"And when would that be?"

"Warriewood 11:20. To arrive Spit Junction 12:19"

"Would that be from the first stop at Samuel Street?"

"Yes."

"What's after that?" Gramma Chatty kept at this until I firmly asked the exact time she needed to go.

"It's for my granddaughter's birthday, dear. She's turning eight! I've bought her a lovely wide-brimmed hat for the summer. She's going to really look stunning wearing it. It has these lovely pink rosettes that she'll be crazy about. I remember her second birthday. Her hair was just long enough for pigtails then. I gave her hair bands with pink rosettes. She looked so adorable, I took a picture and it's now on my wall above the fireplace. I put it in a nice filigree frame. So I saw this hat at Warringah Mall last Wednesday and I just had to buy it for her. Actually I'd already promised to take her to the zoo for her birthday present. But it's almost summer so she'll need this wide hat walking in the zoo, won't she? I—"

"Absolutely. She'll look fantastic! Now you wouldn't want her to miss the Seal Show, would you? Please take the next bus. Ten twenty, Ma'am. Happy birthday to your granddaughter. Thanks for calling!" I hit the RELEASE button.

"You're very patient," commented Pete from across the workstation.

Since Pete rarely talked, I was pleasantly surprised.

"She was actually lovely," I threw him a smile. "But she can't help being old."

He tilted his head, contemplating me with his very beautiful eyes.

"Join me for a smoke Sydney." Friendly Kevin offered his cigarette pack to me in the lift during a morning break. "Here, have one."

Many colleagues, young and old, had been pestering me to take up smoking each time I went outside the building. It was their life mission to initiate all young agents to drinking, smoking, and sex. Kids did not leave here a virgin or a non-smoker. Everyone drank. The Aussie office culture.

"No, thank you. I'm going to the library."

"But you never turned the page of your book yesterday," he winked. "I saw you through the glass wall."

"Perhaps I was thinking. Bye."

It was overcast outside. I walked quickly away. To the right. And spotted Lindsay enthusiastically kissing Flo, a young Aussie agent, in front of Hornsby Library. This, the guy who had forever asked me out?

He grew sheepish when he saw me. Busted. I held eye contact and smiled. Back off from me now, Lindsay.

Kevin joined me in the lift up, checking the book I had just borrowed from the library.

"Lighting techniques for photography?"

"Just for fun," I told him. "I need to improve my photography."

Upstairs Justin appointed me to be the Floor Walker of the hour to assist with agents' queries. I was actually wary of people and hesitant to initiate a chat. In this instance, my colleagues were the ones who flashed a light summoning help.

"Hi Sydney, how's it goin'?" Pete always greeted me with a smile before launching into transport questions. It did not reduce my nervousness caused by his proximity and masculinity, though. "This mom with baby in pram has been waiting for the accessible 380 scheduled at 12:10 from Dover Heights to Bondi, but the one showing up wasn't accessible. The baby's very sick and has a doctor appointment. Where's the accessible bus?"

On the floor we had several accents. Some lovely and some—

well, not lovely. British accents were abundant—sometimes I teased Pommy agents that our greetings should be "Welcome to the UK".

Today, as I floor-walked, I could hear snippets of between-call conversation here and there.

"A Blackheath customer complained that his train came only every two hours," grumbled Valerya, a Russian lady, "They should go to a place in Russia where the train only comes once a day!"

"My daughter is sick," shared Eugene. "I made my husband stay home with her. He's with the Public Service—they get to go on carer's leave even when their dog is sick."

"Are you wearing your brand-new push-up bra, dear?" asked elderly Lynn of Flo, who looked ready to—spill, sort of.

"You from Sumatra?" Pete asked Nina, his eyes shone with fond memories. "Great surf. Beautiful food…"

I took note of this agent. When I wasn't busy answering flashing lights, I approached her, "Can you tell me anything about Borneo? Balikpapan?"

Nina looked up at me with surprise. "Why, that's a very specific place to be. Only the oil people go there."

"My Dad is there," I told her as Pete, who seemed to have overheard, turned to us from the adjacent pod. I nodded to him. "He's a geophysicist."

"Really?" Nina asked. "I used to be one. Always wondered why many of my colleagues were Australians. Now I know we don't have petroleum in Aussieland."

"*Really*? Then what are you doing here in a call centre?"

"Love. This is five minutes' walk from home. My kids are young. Besides, there aren't any petroleum-seismology jobs."

"True, Dad used to work offshore from Perth. Definitely not for a mum."

I kept coming back there, curious about my father's new world. Between calls she told me about the seismic exploration around Mahakam Delta. Mahakam was a very wide river sparkling in the sun, with the world's best lobsters. Going to work on a speed boat was a never-ending holiday. No civilisation. She had been the only female in the middle of nowhere, apart from an *'all-rounder'* maid.

"The nearest town was Balikpapan. We flew to and from an oil rig by helicopter. Half of the city is a very well-designed upper-class area for the rich oil people, with their posh country-club and such. The other half is poor, crowded and disorganised."

"Funny," I told her. "My parents have taken me to Canada, USA, Thailand, and Singapore. But not to our nearest neighbour."

"Don't worry. All Australians will eventually end up visiting Indonesia. In 200 million years, that is."

"How come?"

"The geodynamics. The Australian tectonic plate moves north at about 15cm a year. It melts underneath Sumatra and Java, causing so many volcanoes there."

"You mean the heat comes from the melted Australian plate?"

"Yes. The mountains are tectono-volcanic."

"And in 200 million years, we'll be no more? Interesting. So I won't end up being a museum object like the African 'Lucy'."

I did not ask Dad anything when he rang, though. At this stage, I was jealous of his English geologist girlfriend. When he squired me around I had thought I was his precious princess instead of a burdensome obligation. I felt disillusioned. I didn't say much except "Yes", "No", "Ah-ha", and "Don't know".

"Typical teenager," Dad sighed. Frustrated. "Please say something."

"Something."

I did not chat with Mum either. She used to look after my every single need, always resourceful and so thoughtful, and very dependable. All I had to do was enjoy life while Mum tirelessly and competently arranged and organised every single detail of whatever I might need for every occasion. She did none of that now. Like, did you know that a sunscreen tube could get empty? I did not approve of the new Mum so I refused to talk. Yes. No. Sure. Okay. In the end she became fed up and voiced a forceful "Grow up!"

They told me to read my emails, having written to me many times... the precise reason I stopped checking my emails. Just to be perverse.

I didn't even touch the computer. Weird, come to think of it. All through my high-school years, Mum confiscated the modem at 9pm. How I used to seethe, watching her unhook the cables one by one and walk away with the modem. A mean mother, was she not? I'd had to make sure all homework requiring the internet was completed by nine. To my surprise, now that I had the internet all to myself, it ceased to be interesting.

I spent long hours drawing instead. And I took photographs, endlessly arranging and rearranging lighting. I did need to know more about this before uni started.

My neighbours enquired about my parents but they did not think it odd for a high-school leaver to live alone. I was an adult now, supposedly.

Now why would an adult feel devastated by her parents' decision? Someone enlighten me. Should I have had counselling? I could not get used to the hurt although it was constantly with me. Pain was a heavy chain tied around my neck. Often it jerked me awake at 4am. Pain robbed me of my voice, making it barely audible. This chain was tied to an invisible pole. You couldn't shake it off. You could only go around and around it.

I felt someone was wielding a sharp knife, slashing my heart into ribbons. The hurt was astonishingly physical. Somehow I could feel it at the tips of my fingers. At the ends of my nerves. If you have never experienced this, then you don't know what heartbreak is like, and I would never wish it on you.

More bad news came to me.

"I got admission to study music in Melbourne!" Brenna announced in excitement after their Queensland trip. And now her artist aunt had invited her to her home near Creswick Forest, Victoria. She would holiday there until January.

"I'm doing the Army recruitment exams," Lucy beamed. "And my ballet company has a new production. We are to tour Australia this summer!"

The girls were deliriously happy when I was horribly depressed. I so needed a friend but could not bring myself to speak up. I was ashamed of my parents' divorce. And I was happy for my friends. I could not sing, dance, or play any instrument that I had great respect for people talented in these arts.

With a feeling of loss I watched them leave. And I walked the empty rooms and hallways of my home...

My old dog knew all about my tears. We jogged and we talked and I hugged her a lot. Dimity, the love of my life.

The Bloody Bus Just Drove Past Me!

"The bloody bus just drove past me!" I yelled on my phone to Nicholas at the administration desk. Although it wasn't considered a profanity in Aussieland, earlier I could not bring myself to use the b-word. It definitely took Sydney's public transport to force it out of me. "I'm going to be late!"

"Sydney... you shouldn't..." This week my rolling shift began at the indecent hour of 6am again. "You'll lose your Attendance bonus."

"I know I know. Can't help it. Sorry."

This was a Saturday morning in December. I had planned to take the N80 bus because the first Beecroft train would arrive in Hornsby at 05:56. I still had to run up the station stairs, and cross the George Street pedestrian bridge to my office. Fat chance I could make it.

I was furious with the N80 driver. Nightride buses were supposed to help customers while the trains stopped between midnight and early morning. I had planned my trip meticulously. But I had stood there in my bright jacket—impossible to miss!—waving, and the inconsiderate bus driver ignored me!

Unhelpful people should never apply to be bus drivers!

I sat on the first train feeling *sooo* upset.

My miserly office only paid the lowest minimum Australian salary. They gave us various bonuses if we were disciplined and good at what we did.

Attendance bonus was yours if you didn't call in sick *at all*, and were *never* late even for a single minute.

Adherence bonus was yours if you logged in to take calls the *precise* minute you were supposed to.

If they monitored you, and you gave out *accurate* info in a *polite* way, you received the Quality bonus.

If you received the Quality bonus, and your Average Handling Time was less than 106 seconds, you would also get the AHT bonus.

But if you did not pass the Quality, you wouldn't get the AHT bonus, no matter how fast you handled the calls.

This Saturday, because of a nasty bus driver, I lost my Attendance bonus for the month. It meant my pay would be nowhere near decent.

As I logged on a few minutes late, I noticed a spill-proof computer mug on the desk next to mine: 'PETE's. DO NOT TOUCH'. Its handsome owner was talking on the phone, his tenor voice soothingly pleasant, and his tone of speaking lovely. Somehow it calmed me down a bit.

My manager Justin called me. He talked for 15 minutes because he was obliged to admonish me for arriving two minutes late.

My mood worsened when the Newcastle Line trackwork victims whinged. The maintenance crews were required to check the tracks on a regular basis to avoid accidents. There was always trackwork on some line every weekend. Except on election days.

A very rude young boy shouted, "You say your (*bleep*) trackwork bus from Gosford is every *ten* minutes? I don't (*bleep*) believe you! Are you (*bleep*) sure?"

"Would you talk politely or would you like me to terminate the call?" And buy some soap to wash your mouth before the next call.

"I just don't believe the bus is so frequent when your train is only every half an hour," he argued.

"The train has eight double-decker carriages. The bus is way shorter."

"Oh."

"Yes. When a train runs, 2000 cars stay home." There. What was so hard to understand?

Next, "I want to go to Silverwater!" an arrogant lady demanded.

"Which part of Silverwater please, Ma'am?"

"Just show me how to get there! You should know! Why do you work there if you have to ask me?!"

"Anywhere in Silverwater, Madam?"

"Anywhere!"

Right. So I whipped up a travel plan to get her to Holker Street near Silverwater Road. The address of Silverwater Jail. I hoped she would be very happy there. Have a nice life!

But then a meaner lady (two in a row!) wanted to go to Frenchs Forest, address unknown.

"But Frenchs Forest is very big, Madam. Bigger than the City. Where specifically, please? So we can send you to the correct location."

"You should tell me where it is!" she snapped. "It's your duty! Call your supervisor! NOW!!!"

For the next 20 minutes she spitefully dobbed my ineptitude and unhelpfulness to Justin. Since she refused to be put through to Your Say, our feedback section, these 20 minutes added to my handling time. There went my AHT bonus.

It did not stop there. Next, harassed Justin assigned me to assist her *again*, assuring her I had been fully trained to do so. Grudgingly she granted me the dubious "honour" of advising her about *every* single bus that went to Frenchs Forest.

"I plan to buy a house in that area," she announced now, "I haven't decided on what street it's going to be. It will depend on your advice."

Ohmygod, now I'm a real-estate adviser?

"How about we mail you the buses' Region Guide for Frenchs

Forest, Madam? Also all bus timetables there. You can peruse them carefully and decide for yourself."

"No, no, no! Don't you try to get out of this! You're being paid to take this call! Now just tell me what's available!"

So I read her departures and arrivals of every single direct bus as well as every combination of buses—both government and private buses—for weekday mornings, weekday nights, Friday nights, Saturday mornings, Saturday nights, Sunday mornings, Sunday nights.

Of course she just had to ask, "And where would I catch a taxi if I missed them? Where's the nearest train station and major bus stop?"

"Have you written down all this information?" I asked.

"Yes yes, just tell me the nearest place for a taxi now!"

I was dying to transfer her to Pizza Hut. But I duly advised her that the nearest train station was Chatswood. She then demanded I read the departures and arrivals of trains and Nightride N90 bus between Wynyard and Chatswood.

Next I had to advise her that the main bus corridor was Pittwater Rd in Dee Why. For this, too, she made me read the schedule of the nightride 151 bus between Wynyard and Dee Why. Weeknights. Weekend nights.

"Right," she said after all that, "What bus was it again that went direct?"

"But you said you'd written them down." Ma'am, I'm about to kill you!

"No. No… I think it will be better if you send me that Region Guide after all. And all the bus timetables of course. Please take my mailing details now. My name is Fu Lyn …"

I looked away to the streets of Hornsby, visible from our northern glass wall, remembering Winston from Pennant Hills High School. A brilliant Chinese Australian, he was one of the most pleasant people alive, even when we always badgered him with questions. If only Mrs Fu was half as nice.

Mrs Fu then felt justified to end her call with the following farewell, "I'm very disappointed with your service today. Not good customer service at all. In the beginning you deliberately pretended not to know anything about the services in Frenchs Forest so you could get rid of me. You're such a lazy person you tried to get out of your duty to provide me with information. I've spoken with your manager and reported your refusal to help a customer seeking assistance. People like you should never get a job in customer service. You're a disgrace to your company and to Sydney's public-transport provider. I'm extremely appalled at you."

She railed on and on in this condescending tune for the next ten minutes while my bruised heart was screaming, *"Daddyyyy... can you see me? Can you see me now? Would you allow this person to batter your daughter to pieces? Daaad... take a look at me now. How can you let this happen to me? Daad... you promised to always be there for me. I need you now. Dad, heeelp!"*

"I hope my words will stay with you and help you improve, because I feel very sorry for all your customers. I pity those unfortunate people who call this number and get you on the line. I've never before encountered such a lazy and deceitful customer-service person such as you."

Very thorough, was she not? Blah blah blah. Ra ra ra. Mrs Fu was simply unstoppable.

"You're also disgustingly incompetent. You dawdle when delivering the information, taking over an hour of my very precious time. Do you know I get paid over 200 dollars an hour at my work? Would you care to compensate me? I don't think so. I hope never to talk with you again."

Though reaching the end of my dwindling patience, I closed the call with a cheerful "No worries. Thanks for your call!"

Surprised? It was obligatory to thank callers, even revolting torturers, or you lost your Quality bonus. I had become so robotic I even hung up my home phone automatically saying "Thanks for your call!"

I logged off the phone despite having missed my allocated break. Hang my Adherence bonus! I had been abused by a malicious woman. I was feeling very sorry for myself. I had nobody to talk to while somewhere in the world my parents were blissfully happy. How could they be?

Blurry-eyed and depressed, I ran to the disabled toilet in anguish. I locked the door, closed the toilet lid, sat down and cried. And cried.

One heap of a mess. That was me. I had been there at the office every day, battling my depression. Tears could still well up when I thought of my parents.

I was scared of being home alone. I dreaded my loneliness. Feared my suicidal thoughts. To keep playing with a full deck, I had to get out of the empty house and keep working before uni started.

With my limited talent and abilities, hardly any appealing career path was available. This job sucked, but at this stage of my life I was not ready to cope with anymore changes. I had no mental energy to enter a new work environment. Or to face contemptuous strangers. I had to stay within the current sphere because I felt safer with the devil I knew.

Soon fury began to stir and flare. Tears subsided. I was now angry with myself. I shouldn't let hostile people shake my composure. Shouldn't have allowed a mean bus driver to make me cross. Shouldn't have disintegrated when aggressive customers insulted me. I was above all that! Nobody would ever, ever have the power to make me swear again. No customer would bring me down.

I would not allow them!

Chin up. I would face my problems. I would not hide, cowering and morose. They would not beat me.

Sadly, from the 5,219 calls I had taken, the majority of torturers were of my own gender. I decided not to copy them. I was very determined to grow up NOT to be difficult like them. I would be kind and wise. And I could not wait to be a wonderful old lady of 70...

I looked into the mirror and cringed when I saw my mutinous eyes. Taking a deep breath, I tried to soften my expression.

The open-floor call centre was accessible either from the rest rooms through the reception, or through the busy break area with its internet café and table-tennis room. I was intensely private. To evade nosy co-workers' interrogation I opened the opposite door.

Pete was sitting right in front of me, long legs stretched out from the reception's black-leather sofa. He made eye contact, scrutinising me with an expressionless face but thoughtful eyes. As always I could not help but notice how beautiful his eyes were. Along with the rest of the package, actually. With skittering heart I nodded and strode briskly to the centre door. I swiped my electronic security pass and went in.

Our American management introduced a system called E-time. Excused time. It meant agents could take an unpaid break or go home early if the floor was over-staffed when we were not busy.

Not busy meant there was no possibility of a call queue. Also no special events, games, concerts, bushfires, flood. No wild wind hitting signal wiring. No hurting soul committing suicide on the rail track.

Businesswise, E-time was a sound cost saver. Only willing agents volunteered to take it. Ranging from 10 minutes to many hours, we took it to go shopping, watch movies at Hornsby cinemas, or simply go home.

"Yellow pages," I requested with fake cheerfulness. That was where they recorded E-time.

"No deal," red-haired Nicholas replied. He was monitoring the call volumes and the graphs showed we were on red. "It's Saturday, our busiest. No way can we give agents E-time. Sorry."

Just my luck.

Tall and slender Justin approached me with a beaming face. Some managers had an abrasive personality, but Justin was your friendly Aussie kind of guy—down-to-earth and always helpful. Very gay, too.

"Tough one, wasn't it? Poor Sydney. I feel for you. Some of these customers are pains in the butt. Man, you guys earn your money. The good news is, though you may have lost your AHT bonus by that long call, and Adherence bonus by having to talk during your scheduled break, you've definitely passed your Quality for the month! Ryan was monitoring your calls then. He was very impressed by your handling of Mrs Fu. Well done!"

Wonderful! I mentally gave myself a pat on the back. With the Quality bonus in, I just saved myself from being the lowest-paid Australian. Oh Dad, weren't you happy for me?

I sat down and logged in.

Soon I became aware that my co-workers—who on other days sat elsewhere—were gossiping about Sinead. As Sinead had the weekend off on this roster, her followers didn't camp around me. Except for Pete, who was still on his break.

One of the gossipers was Monashi. Unlike several other Indian agents, Monashi seemed to think it was cool and very Australian to use a swear word in every sentence. She even swore—while pressing MUTE—when callers were difficult. What if the expletives slipped the MUTE state and got to her customer's ear?

"So our single agents, managers, and IT guys have been hitting the pubs frequently?" elderly Susan queried.

"Yup," Thomas clarified. "We have Friday social drinks."

"A hard night's drinking will end with pairing within the group," Monashi added. "Sometimes they can't even (bleep) look at each other the next morning!"

"Agent-manager pairing is against our workplace policy!" Susan protested.

"Who's going to play law enforcement on consenting adults outside office hours?" Thomas countered.

"Sinead drinks the hardest and f(bleep)s the wildest!" Monashi announced. "All the boys are (bleep) crazy for her! They all wait to see who'll be chosen to get (bleep) lucky. It's (bleep) pathetic."

"Wow," Susan was wide-eyed. "You never know, do you? Sinead's not a flirt. Here she's very decent and friendly. Smiles at everybody. She respects us oldies."

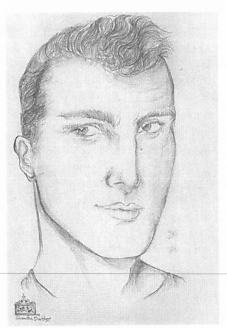

Justin was your friendly Aussie kind of guy— down-to-earth and always helpful

Monashi seemed to think it was cool and very Australian to use a swear word in every sentence.

"She's enjoying her backpacking heaps," chipped in Thomas. "Said she was going to uni in Dublin and would be sober by then."

"She likes to choose her own moments," Susan commented good-naturely. "It's up to her who to drink with. Or to be with afterwards."

"It's been Jack," Monashi gleefully imparted her broad knowledge of others' private lives. "Earlier it was Kevin and some of the (*bleep*) managers. But Pete's often around her at the office." One shapely eyebrow arched, "You think?"

No one could exclusively own Sinead who valued her freedom. I remembered her flirting with Kevin while Pete looked on with possessive eyes. Did he have a thing for her? Foreign agents loved to flirt with the locals, but Pete sort of sat with expressionless dignity near Sinead. Now, why would I bother about other people's lives when I had my own to live? This flitted through my mind as they gossiped. Until Pete returned to our pod and silenced this line of conversation.

Noting Pete's permitted-only-on-weekends casual clothes, I remembered him complaining that this was the first time he had been forced to wear a tie outside the US. Absently I wondered what he was doing working at a call centre. Or in Australia, for that matter.

And I wondered what my fun-loving rowdy co-workers would be doing after work. I loathed my isolation, yet feared mingling with others. I was not a fan of my appalling self. In my misery I could hardly relate to people and, being 17, I still had a legal excuse to dodge their invitation. I did not want them too close to see the real me. I could not be like Sinead who was enjoying life immensely with lots of friends. Lots of sleep partners too, by the sound of it.

I did not judge people or begrudge their choices. Before my parents' divorce, I'd only hoped to save myself for that special someone who might happen by, strolling into my life. Since it was obvious true love did not exist, shouldn't I go party and throw my reserve to the wind? That was what my friends would do with their freedom—instead of endlessly taking photographs or sitting among my roses drawing cartoons.

But I lacked courage. I was terrified of getting hurt. A coward, still.

With and without friends, I was a loser.

One of my callers wasn't a coward though.

"I want to get happy tonight," she confided in a hush-hush tone of someone imparting a secret. "I'll go pubbing. But if I don't pick up a guy, how safe is Campbelltown Station after midnight?"

It *was* a secret. I was the only one privy to her thoughts. Her first time to step out? Alone? She sounded cute, shyly deliberating her wild night out but determined to carry it out. Who was she rebelling against? Strict parents? Revenge against a faithless partner? Or simply to break free from boredom?

After my shift I walked fast to the station. My Northern Line train—the red line on   Sydney's Rail map—departed Hornsby from platform 3. While waiting, I saw Pete going down the stairs to platform 1 for his North Shore train to Roseville. No Sinead today, they had different rosters.

Pete lifted his hand to wave. His beautiful eyes still looked at me in thoughtful assessment. I had the impression he was trying to really *look* at me. As he held my gaze with his appraising one, I felt stripped of all pretensions. Time stood still. I felt, *he saw me. He knew what loneliness was like.* I sensed he understood what it took to present a dignified front when all you wanted to do was howl at the moon.

Had he seen me running from the pod in a terrible state? Had he sat at the reception area waiting for me out of concern? How mortifying! I was normally cautious and shy about showing others my feelings.

Heat rushed to my cheeks as I jumped onto my train.

Stop Working!

The low, sleek, flashy sports car of Mum's boyfriend was parked in my driveway. My beautiful mother—who did not look a year older than her younger boyfriend—greeted me with sparkling eyes and vibrant smiles. She practically oozed with happiness, good health and wellbeing.

"Darling," she gushed, "How good to see you!"

Hoarding my grudge, I put forward a composed, unaffected, impassive face. So far it had been very effective in keeping my co-workers at arm's length, preventing them from seeing the person inside. I knew I looked polite but aloof. But what the heck, my smart, sharp-eyed mother looked straight through me.

"Did you think I wouldn't see you again before you turned twenty-one?" she led me to the family room. "Cheer up, darling. We've come to pick you up for the concert you nagged your dad about. Awful man, away in Borneo! But enjoy yourself. Ettoré here will take you. He's young enough to enjoy it."

My eyes flew to Mum's breathtakingly beautiful Italian boyfriend. Him? Replacing Dad? As what? He looked to be only in his early 30s.

"My pleasure," he said with a lazy smile.

"I don't want to go," I declined politely. "I only wanted to go with my friends and nagged Dad to buy us the tickets." Their rule had been that I could go out with friends at night when accompanied by my parent/s. "But they aren't even in Sydney and I've forgotten it. You shouldn't have bothered."

"Oh but I have. And I reminded you a few times, too. Darling, you should've read your emails," and she went on making me feel guilty. "Have you been alright? You made me worried. The other day I called your office but you were working on the phone. I left a message—you didn't return the call. Well, at least if you were at work, it meant you weren't sick or anything."

"I've been good. Thank you."

She looked me up and down. Now Mum looked a lot like me— or was it the other way round. I was an Aussie girl with a quarter Canadian-French, so Mum had a half—or was it the other way. Whatever. We both had delicate Frenchy bones, long and willowy and narrow-shouldered. We weren't shorties and not giantesses either.

"Saturday dress code?" One neat, beautiful eyebrow lifted. And no, we didn't need to pluck our eyebrows. Each strand in them knew precisely where it was supposed to grow.

I nodded.

"Now please change into something decent. Ettoré has made a reservation for dinner before the concert. Celebrities dine there. They won't allow you in wearing those jeans."

"But—," when had I agreed?

Had you known Mum, you would understand why she was a very successful executive. She was brilliant, shrewd, and ruthless. Fat chance you could escape being manipulated. Her persuasive, focused, purposeful character was never to be denied. When Mum ruled, things got done.

I hated myself being talked into capitulating.

I hated it even more when I sat stupidly in the fanciest car I had ever been in. I tell you what—there was nothing great about witnessing your mother and her new lover gaze in adoration at each other at every red traffic light. The lovey-dovey scene of them each placing a hand on the other's thigh was gross. Highly repugnant.

I wouldn't bother if they were strangers. But Mum? Call me narrow-minded or childish—still I loathed seeing *my* mother acting in love.

In short, I would never wish this revolting experience on you.

But there was nothing a child could do, was there? So I dumbly endured. Feeling sickened. Missing my dog. And it all brought back the unfortunate events of my day.

We dropped Mum at their McMahons Point penthouse. She was to dine at her best friend's. Kate and Mum had been thick since high school. Through many phases of life, the ups-and-downs of changing jobs and partners, they had remained close.

Afterwards Ettoré took me in a water taxi to Darling Harbour.

We had a stilted conversation. Ettoré, who seemed to sense my discomfort, was trying his best to be, what, a good stepfather? Come on, although I considered him ancient, some 18-year olds had boyfriends his age. I did not like feeling unsure about what category our acquaintance fell under. I wasn't sure how to take him. He was not my father. He was not my friend.

Well, he was Mum's boyfriend. I took a mental note to label him my stepfather. There. A ridiculously young stepfather, with his Latin good looks too. He oozed success, as well as... unexpected kindness. And his speech! So impeccably cultured. Awesome.

At a few inches taller than me, Ettoré was not tall like Dad. His eyes were chocolate, whereas Dad's were gleaming silver. His hair was brown, unlike the gold-blond of Dad's. His facial bones were delicate, instead of decisive-bold like Dad's. His frame was wiry-slim, while Dad's hulking-robust. He wore his clothes with the ease of a male model.

It was still daylight in this early summer. The soft-pink colour of the sky was reflected in the buildings and water.

Darling Harbour was rife with activity. There seemed to be a free concert by the water's edge. People of all ages milled about. Young people in great numbers.

The water taxi did not take long to reach our pier. Mr

Handsome of the immaculate manners courteously helped me out. I nearly tripped when I looked up to see Sinead, Pete, Kevin, Jack—with several other co-workers—watching me getting out of the water taxi with interested eyes. They were sitting at the platform by the free concert, eating fries and Maccas take-away.

I felt very embarrassed being seen with Ettoré. He still looked overdressed even in casual attire. His stylish clothing shouted designer labels while my backpacker buddies wore—well, backpackers' you-know-whats.

It looked like they only scrubbed up when adhering to our strict office dress code, and could not wait to shed all formalities immediately after. I guessed that was the fun and freedom of being backpackers. Quietly I envied them their happy carefree ways and confidence. Sinead was wearing patchy merry jeans with a barely-there top. Jane, a lovely English girl from Sheffield with whom I often lunched sported a belly-button ring and cut-off jeans. Severely cut off. And Pete. Man... didn't he look good in a tank top... all beautiful firm muscles and glorious tan.

I wore bone linen pants with a very pretty but simple white linen shirt. It was a very hot day—I had chosen this ensemble because of the fabric. It had not even occurred to me how I would look. Since Mum had not protested, I guessed I passed. Mum had a knack for fashion, I would give her that. She had fine aesthetic sensitivities. Except in shoes. Not that her taste in shoes sucked, but she could never get it right for my age group.

My friends were some distance away from us, and as Ettoré was guiding my elbow in the opposite direction, I turned to them and waved because I didn't want to be considered a snob. Kevin wore his ear-to-ear grin, Sinead her dimpled one. The others also smiled. But Pete just looked back with direct, unreadable eyes.

I fervently hoped they wouldn't think me and Ettoré were an item.

Ettoré embarrassed me further by whisking me off to an up-class harbour-side restaurant. My friends' eyes bored a hole in my back. I kept remembering their Maccas take-away bags. Before our first pay even Maccas was beyond Sinead's reach—she'd had only hot chips for lunch.

They were poor young people. Yet they were so pleased with
life. So disgustingly happy. I knew they would all get drunk
tonight and—yeah, get lucky.

Which shouldn't bother me. I had decided never to fall in love
in my life, right? Had even told my dog why.

I noticed several famous faces in the restaurant. But my mind
was wandering. I shook my head when Ettoré offered wine.

"Too chicken. If I choose not to drink even a bit, there's no
risk I'll ever consume too much, right? I don't think I like the
idea of getting wasted."

"Are you scared you'll be lured to drink for the sake of
drinking itself?"

"I'm scared of not being in control of myself. To prevent it,
I've just decided not to drink. Even after I turn 18. Let others
have their fun. Or make fun of me. For me, I'll have the
coward's choice, thank you."

"You have it wrong. Here in our society, it's not cowardice but
very brave not to drink. It requires strength of character. If it's
your personal choice, let the others bleat. Dare to be different.
It's okay to decline your host's offer. There's no shame in not
frequenting pubs. Myself, I'm a connoisseur of wine, but I only
drink a glass or two, and only when I'm having food. It's the
Italian way."

He refrained from mentioning the trendy Aussie way was to
drink for the sake of getting drunk itself.

I thought again of the close friendship Sinead enjoyed with her
gang. I coveted their cheerfulness. Should I leave my comfort
zone to join them one of these days? Would a wowser teetotaller
ever be accepted? How would it feel to be the only sober one
among friends who had written themselves off? Would I ruin
their fun by being the odd one out?

And did I really need the torture of exposing myself to new
elements when it was easier to bury my head in a book? Would I
ever be ready to open up?

"Why the long face?" Ettoré asked as my thoughts drifted
away.

"Whaat?" Now I felt worse. It was anyone's bad luck to know

me at this time of my life. "Bad company, aren't I? And here you're being really kind to take me. Thank you. And sorry," I babbled.

"I'm no monster," he smiled.

"Oh?" I rolled my eyes at this absurdity. "Checked your mirror lately?"

He chuckled.

"Tell me about your day," he prompted.

"No way. You wouldn't want to know." Like I didn't want to know how you woke up with my mother.

"Try me."

I groaned. Reluctantly I started telling him about the absolute cruelty of the N80-bus driver. Somehow it became easier. I told him of my unforgettable calls. And the constrictive rules of the incentive system. He was laughing so hard when I detailed the Silverwater Jail and the Frenchs Forest quests.

"They made my day!" I also laughed now. "With my Quality bonus in, they saved me from being the lowest-paid Australian. I'll never forget them all my life."

"That's very cool, Sydney. I'm glad you see the funny side of your job. So the horrible calls are the ones you'll treasure because when you think of them you'll laugh and laugh. You have to tell me more next time we meet. Unless you want to quit? I could perhaps find you a position at my office. As a receptionist? Admin staff?"

"Thank you. But no. Not at this stage. This is my fight. I have to win it. I have to conquer myself and my denigrating callers. One day, they will never forget me."

"But your pay is too low. How much bonus are we talking about here, if you can pass all the hurdles?"

"They vary depending on the call volumes. The company sets aside money in the bonus pool according to how much work we get. The more months you pass the hurdles, the more percentage of bonus shares you build. After a time you can get 600 or 800 dollars a month from the Attendance Bonus alone."

"So you're determined to show them you're unbeatable? Your own personal Olympics?"

I laughed. "The challenge of a horrible job."

Little did I know that 2000 *was* going to be my personal Olympics.

We chatted more easily. I asked about his work and he taught me some general business rules. He explained the benefits of exports besides gaining a wider market and spreading the risks.

"To compete in the international market, you have to be better than others. So you'll develop ways to improve your products. This eventually keeps your company on top even in Australia."

"So, are you an Aussie now? There's the faintest accent there."

"My family moved here when I was twelve. But we went back home for holidays frequently. So I'm both Italian and Aussie in many ways."

"Which part of Italy is your hometown?"

"Borgo San Lorenzo. Near *Firenze*, which you call Florence."

"Borgo—whaat?"

"Borgo. San. Loren-zo."

"Borgo—San—Lorenzo," I repeated slowly. "And what's special about it?"

"Apart from the fact that there are so many soccer fields and everybody is mad about *real* football? I could talk about football for hours. But Borgo San Lorenzo itself is magical. The country is simply beautiful in spring and summer. The area is quite hilly. It shines in spring with so many colours. And in summer you can catch moments of amazing view, especially at sunrise and sunset... I have great memories of my hometown."

"Go on. I don't know anything about Florence except Dante."

"Well the streets are narrow. Shady. The town centre could be defined as a perfect example of medieval architecture. It was built with an ancient kind of stone called sampietrino, which gives a pleasant feeling of antique and elegance. Same as the houses. They're painted with the typical colour of Florence, Terra di Firenze. A sort of old-gold colour."

I felt better when we left the restaurant.

My friends were still by the free concert, singing along and holding liquor cans now. Sinead flashed me teasing eyes. But I was annoyed at Pete. He stood motionless, except for a polite nod.

"What now?" Ettoré arched a brow. "You just lost your smile again."

"I like my friends boisterous and sincere," I declared without thinking. "I don't like it when people give me a polite, indifferent nod. It's heaps annoying!"

We stepped aside to let a people-mover Li'l Train pass. Ettoré turned to me, eyes searching, contemplating. Slowly he said with a deadpan, straight face,

"I agree. How dare anyone do that! Don't they know it's your sole prerogative?"

I broke into a laugh, feeling an instant shame to realise how badly I must have acted.

"Exactly!" I joked. "How dare anyone!"

"So?" he asked. "Who was the handsome guy?"

"Who?"

"The one who looked at you."

"They all did. How could you notice any difference?"

"Come on. The cool one. Who pretended to be indifferent."

"Pretended?" This news made me feel better. "Did you really notice that?"

He needled me about Pete. And I could not tell Ettoré anything about him. Pete and I were not normally given the same break. The short chats between calls could only be superficial. We had no chance to get to know who our co-workers really were as individuals.

I kept thinking of them singing and dancing and getting totalled by the water's edge. They were *so* happy. So together. So—*belonging*.

Why was I jealous?

We reached our expensive theatre. Before entering I looked around searchingly.

"What is it?" my baby-sitter-of-the-moment asked. He was an excellent escort. There was no doubt why Mum fell for him. Almost any female would be interested in a handsome god who happened to be cashed up and distinctly of good breeding. "What are you looking for?"

"I'm trying to find the exact bus-stop location for the 443. So I'll know how to properly describe it to my customers."

"Sydney, stop working!" He shook his head and steered me away.

Right. Here I was. Loving my city. Forever trying to be an advocate for our public transport when I knew for a fact that the bosses of Sydney's trains and buses never used one. They never did when visiting my office, despite the fact we were conveniently located near Hornsby Station. Obviously, Sydney's public transport did not suit their bosses.

I Lost My Dress On The Bus!

"Grand date. Where did you find him?" Sinead, already taking calls, asked when I arrived on Monday morning. Many agents had left as casualties of yucky shifts or abusive callers. But the remaining agents were by now skilful, had lower AHT, with better information accuracy.

"Not mine. He was only on child-minding duty 'cause my parents weren't available."

"Blessed," she smirked. "Pass him to me anytime."

Pete's unreadable eyes bored into mine from across the desk.

I liked his constant, unobtrusive presence. I liked his very pleasant voice. I liked his tone of speaking. But why did he prefer a silent method of communication? A look. An enquiring look. Why did he shroud himself with an aura of mystery?

I had to admit I had been thinking of Pete rather a lot lately.

"They took away my driving license!" sobbed my first caller, an elderly St. Ives man. Fury and helplessness coloured his voice. "Please send me the bus timetable."

It was December. Parents asked for next year's school transport. I gave a mum in North Strathfield a detailed travel plan to James Ruse High School.

"No! My friend suggests a different way!"

I showed her that her friend's suggested route took considerably longer.

"Are you sure?"

Gosh, I always wanted to murder a customer who asked whether I was sure. This one ranted on and on.

"Your choice, Ma'am. Please feel free to give your friend a call. Consult her. Sounds like she's better able to advise what to catch. Thanks for your call!" And I pressed RELEASE.

"Good one Sydney," Pete gave me a thumbs-up, his eyes now laughing.

"Thanks," I smiled back. "Do you always listen to my calls?"

"I like listening to your voice," he replied, looking into my eyes. *Wow.* My heart beat faster. My intuition said Pete was interested in me. I could see it in his eyes. But I wasn't brave enough to confess that I liked his voice too. It floated across the workstation in a soothing tone.

In his quiet confidence Pete was different from the other guys. The others, Aussies or Brits, did their best to dance attendance and be charming. They hoped to win female hearts through their posturing, clothing, facial jewellery and hair styles. Sometimes I wondered how long it took Mike to gel his hair. Or how much it had hurt Kevin to have his tongue pierced in order to install the tiny ball he called a toy.

Pete was the antithesis of all that. He was uniquely unselfconscious and cool. So yeah, although I was determined to never fall in love, he had been troubling my dreams quite a lot lately.

The calls rolled in.

Melburnians, Queenslanders and overseas visitors were coming in for the holiday season. 1300500 could be accessed from interstate. Or from overseas by dialling our country code first. I had direct calls from England and Canada. At times I sounded like a Sydney tourism advisor because callers required it of me.

"From Central take bus 372 to Coogee. Stunning view along

the cliff-walk up to Bronte, Tamarama, and Bondi. You can swim on these famous beaches, yes. Then take bus 380 to Watson's Bay. Great seafood. A fabulous ferry ride to Circular Quay. Interesting buskers, fascinating Opera House, Botanical Gardens. Take a ferry to Darling Harbour. Casino. Aquarium. All on a day pass. Call us for timetables, we're here to help."

A guy from Newcastle was very impressed by me.

"Great service. You're the nicest person in your office I've ever talked to, Sydney. May I have your phone number?"

Whaat? He was flirting with me? So I said, "One-three-hundred five-hundred."

He burst out laughing.

I wondered if these callers imagined how we looked. Some of us were blond. Some bottle blond. And we all resembled Miss World contestants, you know. Just... some had to join our in-office Biggest Loser challenge.

When a nice old lady called, I imagined my smiling Nanna Véronique. Or my cousin Kirsten, a hairdresser on a cruise ship, each time a grumpy girl called. Whenever a pleasant young man called, my mind envisioned Christopher Reeves, strapped in his wheelchair, looking up at me with the brightest, most-peaceful, clear eyes. Eyes reflecting his tranquil soul despite his terminal illness. That was how I met him once. At the Queen Victoria Building in the City. He was my model for polite callers.

And no, you don't want to know how I imagined a rude caller.

This particular morning I still received the you-wouldn't-believe-it calls.

"I lost my dress on the back seat of the bus Saturday evening," a girl announced. "It was the L90." Right. I gave her the number of Mona Vale Depot's Lost Property. I wouldn't even ask how she lost it!

"What the (*bleep*) do you think you're doing???" screamed a woman from Perth." (*Bleep*) trackwork so close to Christmas?! Can't you (*bleep*) pick a better time? I'll be arriving in Sydney with luggage, a toddler, and a baby in a twin pram! How will I get on and off your (*bleep*) replacement bus to Scarborough? And I'm a single mother! Who'd (*bleep*) help me?"

In lashing tones she raged against CityRail, swearing her head off. We weren't paid to take abuse. If she had not mentioned the babies, I would have terminated the call immediately. Her kids—like myself—had not asked to be born, right? They could not choose their parents either. It was these helpless children I was determined to help. I gave her the station's phone number for assistance in moving her luggage and kids.

Now what exactly was the privilege of a single mother? Did it entitle her to unrestricted tolerance? Was her offensive language justified? Could we take a poll on this? Or, was she a single mother in the first place because she was so vicious her man couldn't stand her?

Eating alone had to be one of the saddest and loneliest activities on the planet. Eating alone forced on you the excruciating fact that you had nobody to love and nobody was there for you. Simply unbearable. At home, I never ate except a bit of fruit on my days off.

I forced myself to eat while I had company, whoever was scheduled to have the same lunch break. Yesterday it was Bristol's backpacker Mark, who looked so English like a young Paul McCartney. Before that it was new manager Ratko, a Czech. 1300500 was a revolving door. My manager Justin would soon disappear to a lucrative job in Kings Cross, where the lifestyle was also convenient for his sexual preference.

Today I lunched out with former-geophysicist-turned-mum Nina. In the lift we encountered our then Immigration Minister, whose office was one floor down, with his hulking bodyguards. He nodded quietly and we nodded quietly back.

"I don't think he likes migrants," I told Nina.

"On the contrary. He's friendly with our community because we're migrants-through-the-front-door. He occasionally attends our events."

Hornsby's Mall makeover was a complete mess, with only takeaway food. We ordered grilled fish and sat in the Florence Street promenade.

"Aren't you scared racist people will treat you badly?" I asked Nina.

"No. Australians are *very* friendly. I've heard of some racist ones. Perhaps I've unknowingly encountered some, but when you behave like a model citizen they wouldn't have any reason to express their leaning, would they now?"

She explained migrants-through-the-front-door meant the UN gave them priority due to the persecution against their religious community. In their homelands others attacked and killed them and theirs, while authorities watched. As they were an anti-violence community with the principle *"Love for all. Hatred for none"*, they peacefully left.

"This is home now. It's no hardship to show gratitude to Australia."

"I'm proud Australia assists the oppressed," I offered. "But some people look down on people they don't know, thinking the women are backward and oppressed by their men. They wouldn't know you're very smart."

"It's no big deal. No one will think badly of me, except the low people. And no one will honour me, except the honourable."

She further told me there were over 1100 ethnic-groups and over 700 *active* languages in Indonesia, which made me sad thinking of our vastly diminished Aboriginal languages.

Nina belonged to the Minang ethnic-group of West Sumatra, a strongly matriarchal people. For over a thousand years women had been the heads of families. Only daughters can inherit.

"How cool! I've never heard of that before. Western suffragettes were only a hundred years ago. But who is persecuting the Minang people?"

"No, I didn't explain it well. Minang is my ethnic group. But the one being persecuted is my religious group, Ahmadiyya. In Muslim countries we're persecuted by other Muslims, the majority, who refuse to accept us as Muslims."

"Why?"

"Many issues. We don't believe in any form of violence."

In her sect women received equal treatment to men, with most of the women highly educated. She had a cousin who was an actual rocket scientist in the literal sense of the word. No kidding.

Pete flashed his light when I floor-walked after lunch.

"This guy's yelling his lung out 'cause his 178 is shockingly late," he told me. "What's happening?"

I checked with Ratko. He walked to Pete while calling Sydney Buses on the cordless phone.

"No reported delay," Ratko reported.

"Whaat?"

"Sydney, that's what we're told. We're under the obligation to tell customers exactly what we're told."

"But Radio Room fired that out right away! They didn't check first!"

Ratko lifted his arms, giving up.

In helplessness I turned to Pete, who was watching me closely. We looked into each other's eyes—feeling bad, guilty, very sorry for the caller. There was a shared understanding there...

Tuesday was my day off. I had asked our cleaner Vivian to come only every fortnight. Her pay came automatically from Mum's bank-account—Mum's way of showing me she cared.

"Rent out some rooms to students," Vivian suggested. "Extra money."

"No. The house isn't mine." Mum earned a lot as the finance director of a multinational trading company, while Dad earned obscene pay with an American oil company in Indonesia. But the house still belonged to them.

"You Aussies are particular," she chided. "We Asians never set boundaries. We help kids all through their education, and they never pack elderly parents off to nursing homes, isolated and lonely."

"Can't choose our parents," I shrugged.

Today I finally read my emails. Oh dear, there were hundreds unread, excluding spam. Alex wrote about being overseas for the first time. Mum said she and lover boy were going to Europe for a month. Dad invited me diving in North Sulawesi/Celebes. As a third wheel? Learnt my lesson, thank you. Vying for a parent's love was the outside of enough.

Panic assailed me. I absolutely refused to be alone during the holiday season. Moping. A single soul in an empty house.

My paternal Grandad Geoff had moved to beautiful Coolangatta after losing Granny to cancer. Retired, he spent his time fishing and gardening. He always found something to fix in his tiny house, too. The last time we were up north, the shape of tiles in his extra bathroom annoyed him so much that they had to be replaced.

He had called when my parents just split. Today, his answering machine said 'Gone fishing'.

My maternal grandparents now lived in Canada, Vancouver-born Nanna dragging Dorrigo-born Grandpa Stuart over there. We had been visiting them every April school holidays, but my fond memories were of Dorrigo and horse riding on their old farm.

I loved Dorrigo, a tranquil tiny town with rolling green hills and waterfalls on the North Coast of NSW. Thinking of it now, I felt another loss.

My cousins too had left Sydney. Stephen, a commercial pilot, followed his Pommy fiancée to work in London. Kirsten, a hairdresser on a luxury-cruise ship, was having the time of her life on the ocean with endless blue water and blue sky. With her fixation on everything blue she had even worn a blue wedding dress. Currently she was *so* in love with hubby, gorgeous Third Engineer of her ship.

Their mum was Dad's much older sister, Aunt Olivia. She was a very tall woman with a booming voice, and was a professor of nursing in a university in Cairns. When we stopped by before holidaying at the Great Barrier Reef, she told Mum about peeling a victim of a failed suicide from a burnt mattress. There and then I decided I would never become a doctor or a nurse. No nerve for that.

There were other relatives but none in Sydney.

Brenna had gone to Victoria. Lucy was touring Australia with her ballet group. I wrote to several other friends and to my disappointment received prompt replies that they all had plans of their own for the holiday season.

I felt very distressed.

I dreaded being alone and feeling suicidal. I so needed to be near people that I ended up calling my office to tell them I would be available for work from Christmas to New Year's Day. Yes, they appreciated it as many agents wanted this period off.

It was mid-December.

Pete's eyes lit up—with gladness?—when I arrived at work very early. I couldn't help feeling elated. Someone breathtakingly gorgeous was happy to see me. So yeah, I smiled my rare, genuine smile at him.

"Morning Sydney." Matt, who was chatting with him, greeted me. "Why so early? You usually show up very close to your start."

"I was awake. My dog wasn't keen to go jogging, somehow. I figured I might as well catch the earlier train." I did not tell them that my depression had jerked me up with pain at 4am. Since this occurrence had become less frequent, I hoped to be free of it soon. "You guys are early too."

"I'm the only manager who lives nearby," Matt explained. "They often schedule me to open the shop at 6am."

Pete did not say why he was early.

I was in the kitchen about to make tea when he declared from behind me, "When I see you so skinny I feel like giving you loads of chocolates."

Surprised, I whirled around.

"Tea is good, but you sorta look like you could use more nutrients. Here. Wanna try some chocolate?" He held out his hand for my cup. Again, a hint of clean citrusy scent wafted from him. Like a robot I handed him my cup. "Watch, so you know I don't drug your drink." His smiling eyes twinkled with a teasing glint.

"You only have to press a button, y'know," he pressed the hot chocolate milk button on the drink machine. "Faster than making tea."

"Thanks."

"No worries." He poured himself a cup of coffee and went to turn the TV on, keeping the volume low. He was silent again.

I stood awkwardly, sipping my chocolate. It was a bit heavy, but apparently I needed it. I had lost too much weight.

"You don't do drugs, do you?" I blurted out. Still 15 minutes to 6am. Soft morning sky outside the glass walls.

He turned to me with a smile.

"What do you think?" He flexed his arm, showing off healthy muscles. Today he was wearing a short-sleeved shirt with a tie.

"What about the other kids? The backpackers?"

"Those with Sinead are clean. They party hard but they don't do drugs. At least, not as long as they've been with us." Us. So he and Sinead were 'us'? How? Sinead was into lots of boys.

"Why are you with them? The Pommies?"

He looked surprised and gave it some thought.

"Actually, when I make friends, it never occurs to me where they come from..." he reflected. "It doesn't matter to me what backgrounds they have. The Pommies are friends from earlier jobs. But I have Aussie friends too. Here we have Jack, Kevin... How was it that Aussies call the Brits Poms?"

"No idea. It's a friendly nickname though. Not a racial slur."

"So you aren't racist... What do you think of our multi-racial callers?"

"They all have distinguishing traits," I smiled. "But yes, I'm not racist. I give all callers equal deference. No one is more equal than the others."

He laughed out loud. I was pleased to hear the wonderful sound.

Matt joined us in the kitchen. He was a funny guy and we ended up gossiping about callers. Pete and I had actually spoken with tens of thousands of people from all races, while Matt monitored calls.

We talked about one particular race who repeatedly asked

"What's after that?" to torture us. Just because they could and because it was free.

We talked about another race who asked "What ifs?" over and over, worrying unnecessarily. They were the most meticulous race who didn't like surprises and scrupulously planned every possible detail imaginable.

We all agreed that the Poms weren't whingers. They promptly accepted the information we gave them. Perhaps they desperately needed money for grog, but they happily travelled long distances to work. Or at least, they thanked us politely and cheerfully.

And no. I won't tell you who did not do that.

Rain came pouring down later that week and the temperature plunged. I floor-walked during a managers' meeting and had to check out on problems myself.

"Sydney," Pete said when I answered his light. "This guy's at the Cricket Ground. The match has been cancelled 'cause of the rain. His boys are soaking wet and it's the coldest day ever for summer. They wanna go home, but no Special-Event bus can be seen. They've paid for return tickets and with the other cricket crowd are waiting to go home."

I stood near him as I phoned Sydney Buses. The contact there replied with an icy voice, "The return service is only scheduled from 4 o'clock."

"But the game's been cancelled *now*. The customer said they've paid for return tickets and the cricket crowd are waiting in the rain to go home."

"I DON'T CARE!" he snapped. "The return buses will be from four!" And off he went.

What a horrible man! Arrogant beyond belief... I was shaken. Taken aback by his contempt.

"Sydney?" Pete enquired in a gentle note. "You look like a kicked kitten." *Don't cry.*

There was deep understanding in his eyes. His concern loosened up my tight emotion that I opened up. In wretched voice I told him about the self-centred, obnoxious Radio Room man.

"Can't he phone the event's organiser who's chartered the Special-Event buses to work this out? Like, show some interest in helping customers? I'm just out of school here—how was I to know our public service was so non-customer-service focused?"

"Sydney... I'm sorry you have to take the brunt."

"Never mind me." I worried about those kids—and about Pete. Sydney Buses never gave a damn that we were constantly on the receiving end of the filthiest profanities imaginable. "What are you going to tell your customer with poor, soaking children?"

Calmly Pete spoke to appease his caller, his sympathetic tone and mesmerising voice 'hypnotising' them to walk far away to catch the non-special buses. Marvellously he avoided the caller's anger by being helpful. All the time his eyes held mine. Again, I felt that connection...

"Hello?" A balled paper hit me. Sinead grinned. "My light is flashing!"

December continued to be hectic. One distasteful thing was that the company made more money when a disaster struck. Of course it was not their fault, but the call volumes always jumped significantly at these times, bringing in a lot of money for our centre. Since this would increase our bonus considerably, I could not help feeling guilty. I felt compelled to go out of my way to be helpful.

One morning, somebody figured the railway track was the-place-to-be for committing suicide. Successfully, too. Many had done this and we weren't supposed to broadcast it. I personally thought Sydney trains should copy the stations of other world-class cities such as Singapore's. There wasn't the slightest chance anybody could jump onto the rail tracks there.

Another morning, there was an oil spill. Somewhere else, there was a burst water main. Both causing major traffic diversions.

On another day, raging bushfires in Berowra cut the railway line and the motor freeway. The calls slammed us non-stop. We had fewer agents because many of them lived on the Central

Coast and could not pass the fire to get to work. The centre called in Pete and others in Sydney who were on their days off for overtime.

In panic, thousands of stranded passengers asked, "When will the train service resume?"

Sorry guys. Sydney trains had not faxed us the "Bushfire Schedule". They didn't give us a crystal ball either.

"How am I going to get home?" asked exhausted Lynn. "I drove to work because the trains were already out when I left. Now the roads are closed, too."

"Would you like my house key?" I offered. I gazed down the northern glass wall. The streets were choked full, the traffic stationary. The long traffic jam from Berowra had reached Hornsby. "Go there and have a rest."

When I turned around Pete was looking at me. His eyes thoughtful.

The Bus Just Drove Off With My Christmas Shopping!

I was busy at the office answering calls all morning on Christmas Eve and Christmas day.

"The bus just drove off with my Christmas shopping!" screamed a lady, "I forgot to take it with me when I got off the bus!"

Christmas Eve was also horrible with last-minute travel plans. Several callers were disturbingly heart wrenching.

"To Pokolbin Prison, please," requested a woman in a very weak, barely audible low voice I could well relate to. A vision came to me of a gaunt, sickly, very depressed lady.

I worked out her travel plan. She had to catch a bus, two trains, and a bus again, for a three-hour journey. Then she asked, "How much would it cost for a pensioner and a three-year old?"

Tears gathered in my eyes. A poor young mother with a young child trying to visit her worthless husband at Christmas!

And she was not alone. "To John Moroney Prison, please," said a miserable mother.

"To Silverwater Correction Centre, please." A sad girlfriend.

"To Long Bay Jail, please." A wretched daughter.

Long-suffering souls requested travel plans for Lithgow Jail, Parklea Jail, Goulburn Jail—you name it. I do have a word to anyone out there planning to commit a crime. Please, please stop and think of your loved ones... Consider their feelings. You don't want them to call 1300500 on Christmas Eve. You want them cooking your special dinner!

Come to think of it, there was hardly a male caller wanting to visit a female prisoner. Either the men did not use public transport or they didn't bother to visit. What did this tell you?

The next day chocolates flowed on the floor. The managers and floor walkers went around offering lavish Christmas goodies.

My backpacker friends rejoiced in the special feast laid out by the management in the break area. Sinead and gang had chosen to be rostered on Christmas so they could have New Year's Eve off.

"What are you doing at work?" Lindsay heaped his plate with delicacies. "Our families are far away, but yours are here."

"They aren't," I confessed. Thinking of all the empty promises. That they would always be there for me. One was diving in paradise. The other at a Swiss ski resort.

"No family coming over? No? You aren't going anywhere?"

"No." I speared a strawberry and held it in the chocolate-fondue fountain.

"You have the whole place to yourself?"

"Pretty much."

"Awesome. You mean we can come over and party at your place?"

"Yes! Oh blessed, yes!" Sinead joined in with enthusiasm. The plate she had been delving into was forgotten. "Please Sydney?"

"Dash it," Lindsay apologised. "I was only teasing."

"But I'm not!" Sinead pressed on, unabashed. "What sort of a place do you have? A house? An apartment?"

I was under siege. Around the break area, expectant eyes waited. Pete stood quietly by the window, but why did the silences between us feel very loud?

"It's a house. But there's nothing cooking."

"We'll think of something," Jane urged. "Just say yes."

"We'll bring the grog," Sinead offered, "We'll convert you yet."

"The shops are closed!" Moya interjected, "Where'd we get some? Do you have a barbeque? Any hope we'd get something somewhere?"

"The shops are closed," I told them, still trying to analyse my feelings about having them over. Should I test the water? Was I ready to open up? "I only have blueberry muffins." Yucky frozen ones. Been there for a few months too.

"No grog?"

"Well... There's Dad's... I suppose..." But when would he ever return anyway? Hang Dad. These friends didn't do drugs. I rose to the occasion, "To my place. After work this arvo."

A big step for me... I waited with impatience and trepidation for the end of my shift.

"Next train from Newcastle Station to Katoomba, please," asked a 'Newcastellan'. This was my term for a Novocastrian, no offence intended. I gave him a travel plan with a change-over at Strathfield.

"Darling, I'm in Fassifern. What time will it be at Fassi?"

I gave him the time at Fassifern.

"What time will I arrive at Hazo?"

Why on earth didn't he simply ask for Fassifern to Hazelbrook in the first place?

Another caller requested the Port Stephens 130 from Newcastle Station to Nelsons Bay, while actually she would board it at Mayfield and disembark at Salt Ash. For some reason that eluded us at the 1300500, many Newcastellans had a rather convoluted way of requesting travel plans. Well, Newcastellans?

To my disappointment, Pete was not among the bunch of friends who followed me onto the 14:42 Northern Line that afternoon. Hang Pete. I had decided to have fun.

The day was scorching hot. I lent the girls Mum's swimming suits and the boys Dad's and they helped me to roll away the swimming-pool cover.

I cringed when I saw my reflection in swimming suit. After ignoring the mirror for ages, I was horrified to see my near-anorexic unenviable bony self. It wasn't news that I had lost weight, but frightening to notice how much. Self-conscious, I covered up by putting on my long-sleeved rash-shirt.

"Grand Christmas in the sun!" Jane squealed happily. "If this doesn't beat all."

"Enjoy," I commanded. "Hang on, I'll get towels."

I was at the linen cupboard when the doorbell rang, and answered it with an armful of towels on my hip and Dimity barking by my legs.

It was Pete. How my heart sang with joy.

"Barbeque," he put a bag on the foyer table and helped me close the door. "Raided my uncle's freezer."

"Uncle? You have family here?"

"Yep. Wife an Aussie. Made a wicked roast dinner last night. They've gone to her parents' in Cessnock."

He looked around. Pete was in my house! For a long moment I stood transfixed, flustered by his nearness, his masculinity, his scent.

For quite some time now we'd had this *thing*. Besides our occasional chats we had a tacit communication. As if I could tell him about my life without a word. As if we understood each other just by shooting looks across the room. Or across the workstations in our pod.

What did he think of my empty home now? Proof of the vacuum in my life, my hollow world, as he had perceived? I was almost certain he could see me going to sleep at 5pm yesterday, anguished over being alone and hungry on Christmas Eve.

He turned to me. Dazed, speechless, my wit deserted me. He searched my face.

"You're trembling," he stated.

"Nervous," I replied stupidly.

He laughed, the beautiful sound filling my heart with so much warmth. Then without a by your leave he gave me the kiss of my life.

I won't tell you about it.

I will not tell you how to do it if you don't know how. Or how special the kiss was.

But of course my dog felt left out and came barking between us. I jumped away. Dimity!

Suddenly I remembered all the (one-sided) nightly conversations I had had with Dimity these last few months. No falling in love. No boys. I would never marry. Never bring a child into this cruel life. I wouldn't.

I shouldn't.

With thundering heart I picked up the towels that I had dropped to the floor.

"Sydney?" Pete asked with an enquiring tone.

I didn't look at him. I did not know what to say. I did not know how I felt, except very scared.

I stood up and walked quickly to our friends by the pool. Sinead was eyeing us intently, studying our faces. I set my mild, expressionless mien.

My friends asked me to take their pictures, to brag to their loved ones back home that come Christmas, Sydney was the place to be. Swimming in the sunshine. No freezing winter to whinge about.

"We're in this contract fulltime until Australia Day, January 26," Sinead told me as we idly paddled a backstroke. "We're saving to continue our way north."

My eyes darted to Pete as worry started to gnaw. Was he going away with them soon? What about the earth-moving foyer incident?

After swimming he walked across the lawn checking all the flowerbeds, shrubs and trees, and looked around with interested eyes. I watched him covertly for a while. Then I followed him and answered his questions with reserved politeness.

"Jacaranda. It's Australian. Flowers only in November-December. Students call it the examination tree."

He liked the jacaranda, with its beautiful purple flowers strewn across the grass. Next he asked about the kangaroo paw, wattle, and other native plants. Mark and Moya joined us and I ended up giving a botany lesson.

"You don't have a bottlebrush," Mark commented. "I remember that from a book on Captain Cook."

"I do, actually. But the one I have is Heath Banksia, that plant with rosemary-like leaves. As it only flowers in winter, you can't see bottlebrushes now."

"Is it true they need fire to release the seed?"

"One type of banksia, yes. Mine here can't stand fire. See that plant? The waratah. It's Aboriginal for beautiful. In spring it will have vivid red flowers. Waratahs thrive after bushfires."

"Gosh," Pete exclaimed, "I hope you don't have a fire in your backyard!"

"No," I laughed. He tilted his head, looking arrested. Then he smiled, as if pleased that I laughed. "No fire except the barbecue."

"Speaking of barbecue, Pete," Mark nudged him, "I'm hungry. Can I start it?"

"Yes. It's ready for cooking, I've had it marinating."

Mark walked eagerly away.

I asked Pete, "You marinated it? You know how to cook?"

As we walked towards our friends, Pete told me about his cooking. He had travelled to several countries and knew many recipes. "For any meat dish, add a teaspoon of garlic, a teaspoon of ginger, and something sour."

"Something sour?"

"Tomatoes. Vinegar. Pineapple pieces. Pureed peaches. Chopped green apples. Sour mangoes. Tamarind," he listed. "Any of these. For this barbecue, we will use lemons."

"Garlic, ginger, something sour. Is that all?"

"Well, that's the basics. You can always add other stuff like salt, pepper, herbs, spices."

"Easy. Right?"

I took them to visit Dad's thousands-of-dollars, lavish-choice vintage cellar and told them to make free of whatever they fancied.

"You really don't drink at all?" Lindsay flipped lamb ribs on the barbie. To my astonishment, the aroma of food in that simple marinade—garlic, ginger, lemon... and a smidgen of Vegemite! —was heavenly. "Not even a bit?"

"By not drinking even a bit, I'll never risk drinking too much. I just choose not to. Sort of, why drink when you can live without?"

"Because it's fun!" Sinead promptly piped in. "Makes you mighty happy."

"Nothing quenches thirst like a beer," Lindsay topped.

"Good on you. Just for myself, I'll pass, thank you."

"That's bad!" Mark, an economics student back in Bristol, sucked on his coldie. "Dire for your economy. Imagine if Aussies stopped drinking. Your great wine production, wine tours, and beer industry would collapse! Unemployment would increase. Your government would lose all those beautiful taxes. They'd rather have young Aussies die on the roads, don't you know?"

"And we backpackers would lose the fruit-picking jobs," Lindsay added. "You should at least drink responsibly."

"And that is?"

"Do not get foxed as bad as Sinead." Lindsay smirked at Sinead, receiving a punch on the arm in return. "And don't drive when you drink. Call 1300500!"

Everybody burst out laughing, except Mark who was prone to turn any conversation into a debate.

"I'm not joking, you know," he argued enthusiastically. "As long as Australia produces wines, there's no way you can stop drink-driving. Your government can't afford to ban the alcohol ads here because too many people are dependent on the industry. Just like some other countries can't afford to ban cigarette ads."

He was a convincing speaker with a forceful intellect, but in today's holiday mood not everyone cared for his opinions.

"Then thank God they don't produce tobacco here as well," Moya cut him short. She slouched down next to me, crossing her legs. I noted black nail polish on her toes. "Hey Sydney, we'll put up with a teetotaller like you any day. Tell me your plans. You staying on with 1300500?"

"Probably. Now that I have the hang of it, I rather like knowing what's happening in Sydney. Need to switch to part-time, though. Uni starts February."

"*Uni*? Indeed?! Aren't you going to take calls until you're 64?" Everybody guffawed again.

"Are you really going to uni?" Sinead asked. "Oh blessed! What will you study?"

"Animation."

"Why animation?" Pete asked, just when I thought he would remain watching in silence.

"Well... I want so much to draw or paint. But I'm hopeless at those. We had a school excursion to the Design Centre in Enmore. And hey, I thought I could learn animation. Digital technology makes it possible."

He waited. Nervous, I plunged on.

"Animation is fun. It'll be challenging too. I dream of creating stories and peopling them with my own characters." I sensed his penetrating gaze could see my dreamland... No Mrs Fu yelling. No manager breathing down my neck for lower AHT. No one to dictate what I should create... "I'll learn the basics of 3D animation, visual effects, basic game programming. If I can't create stories, at least I'd get a job in media advertising."

"Good choice," he agreed. "Seeing how rapidly the online technology is advancing, you'll always be in demand."

Respecting my parents' house, the friends drank moderately. No mayhem.

"Come often Jane," I teased Jane when she washed up after us. She even microwaved the wipes for a few minutes to kill the germs.

The friends used my computer to email their "Grand-Christmas-In-The-Sun" pictures back home, showing off to families suffering snow in the northern hemisphere. They invited me to their homes too, giving me their details.

"Keep in touch *when this is all over,"* Sinead suggested.

My head swivelled to Pete at this. He held my gaze from across the room and my heart thundered at what I saw in his eyes. *I don't want this to be over...* Time stood still as we became oblivious to the others. The rest of the room ceased to exist.

Until Sinead whistled aloud.

She turned on the music and we moshed on the back veranda. I danced with all the boys including Pete, heart thumping loud, gaze averted. Too fragile and confused, I was not in a fit state to make decisions. Not ready for more than friendship. He did not push me, giving me breathing space. But what an effect he had on me... I was a bundle of nerves.

His eyes, charged with a strong current, bored into mine as they were leaving. I was rather unmindful when the others said "Thanks a million" with their Pommy accents.

On The Porch To My Heart

One day, I would be free of pain. One day, I would bounce back and be happy.

But why on earth couldn't it be today?

I smiled at the ceiling when I woke up, reliving the rioting sensation of my very beautiful first kiss. Until I remembered today was Boxing Day.

Dad was thousands of miles away diving in Sulawesi. This reminded me that Pete was not from Sydney. Just like Dad, one day soon Pete would be thousands of miles away from me. In a few months he would not be here. No more gazing with tender feelings or electric promises.

Gone.

And he would spare me no more thoughts, just like my parents.

Suddenly Boxing Day slammed me with acute depression.

Now in case you don't know what Boxing Day is, it is the day after Christmas, when long ago rich western aristocrats sent boxes of gifts to the houses of their workers. Of course, if they happened to be miserly landlords, they boxed their Christmas leftovers to send out.

And in case you haven't been to Sydney on Boxing Day, the start of our annual Sydney to Hobart yacht race is a vision to behold.

Dad and his buddies used to be racing participants. When they dispersed, Dad took us to watch the start from his small boat. You could feel the excitement of the race as your sail flapped in the wind. And if your parents had brought you here since you were in a backpack baby-carrier, it felt weird to miss it when in Sydney.

Today I couldn't help feeling like a little wounded bird.

Divorcing parents are deluded if they think that their older kids would not suffer as a result. Divorce taught kids not to trust. Like, how could I have confidence in Pete when he was a drifter? Was there any guarantee he would not get bored and leave? My own parents left.

I avoided looking at him all morning.

Struggling to sound cheerful, I directed callers to North Head and Watsons Bay—the places to be on this beautiful day.

I didn't dare to smile at Pete. But I did notice Flo—the pretty, blond Aussie who today sat in our pod—flirting with him and flaunting her assets, blatantly trying to wrangle a date. So far he had not flirted back. Still, I shouldn't worry, right? It was I who wanted to be alone. I was the one doing my best not to look his way. But my feelings towards him were in turmoil.

The kiss! How could I dismiss the glorious feeling? Or the looks from such a fine man?

And so I vacillated.

I did notice that Jack had an incessant cough. He drank water. Talked. Pressed MUTE. Coughed. Drank water. Released MUTE. Talked. Pressed MUTE. Coughed. All because he refused to take sick leave for fear of losing his Attendance bonus. That was what happened when you were an almost-lowest-paid Australian. And it was what happened when the government outsourced their agencies to the cheapest bidders.

Instead of being impressed by Jack's $800/month bonus from Perfect Attendance, today I felt sorry for him. I sincerely hoped he would find further education and advance his career.

Having driven to work in Dad's huge car, I carried my heavy heart to North Head after my shift. No, I wasn't taking public transport today: I was copying our transport ministry bosses!

I drove to Manly on my P-plate.

Though the racing participants had sailed away, the water was still dotted with hundreds of beautiful sails. I parked near North Head, then walked and walked very fast. I found that if you walked like a woman on a mission people did not bother you. The wind whipped at my long hair. The seagulls shrieked. And my heart writhed in agony.

"Dad... where are you? Dad... the Harbour is still as breathtaking as always. The crag of North Head still majestic. And we would never sail out together again..."

As I walked, wishing I had never been born, I questioned life. Right now, I had no sense of purpose, so why was I here? Why did people have kids? Apart from nature's way to ensure the continuation of the species, why were we here? For what purpose? Since we didn't ask to be born, did we even have to stay?

I walked and I cried angry tears. I was furious with myself for not yet bouncing back to normalcy. Felt like I had been in a state of arrested development for two months. Where was my youthful spirit? My joie de vivre?

I wanted it back!

When I returned to my car at dusk, another car was parked next to mine. Pete leaned in front of it, arms crossed, watching me with concerned eyes. My heart flipped at the sight of him. My steps faltered. We looked at each other. *Don't lose it now*. His gaze implored me. *I care*.

Swiftly he unfolded his arms and walked to me—both hands outstretched reaching for mine.

"I was at Hornsby Library's car park after work when I saw you running to your car." He squeezed my hands comfortingly, looking into my eyes. "I was worried for you, so I followed. Just to make sure you're alright."

He searched my eyes and then pulled me into his arms. I was surprised at how soothing it felt. It felt—*safe*. It was true nobody had hugged me since my parents left, but still I didn't remember feeling a hug this good. He was warm, strongly solid, and smelled wonderful. He was real.

"Wanna talk about it?" His nose nuzzled my hair.

No words could come out of my mouth. I just wanted to be held. Forever. As if he understood he tightened his hold, tucking my head in his throat, his hand soothing my hair. Gingerly, I put my arms around his waist.

"You're wonderful," I admitted after a while.

His hands lifted my face towards his.

"Do you have my number?" he asked quietly. "I wrote it down in your little phonebook last night when our friends were writing theirs. Don't hesitate to call me any time."

I nodded. He bent down and kissed the tip of my nose.

Pete followed me home in the car he borrowed from his uncle. At my place he came out to meet me. Before we could say anything the landline rang, and I let him in while I went to answer the phone. It was Mum's friend Kate. I listened to her as Pete flipped his own phone open, talking quietly away from me.

"Darling, we're all down on the South Coast. Come over to our holiday home in Broulee now. I didn't realise you've been home alone."

"Now?" Get real. Why hadn't she invited me earlier when I had no plans for the season? Because you-know-who just rang from Italy asking her to check on me? It hurt to be treated as an afterthought.

But wonderful Kate was a mean cook. Really. Don't laugh. This was very big to me. Her house always smelled of heavenly baking. Each time we visited when I was a little girl, I used to ask after hugs and greetings, "Can we eat now?" and received more hugs and kisses.

In my very secret wish, since childhood I had always imagined my dream home. I had never bothered to visualise how it would look, but I knew it would smell like Kate's heavenly baking.

Thinking of her food, I forgave her for not knowing I had been home alone. That was how badly I'd missed home cooking.

"Let me think..." I considered my schedule as I looked at Pete, who was now crouching down patting Dimity. Should I cram this in? "Kate, I'll be having Your Say training for the next three days. If you still want me over, I could drive down after work on the last day. Have to return to take calls for New Year's Eve, though. I've agreed to help out until midnight."

"Midnight? But 1300500 closes at ten!" Kate, who often used public transport, knew this. Only much later would 1300500 be open 24 hours.

"Special occasion."

"But darling, it means after five hours driving you'll be with us for only—what? A day and two nights? I guess... that's better than nothing... We'll have a full day at least. What would you like me to cook?"

Pete looked at me when I hung up.

"Your Say training? Seriously? Why'd you be willing to take complaints when Sydney is notorious for late running trains, buses, and ferries? Sydney's rail network is complicated. One problem train can cause a hopeless domino effect on many lines." Probably sensing my reluctance to talk about my problems, he talked shop. "I was shopping in Chatswood before Christmas. I know what it's like when the trains make passengers wait in the extreme heat of your summer. How on earth can they call it a minor delay when no trains show up for half an hour? Chatswood trains are supposed to be every 8 minutes."

"I've been stranded with friends at Parramatta River, not only once, but twice," I topped, swapping experience. "The Rivercat was cancelled."

"Exactly! So why'd you join Your Say, Sydney?"

"Oh come on Pete. This is my hometown, I'm entitled to love it. It never fails to hurt my feelings each time a Melburnian yells about how stupid our city planning or transport is. Criticism should give Sydney the drive to better itself. I'll start with myself. I'll listen to our transport feedback."

At that moment the doorbell rang and I turned in surprise.

"Don't worry," Pete went to answer the door. "It's pizza."

"Pizza?" I asked stupidly.

"Yes. Y'know, what some people eat when they don't have the time to cook?"

Of course.

Darkness had just descended on the long summer day. We sat on the back veranda, listening to cicadas and eating pizza under the Southern stars.

"You genuinely believe people's complaints will improve dodgy services?" he asked.

"It could. For example Sydney trains has this habit of saying over 95% of its services are reliable. Meaning it needs input to make travelling a better experience for the unfortunate 5% of its passengers. Faulkner says it's not enough to be better than others—you should be better than yourself."

He looked at me with wondering eyes.

"I like that attitude," he smiled softly, handing me more pizza.

His smile stayed with me long after he left.

At the office, my American boss had invited us agents to develop our skills.

Those who aspired to managerial level went through a selection process. I later understood this involved intrigues such as elbowing, backstabbing and denigrating other candidates (you know, just like in most workplaces). The survivors were called Seconded Managers. Numerous co-workers would successfully advance their career through this scheme.

I didn't want to be a manager because you had to work full-time and I was to be a part-timer when uni started. I agreed instead to handle feedback. For the following three days I had my training with Matt, its trainer/manager.

Your Say was a happy, high-spirited team. They nicknamed it "Yellow Submarine" team and decorated their pods in a deep-marine theme. Once they noisily sang the Beatles' "Yellow Submarine" until the management told them to curb it. After all, it would not look good if callers knew Your Say—where passengers phoned to vent their anger and to relate their woes—

was the happiest team on the floor. Once a guy on a Newcastle train was hit by faulty toilet's pressure burst. After journeying almost three hours many people had been using it before him, building up the pressure too high. When he pressed the FLUSH button, this high pressure caused the receptive tank to burst and throw out its contents on the poor man. Shit happens. He ended up screaming on his mobile phone straight from the toilet... and Your Say team laughed and laughed all the way home.

During training I listened to Your Say agents for a few hours every day. I used to think Your Say line was scary, assuming that was where abusive callers went. Turned out callers on the Information line were more abusive. Not getting what they wanted, they just lost it because they didn't know how to channel their anger. In contrast, most Your Say callers knew their complaints would be forwarded to management.

Some of the calls made me smile though. A girl had a crush on a helpful staff member at a Lost Property office, so he received a flowery compliment.

There were serial callers. An ex-girlfriend stalked a bus driver. Every week she lodged a complaint about him. She knew everything about his driving and his whereabouts. She simply could not get over him. Must be a great bloke.

Away from Your Say pods, one fine bloke rarely took his eyes off me as he talked on the phone. I knew, 'cause I constantly looked his way. There was honesty there. The distance between our pods could not stop the electric current. *I wanna be with you...*

On the day I was to go to Broulee, I left Dimity with Vivian and drove to work. When I signed out Pete was waiting quietly by the lift, looking very good. I faced him saying, "Don't follow me. I'm going intercity today, not just to Manly."

"Alright," he agreed, probably because he had overheard me ordering prawns and pineapple chicken from Kate. I appreciated the fact that he was subtle and polished, never coarse or dull or blunt. This week I had come to know he was also caring. I sensed Pete wasn't just a pretty face. Deep inside there were more interesting things about him to learn. Surreptitiously I observed him in the lift down, wondering, how had he lived his life before today?

He walked me to the car. When I turned to him, he opened his arms without a word. I went to him and we shared a wonderful long hug.

Robbed of his warmth when we parted, I was overwhelmed by the loss assailing me. Oh I was going to miss him!

"Keep safe," he kissed my nose. Our eyes were saying "I'll be thinking of you."

He was forever on my mind as I drove across the city to go south. Pete had been tapping delicately at the door to my heart for some time now. He was there. I knew he was there. I could hear his footsteps approaching. I could sense him softly calling to my soul. But I left him standing outside. On the porch to my heart. I did not grant him entrance.

A few times I met him there. His eyes would enquire about *me*. Worry about me. Full of concern for me. And convey deep affection and love. I would look into his eyes and dream of forever. I would steal a few moments of closeness before retreating. But it was getting harder to keep the door to my heart closed.

He was kind. Patient. He was breathtaking, beautiful. Well—in a masculine way.

He had this strong, chiselled manly jaw. He had a straight, firm, masculine nose. His mannish brows slanted in perfect arches. His wide, beautiful, sculpted lips had given me my unforgettable first kiss. And oh—his clear, gorgeous green eyes were definitely not girlish, because no girl's eyes had ever sent my heart throbbing wild with a single glance.

Could you not tell I was smitten? I could clearly envision every line of his face even when he was far away.

Still, I had not let him in. I left him standing on the porch to my heart. Perhaps he would always wait for me out there. In the cold. In the rain. In the wind. Or in the heat of our Australian summer. Perhaps he would be gone. Never to come back again. Was there any wisdom in letting him in?

I thought a lot about him as I listened to my new music in the warm dry car. Outside, it rained a deluge from Unanderra onwards. But I loved rain, finding it soothing either as a cold mist or bucketing down.

The drive was without drama, apart from getting nostalgic when passing Milton. Dad and I had climbed the nearby Mt Pigeon House when I was twelve. It had been my idea, "Let's check out what Captain Cook found interesting!" And Dad had indulged me, explaining the geological and geophysical aspects of the formation. Dad, who used to be my best buddy...

"SYDNEEY...," Kate hugged me like a mother bear when I pulled in at her holiday house. It was still daylight at 8pm. "Darling, how great of you to brave this rain!"

"The welcome's sure worth the trouble."

Her genuine love was balm for my soul. Warm hugs. Delicious food. Pressies. Games.

Pristine Broulee on the NSW South Coast was beautiful and tranquil, much nicer than noisy touristy beaches. The next morning we jogged along the untrodden expanse of white sand. I surfed the glorious water, and the kids thought me cool because their dad Holger didn't surf. I ended up teaching them surfing and earned worshipful looks from eight-year-old Frank.

Holger was Swiss through and through, except that he hated cold and migrated to Australia for the climate. While fishing later, we engaged in friendly banter on how to pronounce Broulee. I said it the Aussie way, Browlee, but he kept saying Broolé.

"Aussies aren't actually consistent," he argued. "We say names any way we want."

"Touché. Newcastellans pronounce Beaumont Street the

French way, while Sydneysiders pronounce Beauchamp Street the Aussie way—Beacham."

"And how did Sydney come up with the name Railway Square when it's a triangle?" he topped. "Or World Square when it's round?"

It was a day jammed with activities. I felt invigorated. Lovely Kate, who was genuinely concerned about how thin I had become, made it her mission to feed me well. I was pampered and fussed over.

Kate had three children. The eldest was Frances, a daughter from her first marriage. Frances' dad used to be a dancer for a famous American singer. If you are of Kate's generation, you most certainly own this singer's records. Kate had been a music journalist, chasing after great musicians all over the world. The dancer was a very charismatic graduate of an American dance academy. The super-famous singer had been very busy. His dancer had not. That was how he and Kate had ended shacking up at his hotel.

Frances, a chocolate-eyed 12-year old with olive skin and very black hair, considered herself a lucky girl because every member of her very big family spoiled her rotten. She had two younger half-brothers from her dad's second marriage, two younger half-brothers from her mum's second marriage, three older stepbrothers from her mum's husband's previous marriage, and two older stepbrothers from her dad's wife's previous marriage.

"I'm the prettiest girl in the family," she beamed. "So many boys love me!"

Would I be less bitter if Mum and Dad had split when I was that young? Less sullen? Would it have been easier to cope?

Which Girl Are You Trying To Impress?

New Year's Eve hit 1300500 like a cyclone. It felt like all Sydneysiders and tourists were making last-minute plans to greet the new millennium.

The contract specified 80% of the calls had to be answered within 20 seconds. It meant the Ministry of Transport fined us when we kept callers waiting for longer than 20 seconds. Now, the agents' bonus was based on how much money came in. When we were fined, less money would be thrown into bonus pool. So everyone on the floor panicked. Nobody wanted to be the lowest-paid Australian, remember?

"My bus is diverted! Where should I catch it from now?"

I guided them step-by-step through the bus diversion. "Thanks for calling!"

RELEASE.

"Darling, the signs say the Harbour Bridge is closed for buses and all traffic from six o'clock. But how come ferries continue to operate?"

"The ferries don't go on the Bridge." They go under it, in case you didn't know." Thanks for calling!"

RELEASE.

© la Uaro

"The ferries don't go on the Bridge."

They go under it, in case you didn't know.

"We only have to pay for one child and the other is free?"

"Correct. On our public transport you only pay for one child, regardless of the number of children."

"But my kids are twins. Which one should I pay for?"

"It doesn't matter, Ma'am. Thanks for calling!"

RELEASE!

"What a hot voice! Babe, what colour is your underwear?"

RELEASE. Didn't deign to say a word.

"The taxi driver is refusing to help with my luggage," a soft-spoken trannie whined. "We've been arguing for ten minutes. He scares me. Could you put me through to complaints, please."

"Will do." While I clicked the Your Say extension, I could hear the taxi driver abusing her because she was a trans. He argued that he never helped a male passenger who only had one suitcase, but he would when there were many suitcases. He adamantly refused to acknowledge that she was not a male anymore. So they were at a stalemate.

While I was definitely straight, I respected others. I believed people of different races, religions and sexual-orientations are entitled to a decent life just as you would want for yourself, even when you disagree with their views or choices. I did not condone this driver's language as nobody in the world deserved it.

"Please get his driver's ID," I told her. "Thanks for calling!"

RELEASE.

Of course, the bulk of NYE calls were about how to get to parties and the best vantage points to watch Sydney's famous fireworks. Mrs Macquarie's Chair. McMahons Point... You name it.

The non-stop calls banged our ears fast and furiously. At the start, the managers offered chocolates to console agents. That was plain unintelligent—how could you eat when you were this busy? Everyone felt the pressure. Very soon even managers and administration staff sat down to take calls. Still the calls continued to drop in like a storm. Why on earth did thousands plan their night at the last minute?

So I talked. And talked. My voice was tired. Before I worked at a call centre, I had not known a voice could get tired, just like it could grow old. I drank water. And talked.

And I missed Pete terribly...

Why did he have to be so wonderful? Should I continue keeping my distance? But how much longer? Worse, could I?

I was torn with indecision.

He would be gone soon. Never to return. Wouldn't it hurt to be treated as a fling? This thing between us could go nowhere. Who was going to jump into the abyss at 18 anyway? He was an American. For God's sake, he had gone *downtown* to party.

I logged off the phone at midnight. All television screens changed from transport-information updates to bursts of beautiful colour from new-millennium fireworks. Everyone on the floor cheered. Champagne erupted.

"Under 18," I smiled, shaking my head when offered a flute. Felt like I had said it too often lately, hounded by friends to drink. They would leave me be for a while before trying again, because in their kindness they wanted kids to discover the joy of booze and cutting loose. So I smiled. And smiled. No thank you.

Ours was a society which regarded me a freak for saying no. To many, drinking and casual sex were mere forms of entertainment, meaningful or hollow. During high school, friends wanted respect for their choices, which was fine by me. But they labelled me prudish, killjoy, un-Australian. Do you know how intimidating it was for a teen to live and breathe among the majority of prude-haters? Well, human rights belonged to each and every one of us. Ours was a free country. I was permitted my choices.

My office friends cheerily wished me Happy New Year. *Friends*. I did not regard them as "co-workers" anymore. They were now "friends". Young and old.

We weren't a bunch of lazy bums, you know. Some were elderly pensioners. They returned to work because staying home was slower than a wet week after a time. They loved to meet fellow human beings at the office. They were wonderful to chat with. They had interesting thoughts, feelings, and rich histories to stimulate your mind.

Several were mothers. They worked while their kids were at school, refusing to stay at home sucking tax-payers' money through welfare benefits.

And several were students, working hard to support their study.

The lift down was noisy with best wishes.

We crossed the pedestrian bridge over George Street still munching chocolates from the office. As my friends went to party in Hornsby first, I descended the stairs to the platform alone. A few police officers stood around to "welcome" the (totalled) NYE revellers. One of them was extremely good looking and he winked at me, "Happy New Year!"

My train was empty as it was going to the City to pick up party-goers. I checked my SMS and they were all from Pete. Immediately I felt euphoric.

"Wish u were here"

And, *"Happy NY!"*

And, *"Can't talk. Too noisy. Thinking of you"*

I alighted in Beecroft blissfully happy and had a very restful sleep... Until I had to sit down at my workstation at 6am taking calls.

"Sweetheart, I wanna go home," a written-off guy slurred.

"Give me a clue where you are."

"In the City... near a big building... Whaat? No... Dunno what building. It's big." Right. In the *City*. Near a big building. Really narrowed it down, ya think?

"I lost my wallet on the train," another soused one reported. "It was on the City Circle." And did you know there were hundreds of trains in the City Circle last night?

"I lost my wallet, not sure where."

"I lost my wallet!"

There. Don't get drunk when you go out on New Year's Eve. Pickpockets are out too.

Happy New Year Sydney!

"You wouldn't *believe* the amount of roobish at the Opera House!" Sinead cornered me near the lockers, looking exhausted *after* her days off. We gave each other Happy-New-Year hugs and she urgently whispered that we must talk.

"Sydney and Sinead," our very pretty American boss passed, and played with our names. She stopped to chat about the New Millennium. The feared millennium bug did not happen. Our computers were safe.

When she left, Sinead whispered with determination, "Let's go somewhere after work."

With Hornsby Mall's makeover still a mess, there was no good place nearby except Hornsby Library next door. Which was closed.

"Come with me." I took her across the station to William Street and turned into Lisgar Rd.

"Oh blessed! A secret garden!" Entranced, her eyes widened when we entered Lisgar Gardens. Once upon a dream, Dad and I had brought Mum here to celebrate a Mother's Day. "How loovly!"

As we walked down the winding pathway of the terraced garden, Sinead looked around with fascinated eyes. "So tranquil... Soothing..." she twirled around. "Feels like we aren't in Hornsby! D'you know how ugly Hornsby Station is? They could've made it greener, but no. With such an eyesore to welcome visitors, who'd have thought of fantastic gardens and a forest so nearby. This is grand! If I ever get married, I'll get married here!"

"You'll have to marry an Aussie! And get married in August. Hundreds of camellias will bloom then."

This summer afternoon, it was very cool and peaceful in the leafy garden. We left the upper gardens and went down the valley to the quiet lower gardens, which was rather dark under soaring trees as it bordered native Australian bush.

I sat on a boulder by a trickling waterfall and raised an eyebrow.

"You need to give in to Pete," she ordered bluntly. "I saved him for you on New Year's Eve! He was drunk. That horrid Flo would've liked to get on to him. But I like you so I kept him with us. That bitch kept trying to lure him away. I even drank less to keep my wits about me for you!"

What the?

"Wait wait wait... You drank less to keep your wits for me?"

"To save your boyfriend for you!"

"*My* boyfriend?"

"He's our friend. He's good to us. We all like him." She looked into my eyes seriously. "We like you, too."

"Why, thank you." But my mind started to assimilate what she was telling me. "Flo and Pete?" Jealousy reared its ugly head.

"There is no Flo and Pete! You can thank me for that. We kept him dancing with us all night. We ditched Flo at Circular Quay, she was rather high then, so we could shake her. Pete crashed with the boys before going back to his uncle's. How dare she? Join us, I mean. We'd been out there since early morning to secure the best viewing place. We took turns going far away to the toilet, the others guarding our little spot of prime real estate. We were all prepared with food and cards and things. Waiting for hours on our picnic rug. Then she came, sauntering in late-as-you-please, clinging to Pete. He just didn't want to be rude to her. Then we were all foxed. I mean, not me. I was determined to keep Pete safe for you. I hate that girl. She's been awful to me. She does drugs too, you know?"

What was it about me? I had been so out of touch. Selfishly wallowing in self-pity. Never taking any pain to notice my friends' problems.

"Would you like to tell me?"

"She's been a bitch for months!" she complained, her Irish brogue thicker with emotion. "She's selfish and a bully. She comes between me and my guy, elbowing her way in, literally, no matter whom I'm with, everywhere we go pubbing.

"Last month in Lindfield I told her politely that wasn't the way to go. But she pushed me, yelling. Kevin told her to back off then. The things she said, they were too obscene to bear repeating! She so looks down on me because I'm Irish and I'm backpacking.

"We've been trying to avoid her. But now she hunts us because Pete's often with us and she's trying to get him. I feel so disturbed when she's near. True, our contract here is nearing the end, but I want it to end splendidly. Hell, we've come all the way to Australia to have the time of our lives! We want to remember this with joy. In Ireland it'll be boring studying. Pete doesn't give in to her but he's not rude enough to her for my taste."

"Pete can look after himself. He's a big guy. He's tactful and reasonable."

"We only have one month. She wants to get her claws on Pete before we go. Now Sydney, the air fairly sizzles with electric current when you two are in the same room. Sparks fly. So take action!"

"I'm worried... She's so pretty and I'm near anorexic. I have nothing to offer. I'm not cool."

"You won't be anorexic if you'll just let Pete cook for you. He's an excellent cook!"

She looked at me grimly and I truly felt sorry for being unaware of any undercurrents between her and Flo.

"Sinead... I want you to be happy."

"Oh blessed! Famous! So you coming to the pub with us now? Keep Pete company. That'll get Flo to back off. I don't want her near!"

"But how will I stay happy when you're all gone?" Was I to help her be happy for one month by endangering my own heart? "I'm feeling sad just thinking about it."

She looked up at a slither of sunlight among the tall gum trees, her hair shining red, and smiled.

"Sydney, seize life by the moment. You're young only once and only for a short time. Make the most of what's presented to you. Live life, embrace it. Be joyous. Let's be grateful for what's within our reach." Amazing. Devil-may-care Sinead sprouting philosophy. "Live with no regrets of what-could-have-been."

I thought about her and her group singing at Darling Harbour. Living life. So poor. So blissfully happy. Appreciating whatever was within their reach. No regrets.

© la Uaro

*"Oh blessed! A secret garden!" Entranced, her eyes widened
when we entered Lisgar Gardens.*

"Give in," she urged. "Travelling can be lonely, you know. Haven't you wondered about Pete always being alone? He feels this thing for you. Aren't you thinking of him?"

Didn't she just know how to clinch it.

We went back to the office. I was deep in thought.

The next day I started taking feedback.

"Welcome to Your Say, this is Sydney."

"Yes Sydney, I want to complain about your bloody bus!" A guy with Holger's Swiss accent. He went on to detail his suggestion. "My name's Bru. Tell your boss to call me back. I want to give him a piece of my mind on how to run a bus!"

"Somebody graffitied my phone number at the back of your bus," seethed a young man in a low, gritty voice of restrained violence. "It says to call me for some obscene sexual services. Please remove it at once. I've been harassed by people asking for those services." He was very angry, yet his speech was unfailingly polite. So courteous.

The caller after him hollered and swore viciously in offensive language. I terminated the call. He called again and got me again.

"I wasn't abusing you," he pleaded in profuse apology. "This is just the way I talk. The way I was brought up." And for the rest of the call he cautiously struggled to speak with respect. "I have a few choice words for Sydney trains," he confided. "But you couldn't close your ears, could you?" I felt sorry for this bogan because he was actually nice.

"The staff's treatment towards my elderly parents was absolutely horrendous!" A furious gentleman described what his beloved parents had to suffer on their recent Country train trip. It sure was a genuine issue to turn any decent man livid.

At my next performance review, I found out he later lodged a compliment about me for being very helpful in handling his feedback. Wow... That very, very, very angry gentleman? The magnificent defender of elderly parents? I felt honoured. Hopefully one day I would have a son to look after elderly me half as well. Wait, wait. Did I just envision a child in my future?

The Your Say team occupied pods along the western glass wall from where the entire floor was visible. While documenting the cases, my eyes swept around the room. Flo sat far away at the pod where I used to sit taking Infoline calls, no doubt waiting for Pete, who just had his days off and was scheduled to start later. As casual temps, my backpacker friends did not do feedback. Paid higher casual rates, they didn't get bonus either.

I knew the precise moment Pete arrived for work. I could sense him in the room. My heart thrummed, and did a flip when I turned towards the door. He was walking towards me in his graceful gait, so gorgeous with a new haircut.

A surge of gladness swept through me as he smiled his potent smile right into my eyes.

I felt joy!

I had a smile on my face because Pete was happy to see me.

"Where on earth is your three-late-nine?" screamed my customer, asking for the 389 bus. Pete took an Infoline seat nearest to Your Say next to a bunch of merry old ladies. "Oh, now, now here they come... Three buses turning up at the same time!"

Lynn teased Pete about his stylish haircut. "What a handsome, respectable young man you are. So, which girl are you trying to impress?"

With the hot seating, you never knew who had coughed his life away at the workstation. Pete wiped his computer with disinfectant and joked in calm tones with the oldies. Come to think of it, he was friendlier with them than with Flo, whom he had not spared a glance. Seemed I had nothing to fear there.

But I was fearful that he would soon leave Sydney. Both Sydneys.

Instantly I knew I did not want to waste any remaining time. I must get to know Pete. I needed to. I refused to look back with regret someday, wondering about the "what ifs".

After some deliberation I daringly sent him a note through Val, the Floor Walker: "*Library. When you finish work.*"

"I'm in the taxi, waking up the driver each time he dozes off to sleep at red lights!" a brave Queenslander reported.

My hands shook when Pete sent me a reply, "*OK. Can't wait.*"

Val, a very lovely girl I liked very much, smiled down at me, "Any more post?"

I shook my head, smiling back.

"Postage?" she prompted.

I gave her a lolly, "Postage."

She ambled away with a happy smile.

"You ask if I'd like to leave my details?" shrieked a hysterical grandma, her ancient voice cracking. "What details do you need, love? That I was born ninety years ago? That your hourly bus didn't show up so I had to wait two full hours at your rotten bus stop? That I'm suffering a medical condition and this wait has caused me a set back? That I've been in extreme pain since?" Her shrill shouting escalated in crescendo. "Are those enough details for you?"

My next caller spoke with serious stutter. Raging against a rude female station attendant, he expressed his fury with great difficulty. It was as challenging for him as for me. Gently I probed for details. After some time, he calmed down and hardly stuttered at all. I verified the details. By now his speech was slow, the words clear. He was very delighted with my assistance, he said, and it would be marvellous if the station staff were half as patient. No worries, Sir, glad to help.

He was okay. But sad to say, some people with disabilities liked to flash their limitations like a badge: "*No Sydney. Not fair to compare us to radiant, peaceful Christopher Reeves. He's rich. He has a lovely wife, paid attendants, adoring fans. We suffer like he does—minus all the pampering. So we have every right to be bitter! It's our privilege to snap off everyone's head! We have disabilities. We're entitled to be mean!*"

Later, due to the abuse we received, our centre offered a confidential psychological counselling service. And what did I think when callers hurled insults at me, all high and mighty? Nina told me it wasn't worth getting upset.

"No one will think badly of you, except the low people. No one will honour you, except the honourable."

I had a quick chat with Sinead after work. I would step out with Pete. But not to join her group binge drinking.

"As long as you keep Pete with you," she agreed. "Happy dating!"

When's Your Birthday?

I waited in Hornsby Library for Pete to finish his shift. At the start of 1300500, I had come here to dodge co-workers when I was an emotional wreck. Later, to hide from those who tried to initiate me to smoking. I used to pretend to read, but today I was actually engrossed in reading.

Pete raised an eyebrow at my book when he came. "A horror book?" he teased, eyes twinkling.

I scrunched my nose at him. "And what did you expect me to read?"

"No idea," he took my trembling hands and pulled me up. Pete was bad for my state of health—my heart now beat in erratic thumps. He smiled disarmingly into my eyes. "But there are books I'd like you to read."

He pulled me along and I burst out loughing when we stopped at the cookery section.

"Pete! This is rich."

A tall librarian with short curly hair appeared at the end of the aisle, motioning us to be silent. I knew her from high school. When friends and I noisily met here before going to the movies, she would try to instil some manners in us. But I liked her. She was very lovely at Lisgar Gardens, where she sometimes assisted people with disabilities with the inclinator.

"Sorry," I apologised, bashful.

She nodded and left us.

"I like it that you laugh so freely," Pete smiled. "Uninhibited."

"Not for a library," I whispered, motioning to the direction the stern librarian had gone.

"Right. Take life seriously," he smirked. He gestured to the cookbooks and asked me in earnest, "Will you eat? Will you look after yourself for me?"

For him? My heart thudded. All laughter left me. Was this a declaration?

"I love you".

It was a declaration. I had *sensed* something. But why? Why had he fallen in love with me? I was dying to question him. But I was struck speechless.

"You've known it," he stated, his gaze boring into mine. "I'm just verbalizing it so there's no doubt."

He bent down—Pete was about four or five inches taller than me—and kissed the tip of my nose gently. "I have to go away at the end of this month. Not for long, but there's something I need to do back home. I need to make arrangements to move here. But I don't want you not eating while I'm gone. You're gonna do it for me? Will you look after yourself for me?"

He *cared* for me. He was worried about me. Well, what could I say. Except, "Yes."

I felt an unexpected gladness. Ecstatic. "Yes," I said with more conviction. "I'll do it."

"For me?"

"Yes," I promised, looking into his eyes.

He squeezed my hands. We stood there in the aisle between books grinning like lovesick idiots. Gazing at each other. Feeling elated. Bubbling hearts overflowing. Eyes shining with absolute joy. All sorrow wiped clean.

I did not remember what pain was like. All was right with the world.

"Cooking lessons," he smiled. "We'll start with your favourite food to make sure you'll eat it. What is it?"

Pete picked up a Margaret Fulton that included continental and oriental recipes, promising to simplify them, saying, "You won't mind cooking so much when it's easy". He liked to try mixing recipes from one country with another according to available ingredients, and if it turned out okay he would continue to use it.

We bought a few slabs of barramundi fillet for that night's dinner because I liked it and because Pete said grilled fish was one of the easiest and quickest dishes to make.

"For a dish to taste good, the ingredients must be very fresh and of very good quality. It's not hard here. In some countries you have to scour the whole market to find the freshest." He picked up several tiny tubs of herb plants. "Here. You'll use them heaps."

As we waited for the train on platform 3 with Pete's arms snaking around my waist, inadvertently I met Flo's eyes spitting fire from platform 4. If looks could kill, I would have been dead. Pete sensed when I flinched and he kissed my hair,

"Don't let her worry you," he whispered. "No one can come between us. No one. There's only us. 'Cause nobody else exists."

"But Pete, she's interested in you."

"Honey, she's gone through most foreigners on the floor. She only wants to add me to her statistics of conquests. She's not interested in *me*. So I wouldn't let her bother you."

That did not explain why he was interested in *me* though. Why had he singled me out? Why had he fallen in love with me? I opened my mouth to ask. But what came out was,

"But Pete, she's so beautiful."

"True. That means she'll easily pick up someone else and forget me."

"Oh." I thought about it. Of course. I knew Flo was one of the girls who went for boys just to see how many she could score. "Pete, do you know you're very practical?"

"And you smell so good," he murmured into my hair. "Now, here comes our train."

He showed me how to marinate the barramundi and afterwards we planted the newly bought herbs in the backyard.

"You have the most beautiful garden. I would've bought you

fresh flowers except you can open your own flower shop." He scooped a handful of fallen rose petals and inhaled. "Don't you just love this scent?"

"I'm ashamed I don't have any herbs," I stood shuffling my feet. "I don't even know their names and what they are used for."

"That's okay," he looked up at me, his smile and his eyes so beautiful. "When I was your age, I didn't know their names and what they were used for, either."

I asked him all about his travels as we took Dimity for her afternoon walk. He had visited several countries in the past few years.

"Um—Pete? When's your birthday?"

"February eleventh. Yours?"

"February the fourth."

"You're kidding. A week before mine? Too easy."

This was an awkward moment, exchanging birthdays. We knew so little of each other.

"So," I asked shyly, "Are you going to be twenty two?"

"Twenty three. And you?"

A few hours later Pete asked, "Shall we talk about the big elephant in the room?"

I started.

We had dined on the back veranda and were now watching an American sitcom on the lounge-room TV. I supposed it was a funny show, but I found it hard to concentrate. Ridiculous. Since when did watching a comedy require concentration? But my heart was hammering. My hands felt clammy. And I had been fidgeting.

There was a very big elephant in the room.

I threw a glance at him. And quickly looked away.

This long summer day I had been so ecstatic to spend time with him. Sitting across the table at dinner had felt so good. Chatting with him had been very, very pleasant. I had savoured our closeness and a sense of deep connection.

But never mind the laughter from the TV now. The silence was simply too loud. There was a very big elephant in the room.

Was he going to ask for sex? In this time of ours, when it was commonplace, would you label me outdated for feeling petrified?

"Sydney, don't be scared."

I glued my eyes on the idiot box.

"We're not gonna sleep together."

Oh.

He chuckled. "Sydney, look at me."

Shrivelling in fear, I turned to him warily. We were sitting on the same sofa. He was in the middle of it. And I had taken the farthest possible place to his right without toppling over.

He smiled his breathtaking smile at me. His wide, perfectly sculpted mouth was bracketed by slight dimples. Sparkling eyes looked into mine with fondness and understanding.

"I have a strong belief that this connection between us is true and gonna last for always," he said gently. How I loved his charming, unhurried way of speaking. "No one's gonna take it away from us. Ever. Someday we're gonna be together in every way. But that someday isn't today."

I breathed a sigh of relief.

"You aren't ready, Sydney. Everything is too new. I don't know what your problems are. I hope you're gonna open up to me and let me give you a hug or a shoulder to cry on. But I sense there are too many complications in your life at the moment. I feel that sleeping together will only add to the confusion, making things worse for you."

I nodded.

"One day I hope you'll agree to marry me. 'Cause I'm crazy for you. You and only you. But I'm not gonna shock you now. We'll talk about this again someday. When you'll be—what? A proper grownup?"

I looked at him dumbly.

"What d'you say?" he asked, one very beautiful eyebrow lifted.

I shook my head. "I don't know what to say. Except... how intuitive you are!"

He smiled shyly.

"Some years from now you're gonna be mine, sweetheart. Mine to cherish, night and day. I'll be yours and you'll be mine. I never doubt it. For now, I want your company because I feel good whenever you're around. But let's take it easy, okay? One step each day. Now, don't hesitate to talk about anything with me. Or question me. Or ask for my time or my help. Whenever. I'm all yours."

"All these weeks..." I wondered. "I've tried to ignore you. Really I tried." He smirked at this, but I plunged on, "What a waste of time."

"No. You're too young." He readily excused me. "You needed time to get used to the idea and the feelings. But man, did it take you so long! What a relief it was to read your little note today. My heart stopped beating. Then it went racing. I thought, at last..." He took out the little note from his shirt pocket and kissed it, holding my gaze. "I'll treasure this always."

And he moved back. Just when I thought he was about to kiss me.

"I shouldn't touch you when we're all alone like this," he smiled ruefully, as if reading my thoughts. "I won't be able to stop."

He was tempted? I grinned at this. "A teacher in high school told us kids to only go on a date to places that are bright and crowded."

"Very wise."

So Pete was cautious. It made me realise he valued me as a person, not just a sex object. Despite his heated gaze, he only kissed the tip of my nose when he said goodbye. Trying to control his passion instead of being governed by it.

"I'll wake you up in the morning," he promised. "No need to set your alarm clock. When you hear the phone ring twice, that will be me waking you. You don't have to pick it up."

"And if it rings thrice," I looked into his eyes, challenging, "I'll pick it up."

"Yes," he grinned, eyes dancing, "It means I wanna speak with you."

I Changed Her Nappies!

I could tell you about euphoria.

It was walking in the clouds. It was happiness so engulfing, elation so joyous. It was sunshine in your soul, brightening every corner of your heart. It was a supreme delight when your love was smiling into your eyes. Or simply when he was saying "G'day," trying to imitate your Australian accent.

I could tell you about love.

Love was squirming with fear that you might not look your best for a date. Worried to the bone when he was late (well, what could I say, he was catching CityRail—for God's sake). And babbling like an idiot when the perfect Adonis showing up at your door robbed you of speech. Love was feeling cherished when he was cooking your dinner.

I was now acutely aware of my surroundings. If I had been a zombie in November, half-awake in December, all my senses were tingling with life this January.

The world was suddenly a vibrant place to live in.

At the office I noticed Valerya's eyes were the lightest shade of blue, instead of just any light colour. I noticed there were four types of greens in the enormous bowl of plants by the entry door.

I noticed my newly married boss, previously impeccably dressed, now came with her business suit dishevelled.

I noticed many callers were actually very pleasant to talk with.

There was this sweet Russian grandmother in Liverpool. A humorous Rose Bay lady who wished Newcastle trains provided sandwiches. An elderly Neutral Bay gentleman with the wickedest way of spelling his name. A was for Awful. S was for Shocking. G was for Gross. E was for Evil. I was for Irresistible. R was for Risky. H was for Horrid. V was for Vile. N was for Naughty.

And many other witty callers.

On Your Say I dealt with more angry customers.

"The Premier would do Sydney commuters a favour by jumping from the top of Sydney Harbour Bridge! We're all paying customers here. You must lift your game." A guy whose bus did not show up had to ask his very sick wife to drive him to work. As she was suffering from a terminal illness, he felt like a cad. Me too. You wouldn't believe how heavy my heart was each time a floor manager forced me to tell callers:

"The Radio Room has just confirmed, there are no reported delays."

They said I shouldn't feel bad. That I wasn't lying. Because that was exactly what our centre was told.

"Look at other world cities! Their public transport shames Sydney any day. We all pay tax as they do. Why the hell can't we get a credible service too?" A famous journo yelled and yelled in raging fury. "Sydney's public transport is run by a bunch of spoiled kids of low IQ with a total lack of vision and commitment! The transport ministry is peopled by inconsiderate selfish morons who lack the intelligence to know what they're doing! By continuously delivering poor services, the NSW government insults thousands of commuters who have paid their taxes for years!"

But this public figure turned out to be decent, pushed to anger only by valid reasons. After venting his ire, he calmed down and became a very pleasant bloke. We had a bit of a chat. He ended by telling me the best place to buy coffee in Sydney.

A retired ex-serviceman of Kensington rang. Cheerful and pleasant, he was positively a happy person who viewed his blessed long life a wonderful experience. A regular, he had very kind words for everyone. He rang to compliment agents, bus drivers, taxi radio-rooms, and everybody else he happened to get in touch with. Including me.

Those weeks before Australia Day flew with incredible speed. Before, Pete just stayed nearby. After my gesture of surrender he was in my life with full force.

He even talked more.

After that first morning he had woken me up, the phone always rang thrice. And I would snatch it immediately.

We would laugh and say good mornings and start the day saying I-love-yous. We talked about our plans for the day. About our feelings. About the kookaburra perching on my window sill. Once he asked me not to cut my hair. And we hung up, knowing we would soon meet to spend the day together.

He would ring again at night, both of us very sad to be separated until the morning call. Saying goodbye was always extremely hard. Once I timed it, and it took us 70 minutes.

I loved listening to him. In my job, few callers had very pleasant voices and were great to talk with. Pete eclipsed them all. Some people would say his tenor voice was very sexy, except that he never steered near risqué conversation.

He told me his Dad, Clive, was a professor at Massachusetts Institute of Technology, teaching Civil Engineering, specifically bridges: "I saw him marking his students' exam papers very hard. He said they must be careful because public safety was involved".

His Mom, Emmanuella, was a piano teacher at a Catholic girls' high school in Boston.

He had a sister, Eve, 6 years older, an Oracle database-administrator, recently married to a family lawyer.

He had a brother, Lance, 6 years younger, who used to dream of joining Boston's Red Sox, but was now more interested in playing drums for his high school band.

"Just happened, my parents said. They didn't plan to have a child every six years."

"So you didn't have anyone to fight with, growing up?"

"Plenty. Eve used to think I was a real pest, being much younger. One of my first memories was her screaming after I *helped* her doing her school homework—she obviously didn't appreciate the handwriting of a two-year old."

And he talked about his dreams. "My travels inspire me to help others. When I settle down, I'm gonna volunteer part of my time—and whatever else I can give—to ease some of the suffering around us. And I wanna have a life partner with whom I don't fight, so that together we can spend our energy and resources in caring for others. I believe, to glorify God means to have a good relationship with all of His creations".

God? He believed in God? Because I had no knowledge on this topic, I saved this line of conversation for later, planning to ask him someday.

When Pete came to my house, which was now every day after work, he taught me how to cook my favourite dishes.

"Can't you just accept me as I am?" I asked him while chopping some thyme. Pete himself cut a lot of things with scissors instead of a knife. "Why fatten me up?"

"Sydney, to be 80 pounds when you are five-seven can't be healthy. 'Course I accept you no matter what, but you'll be much happier healthy." He combined the herbs and spices and looked at me, his clear, earnest eyes marred with concern. I knew what he was thinking. That my depression and anorexia had been clinical but I had not bothered to get any help. Nobody had bothered—until now. His gentle voice called to my stubborn heart. "I worry about you."

"Aaargh! Your eyes... Like Dimity's. When she asks for something that I can't refuse..." I turned away from those mesmerising eyes. "Now, how long should I cut these fillets?"

"Satay cubes. One inch." His eyes gleamed with mischief. "It has to be exactly two point five four centimetres."

"Why?"

"It'll taste better."

"Pete!" I elbowed him.

"Darling," he laughed. "Don't worry so much."

So we marinated chicken satays for dinner and Pete said to leave it for an hour. It was still the bright daylight of summer. I took out cold juice and colourful tall glasses, green and blue. Pete poured the drink and offered me the blue.

"No," I objected. "The green's mine."

He lifted an eyebrow.

"Because it tastes better!"

"Right," he winked. "And you always sit closer to the window because the food is tastier there."

"You've got it. That's why it's my favourite chair."

As he sat to my right, I rhapsodised about Auntie Kate's satay sauce which was tastier than in any restaurant.

"So we call her."

"No Pete, that's the most useless thing to do! Kate just throws in her ingredients without any particular measurements. And somehow it turns out great. But I'd be lost."

"She sounds great. We'll figure out the measurements."

I had the feeling that he was curious to get to know somebody from my life, and I did not discourage him. So we had Kate on the line. On speaker.

"Darling," she gushed. "I saw you on the 501 from Railway Square a few days ago." Kate now worked as an ABC journo in Pyrmont. "What were you doing out there? I was about to catch that bus, but I arrived late, just in time for the impatient driver to slam the doors in my face! Then I saw you on it. But you didn't see me. I doubt that you could've known other people existed anyway. You were with this most gorgeous specimen and had eyes only for him. So darling, how's the love affair?"

"Kate, you're embarrassing me. The gorgeous specimen is here, listening. The other day we took the 501 to the Fish Market. Had lunch there. He's been on a mission to feed me."

"Good on him! Darling, I'm so happy to hear this. In Broulee I was so shocked to see how much weight you've lost since—since… you know."

"Yes Kate—life happened... So, Pete here wants to speak with you. About recipes." I nodded at Pete. "Over."

"Hi Kate, how do you do? It's Pete here. I'm sitting in Sydney's kitchen. And she's been going on about your wonderful cooking. Could you please help us with recipes?"

"An American!" Kate's voice was laced with disappointment. Oh dear, this must bring back the memories of her American dancer. "What are you doing here? Are you going to hurt my Sydney?"

"Kate!" I protested.

"I'm her second mother," Kate insisted. "I love her! Are you going to be good to her?"

"Aw Kate—," I began, but Pete caught my hand and squeezed it in reassurance.

"I'm planning to live here," he informed her calmly. "If you love Sydney, we're on the same ground. You've known her longer—"

"All her life! I changed her nappies."

I choked.

"Super," Pete was smiling at me. "Tell me all I should know. Starting with tonite's recipe."

Kate told him two for satay sauce: the proper one and the cheating one. The cheating one was from ingredients easily available in most houses and easily accomplished within two minutes. Soon she proceeded to grill Pete again.

"Kate," I protested, "I'm not yet 18. There's no need for serious talk."

"Do you know anything about contraception?"

"KAAATE!"

"Don't get knocked up," she was unrelenting. "*Some* Americans can be too charming. *I* should know."

I looked at Pete in mortification. His eyes were dancing with merriment.

Diplomatically he put Kate's concern to rest and she let us go after extracting a promise that we would dine at her place. We were to have a big dinner. She and Pete together would stage a many-course culinary feast.

Pete and I grilled our satays in the backyard, with Dimity looking on with weary eyes.

"She hasn't touched her dinner at all," Pete commented. "Reckon she's sick?"

We knelt down and checked her. Nothing seemed to be wrong at first, except those very old, tired eyes. Had I neglected my one true friend while falling head over heels? Had I stopped to really look at her while I thrived and basked in the glow of Pete's love? I looked up in fear—and mortification.

"She can't get sick!" She couldn't die! "I won't have it!"

Pete gave me an assessing look.

"Best take her to the vet," he pulled me up. "After dinner."

That beautiful summer evening, during the interminable wait while the vet was conducting blood tests and biopsying a small lump he found on Dimity's thyroid, I finally told Pete about my parents' divorce and how it affected me.

"I can't lose Dimity," stupid tears threatened to spill out of my eyes. "She's been the only constant in my life."

"I can't be your past, honey. But I love you. I will always love you. Forever." He squeezed my hands in comfort. "And forever is never over."

The vet appeared. He told us Dimity suffered from a virulent form of cancer.

"It's my fault," I anguished, sobbing now. "I've been so self-absorbed. Should've brought her to you earlier... Should've noticed the lump..."

"There's nothing you could've done," the vet gently advised. "It would be the same outcome whether you'd come three weeks or three months ago. Dimity is over 16, which is a good age for any dog her size. The cancer she has developed is particularly aggressive, and will spread rapidly. It's actually amazing that she has remained as active for as long as she has. No doubt due to your special bond."

In a kind tone he told me I would save my lifelong companion a lot of pain if I surrendered her to a lethal injection. It would put her to sleep in peace, never to wake up again. "It doesn't have to be right away. If you want to keep her several more days, I can prescribe some pain killers."

"But she's in pain without it?"

"Yes."

I felt so bad. Dimity had been in pain all these months and I had not known it. I had attributed her fatigue to old age, her sad looks as deference to my own sadness. What a selfish and stupid dog owner I had been.

"No," I decided. "You—you can have her tonight. I don't want her to suffer."

I turned my face into Pete's strong shoulder and crumpled, sobbing uncontrollably, beyond caring about what he thought of me slobbering.

Like in a bad dream numbness returned as I stroked and cuddled my thin, beautiful Dimity for the last time. I held her as the vet gave her the injection. She looked at me with her trusting eyes and did not make a whimper as she slowly closed them and became limp. Vaguely I remember Pete helping the vet prise her out of my arms and speaking in hushed tones about cremation for my beloved dog.

Pete must have called Kate. She and Mum always had each other's house keys and she was at my home, waiting. She took me into her arms and stayed the whole night, even after she knocked me out with a sedative.

Mum was on the phone the next morning. She was in Firenze. She had picked up some pretty things and perfumes for me in Paris. Would I like anything else?

As if material things could replace the love of your life.

My American Pete had a fight with our American boss about me. She told him it didn't matter whether it was your parent who died, to be fair with all of your co-workers, if you could not attend your shift, you would still lose your Attendance bonus.

"But she's a very good agent," he protested forcefully into the phone, his gorgeous eyes flashing green fire. I felt touched that he would fight for me. Privately, I had sometimes thought this particular boss had no flaming idea about how Aussies worked. Pete listened some more, shaking his head.

He had arrived early bringing fresh bread from the bakery, saying, "Next time we'll do proper baking, honey. This morning is a short cut." Its heavenly aroma now wafted to my nose. The coffee was ready and he brought it to the table. We were sitting in the sunny kitchen, with the French doors open to the back veranda. A pair of lorikeets hopped on the floor, green and happy.

Pete sat to my right and practically hand-fed me, taking his self-imposed mission to fatten me up in earnest. He and Kate seemed to have a seamless phase of introduction. No, they agreed, we were not going to have the planned elaborate dinner, but both of them would come here and whip me up the traditional Aussie casserole.

Thus Pete and Kate—who never counted (or mentioned) how much they gave—held my hands as I grieved for Dimity.

Do You Tell That To Your Customers?

"Sinead, please swap our days off," Pete asked.

"Or?" Sinead teased. She was eating lunch while checking her emails at the office internet café. Her long hair was tamed into a simple ponytail and three tiny stud-earrings winked on her left ear.

"Or else!"

"Ooh, I love this," she swivelled her chair to face us. "Sydney has Tuesday off? You two are going out on a date?" she beamed. "This is all my doing. I brought you together. I should get a commission! You owe me ten-thousand dollars."

"Swap days off?" Pete passed her the shift-swap form.

"How much will you pay me?" She scribbled her signature. "That's another ten-thousand dollars."

"Keep counting."

Sinead had this huge grin and toasted me with her water bottle as we left.

"She claims we're an item because of her?"

"Let her think so," Pete winked. "Easier to get her to swap shifts to suit us."

I smiled. Although I ached inside for my Dimity, it was easier to bear having a gorgeous, undemanding man looking after me. Feeling safe and sunnier with him around, I knew I was not going to fall into that pit of despair again.

"Shall we take the L90 tomorrow?" he asked.

"Surf boards and all?" The bus driver would only permit it when the space was available.

"It's not gonna be peak hour, honey. The bus won't be crowded."

Breeze lessened the heat of summer on Tuesday. We lunched by the blue water of Newport Arms. The food was superb. And above all else the company was excellent. Pete could discern what ingredients there were in each dish, making me shake my head in wonder.

We continued on north to Palm Beach by taking the L90 again.

"This gives me palpitations. A long bendy bus, up and down these steep hills." I gripped the seat in front of me when the bus lurched, not daring to cling to Pete. He was too gorgeous. I had to wrestle the temptation to climb all over him. Remember my caller who lost her dress at the back of an L90?

"Never fear. The driver's brilliant. Such smooth driving. He obviously knows what he's doin'." He took the driver's ID and phoned Your Say to lodge a compliment.

Lynn, one of the friendly motherly agents, was on the line. "Happy surfing, dears. Don't forget your sunscreen. Slip slop slap."

Happily surfing, Pete and I did not mind the strong sun. We soared along the fantastic waves in joyous exhilaration, adrenalin running, with an indescribable feeling of freedom and total ecstasy. Really, who needed drugs to be on a high?

"Thank you," I breathed as we collapsed on the sand later. After peeling off my wetsuit I kept my sun-shirt on, to hide my still-countable ribs. "I used to surf here with Dad. I was a bit afraid I'd feel sad today. But I don't."

"Actually your Dad sounds great, you know." He took my hand and kissed it. "He played quite a role as you grew up."

Then he looked at my hand. Played with my fingers. Stared at them. He was wearing very dark sunnies, but I could tell his thoughts were churning.

"What is it?" I asked.

He kissed my fingers again, "Will you wear my ring someday?"

"Pete! We're still kids."

"Will you?"

I faced him. Wrong move. He had peeled off his wetsuit and the sight of his muscles gave me a shiver. Unsettled, I turned on my stomach and looked at the blue ocean. We were too young for serious talk, but I sensed this was important to him.

"I'd love to. Someday. But, Pete? Aren't we supposed to get to know each other? I mean, I know your shoe size and I know which one is your favourite tree in the whole of Centennial Park. I know you're very decent. And I'm touched by how kindly you care for me. But who are you, really? So far all I know is, you've been drifting for way too long, travelling the world. After high school?"

He choked.

"I've heard a lot about your travels. The places. The locals. Holland. Serengeti. Himalayas. But what would you like to do with your life Pete? What do you want to work at? Or study?"

He was silent for a very long time that I wondered if he would not answer. Or if he had fallen asleep.

"I'm a musician," he managed, his voice sounding reluctant.

A musician. His Mom taught piano. His brother played drums for his high-school band. My imagination formed a stage. With Pete on the keyboards or the drums or guitar, singing rock and roll. Weird. But not too bad.

"I'll move here," he promised. "Or wherever you're near."

"Will you be able to find a job with a band or something?"

"Or something."

"Good. I can't imagine being away from you."

"Come to the US with me next month? For a short holiday?"

"I'd love to. But I can't. Uni starts."

"Then I'll go only for a very, very, very short time. I worry thinking you'll be alone. Hey—Sydney? Would you like a puppy?"

"Pete," I sighed with an ache of sadness. "No other dog can take Dimity's place."

"I know. The new one won't replace her. But it'll give you company while I'm away. If you want, I'll show you this new litter of puppies I know about. See how you feel after that."

We dozed off lazily, enjoying the lassitude of Palm Beach's tranquillity. The waves today had been splendid for surfing. Now the sun felt really good on my back. I definitely prescribe this as therapy for all sad people whose beloved lifelong pets have just died. The sun and the beach were great for inducing good feelings.

"Pete?" I turned, keeping my eyes on his face.

"Mmm?" he mumbled sleepily.

"The litter of puppies?"

"They're at home. Rough collies. You know, they'll grow to be like Lassie? The mom gave birth to six puppies. One died. Two were given to some friends. So they have these three very adorable puppies. One is more merle—greyish—and white. The other two more sable and white. Angus, he's my young cousin, is considering the merle. Boyish colour and all that. His sister Lauren says she's happy with any." He traced the bridge of my nose with a finger. "Wanna stop at Roseville after this?"

"So I have to meet your relatives? Scary."

"Don't worry, honey." He played with a string of my hair. "They only cook pretty girls with shiny chestnut hair for dinner on Fridays."

That was how I met Bronson that evening. In the backyard of a house on Bromborough Rd. He was sable and white.

"Pete, he's so tiny!"

"He'll be thirty k-g soon enough."

The puppy wriggled in my hands. Oh yes. I fell in love at first sight. When I looked up at Pete, he was watching me fondly.

"You're smiling," he grinned. "I'm so glad."

His cousin Lauren was an eight-year old with very long light-brown hair. She held Molly, Bronson's twin sister, and pulled me to their open-air backyard gazebo. While the men started a barbecue, we had a girl-to-girl chat about how to look after puppies. We promised to see the same vet so we could compare how the puppies were doing.

Pete brought dinner and the others joined us. Bridget, Lauren's dainty mother, was a sport journo. Craig, her dad, a specialist in disability nursing. Everyone welcomed me with enthusiasm. Tuesday, right? They only cooked chestnut-haired girls for dinner on Fridays.

"Glad to meet you at last," Bridget smiled "Pete has been asking his uncle all about having an Aussie partner. Tell her, Craig."

"I told Pete his kids ain't gonna sound like him." Craig gestured towards his shy son, "Angus is only six, but he has a very Aussie accent already."

Hang on. Kids? I darted a look at Pete, cheeks burning. He shook his head with a smile, tacitly saying "Don't panic, darling, that's not ours to worry about until a very far, far away future".

"Dad's been in Australia for much longer than us!" chirped in Lauren. "But he still can't speak like us."

Afterwards Craig lent us his car because NSW only allowed guide dogs on public transport. I held my very soft and very warm new puppy all the way home, and he cuddled up trustingly. I felt so enthralled I couldn't stop smiling, while Pete kept turning to us while driving.

"I could grow jealous," he sniffed, but his eyes shone in fondness.

"Thank you," I said with all my heart. "I won't neglect you. Promise."

"Does that mean I get to cuddle up too?"

"Mmm."

"You'll hold me? All night?"

"One day. In a faraway future."

He burst out laughing. "I'll keep counting."

I put my arms around him as we watched the Australian Open

on TV. We normally watched science shows or sports to prevent getting carried away watching romance. Pete said he didn't watch anything R-rated at all, because, "One day honey, I may have a daughter. Would I want people to watch my daughter? No, I'd probably commit murder! So no, I won't watch other people's daughters."

In the next few weeks, we watched Bronson grow. He was playful and cute. And a handful. I had to toilet train him—which wasn't fun. He loved going outside, but was not interested in running. He kept stopping, sniffing out everything with curiosity. Yeah, he was so different from Dimity, but totally adorable.

Pete and I went out a lot. We used public transport everywhere. Our specialty. The 1300500 dates, we dubbed them.

Sometimes our backpacker friends joined us. On a few nights we joined them in the city. At 1300500, you always knew what was happening in Sydney. The backpacker lot knew more about which entertainment was free. Heaps of free quality ones all of January. Music. Plays. Some by world-class performers. Many celebs were here, jetting down as part of our summer-long Sydney Festival.

"I've never seen Pete so happy," Jane wondered aloud one evening. We were sitting on the grass enjoying a concert at the Domain. Surrounded by the crowd's warm camaraderie, you felt a *real* sense of belonging to Sydney community. Pete said in several US and Europe cities, the locals only partied among themselves for themselves—while Sydneysiders embraced visitors. "What have you fed him, Sydney?"

I glanced back at Pete who sat cradling me. His hold on me was more relaxed when we were in a bright and crowded place. With our strong chemistry, the presence of others relieved us from being constantly on guard against ourselves.

He *had* changed, I realised. Pete's face—glowed, sort of. He looked radiant and very much at peace, instead of politely aloof. And there was a sense of purpose in his step.

Pete winked at me and pulled me back to his chest.

"You've got it wrong," I told Jane. "He's the cook."

"Actually, both of you have changed," Jane marvelled.

"We're living our life," Pete summarised it for her as he tucked my head under his chin again. "Not just bystanders."

Life was empty no more.

We were inseparable during our entire waking time.

Once the British boys and I even took Pete on the 339 to Sydney Cricket Ground and he watched cricket for the first time in his life. To my surprise, he enjoyed it after we had explained the rules.

Another time we took a ferry to have lunch at Abbotsford, and continued on up Parramatta River to swim at Olympic Park. The exciting water-park was so much more fun than the place where great Olympians would compete.

And we took his six-year-old-cousin Angus on the 376 to South Coogee. Had that fabulous coastal walk all the way north along the cliff. Stopped to swim at Bronte Beach. Here, like at all Sydney beaches we visited, Pete presented me with a single perfect shell. As usual we argued a lot in voting which shell was the best looking. Luckily we had Angus, arbitrator-of-the-day, to help us decide.

As we savoured scrumptious seafood at beautiful Watsons Bay, Angus, who had black hair and green eyes like Pete's, declared he had enjoyed the day heaps. I asked Angus to join me on the next City2Surf, and he promptly accepted.

"You're good walking Coogee to Watsons Bay," I praised him. "You'll easily make it up heartbreak hill."

"Heartbreak hill?" Pete raised an eyebrow.

"Rose Bay's steep hill."

"I see. But Sydney, what *is* City2Surf? Why do you like it?"

"It's a 14km annual running event from Hyde Park to Bondi Beach. Or you can walk with hundreds of thousands of others. You have friendly chats with those around you, strangers and all. So it's a warm and friendly community event. Gives you a fine sense of belonging."

He talked about the Boston marathon then, "Not my cup of tea, but a fascinating event."

I had the surprise of my life when we watched a concert at Walsh Bay.

It was very expensive, but Pete was keen on going. Normally we shared expenses, throwing our money together before going. This time he turned up with the tickets, insisting the outing was his treat.

During the performance, the symphony's conductor caught sight of Pete and sought him out during the break. I watched in fascination as the big man strode down to us and extended his arms to Pete excitedly.

"Peter Peter Peter! World's best violinist! As I live and breathe! Where, oh where, have you been?!"

And they hugged and shook hands and clapped each other's backs.

Was this even real?

Pete? *My* Pete? World's best violinist? How could that be? He had been taking calls at 1300500 for almost three months now. And before that he had been planting pine trees near the Snowy Mountains. And before that training kids at Mount Buller's ski resort. Was I missing something here?

Pete had said he was a musician, but I didn't see this one coming.

I sat there stupidly.

The intermezzo was playing and the men talked like long-lost friends reunited. Like in a dream I heard Pete say, "... a whim to travel the world on my own without any strings... yes, I'll be back to music... No, not to New York Philharmonic... in the process of applying for a position with Sydney Symphony, I hope to hear from them soon..."

And he turned to me with a cheerful smile and pulled me up. "Honey, meet Guido, an old friend."

Guido the old friend shook my hands vigorously with long, beautiful fingers.

"We were together at New England Conservatory of Music," Guido beamed. "Of course, Pete was much younger. He was the only one of us graduating at seventeen!"

I looked at Pete in amazement. New England Conservatory of Music? In Boston? I had heard of it because Brenna had dreamt of studying there.

My slow brain grabbed at something else, "At seventeen?"

"A genius, our Pete," Guido praised, thumping Pete's back again. Then he shook his ginger head, dumbfounded. "Can't believe he put his music on hold to turn backpacking."

"Youth craves for more from life," Pete shrugged. "But I'm good to return to music now. Where are you staying, Guido?"

I turned to Pete big-eyed when Guido had to return to his duty. "What a collection of people 1300500 has," I said in amazement. "You're the world's best violinist?"

"Not the world's best," humble Pete was adorably embarrassed now. "Guido exaggerated. One of the good ones in the US, if you like."

"Were you ever going to tell me?"

"Honey, we've been together only for three weeks. I've been dying to tell you... without seeming to brag. I told you I was a musician. You weren't interested in knowing more. You didn't even ask what I played."

"Aw. Pete... Did I offend your feelings? I'm *so* sorry. It was just that I played no instrument whatsoever, so I thought anyone who could play was awesome. When you told me you were a musician, I automatically imagined you could sing karaoke or play a bit of guitar, enough to join a band of a local pub. I thought that was good enough for me, as long as you could land a job here in Sydney. How awful of me to think that. Pete, I'm so embarrassed."

He laughed and hugged me. "But darling, I'm glad that you still wanted to be with me even thinking I wasn't that good."

We talked and talked about his music career all the way home. He escorted me to Beecroft on the Northern Line, even though his place in Roseville was on the North Shore Line.

"This is so out of your way, you know," I had told him once before. It was actually safe to travel alone on Sydney trains at night.

Nevertheless, gallant Pete insisted on seeing me home safely. This was not always wise. Late at night, there was hardly anybody else around. The previous week we started kissing just before the train reached Beecroft, and missed the station. Or stations. Had to end up disembarking at Normanhurst.

When we stepped down at Beecroft Station tonight, Pete commented on the proposed Airport Link Line. The government planned to open it in July, just a few months before the Olympics.

"What a shame," Pete said. "In a few more months I'd be able to take the train all the way to the airport."

"I'll pick you up," I volunteered. "And drive you there."

"You sure? We can always take a train to the City, then a bus to the airport. As long as you'll be with me a few more hours."

"Pete, I'll drive you. When you travel from the Airport, you can catch public transport. But when you go *to* the Airport and have a flight to catch, don't ever risk it. You'll easily miss your flight if the trains don't show up."

"Right," he squeezed my nape. "Do you tell that to your customers?"

We still talked about his music the next day. Perhaps because it still amazed me, here in my simple world, to actually *know* someone who was bigger than life. Someone who was seriously talented.

"Any other surprises up your sleeve, Pete?" I smiled into his eyes. My heart was overflowing with happiness, feeling *so* in love. "What's next?"

"'Kay. About time you know. I've been dying to tell you this one in the last three weeks too, but couldn't find an opening."

"You mean, I've been too immersed in my own problems, so you've been too busy trying to cheer me up and look after me?"

"Not your fault, darling, things happened." Affectionately he traced my cheek with one finger, his eyes shone with so much love. "But I don't want any more secrets. I don't want any lies or deceit between us. Ready?"

"Shoot."

In a calm voice he told me.

And here came the shock of my life.

Pete was married.

He did not have a girlfriend. He had a wife back home.

Once Upon the Great North Walk

"Married?" I whispered, the wind all knocked out of me. There was no way I could believe this.

"Separated," Pete corrected calmly. "Divorcing. I have the forms from my lawyer even now that I'm filling in. It should go through shortly."

Gosh... What on earth had I done?

I threw my strawberry milk carton at him, but he caught it easily. Nothing spilled. How I had wanted his white shirt to turn all pink!

I stood up and ran. We had been sitting by the park's rose arbour in front of Hornsby Aquatic Centre after work. Sipping chilled milk. Planning to swim here on this sweltering summer day. And he imparted this horrific news in a remarkably casual manner. Like a friend telling you what he had for breakfast.

Married! For God's sake. The first thought crowding my mind was the memory of me raging at my parents. My outburst the night they announced their divorce. I distinctly remembered asking them, in self-righteous plea, not to throw their marriage away. And now *I* myself had been dating a married man? And a divorcing one to boot. Ohmygosh...

I reached the corner of the park. Pete was right behind me. Perhaps I should have run to the pool and swum. I definitely needed to cool off or I would kill someone.

"Sydney. I'm sorry. God knows all these three weeks I've been trying to find a way to tell you. Having this hidden made me feel like a devious cad. All I've ever wanted between us is total honesty."

I kept on walking. Abruptly I thought of Dad. I wanted my dad. And I wanted Pete. And I wanted to murder the both of them.

Some part of my mind warned perhaps I was behaving like an unreasonable youth. The other part said the shock entitled me to be furious. Whatever! Right now I was mad with jealousy. I did not want Pete to have a past or to have known happiness with any other girl. I had strongly wanted to have only *one* love in my life. One! And it had to be special, absolutely perfect, and totally unblemished all at once.

How dare he have been married!?

Somehow my steps had taken the right turn and brought me to the beginning of the forest behind the swimming pool. I kept on walking very fast following the track into the woods. Pete, of course, was unshakeable, walking next to me. I hoped to God he would have sore feet following me through the bush in his office dress shoes.

All kinds of thoughts churned in my head. To wring his neck was the foremost.

"Honey, talk," he urged when we neared the Rifle Range.

It was dark and cool in the bush despite the summer heat, gum trees soaring high. I picked my way across the creek and glanced at him for the first time. He was looking around with those exquisite eyes of his. How good looking he was. My heart did a flip each time I looked at him. He observed the path curiously, noting the vegetation and searching for a glimpse of the birds we could hear chirping.

"I've never really walked in the bush before," he said

reverently. "This is beautiful."

And his face looked so calm. So unruffled. While mine must have shown the onslaught of a million emotions.

"Pete," I glared. "This is not sightseeing!"

He turned to me, love and tenderness swimming in his eyes. "We've visited so many places in Sydney these past few weeks. Yet this is the first time we've explored Hornsby when we've worked here most days. Look around you, Sydney. Isn't the bush amazing?" he wondered aloud. "Doesn't feel like we're in Sydney."

"Many Sydneysiders are yet to ever step into the bush," I snapped. "A lot have never even heard of the Great North Walk."

I turned around and walked again. Still simmering with rage. He had been another woman's husband.

"Sydney, I can't change what I have been before I met you," he reasoned, unfazed. "But the past is past and it's over. I only want to be near you now. You and no other. What we have is very rare. I've never known this connection with anyone before. And I'm not about to let you throw it away. I'll fight for you."

"But you've never told me about any of this before. The whats. How. When. Who."

"I'm sorry. How I wanted to tell you, but couldn't find a way." Never once did he blame my own vulnerability as the reason, taking full responsibility on himself instead.

But I was not done having our first real fight. I whirled to face him, scolding.

"For God's sake, you're only twenty two, Pete! And you've been married. Married! If you're married and divorced by twenty-two, it means you haven't been a good judge of character or have been extremely reckless in making important decisions! It makes me feel I don't know you at all. Before this, I thought we knew everything about each other without even having to spell it out. And you know what? I hate *everything* about a divorce! I hate divorcing people. Just hearing about it sickens me. The word divorce itself gives me an allergy. Ohmygosh... you don't have kids, do you?"

"Whoa. No. Not any."

Gosh, what a relief. But tears were running down my cheeks and I swiped at them fiercely.

"I've been angry at my parents. To my mind they've not bothered to fix whatever was wrong to preserve their marriage. They've smashed my model of everything good! Carelessly. I promised myself never to fall in love. Never to get married. Never to have a child of my own. Because when I'd be no more, my child would cry in heartbreak and loneliness. But then I met you. I thought you were Mr Maybe, hoping in future you'd be Mr Definitely. Before today, I'd entertained the possibility of someday having a family. Because I've been so happy with you! Because I couldn't imagine living in a world without you! You'd been so good you took away all my insecurities. But now—now you heap doubts on me again. How can I trust you after this? I hate you!"

Pete was looking at me with fascinated eyes, a slight smile tilting his lips.

"You're not even paying attention to my words!" I yelled. Man, all the birds and wallabies of this bush must be offended by my ruckus.

"But Sydney, you're gorgeous when angry. So full of fire. So adorable. I love you so much!" and he wrapped me in his arms.

"No you don't," I beat at his chest with fury.

"Believe me darling," eyes dancing. "I do."

I pulled free and scrambled several steps away.

"Pete, when a person loves, he'll protect her from hurt and never hurt her himself. He'll be her rock, her support, her defence against the world. He'll *always* stay with her. Now with your divorce history how could I be confident that you'd *always* be there for me? You yourself said we wouldn't spend much time quarrelling 'cause you wanted us to give something of ourselves to the world. You dreamed of a life partner who wouldn't fight with you but instead walked with you caring for others. I agreed 'cause I saw the bigger picture in much the same light! Together we were meant to devote ourselves to humanity. So we weren't supposed to have problems between the two of us! Now with this proof that you view marriage so lightly, how do I know you'd never desert me or treat me badly?"

He considered this. And said reflectively in unruffled calm that just now I found highly exasperating, "By knowing for sure that I know what it was like and would never wish it on anyone. By knowing for sure I'm going treat my love the way I've always wanted to be treated. By knowing for sure that I'm a much better person today after my experiences."

I stared at him. My heart ached thinking he had been hurt. I did not like it that someone had hurt him. How could anyone want to hurt such a lovely soul?

"So who was she?" I seethed with anger at this unknown identity. Gosh, how could she hurt such a fine man?

"The orchestra's cellist," he answered.

A musician! More talented than my best friend Brenna? My insecurities and ire doubled. I did not know how to play a single instrument. Except a triangle.

As close as we were, I actually kept one BIG, dark, mortifying secret well hidden from Pete. I had never ever let him hear me sing. Never let out that I loved to sing. While he sang out loud when he liked a song on the radio, I sang in my head, tiptoeing carefully. Or my tonal failure would cause me to die of embarrassment.

"Well?" I pressed. "Aren't you going to elaborate?"

"I don't like talking about her. I don't like her. Past is past, Sydney." He darted a glance around us. "How far does this track go?"

"Berowra." Privately I had started to think I would exit the bush at Hornsby Heights before Galston Gorge and catch Shorelink's 596 bus. But I wasn't about to let him know. "That's nine hours' walk."

"It's gonna be dark in five." He inhaled, savouring the scent of the forest. "I don't mind spending the night in the woods with you. Have you ever been in cadets or something like that? Any bush survival skills?"

"Pete," I hissed, "Don't change the subject."

"Right," he capitulated. "I don't like talking about it, but I care for you—so I'm gonna tell you anything. What'd you like to know?"

We had passed the Rifle Range and picked our way across the winding creek again. The trail branched out to several paths here and I picked the left. Dad and I had occasionally walked through this bush, but we normally started in Berowra and came out in Hornsby at the park near Rosemead Rd.

"Why did you marry her?"

"We met when we joined the Symphony at the same time. But she was four years older." Of course. Not many people graduated from university at 17. "She was a wild thing and full of fun. I was hooked. We married three years later. I mean, I did get her to agree to marry me. I wanted this sole right to sleep with her. But she was very outgoing. Turned out she still wanted freedom to do as she pleased, even when wearing my ring." He shrugged. "She—she liked *men* and social outings."

"Oh."

"Does that answer your curiosity?"

"But didn't you fight to keep her? Didn't you try to save your marriage?"

"Sydney, I reached my limit. It came to a point when I just shrugged when I came home to find her making out on the couch with some other guy. She had left me three times before, but I'd fought to get her back. That day, as I passed them on the way to my room, I realized that I didn't feel hurt or anything. I didn't care anymore. I realized then I didn't want to live with her anymore. So I walked out. Dropped my wedding ring in the first beggar's bowl I encountered."

"Oh."

"But I figured there must be something more to life than just a crap marriage and a world chained to music. At least I knew that *I* wanted something more. I wanted to find *how* and where I could be happy, so help me God—one day I *would* be happy! I also had this firm belief that a real marriage was meant to make you happy, and one day I would find somebody who'd love me back. Up till then I'd been totally immersed in my music. I'd been playing music since I was little more than a toddler. When I was 20, I found I wasn't happy. I wanted a break. Not to give up my career of course, just to explore what else there was in this big wide world. I didn't set any goals. I didn't set a time limit. I just wanted to see how others were doing. I wanted to observe life. To broaden my horizon. Learn what I could."

"That's it? And am I to take you at your word just like that?"

"Sydney, you're a hard young woman."

"But I did notice you looking at Sinead. Possessively. When she was flirting with other boys, when the centre was new." I stopped walking and leaned on a gum tree facing him. Watching his eyes, his expression, searching for possible lies. "Did your travels include having sex with whomsoever you could?"

"'Course not. That would make me like my ex, don't you think? Sex with every person you're with?" He regarded me with earnest eyes. "I'm not into casual sex. Go ask the backpacker kids. They call me a stitched-up wowser. The interest just wasn't there. That day when we were introduced, I only wanted to warn you what kind of followers Sinead has.

"I met Sinead in Victoria. We were ski trainers at Mount Buller last winter. Your Aussie winter. At night we went to a disco and she was wild, but nothing happened. I didn't sleep with her. Then we travelled north. Those other friends were strangers at first, but they joined us and we sort of formed a group. And you know, when you travel, you really get to know everybody for what they truly are. All their bad habits will come out. I told you about getting lost with a bunch of friends while climbing Sumatra's Mount Kerinci once, how some friends turned out to be terribly selfish.

"In travelling, you get to know who takes advantage when a person is being kind or generous. And Sinead's okay to travel with. She's become like a sister to me. I do watch out that the guys she sleeps with don't give her drugs. She doesn't want to be a user, but what happens when she's too drunk to know?"

"Well don't get drunk in the first place!"

He grinned at that. "I won't. I've given up on drinking now. But the fight is harder for her 'cause she happens to be Irish."

I pulled away from the tree and walked again.

What could I say? He had made wrong choices in the past—

when he was too young to know better—and had learnt his lessons. Should I stay churlish and narrow-minded? I thought of Dad telling me, "Honey, don't fight too hard."

I turned this over and over in my mind.

First and foremost, my anger could not alter the fact that I needed Pete like I needed the air I breathed. There was no way we could separate without HUGE emotional damage. How, just how would I ever survive without his wake-up call every morning? How would I ever go to sleep without him on the phone saying he loved me?

I had been so at peace knowing I was truly loved. I couldn't face it being taken away from me.

Should I condemn him, and myself, to a life of misery because he had a history? He had had to live his life somehow, all the years before he met me, hadn't he? Just because I had this divorce-phobia didn't mean all divorces were bad, right? At times one had to differentiate being stupid from being patient or face peril. Lucky Pete had the option to walk out on his dreadful mistake.

No wonder he had talked more about his travels than his life at "home" in the US. Really, he did not even behave like an American guy. Or had I been prejudiced in thinking many Americans were unpleasant and so full of themselves? Like, why did they always talk so loudly on their *cell* phones?

So far I had never pestered Pete about his home because I had visited the US for Dad's conference. I had seen a bit of it. Besides, we were so alike in our views that I "forgot" to think of Pete as a foreigner.

He was now in the middle of applying for a job as a musician here because of me. Because he loved me. He wanted to be near me as I studied and became a mature adult. He dreamed of us sharing life: the ups and downs, laughter and tears.

We had grown very close. Dependent on each other. Emotionally, we were never stingy. We never counted what we gave. Never calculated before we gave. Emotionally, we honestly gave each other our all, holding back nothing.

And I knew he loved me passionately. He could turn me to

jelly by just a single look.

I had to admit I loved Pete.

He did not have the slightest bit of rudeness or deceit in him. He did not have a single mean bone.

Nobody—nobody!—could ever be more wonderful than Pete.

Slowly I became aware that my rage was diminishing the further we walked. We trudged up a steep incline, savouring the sound of shuffled leaves under our feet in the quiet, tranquil forest.

Yes. I still wanted to wear his ring someday. I was pretty certain that when I grew older, I would still love him. Someday we would be together night and day. I would be his, and he would be mine. For always.

I stopped at the top and turned to face him. Pete had picked up a perfect laughing Banksia man from the forest floor and lifted an enquiring brow.

"This is a cone of Old Man Banksia," I explained. "It's the only bottlebrush that flowers in summer. This particular one has been burnt and the seed released, forming these gaping mouths. Many Aussies are wary of this cone, imagining it as the scary, bad Banksia Man from May Gibb's stories. But positive thinking Aussies call it the Laughing Banksia Man because the mouths can look like they're laughing."

"I like that better. Kind of the optimistic way of looking at it." And he quietly presented it to me as the memento of this "outing". See? My love *knew* how to turn the blues around.

"What exactly were you doing here in Sydney, Pete?" I dropped it inside my bag without removing my eyes from his.

"I was just drifting by," he replied. "But one morning, I found you. I was sitting next to you. You were talking with one caller about every bus in Frenchs Forest for over one hour. I had over twenty callers while you were talking to this person. You had this most lovely voice. You had this big, wonderful heart. I'd never known anyone more patient. Your inner beauty so touched my soul. I couldn't help myself. There was no way I could've stopped it from happening. You were you. Just—you. I was knocked out. Everybody knew you weren't a girl to trifle with.

Everything about you shouted it. I knew there and then I'd go through fire and water to get to you and be with you."

He looked into my eyes with burning intensity, "I would never give you up for any reason."

My jaw had dropped to the ground.

"Mrs Fu..." I whispered.

"Pardon?"

I laughed out loud, tears running down my cheeks. "This is rich..."

I laughed and I cried—I couldn't decide which.

"Sydney?" he was befuddled.

"You've just said the most hilarious thing! And most touching. Wait until I've told Ettoré—you fell in love with me because of Mrs Fu!" I doubled over with laughter, holding my sides. I never did get around to asking him why he had fallen in love with me. "Who'd have guessed?" I pulled out some tissues from my small backpack and cleaned my nose. "She wasn't my jinx! That woman was a heroine. She saved me my Quality bonus. And she gave me—you."

Somehow I was grinning into his gorgeous green eyes and had forgotten all about being angry or any lingering doubts. And when Pete opened his arms I just walked in without a protest.

"One-three-hundred—five-hundred," I smiled, my nose nuzzling his neck.

His chuckle rumbled on his chest,

"One-three-hundred—five-hundred," he agreed.

Men and Their Mood Swings

It was Australia Day. Sinead and Jack had a major disagreement.

"That's the most offensive T-shirt ever!" Jack hissed under his breath. I threw Pete a look, eyes sharing smiles, faces straight, while eavesdropping on trouble brewing in paradise.

I had walked to their pod from Your Say, waiting for Pete to finish his call before going to the office barbecue. Today everybody was wearing Australian green-and-gold, except Sinead. She had a white T-shirt on, with "I SURVIVED 1300500" emblazoned in happy colours.

"Our last day!" she taunted, grinning broadly. "Freedom! Hooray!"

"Cut that out!" Jack seethed, gripping his pen.

"Jack can have the yucky callers all for himself!" Sinead's eyes glinted mischievously. "Yeay! Celebrate..."

Jack's firm jaw was set in obvious disgust. He abruptly logged off and cleared his desk.

"Wait!" Sinead ceased gloating. "Where are you going?"

"E-time!" he snapped. The centre was over-staffed and not keen on paying agents the higher public holiday rate. "I'm going to get roaring drunk!"

"Don't go!" Sinead begged, panicking. "Wait till I finish my shift!"

"You can enjoy all the yucky callers for your last day!" Jack spat contemptuously as he stomped away.

Sinead's blue eyes followed him, worried and bewildered.

"*Men* and their mood swings," she muttered.

"Don't be evil," I chided. "Men have feelings too."

She looked up at me. Her eyes troubled.

"I don't think she really survived 1300500," Pete commented as we walked out of Sinead's earshot. We reached for each other's hand, feeling fortunate for understanding what we had. There was so much peace swimming in his eyes, and I hoped I have helped putting some of it there.

We arrived at the Australia Day barbeque for lunch and our American boss smirked when she noticed the handholding. She told us to have our pictures taken with the Olympics' torch, which today had been brought in by some visiting Olympic officials.

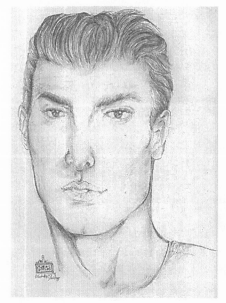

"E-time!" Jack snapped. "You can enjoy all the yucky callers for your last day!"

It was a very fine afternoon and we walked in my favourite secret garden after work.

Pete wanted to be with me for our birthdays and our first Valentine's Day before returning to the US. I myself had taken leave for the next few weeks before switching to be a weekend part-timer. Although I had a digital-animation-for-fun workshop before my formal lectures start at the end of February, for now we had several days of holiday together.

As we walked through the tranquil, soothing glade Pete told me he had submitted his divorce papers. His lawyer advised him to be there when they would fight for his New York condo.

"It's mine," he reasoned. "I've been playing music for as long as I could remember. When I was a minor, my parents invested all my earnings for me. After I graduated at 17, I used it for the deposit to buy this cool apartment."

"Umm... aren't New York apartments very expensive?"

"Yes. It isn't big, but very expensive because of the location and—well, it's kinda posh. During the first three years of working full-time, I lived frugally and paid it off. Then I asked my ex to marry me. She's been living there and my lawyer has the impression she wants to keep it. Well, she can't. It's my lifetime's hard work. Earned it solely on my own. I'll be very cranky if an undeserving woman wants to hog it. Besides, it's my only asset. I have no money anywhere else. I need to sell it to start over here."

"Why didn't you do it before? Like, before you left the US?"

"Couldn't be bothered. Reckoned I could make my own way during my travels. Kinda too lazy to care, I guess."

"Should've could've didn't?"

"I know I know ..." He squeezed my fingers, "How I hate having to go back for this now."

"Pete? Why didn't you join the Boston Symphony? Why New York?"

"A mistake," he sighed. "At 17 I thought I was very grown up and should move away from my parents. Stupid move."

I stopped and faced him, "Dad says we're allowed mistakes as long as we learn."

His hand came up to touch my face. *I love you. I am so happy you are in my life.* We stood in the quiet lower garden, our eyes communicating a million things. Then we embraced one another as we savoured the closeness.

At a loud squeak of a bird from the tall trees I looked up and saw an eagle perched on a branch high above.

"Hey Pete, if you were king of the world, and you could do anything you want, what would you like to turn yourself into?"

"A bird," he promptly replied. "So I can have a bird's-eye view. See things better. Easier to comprehend them. And you?"

"An eagle! Not just any bird, but the most majestic of them all."

And we laughed together.

"I like that." He followed my eyes to the bird. "You—strong and wise."

Mum phoned that evening as Pete and I were cooking dinner.

"Ettoré and I are back in Sydney," she announced. "We're on our way to visit you. We'll be there in five."

"In five? Why don't you just turn up?" I asked, puzzled.

"Kate said you have a boyfriend now. I want you to be presentable by the time we arrive." And she switched off.

I turned to Pete, still confused, repeating what she said. And he laughed.

"She thinks we have a more physical relationship," he explained. "She doesn't want you embarrassed if they show up without warning. Just in case you're en deshabille." He mussed up my hair and pinned me to the fridge. "Let's not disappoint her, shall we?"

We were still kissing when Ettoré's car pulled into the driveway. I was still dazzled by the kiss when we greeted them.

"Hi honey," Mum gushed, embracing me. "So good to see you again. Oh what smells so yummy?"

"My friend is cooking. Mum, this is Pete." I made the introduction. "He's—a violinist."

"A violinist?" Her eyebrows shot up. "Kate said—never mind.

Tell us all about it, Pete. And a violinist who cooks? Fabulous."

"We're about to eat," Pete smoothly took charge. "Please join us."

"Are you sure? Is there enough?" Mum asked.

"Just enough for four," Pete took out the food from the oven. "It's moussaka and Greek salad tonight."

"Yum. But Sydney didn't use to eat aubergine." She followed Pete to the table. "We were actually thinking to take you to eat out."

"We can still take them out next time," Ettoré joined in. "This sure smells great."

"It tastes great too." I sliced warm bread as they took their seats. I chose the outer crust for myself.

"Hey, the crust is mine," Pete protested. He was serving everyone the moussaka.

"But Pete, the crust is the yummiest part."

"I know. That's why I like it. Hey, if you weren't so skinny I wouldn't share."

Then I realised Mum and Ettoré were observing our squabbling.

"But you didn't use to eat your bread crust, darling," Mum questioned, sounding puzzled.

"Pete bakes so well. The aroma... The taste... And the crust is the yummiest. Here, have some. He usually throws a handful of any fresh herbs into the dough."

"Any herbs?" Ettoré asked.

"Italian. Asian..." I explained. "As long as it's fresh."

"You know how to cook now?" Mum asked, more puzzled.

"Starting. Pete's teaching me."

"My my... Pete this. Pete that. You're a very good influence, Pete," Mum turned to him. "Where did you come from?"

With considerable social finesse, Pete handled her subtle interrogation. Dinner went down well with cordial getting acquainted conversation. I looked at Pete with pride. He knew how I had withdrawn from my parents. But I began to discover that one of Pete's greatest assets was his ability to see both sides of an issue and to diplomatically negotiate a compromise. He was objective, unbiased, fair, and always tried to bring about a peaceful coexistence among the people around him. Including me and Mum, apparently. With his warm personality and his warm tone of speaking he made people feel comfortable.

"I'm sorry you lost Dimity," Mum said when I introduced them to Bronson in the backyard. Pete insisted on stacking the dishwasher.

"When we saw Pete at Darling Harbour," Ettoré smirked at me teasingly, "I knew there was something in the air."

"That seems so long ago now. How life has changed."

"For the better, I gather."

"Do you always wear jeans when you are with him?" Mum interjected. "I bought you lots of stuff in Paris and Milano."

Ettoré went to his car and brought in Mum's presents as we all moved to the living room.

"So many bags of them?" I shook my head.

"Sydney," Pete chastised, "Say thank you."

"Oh. Well. Thanks then," I offered, without delving into the bags.

"Good on you Pete," Mum told him. "Now make her wear these girlie things." And she opened a few bags herself. Clothes. Shoes. Perfumes. She liked to nag at me all the time to wear dresses. Perhaps the very reason I rejected them. Just to be contrary.

I held a five-inches Manolo Blahniks, one of several, throwing Pete a horrified look. "You aren't going to make me wear these, are you?"

He cocked an eyebrow. Non committal.

"He probably wants to see you in one of these," Ettoré picked a little dress from the top of the pile, throwing Pete a conspiratorial look.

"Enough." I swatted his hand away. "You guys please watch TV. Australian Open is on."

I scooped the bags and carried them upstairs. Mum followed with more. With my toes I slid the middle door of my wardrobe to the side and dumped everything at the bottom. I closed the door. There.

"Honey, don't do that," Mum protested. "You're so childish."

"I'll wear them one day. Promise." When I would be more than skin and bones.

But Mum made me hang everything neatly. She kicked her shoes off and sat on my bed explaining where she found the dresses and who created them. Having the same build, she knew exactly what size to buy me.

"Have you discussed sex with Pete?" she asked. "You're reaching your majority next week. Legally adult."

"*Mum*," I protested, "Did you discuss your sex life with your parents? And here the legal age for having sex is 16. Not 18."

"But you haven't. Going all the way, that is. I can tell from the tension between you two."

"What tension?"

"The charged air. There. I can tell from your blush too."

"*Mum*... Let's go down and annoy the boys. I want some dessert. And Pete's bought a wicked coffee."

"But why haven't you given in to Pete?" She put her feet back into her shoes.

"Frankly, there's no need for now. We're so happy the way we are. Besides, too much is happening. Uni is about to start. He's going back to the States shortly before returning to live here permanently. I don't know. This isn't a great time to rush into things."

I'll Love You until I Die

A strain of the sweetest Brahms violin drifted up to my window at sunrise on my birthday. I opened my eyes, heart thrumming. The most enchanting sound of love was in the air, pulling at the strings of my heart, tugging at my soul.

Pete—my Pete!

I threw open the drapes. Pete was playing under my window, in the misty-grey day with a promise of rain. His eyes grew vibrant with love and elation when he saw me. I blew him a kiss. Totally besotted, we must have looked stupidly like the balcony scene of Romeo and Juliet. Except that it was not stupid music that was flowing. A world-class violinist lovingly delivered a touching sonata from a great master composer.

At the end I leapt downstairs, opened the door, and we flew into each other's arms. He swung me around and we hugged each other tightly, hearts and minds overflowing with joy.

"I love you Sydney, I'll love you until I die."

I was so touched when he gave me his violin CDs and a tape of him beautifully whistling a perfect Dvorak melody for my birthday presents. All this, when he had kept his violin background a secret from others. I sensed he must have gone to hell and back to leave everything he used to be. I started to learn that until you spend your time with someone every day you do not get to know the real person. And the more I knew Pete, the more I was impressed.

"We'll stage your birthday lunch tomorrow at Fagan Park. Saturday." He pulled me to the kitchen and started making breakfast. "I've told your mom and Kate tomorrow will be a good day 'cause the forecast says sunshine and you're an outdoorsy girl. But actually I wanna monopolize your time today." He winked.

"What birthday lunch? Who's coming?"

"Your mom phoned your school friends. And I phoned friends from the call centre. I've recruited Kate and Nina to help me cook. Anybody else you wanna come? We can give them a last-minute shout."

"Call your relatives too," I suggested. Lately we had been so busy spending time with each other that we had forgotten the rest of the world. "But I'm so glad we have today just for each other."

We cooked ourselves a lavish breakfast.

"Those choux pastries look very cute. Let me try one, Pete. To make sure they aren't poisonous."

"I've chosen the recipe for maximum damage. Tastes good?"

"I'm not convinced. Better pass me the whole plate to make sure. Thanks. Mmm... I've died and gone to heaven."

"Wait, Sydney. Spare some space for the croissant. You're gonna love the savoury chicken filling."

"We're acting like kids playing happily in the kitchen." And Mum thought we should discuss sex? "Except that we produce really yummy food."

"And kids don't kiss in the kitchen," he licked lemon butter from one corner of my lips. "You're so delicious!"

We had been going surfing every day, but on this rainy day we roamed the museums instead. He shook his head when I wanted to walk from the Art Gallery to the Museum of Contemporary

Arts.

"How can you think grey, rainy day is beautiful?" But he gave in anyway. It was only drizzling rain.

"Feel it Pete." I faced the sky. "Feel the rain on your face. I don't know. I just love the feeling. Do we really have to explain why we love something?"

"I guess not," an indulgent smile, "But I can tell you a thousand things I love about you."

"Cool," I hugged his arm, smiling to his eyes. "Start telling me when I'm 64."

"64?"

"Sure. What's new about a guy telling his girl how cool she is? If you really mean it, I want to hear all about it when I'm 64."

He laughed out loud.

"Gosh, you really are a hard taskmaster. Now I'll just have to show you instead of telling you. Right?"

Mum and Ettoré picked me up for my birthday lunch at Hornsby's Fagan Park the next day. Ettoré's car had to crawl very slowly through the dangerously winding Galston gorge, but it was worth the trip. Kate, Nina, and Pete did not just throw stuff from the shop onto the barbecue. They planned everything meticulously. All the meats were superbly treated with excellent home-made marinade. The salads and the sides were culinary perfection.

"You three chefs should team up and open a restaurant," I declared. "Seriously recommended."

"Where's the grog, though," Brenna looked at her orange juice with distaste. "It's Sydney's 18!"

The others too turned expectant eyes at Ettoré who was in charge of the drinks, but he had always championed my choice.

"We all have to drive later," he reasoned. "It's Galston gorge, people."

"So can we test-drive your Maserati?" Kevin pounced. He was manning the barbie with Jack.

Ettoré looked around. Interested eyes looked back. He laughed, and gave in.

I had an eclectic mixture of birthday-wishers. Val, Winston, and several more friends were there. Lucy was away, but she rang and emailed. The backpacker kids had gone away and sent emails too. Angus and Lauren ran around with Kate's and Nina's kids. I raced them to the top of the climbing-frame. Mum looked up at us as we were laughing high up in the air. She shook her head and said something to Pete. He smiled at her and said something to appease her. She relaxed and laughed.

Later, Brenna eyed Pete and Nina chatting. Pete had some indelible memories of earlier adventures in Sumatra. Getting lost climbing Mount Kerinci. Terrific big-wave surfing in Mentawai. Exotic, delicious cuisine—rendang etcetera. So Sumatra was big for Pete and he liked to chat with Nina about it.

"What a catch," Brenna observed. "Will you get mad if I try to steal him away?"

"Do your worst," I grinned at my beautiful friend. Mum said Brenna was the best-dressed of us all. But today she didn't have much on. "Come. You're in for a surprise about his background."

As if oblivious to Brenna's charms, Pete only had eyes for me as we approached. He flashed me a loving smile while still mid-sentence to Nina ("That's it. Being prejudice isn't a nation's trait, but individual's...") and tugged me to his side with a comforting arm around my waist. I knew then that he had noticed Brenna's appraising look. He was subtly showing me (and the world) that I was special. That he cared for me a great deal.

As bizarre as it may sound to others, we had this extraordinary connection. A *special* bond. Often we knew things about each other without having to spell it out. Pete was a very deep person and acutely aware of his surroundings. He possessed a small measure of psychic ability. Once he confessed to feeling jealous the first time he saw me with Ettoré, but quickly calmed down because he could *sense* me. ("Nobody could be interested in another guy when she was sending such strong *waves* my way"). Yet he dismissed his intuitiveness and never made much about it.

"Pete, Brenna is going to study music in Melbourne soon. Brenna, Pete studied at the New England Conservatory."

Brenna was so delighted to be introduced to a NEC graduate that she put flirting aside. They talked music. And Brenna made me promise to check my emails regularly.

"It's a great day. I don't feel any different being 18, but I'm happy." I linked arms with Mum and Kate. After stuffing our face with lunch, we all went for a walk before having cake.

"You *look* happy," Mum smiled.

I left them to walk with my friends, but kept waiting for Pete. In this sprawling park he stopped all the time, exploring, curiously checking out the plants and animals in the many international gardens of Fagan Park. As usual I loved seeing the world through his eyes.

"Sydney, I'm so amazed you can name all the plants."

"Only the native plants."

"The world's richer, living it with you."

"And I was just thinking the world's richer seen through your eyes. You delight in every little shape, scent, hue, pattern... And sound. Now it's like I'm seeing them with renewed appreciation."

"There's so much beauty here. Isn't there? This is a massive park."

"Yes, when I was little we took my bike. We used to feed the ducks early in the morning. You know, when I was little I didn't eat the *bones* of my bread. That's how I called the crust. Dad froze them and we fed the ducks here on Sundays."

"Do you still cycle? Wanna go cycling?"

That was why we borrowed Craig's and Bridget's bicycles the next day. We went cycling to the enchanting Akuna Bay. Where we ended up starving because it was in the middle of nowhere.

"Know how to catch one barehanded?" I asked Pete when we saw a school of fat fish in clear water. We were passing a picturesque barbecue area. "I'm so hungry."

"Nope," he laughed. "Keep going Sydney. Didn't you say the nursery restaurant back at Terry Hills has the most sinful desserts?"

A few days later, he was making me a sandwich to take to my animation workshop. Now that he did not have to go to work, Pete only shaved every third day. No matter his style, he always looked good. I took a shot. He lifted his head in surprise. I took another one. He smiled. Another one. I just loved taking his photo. Pete never failed to look interesting.

"What are these?" I pointed to a stack of new, colourful lunch boxes. "Why so many?"

"To match the colour of whichever socks you're wearing," he winked. "The food will taste better."

I burst out laughing. Pete liked to tease me for my colourful socks.

"What is it today?" He bent to lift the hem of my summer jeans. "Ahh. Green..." And he put a sandwich in the green box, handing it to me with a grin.

I looked into his eyes, overwhelmed by this small gesture. Pete had the knack for making me feel good. He was romantic and honest about his feelings and desires. At a very deep emotional level, quietly but intensely he went about forming very strong bonds and attachments between us.

"I'm going to miss you," my voice wobbled. "You do these little things that make me feel special. Why are you so wonderful?"

I had really looked forward to this animation-for-fun workshop. It was a hands-on digital compositing process using 3D animation, lighting techniques, and digital effects for beginners. But as I sat on the train I missed my guy terribly... He was still near me. He was building a cubby house for Angus in their backyard. I would see him again tonight. But how was I going to cope when he returned to the US next week?

Will You Ever Forget Today

Pete made me a wreath of tiny, fragrant roses for my hair.

It was our first Valentine's Day. He came very early with more roses for my garden, latest hybrids of the most beautiful fragrance, "Because you can never have enough of roses".

Bronson lunged at him with joyful greetings and they tussled on the lawn. And sang too. No kidding. Pete sang several notes of a melody, while Bronson answered with two woofs. They repeated it again and again in perfect synchrony,

"Rah-rah-rah-rah-raaah rah-rah"

"Woof-woof!"

Together we chose the location for the new roses, with Bronson yipped and nipped at us as we planted them. He loved chewing my gardening gloves too, so proud and triumphant when he could steal them from me.

Fingers entwined we walked him before he woke up the entire neighbourhood. At a nearby park we played on the swings, soaring high like two happy, laughing big kids.

"Pete, I didn't really understand what the word euphoria actually meant, or what it felt like, until I knew you."

Together we chose the location for the new roses

"Same here, darling. I thought I knew, but I was wrong."

It did not occur to us at all that if you soared to such heights the fall would be all the greater.

It was a wondrous day, even though my puppy wasn't impressed. Bronson slunk away to his doggie house when we turned on our favourite radio station and swam in the backyard pool, rose petals floating by.

"I'll make a salad for lunch," Pete offered afterwards, both of us dripping water on the slate floor.

"Good, I'll just change then I'll help you."

He sucked in a breath when I appeared, for the first time, in a dress, Mum's recent gift from Italy. It was a light halter dress in a bone colour, short and backless. I thought I must have looked stunning. For a while Pete just stood there in the kitchen, speechless. Then several emotions flitted across his face.

"I'm so flattered, honey," he said slowly. "I'd like to enjoy the view, but you're testing my limits here. So please go and change."

"Why?"

"And while you're at it, put on a bra, too."

"Pete! You're not a dinosaur, are you? I only want to show you that I'm not skinny anymore."

"Darling, there's only the two of us here. I'm not that strong. Wear a dress when we go somewhere bright and crowded. Oops—no. I take that back. This dress is for future private viewing, someday. I don't want other guys to look at you. You don't know it, but you may inspire unholy thoughts in some creepy men who like underage girls."

"Aw Pete, you're so old-fashioned, so—"

Without warning he tossed me onto the kitchen counter.

"Pete!" I sucked in a shocked breath.

"D'you know how hard it's been to keep my hands off you all these weeks?" he asked with burning gaze.

I shook my head vigorously.

"You wanna take this relationship to the next level?" he questioned.

I looked at him wide-eyed, my heart jumping summersaults, pulse racing.

"You ready to proceed?"

"PETE!" I shrieked. "No!"

"Scared, are you? That's what I thought," He smiled now. Eyes laughing at me. "Save this kind of fashion until after we're married. Now please go change," he kissed the tip of my nose and effortlessly lifted me back down. "I'm all hot and bothered here."

You wouldn't believe how fast I ran ("Great legs," he taunted)—chased by a myriad of emotions I could hardly comprehend.

I changed in record breaking speed. Now a grownup by law, I could dress any way I wanted. But whenever Pete threw that look at me I couldn't help feeling rattled.

I put on another dress though (our first Valentine's Day, right?)—a floral one Mum bought in Paris. This one had a high shoulder-to-shoulder straight neckline and reached my shins in wisps. It was green like my eyes.

I knew I had inherited Mum's and Nanna's delicate frame and classical features. Clothes hung well on me. Somehow, I wanted Pete to remember that I was a girl. That I could look pretty. I meant, hopefully I did. I wanted him to come back to Sydney at the fastest possible speed.

He was leaving for the US tomorrow... How I dreaded the separation.

Pete was all polite and made only decent conversation when I returned to the kitchen. Not a mention of the earlier episode whatsoever. Just to get back at him, I deliberately brought it up as we sat down for lunch.

"How's the elephant today?"

"Pardon?" he looked enquiringly. Pete always sat on my right-hand side, slightly turned to me, and now and then he would pick up my food and handfeed me.

"The big elephant in the room. Shouldn't we talk about it?"

For a moment he looked perplexed, before breaking into a laugh.

"Pete. You say we can talk about anything. Discuss any topic. The Open Book Management, they say at the office."

"Right," a dazzling smile. "Looks like we've progressed so much. I'm glad you're at ease discussing this with me. Sure darling. What about it?"

"I realise a few times now you've used the shock tactic to scare me into compliance." He smirked at this, but I went on. "But in reality you're old fashioned."

"Sweetheart, I'd never do anything against your wishes. And I only want to protect your innocence. So yeah, call me dinosaur...," he shrugged.

"Prehistoric. Out of date," I continued. "Just like myself."

He laughed. "Glad we have the same moral values."

"Do we? So you honestly believe there's nothing wrong in delaying... um—," blushing, "you know... Before, you didn't want to add complications to my troubled life. Now I'm far from troubled, thanks to you. And I'm 18. I've reached my majority. Are you still okay about saving that fun for later?"

"Yes. You're still skittish that way." He gazed at me fondly. "I could help you overcome it, but I rather enjoy watching you all innocent like this. Very sweet... Let's not rush it. It'll come in time. Preferably with the freedom of an absolute trust that comes with a marriage commitment."

"A marriage is freedom? Really? Not shackles or doom?"

"Depends on what you're after. Some people only want the obvious. But hey, you can even get the obvious without getting into a relationship. But us—we have so much more than the chemistry, don't you think?" he traced the bridge of my nose with one finger. "I want you to fully trust me first, and be willing to commit yourself to me of your own volition."

"Oh"

"I want you to come to me fully knowing you choose me and

only me. I want you to be very, very sure. Wouldn't you like to get physical when you don't have to question why are you even doing it or worry about any consequences? I want you to let go, to give yourself fully and wholly to me without any doubt. In my book, a marriage is liberation. Freedom."

"Oh."

"Sydney, when we take this relationship to the next level, I want you to come to me with everything of you! Heart and mind and soul, without reservation. I want all of you! Everything of you."

I gaped at this impassioned speech.

"Well," he returned to smiling again. "You brought that up." And he popped an olive into my mouth.

I thought about his words as I chewed.

"So what do you think?" he asked.

I swallowed and blurted, "You've been hurt. Badly."

He looked up to the ceiling.

I leant over and kissed his cheek. "Darling, I'll never leave you". Oh what the heck. I threw myself at him and gave him a big hug. "I'll hurt anybody who dares to hurt you!"

Wrapped in each other's arms, I felt an indescribable closeness as if our souls were conjoined together in a very soothing land. As if our hearts beat as one.

"Why do you even believe in marriage?" I asked. "I'd have thought you'd become a sceptic after your experience."

"My travels, I guess. That's how all decent people of the world live." His breath felt warm as his nose nuzzled my hair. "It's the norm, Sydney. It brings order to civilization. Differentiates us from earlier forms of humans or animals. Marriage is commitment with full awareness, knowing we're being responsible and loving to our partners. Since it's been proven a successful institution for all these times and people of all places, there must be some good reasons behind it. It would be arrogant to change it."

"Many will disagree with you."

"They're entitled to their opinion. We're all different, honey. What's right for some can't be right for everybody." He twirled my hair. "In my view, marriage contributes to the harmony of society. Before, perhaps it was just my youthful attempt to harness my ex. Now I view it as a natural way of life... That said, I wanna marry the person I love at a mutually deep emotional level. You're very precious to me. I want you to be certain that I value you as a person. Not just a sex object."

"Hey, I've thought of exactly that before! How our minds click. I trust you. But your insight makes sense. We'll wait."

"You don't have to blindly agree with whatever I say."

"But I find the notion appealing. Beautiful." I returned to my chair. "And oh, logical."

"Nice." He relaxed back on his chair. "So we're agreed on this? Dare to be different from the crowd out there?"

"Ah-ha. I do see our personalities and situation are different from many friends. For now the thrills and fascination of being with you overwhelm me already. So, yeah. Until I'm ready to jump into the abyss. Just kissing is fine with me. Hands off."

"Sydney," he grinned. "You're so innocent. But I sorta know what you mean."

"Cool. So I still have years to consider whether I'll agree to marry you."

"And when the time comes," he captured my hand, "I'm not gonna take 'no' for an answer!"

I burst out laughing. "Pete... I love you."

He played a few violin pieces for me, a Dvorak love sonata and one delightful sonatina. How I revelled in his skills and flair!

Next we went ice skating at the Macquarie Centre.

"I love you," he said again and again as we circuited the ice rink, my flowing dress whipping at our legs. "I'll miss you terribly."

Some couples never expressed their feelings for one another. Pete and I, although very at ease with each other, never before repeated them in total desperation as we did now. Usually we preferred our long and sweet tacit silences. But hey, this afternoon we were feeling insecure.

Truth was, we never wanted the day to end. Harrowing

feelings started to creep in with a heavy sense of doom. Eating at us. Bringing the real fear of our coming separation. How, just how, would we cope?

"Pete," I clung to him in anguish, "Come back. Please come back quickly."

"I will, darling, I will."

He had said not to plan anything for Valentine's Day. As he was creative and inventive, I went along. But a surprise awaited me at dinner. He had taken me by train and bus to the Jones Bay Wharf at Darling Harbour. There was a posh dinner-cruise ship waiting there, and when I looked up I saw Mum and her partner on board.

"They've invited us," Pete confessed under his breath when I stopped in astonishment. "Your mom phoned me. I didn't see any reason why we should decline."

"It's okay, love. I'm just surprised, that's all."

I walked with him towards the steps, very carefully because for the first time I was wearing heels instead of my favourite sneakers or flats. After skating Pete had donned a brand-new dress shirt and pants. How good he looked. I couldn't do less now, could I? That was how I came to be dolled up.

Mum looked at me approvingly. How she would be ecstatic if she knew I had worn three dresses today. Personally I must admit a one-piece dress with a zip had to be the most practical piece of clothing invented for a woman. You could put one on by throwing it over your head in a hurry, zip it while running down the stairs, and look good in it. I even thought boys were not so lucky because it took longer to button a shirt. But I was not about to let Mum know.

"Darling," she gushed as we stepped on board, "Aren't you beautiful! Look Ettoré, this is the fiery-sunset Thai silk we chose for her in Milano. Isn't she gorgeous?" she kissed my cheeks. "So pleased you can join us. Have you been well?"

Beautiful Sydney Harbour was enchantingly swathed in colourful glittering lights. Soon waiters came with canapés and drinks. Pete and I settled for cokes.

We chatted about my workshop and Pete's arrangement to move here.

To my surprise, when dinner was ready, Pete and I were separated from Mum and Ettoré, with them sitting at the farthest possible table. All the tables were set for twos. Your ultimate romantic Valentine's Day dinner. From then on they left us alone and we appreciated this gesture. Heaven knows there were only a few hours left for Pete and me to be together. He was leaving tomorrow.

A band was playing "It Had to Be You" and some other very beautiful, haunting melodies. And I wanted to cry. We danced the saddest dance of my life on the deck.

"I love you so much. Oh darling, never forget today."

The Jade Promise

The next morning I picked up Pete from his uncle's at 5am. He looked so good moulded in a T-shirt of hand-painted gum leaves from an artist at The Rocks, my gift for his birthday. Yesterday I gave him a personalised opal key-ring. And a thin wallet because his looked like it should retire.

In the car the atmosphere was very tense, despite the morning host providing hilarious commentary on the radio. Pete reached for my hand and for most of the drive we laced our fingers tightly.

"Sydney, that's a Ferrari in front of us," he tried to lighten the mood by joking, "Overtake it! Today's the only time you'll ever overtake a Ferrari in your life. Believe me."

So I did, yeay... we had a laugh. Now how could I overtake a Ferrari very early in the morning before the traffic started? Because it was riding on top of a tow truck, of course.

That was one Ferrari driver with a few drinks too many on Valentine's night.

Soon after we lapsed into sorrow again.

"So, you're gonna look after yourself for me?"

"Yes." I faced him at the red light, "I'm yours. Always."

"Super. No flirting with uni boys? I'm not happy to be so far away from you while they can see you every day. So please play hard-to-get. Put on that expression you had when we first worked at the call centre. The one that scared the boys away. It kinda made us feel we were all beneath you."

I scrunched my nose at him.

We arrived at the airport very early because we wanted to spend as much time together this morning. Pete checked in only a single bag, leaving his other stuff at his uncle's. He left his violin at my house because he would return soon to play it again. But nothing made this separation easier.

"Let's get you something to eat." He steered me to an Italian café.

He hand-fed me brekkie, as he rather seemed to love doing. I ate with great difficulty, and not much of it. All the time Pete talked softly in a quiet undertone, his wonderful voice asking me not to worry.

"You look so beautiful sad," he smiled ruefully, "but I want you happy."

"Aw Pete, can you?"

He swallowed. Could not answer.

He took my hand and silently whisked me up the lift to the waving gallery. I looked at him questioningly but he didn't say anything.

There was nobody up here this early in the morning.

Pete leaned on a pillar and buried his face in my hair, crushing me in a tight embrace. I buried my face in his neck, holding him tight. We did not say anything. We stood that way for a very long time. When we pulled apart there were tears hanging on his beautiful lashes and his nose was very red.

"I feel very special," he smiled, wiping my wet cheek with a finger, "because I mean something to you."

"You mean the world to me," I declared passionately into his eyes. "You are very, very, very special."

"Thank you," he kissed the top of my nose. "After this, we

shouldn't be put through this ever again, don't you think? I wouldn't be able to bear another separation. I don't like this at all. After this, we'll only go on trips together. Holidays. Or work. Okay?"

"I'd like that."

He brought his right hand in front of me, curled in a fist. Pete had strong-looking hands, with beautiful long fingers, very clean short nails. I gasped when he opened his palm. He had a thin band of genuine jade. Like a simple wedding ring, about half a centimetre wide, marbled-green in colour. I looked up in askance and he gazed fiercely at me without saying any word. Silently he slid the cool stone onto my trembling finger.

"I love you," he said in a quiet tone. "I'll come back for you very, very, very soon."

We kissed like there was no tomorrow. And then he was gone.

Back at home, I found Pete's email, sent the night before his departure.

"I can't stop smiling thinking of your little beige summer dress, and it's making me think of other things too. I'll let you know one day, in time. And you keep on promising to do this and that for me one day. I'm counting, you know, and one day I'll extract every single one of your promises.

Sweetheart, you looked really grownup in that dress. Except that you were very innocent. Endearingly so. You didn't dress like that to exercise your wiles.

Have I ever told you I love the fact that you're untouched, that you don't sleep around, that you're stubborn and in control, and don't let others pressure you to do as they expect you to do?

Even Sinead respects you, thwarted that she is, failing horribly in her quest to convert you into a boozer. I often smiled watching you two being such thick friends. You allow others their choices, and you don't give a damn about what they think of yours.

You are so adorable.

OK love, I'm going to sleep now, or I'll still be sitting here tomorrow.

I'll dream of my pretty girl in an LBD."
Little beige dress. The wretch! After being sad all day, I went
to sleep grinning like an idiot.

Pete phoned me from New York as soon as his flight landed
and my heart burst with joy as I had been pining for him. He was
about to change for a flight to Boston where he planned to stay
with his parents. He would go to New York only when required
by the court.

"Darling, I couldn't stop thinking of you the whole flight!
Missing you already."

"That true? No lovely lady asking you to join the mile-high
club?"

"Aw Sydney, I'm surprised at you," he chastised. "How can
you even think that?"

"I'm only young Pete, not dumb."

"But honey, for me, there's only you. Remember Flo? There
are many Flos in the world. And I don't want any of them."

"So you aren't denying there are beautiful women around?
Only that you don't want them? Oh Pete, I love you I love you I
love you!"

He was calling from a phone booth, but as we talked I could
hear his mobile phone ringing, I recognised the ring tone.

"Aren't you going to answer it?"

"It's Mom. Okay love, I'll call you back soon."

"My class is about to start. I'll call you back. Perhaps you'll be
in Boston. Wait, what's the time there? Will you be asleep then?"

"Call me anytime, no matter what. I miss you *so* much. Miss
Australia too, it's freezing here. Anyway, don't forget to eat.
Love you, honey."

"Love you too."

A Chinese classmate happened to be nearby as I closed this
call. Smilingly she asked, "Your friend going to sleep? An
international call?"

"Yes, Monica." I was embarrassed that she could hear. Had I
been loud?

"That's expensive, using a mobile phone. Do you know anything about the cheap international phone card?"

Working part-time on low pay, this sure piqued my interest.

"No, but tell me about it."

"You buy them from the shops. Calling a landline gives you heaps more talking time than calling a mobile phone. I call my parents in Hong Kong all the time. Where are you calling to?"

"The US."

"That's the cheapest destination! You get to talk thousands of minutes on a ten-dollar card."

"Really? Quick, tell me where to buy one."

Later that day I found Pete's latest email, explaining the ring.

"The jade is supposed to be a symbol of safety, peace of mind, kindness, and eternity. I want you to stay safe for an eternity. I still have a thousand things to tell you when you're 64, remember?"

A No-Class Australian Bit-of-Fluff

I was eager, highly impatient, looking forward to calling Pete that evening. But because I wanted to chat without interruption, first I walked and fed Bronson, watered my plants, had dinner and showered. This would allow him to wake up at the normal time on a Boston morning. Relaxed, I punched the speed dial to his *cell*. I wanted to ask for his landline number so I could dial it from my home phone using the new phone card.

"Hello," a woman picked up his phone.

For a moment I was confused. His Mom? Sounded like a younger woman. Must be his sister, Eve, who was six years older than Pete.

"Hi," I said nicely. "This is Sydney. Is Pete available, please?"

"My husband isn't available," replied the woman brusquely.

I was stunned. What was this?

"Come again?" I asked, bewildered.

"Who's this?" she countered.

"This is Sydney," I answered, perplexed. Pete had told his sister about me. She should know. Hang on. This wasn't Eve, was she? What did she say? My sluggish mind could not believe it.

"And who is Sydney?" she probed.

All the joy drained out of my body. I felt very, very uneasy. I checked my phone screen, but it did display Pete's name and number. So I had not called a wrong number.

"Look, Pete is expecting my call," I told her without answering her question. "Is he there, please?"

There was a silent moment. This person was digesting the information.

"My husband is in the shower," she announced after a pause. Then she gave a throaty laugh. "We've just had the most satisfying all-night romp after years separated." WHAAT??? "Pete has really missed me and my body! How he worships my body! Just, wow..." she laughed again as I listened in astonishment. "He's refreshing himself in the shower after hours of our mind-blowing sex."

I took the receiver away from my ear, staring at it in disbelief. Did she really say what I thought she said? I saw that my hand was shaking.

"Pete needs me and he's *so* madly in love with me," she continued. "And the sex is so combustive—we've really missed each other! We're so glad we are together again. This time for always." (NO!!! It couldn't be!!!) "And I've missed him so. I'm wearing his shirt now, 'cause I miss his scent so much. Mmm, he smells yummy..."

Singed, I switched the phone off and dropped it like hot coals.

Heart hammering I ran to the backyard and scooped up Bronson. Man, how heavy he was! He was no Dimity. I put him down and stepped onto the lawn, staggered by the massive impact of the conversation. Hurt. Confused. Worried. ANGRY!!!

I looked around me. Paused at the sight of my herb beds. And the newly-planted roses.

Shivering in fear, I touched the jade ring. It felt cool and soothing around my finger. Gosh, was I promised to a married man? And who was I to compete with a woman he had once married and slept with? And still legally married to, at that.

"Pete loves me," I stared at my ring. "He can't be so cruel."

I took a deep breath. More deep breaths. Somebody, help me...

The home phone rang. I let it ring out. But it rang again. Sooner or later I would have to face the music. Since the suspense was killing me, with leaden steps and frayed nerves I approached the house. I picked up the receiver with a visibly shaking hand. Heart thudding. Dreading the hard truth.

"Honey?"

I couldn't say anything.

"Sydney, darling?" Pete asked in a concerned voice. "Are you there? Are you okay?"

Tears were running down my cheeks.

"Is it over, Pete?" My voice was so low and lame. "Are we over?"

"Pardon? What are you talking about?'

I did not answer.

"Love, are you crying? What's wrong? Please, tell me." He sounded very worried. "I was in the shower. I heard my cell rang. But when I called you back your cell was turned off. And now you're crying. Honey... what's happened?"

Very kind tone. Genuine concern. Was he pretending? But my Pete had always been very honest. He did not have a single mean bone in his body. Perhaps this was stupid, but I gave him the benefit of a doubt and asked, "What's your landline number there? I'll call you back."

"Let me find out, this is a hotel room. Let me see... Okay, you ready?" he rattled the area code and number to me. "Please call me immediately, sweetheart. What's up? I'm so worried about you."

His wonderful voice sounded so loving. Concerned and caring. I took a deep breath. Was he going to lie to me? Was our magical love just myth? But why? Why would he lie? Pete had never taken advantage in our relationship. It was him who always gave and gave. He never asked for—well, a *"reward"*. We were very open about it, we had talked it over. But if that woman was to be believed, Pete was craving for—. Had I been too gullible?

In tears I used my phone card to dial his hotel room. Why, oh why was he in the same hotel room with her?!

"Where are you?" I asked anxiously. "Who are you with?"

"I'm in New York. I—"

"New York???" I sounded hysterical.

"Yes. Remember when Mom called while we were talking? She and Dad had just arrived at the airport too. Here in New York. She asked me to postpone going to Boston and join them here. My ex's mother had just died, as it happened. Today's the funeral. Mom wants me to be with them."

"As what?" I cried anxiously, "Your wife's escort?"

"Not my wife. Darling, please don't call her that. She's my ex."

"So the divorce is through?"—hopeful.

"Not yet. I don't know. I haven't checked with my lawyer."

"So you're attending the funeral as her husband,"—devastated.

"No!"

"As what, then?"—confused.

"I only agreed to accompany my parents. Mine and hers have become friends, so I'm just paying respect to the lady. I'll have nothing to do with my ex. In fact, without this funeral I don't even have to see her at all."

"Is that why she's in your hotel room?"—jealous.

"No," he sounded really puzzled. Was he lying or not? "She's not here."

"But Pete,"—suspicious—"She picked up your mobile phone when I called just now."

"Really?"—in genuine astonishment—"Perhaps she visited my parents and came in here when I was in the shower. I don't know. This is a hotel suite with two rooms, darling. One is my parents' and one is mine, with a sitting room in between. I didn't think to lock my door against my parents. She must be visiting them. I haven't seen her at all."

"Really?"—sceptical.

"Yes. Mom did call her late last night when we'd just checked in. She wanted to talk to me, but I didn't want to so I cut it short. Had jet lag anyway."

"Was that all?"—doubtful.

"Well, she said that now her mother had died she'd have more time for me, so I could stop travelling the world. But this wasn't the problem that caused us to separate at all. I've told her firmly that the marriage is over and I don't want to live with her ever again."

"But your Mom is chummy with her?"

Just then someone entered his room and Pete made a startled sound.

"Go away!" he shouted. "Get out! What do you think you're doing? Get out of my room!"

"Pete, darlin', you look so hot in only that bath robe!" I heard the woman's voice. "Could you please help with my bra?"

"Get out!" Pete hissed angrily. I heard a scuffle. Then a door being slammed and locked.

"Damn..." Pete sounded livid. He returned to the phone, "Sorry honey. That horrible intruder! Had to throw her out of my room." He talked with barely leashed anger, struggling to maintain his calm speech.

"What happened?"

"Well, the bitch just barged in and started to strip!" Wow, never heard Pete calling anyone names before. Must be truly angry.

"What? You didn't enjoy the view?"

"No!"

"Why should I believe you, Pete? You two were married once."

"That was in the past. Long over." He sighed. "I can't change the events before I met you, honey. Anyway, enough of her. Why were you crying, my love?" He sounded deeply concerned. "What's happened?"

"Your ex happened. She said she and you were back together Pete."

"No way!" he sounded strongly repulsed by the idea. "Honey, ignore her."

"But Pete, she said she and you had been at it for hours before your shower!"

"God... Darling, she lied. Reckon she was trying to play a mind game on you. Don't buy it, alright? I love you and only you. I'm so sorry you even had to speak with her." And just like that, just by listening to his caring voice, I was soothed. Talking to Pete always felt very good. But why should I believe him? What if he was lying? My own Dad lied to me.

"I would've thought somebody with her qualifications would be classy and well brought up. And she's four years older than you Pete. Shouldn't she sound mature and dignified?"

"Beats me. She's always been wild. I don't like her, hon."

"Does she know about us?" I asked testily.

"I don't think so. Did you tell her?"

"I told her you were expecting my call. I think she figured it out."

"Good. She should know that I have you—"

Just then I heard loud knocks and a muffled voice at his door.

"That's Mom now," Pete sighed. "Give me a minute." He went to the door, "I don't need a dark suit. I'm not going now."

More argument.

Pete came back to the phone, "Sorry honey—"

More disturbing loud knocks.

"Oh no..." a heavy sigh.

This sigh was an eye opener. At that moment, it was very clear to me that he was genuinely miserable. Pete had always been a man of high integrity. Supposing he wasn't lying, supposing I was in his shoes, how would I feel? He was a victim here. I realised my respect for him exceeded my ire.

"Poor Pete. Go answer it."

"But I wanna talk with *you*. Love, I've missed you."

The knocking was incessant.

"Darling, go answer it. I have five phone cards. You know, we can talk for thousands of minutes on a landline."

"I've heard of those cards. But Mark also mentioned cheap calls via internet dialling."

"Really? Let's find out and compare. After we finish these five cards."

The knocking was louder.

"Hang on. I'll have a word with Mom." He went and apparently let his Mom in.

"What do you mean you aren't going to the funeral now?"

protested an older voice as the door clicked shut.

"Exactly that. What's the point?"

"What's the point?" her shrill voice escalated, reminding me of irate Your Say callers. "She's been neglected by a husband who went gallivanting around the world! Totally disregarding her welfare for over two years! And now that husband is back home it adds insult to injury if he doesn't support her at her mother's sad funeral!"

"What sad funeral?"

"She's grieving! She was very close to her mother. Unlike *some* people."

"Her behaviour doesn't show the least grief. She's cunning. Devious. And I've told you we're divorcing."

"No you're not. A marriage is for life! Even if the court dissolved it, our church wouldn't recognize the divorce. But you're *not* divorcing, Pete. I forbid it."

"Well I *have* submitted the divorce papers."

"You. Are. Not. Divorcing. You'll reconcile. Your wife is willing to be everything you ever wanted her to be. You must play your part."

"Mother, I want no more part. That marriage was well and truly over ages ago."

"That's why you need a marriage counsellor! You were too young then. But you're a full adult now. You'll behave accordingly. Find solutions to your problems. I've booked the counselling, we'll do everything in Boston. Your wife is coming home with us to stay while she's grieving."

"No! She can't!"

"I've invited her and she's accepted. It will give you both the chance to be together and make up."

"Then I won't stay with you."

"Don't be foolish. You don't have money or a job, do you?"

"I'll find one. Trained myself while backpacking, haven't I? I've learnt to be resilient. Something always comes up."

"Pete, if you have no more feelings for her then there's no need to avoid her. You can face her and be comfortable about it. Like now. Get ready for the funeral. She's brought in one of your old suits. Looks to be in excellent condition to me. Such a thoughtful wife, she is. Besides being very beautiful. All my friends say she looks like Kate Winslet. She doesn't deserve your neglect. Now please get dressed. We'll all have breakfast downstairs."

"I'm not going to the funeral. I don't want to."

"Why? All your friends from the orchestra will be there. As well as everybody who's anybody. Don't shame me, Pete. It will be a great embarrassment for me if you don't go. If you're not going I won't be able to show my face, then I can't go. What a waste of effort in flying here. And don't tell me that 18-year-old bit-of-fluff you've been telling me about has any say in this. I don't want a no-class Australian in the family."

I heard the door open, close, and lock again.

"Honey?" Pete was back on the phone.

I burst out laughing. "Pete... What a merry welcome!"

"You find that funny?" he fumed.

"Very funny. Don't you? *'So you're a full adult Pete',*" I copied his Mom's speech, " *'Behave accordingly'.*"

Next he was laughing with me.

"Perhaps moms never trust their children to be adult enough." He laughed some more. "Sydney... How I miss you!"

"Good to hear. So what are you going to do with your no-class Australian bit-of-fluff, darling?"

"Love her all my life, of course. Mom's choice drinks too much, smokes too much, gambles too much, and sleeps with too many men. I can't believe that when I was 17, those were the very qualities that fascinated me. I thought her sophisticated, exciting, fun. How naïve! I'm so glad I'm over that stage. Well darling, I'm an older eagle with a wider bird's-eye view now, and I don't like any of the things I see in that direction. You have absolutely no competition there. I'll stick with my beautiful down-to-earth Aussie darling, any day."

"Nice. I love you too. But Pete, you've never told me how haughty your Mom is. I'd always assumed she would be friendly like her brother Craig."

"Don't worry about Mom. She's from the old-school of old Boston upper-class snobs. She kinda considers it unfortunate to marry an academic like my father, having to live a middle-class existence. But her parents lost their money, somehow, and I reckon Dad is good for her."

"What about your ex? Your Mom mentioned everybody who's anybody would be at the funeral."

"Her family belongs to New York's old money. Mom regards that as being very high on the importance scale. All that glitter and glamour. But again, they have a gambling addiction. A few years back they were involved in a dire financial stuff up."

"Aw Pete, this is all so amazing. Makes me realise our relationship has been pretty much two dimensional. Suddenly we're thrust into the big wide world. I've just heard so many things that make me grow up overnight. Should I worry?"

"No. With you in my life, I have a purpose, instead of just drifting. With you, I have something to look forward to. Please honey... don't doubt me."

"Okay... But I'm very, very curious, though. A few things nag at me after listening to what kind of personalities your ex and your Mom have. Question time?"

"Shoot."

"When you quit your marriage, why didn't you explain the cause to your Mom?"

He laughed bitterly. "You heard her, hon. Do you suppose *Mom* would've listened?"

I thought about it. Very gently I probed. Very, very cautiously I asked questions. I didn't rush him.

"Honey, if you must know," he confessed haltingly. "It's never easy for men to open up... and let others know that they're victims of domestic abuse."

Whaat? When was Pete going to stop dropping these left-hand grenades? I took a deep breath. This couldn't be easy for him. I had heard that a lot of men died from easily prevented diseases because they felt too macho to visit their doctors. Many hurting souls committed suicide because they could not speak up.

My heart went out to Pete as he slowly recounted the psychological abuse he had had to endure. Turned out his Mom had demanded so much from him since he was a kid.

"That's why you moved to New York instead of joining the Boston Symphony," I stated.

"Probably. I just wanted to be independent. But in hindsight it could be that in my subconsciousness I wanted to escape living under her thumb, and to my regret, I repeated the experience in that doomed marriage. My ex... threw things at me whenever I refused her anything... once my temple bled quite a bit."

"But why'd you have refused her anything? You're very generous with me."

"Sydney, I did wine and dine her. But I drew the line at paying for her gambling addiction."

"You're kidding."

"No. Honestly. It actually happened that way. Before we married she used to live with me each time she ran out of money. I paid all her credit cards as a wedding present, mistakenly thinking her gambling was over. But I was wrong... Immediately she hit the clubs again. Well, here in the States people can marry at 18 but can't drink or enter clubs until 21. I was 20 then. And even if I were of age, I'd refuse to go gambling with her. She laughed at me and picked other guys. Really honey, the more you are with a person, more traits will be revealed. Often she was drunk before rehearsals and I had to try to sober her up. When I refused to pay more credit cards, she destroyed my CDs just to be mean. She slept with those guys... Well, she wasn't worth fighting for. I walked out instead."

"But you didn't just walk out, Pete. You left a marvellous career you enjoyed and were proud of."

"Very astute."

"So why did you shun everything you ever cared about?"

"Actually, my career was the one thing *they* ever cared about, taking pride of my success. They were too close to my work. Too controlling. Music should be a joy, not a burden! By going backpacking I defied them. Thumbed my nose at them. You see honey, they aren't like you. You always make me feel appreciated. You set me free. I've never known my heart to feel so light, so elated. It's a tangible thing that you do when you love me. You understand me."

"Darling... I *care* for you." I was humbled by his willingness to open up to me. "Is there anything I can do?"

"Sure. Send me a picture of you in yesterday's LBD."

"Pete! No!"

He laughed freely, dispelling the serious mood.

"Don't worry about me, my love," he assured me breezily. "I'm now a proper adult. One without an inferiority complex. I don't crave for Mom's or my ex's acceptance."

Just then the loud, insistent knocking started again at his door. We burst out laughing and we laughed until we hung up.

You'll Always Be Number One to Me

But his ex clung to him after the funeral. Pete couldn't shake her off because his mother—who loved her very much—had invited her over to their Boston home while she was "grieving". His Mom insisted she was indeed grieving and needed all the pampering in the world.

Pete assured me his ex was using his married sister's old room. People might say he would tell me what I wanted to hear regardless of the truth because he was a man. But my Pete was not *that* kind of man. He had my unshakable trust.

Therefore I was incensed when a few days later I found some hate messages in my emails from his Mom and from his ex. They included photos. Lots and lots of photos.

There was a newspaper scan of the funeral. Of her clinging on to Pete's arm—her expression devastated and very grief-worthy—with the caption, *"Acclaimed Violinist Returns Specially to Console the Love of His Life"*. Pete's face was unreadable.

But his face was not unreadable in his wedding pictures. It radiated sunshine. Him, looking so young and handsome at 20 years old. And looking so much in love with his Kate-Winslet-look-alike beautiful bride. These came also with a society-page scan of the lavish romantic wedding.

"Ours is a love marriage, as you can clearly see," his ex wrote. *"Pete loves me. We're together and will stay together."*

"Go away," his Mom wrote. *"Pete loves his wife and they will be together for good."*

"Sydney," reminded my tutor. "Have you finished your assignment? Another group need the PC."

"A moment," I replied.

I forwarded all the hate emails to Pete without any comment. There. Explain that.

As I left the computer room, striving to walk in dignity, my tutor—his name was Trevor—came walking beside me.

"How are you finding it?" he asked with an urban smile. "Very exciting isn't it?" he answered his own question. Next he proceeded to tell me about his splendid animation projects. I was perfectly happy to "converse" with a male who was so full of himself that he really didn't need you to voice your opinion.

Trevor invited me for a coffee at the canteen because there was still half an hour before the next class. I accepted but refused to let him pay for mine. A few other students, who apparently thought the world of Trevor, approached us to question him on some projects and to praise him for his superb latest work.

I listened half heartedly, my mind across the ocean.

Trevor went on his way after asking us not to hesitate to call on him for any assistance.

"Isn't he yummy," commented one of the guys as we walked to our class. "A shame he's not gay." Then he told me, "Lucky you."

Pete phoned me immediately when I arrived home that evening.

"They must have hacked Lance's computer to get your email address, I used it yesterday," he explained. "Love, I'm so sorry. You know the wedding photos belong in the past, don't you? The past is past and it's truly over."

"What about the funeral?"

He sighed.

"You know I only attended it to pacify Mom. She threatened not to go if I didn't and she'd go on carping about it. But don't worry, honey. The press had it wrong. I love only you. It upsets me that they pull this on you. Could you please mark them as spam? You don't have to deal with their games."

"But I don't like you living with them. D'you know what it feels like Pete? To have the love of your heart living with another?"

"I know, darling, I know the hurt. I've been through it all. I should know what it's like more than anybody else. Trust me. I'm all yours, even when you can't see me. I won't hurt you."

"All mine? Pete, I can't even call you, I'm afraid they'll pick up the phone." So far my phone would ring thrice as his all-clear signal before I could dial their home landline using my phone card. I so chafed at this restriction. "I want full access to you any time I want. Are you really mine?"

"Of course, darling."

"So move out!" I bullied him.

"I am. One good thing did come out of the funeral. I told you I met many fellow musicians. I've had a few offers to play as a guest musician in some concerts, here in Boston and a few other cities. So I shouldn't be strapped for cash. I've been scanning ads for short-lease apartments and shared accommodation. I'll check a few out this morning."

Pete woke me the next morning.

"Guess what? I'm in the new place already. Write down the phone number."

Sleepily I took it down and called him back.

"It's a humble apartment, near MIT. I share it with a student."

"Will you be comfortable there?"

"Sure. Trained myself backpacking before, didn't I? This is marvellous and very civilized compared to some of the places I've crashed. The other guy, Mario, isn't a slob either. I'll do splendidly here."

"You sound like Sinead."

"Famously, she'd say. How's she? Had any news from her?"

"A postcard from Noosa, Queensland," I told him. "She's waiting tables and having the time of her life."

"Good for her."

"Good on her."

He laughed. And we chatted and we laughed and life was beautiful again, although we badly missed each other. If anything, the separation and troubles had enhanced our closeness and bonds.

I received more harassing emails. Pete's ex and his mother venomously attacked me. For causing Pete to move out from his family home when they were doing their best to get him to a marriage counsellor. It seemed his ex now realised Pete had grown up to be a wonderful man who was too marvellous to let go. They accused me of being a home wrecker and warned me away. Right. I marked both of them as spam and clicked them away.

Mostly Pete was in Boston. A few times he flew to Chicago and to LA to perform as a guest musician, and to New York to attend the court. By having a girlfriend his ex's lawyers sought to discredit his character, accusing him of wife neglect during his travels.

During all this time, I attended uni.

"*I went out with uni friends again,*" I told Pete in an email. "*Most can't get it that I don't drink, but they're nice because I drive them home afterwards.*"

Again, "*Saw a play at Enmore theatre with Monica, Sandra, Trevor, Ethan, and Stefan. Trevor is a senior student who helps tutoring new kids. Monica is a very pretty Chinese girl. She came over yesterday and taught me how to make dumplings.*"

Another one, "*Monica is a lesb, but don't worry, she respects that I'm straight. She's also close to Trevor. That is, even though she proclaims she's a lesb, she says now and then they casually fall into bed together after drinks.*"

I'm finding that uni life is a real eye opener. It wakes me up and makes me realise how rare it is to find a decent man like you. Darling, you're endangered species. Very precious."

Out of sight, Pete and I now used more words to communicate. The more I knew him, the more I learnt. During this time we started to discuss ideas and philosophy. I told him I did not have enough knowledge to form an opinion.

"In my family, we didn't discuss God," I explained. "My parents respect religious people. Each time they had friends over for dinner, when the guests happened to be Jews, Hindus, or Muslims, my parents were very respectful and meticulous about their dietary requirements. But we ourselves didn't get involved or practise religion. We had chocolates at Easter. We swapped presents at Christmas. That's about it".

"I've met several amazing religious people," he reasoned. "I've read extensively about several very spiritual people too. Their works and their insights. So it's hard for me to say God doesn't exist. But I'm not gonna patronize you, darling. The initiative should be from you. You're the one who must decide if you want to search."

"There are so many things out there, though."

"Honey, the theists claim spirituality is important 'cause while this life is transient, the next one is forever. We know that with material things there are always distinct qualities to differentiate genuine objects from fakes. Like, if you visit a jewellery shop, they have valuation methods to appraise diamonds. Suppose there's a god. This god creates diamonds with key characteristics to separate them from fake stones. If He goes to such trouble for the identification of material objects, won't He do the same for the spiritual?

"Supposing there's a god, it stands to reason that He also provides distinguishing qualities to differentiate His genuine ideas from trash, or His messengers from impostors. In this case, *my* first criterion in discerning a rubbish idea from truth is if it teaches hatred."

I mulled this over and planned to gradually ask him about the other criteria. Pete believed in one God belonging to everybody without exclusivity. He had churchie friends as well as followers of other faiths. He also sympathised with some atheist friends because, "Many are intellectuals disappointed in religion for valid reasons, honey. Fraud and deceit can't remain hidden in this era of science, reason, and wise people." And he said, "When people search with pure hearts without prejudice and arrogance, someday they'll find conclusive answers."

I went to see a girlie flick with uni friends after class at the Glebe cinema. When we came out, Trevor hailed us from a nearby pub. The girls headed towards him, but I said goodbye and walked to the bus stop. The buses were full. It was peak hour and Friday evening too, so I started walking down Glebe Point Rd towards Railway Square.

A car honked nearby. It was that guy Trevor again. I waved at him and continued walking. But he tailed me. The car behind him beeped noisily. I shooed Trevor off. But he opened the door on the passenger side and urged, "Get in."

"No, thanks. I'm only going down the road."

"Get in," he insisted. "You're holding up the traffic."

I wanted to say "Not me, you are", but the car behind him was very loud and impatient. What the heck, I didn't like to be a pain for the other road users. I slid in.

"Thanks for this, but I'm only going—"

"I'll take you," he cut me off, pulling out into the traffic.

"Thanks. You can drop me this side of George Street at Railway Square. I'll cross the road to the station."

"You're such a public-transport queen. I'll drop you home. Which way is it?" he smiled charmingly.

"Too far," I was worrying about the practically static traffic jam. "Let me off here so I can catch a train. The traffic isn't moving. It'll take too long. I need to attend to my dog."

"You have a dog? I have one too. A shih-tzu. I call him 'Li'l Shiht'" and he laughed at his own joke.

My phone rang. Pete. I answered it as I opened the car door—
we had stopped too long in the traffic—and stepped out.

"No!" Trevor shouted, "Do you think I'll let you go when I've
just got you in my car?"

"Bye," I waved to him and joined the crowd crossing the road
towards Central Station. Cold autumn wind blew the street,
whipping strongly at my hair and shirt.

"Darling, who was that?" Pete questioned me amid the din of
traffic and the throng of pedestrians.

"A senior student. He helps the lecturer tutoring us new kids."

"I don't like his way of talking." I could hear the scowl in his
voice.

"Just now? I don't like it either. But he's normally very helpful.
Dunno what's got into him."

"Was he threatening you?"

"Trying to coerce me into going home in his car."

"Well don't get in his car again!"

"Why Pete, getting Neanderthal, are we?" I was pleased to hear
the possessive note in his voice. Pete was a jealous guy. "Don't
worry. I'm catching a train now." I spotted a mum and a daughter
being jostled about in the crowd.

"Honey, I want you comfortable, but that guy sounded sleazy."

"He's not a sleaze. Well, not normally."

"Just remember darling, a decent guy will *never* force a girl."

How caring he was.

"I miss you Pete." I had entered the train and run to a blessedly
empty 2-seater. I threw my backpack onto the seat next to mine,
and motioned to the mum and daughter to take it. Sorry guys...
not all of you have disgusting after-five b.o., but... "Did you just
wake up? I'll call you from home to save your phone credit."

The little girl on her mum's knee was now drinking water from
a baby bottle.

"She's four and still drinks from a bottle," the mum sighed.

"Don't worry," I smiled. "She'll drink her water from a glass
when she goes to uni."

"That was one whole hour," Pete complained when I called back. "Where've you been? I was worried Mr Sleaze was stalking you."

"No. Just Bronson needed feeding. He's still a baby, Pete."

"But I miss you like crazy," he whined. "It's been—," he stopped and laughed. "Feeding Bronson. Guess this is training for one day when we'll have kids, huh? Daddy will be number two."

"Aw Pete, kids? You're kidding. And who's saying *I'll* feed the kids? You will. You're the excellent cook."

"Right," he chuckled. "So *I'll* feed the kids, huh? Easy. I'll teach 'em how to make your breakfast too."

"Hey Pete, why are you even talking about this?"

"Restless. The business here is dragging and sapping, darling. I play chess against the computer when friends are at work. Watch the Discovery channel. Pedal around town just looking at things, but there isn't much happening at the moment. I play my old violin. Join Lance's friends playing music. Read every single thing in newspapers. But they aren't enough... I need you so much. All these years I've craved for something more in life. Didn't even know what. But I've found it in you. Sydney... I'm now so lost without you. I'd be much happier doing exactly the same things if you were here. I always wonder what you do. This is only morning, but already I wanna see you so much."

"I feel it Pete. I can't see you, but I *feel* you. Am I psychic? I *feel* you. Yours is a very strong presence."

"That's because I'm constantly concentrating on you, reaching for you. *Focus*. Soul communication. It's telepathic."

"How can you do that?"

"A few people are sorta... gifted. It works when we focus. But it's no big deal, people don't really need this gift. I only use mine 'cause I'm desperate. Lonely. I need you... I dream about a future home with you. One with a well-tended rose garden..." he trailed off dreamily. "Wherever we'll live, it must have your rose garden 'cause I'm so fascinated by it."

"Ah-ha! You covet my garden?" I teased him. "That's the sole reason why you want to be with me, right?"

"Of course!" he played along. "What other reason is there?"

"Can't imagine what. But that's okay. I only want to be with you because I'm after your fantastic cooking. And darling, my dream home doesn't necessarily include a garden. But it must have your kitchen with the heavenly smell of your baking."

"Right," he chuckled. "We're gonna design it exactly the way you like it. 'Cause you'll always be number one to me. Home number two. Work number three."

"Nice. Um, Pete, your Mom and ex sent me emails again, using different user names."

"Ignore them. Tag them as spam. Did you get mine? Send me your pictures in my favourite dress. A-s-a-p."

"Dream on."

"Oh I do."

"Pete!"

He laughed. "Indulge me. I've practically nothing to do until the court next week."

"Your wife will be there?"

"Sweetheart, please don't call her that. I don't like it. She's my ex."

"But she still thinks she's your wife. She warns me away. She's always very optimistic that you'll reconcile. She paints your marriage as all rosy."

"What a conniving—," he expelled a disgruntled breath. "Honey, an ex is an ex for a reason. I've found friends who were witnesses to how she conducted herself during our very short marriage. The marriage itself was a mistake 'cause she'd lived that way before. I was too simple minded to think that a wedding vow would change her ways. I was a different person then. A naïve no-brainer. I paid. I opted out. It's been over for what feels like a lifetime ago.

"I'm stronger now and honestly not interested in her. At all. In any way whatsoever. I don't wanna live with her ever again. The past is past and it's over. I'm sorry she and Mom are harassing you. Whatever mind games they play with you, just remember you're always number one to me. Sydney... there's no way I can live without you."

11:05am, Tuesday, 21 March 2000

One unusually foggy morning in late March, the sun refused to come out. Cold grey clouds blanketed the city for hours. As I was listening to my lecturer on campus, my chest was jerked by a sudden attack of anxiety. PETE! My first thought was of him and I nearly called his name out loud.

As if from a distance my lecturer droned on about digital programming. I strained to heed him. For no reason my heart was beating too slowly. A sudden cold engulfed me in a freezing embrace. There was a strong, inexplicable fear clawing at my heart. It zapped my brain, sapping me dry, making my vision black. Faintly I heard people shouting. Then I passed out.

A short time later I was on the floor—regaining consciousness.

PETE! My heart screamed. But concerned faces surrounded me. "Are you okay?", "Did you have breakfast?", "Are you pregnant?", "Take a deep breath."

A deep breath did not clear the strange fear clutching at my chest. I felt woozy. I was shaking with cold.

"You aren't well," Monica stated. "Go home. I've phoned Trevor to take you."

"Why Trevor?" I asked in astonishment.

"When he was drunk, he told me—," she looked confused now. "Um, I just thought to call him. He's bringing his car around."

Oh no, Pete would not like it. But it would sound strange to reject help when my head was swimming and my body shivering. Reluctantly I let her lead me to a bench outside where eerie thick fog still blanketed the strange morning.

I and stretched my legs. A bit of my green socks were showing. Pete... lunch boxes... how I missed him! He had woken me up one hour too early this morning, speaking from a very noisy public phone. "...out with Lance's gang," he'd tried to say. "... great news!"

"Can hardly hear you!"

"... call me back."

But I had returned to sleep and woken up very late that I must dash out with no chance to call him back using my phone card. Standing in a crowded later train I could only texted him a TTYL message.

Now the time on my phone showed 11:05am, Tuesday, 21 March 2000 as I pressed his number.

He did not answer my call though.

Pete had vanished.

No calls. No emails. No letters. Nothing.

I called and called. There was no answer. I wrote emails. There was no reply. I even tried his family home phone number and his Mom's email addresses that I had to fish out from the spam. No answer. Just nothing.

My true love, evaporated?

No. This could not be the case. I wouldn't believe it of Pete. No one could be truer than Pete. He would not do this to me. He loved me. This whole situation was impossible.

But how the predicament shocked my whole system.

Pete did not wake me up anymore. And he didn't send me to

sleep with his wonderful voice. My heart leapt each time the phone rang. Lurched because it never was him. Bereft, I suffered like a stranded whale on a beach.

I rang Craig/Bridget, pining for some news of Pete. Their little girl picked up the phone.

"Lauren, you don't go to the puppy school anymore?"

"Molly wasn't really keen the last time, was she? Neither was your Bronson. But I miss you. I miss Pete more. He's supposed to come back soon, isn't he? Why didn't he call us last weekend? First time he didn't."

"So where *is* Pete?" I asked in gnawing worry.

Craig came to the phone. No, he had not heard of anything wrong with Pete, but he was not really in communication with his big sister.

"I'll give them a buzz and get back to you," he promised.

Craig tried and tried. Unfortunately, just like me he did not get an answer.

Dread ate at me.

I missed Pete heaps. I steadfastly refused to doubt him because our hearts beat as one and we were part of each other. No way would he deliberately let me suffer. This was just so not him. But not knowing what was going on drove me mad.

I struggled to hold my head high and appear calm. I still had to complete my assignments and work on weekends too. Early one morning, a storm uprooted a big tree and it fell onto the railway track—and a moron yelled his lung out, "Why wasn't I informed about this when I called *last night*???"

Duh! I was dying to press RELEASE, *'Call terminated due to customer's lack of intelligence'*—but must endure the curses he viciously hurled. My lot, to live and breathe among people who thought it was fine to swear. Why didn't they stop for a minute, close their eyes, and imagine they were the ones who were at the receiving end? Would they still be proud and endorse this freedom of speech?

With waning interest, I dealt listlessly with my callers. Some were lovely. Some belonged to agents' worst nightmares. Some

were so gross—they rang while in the toilet or while *at it* with
their partners. Hello? What happened to decency?

And some had exactly Pete's accent...

One Thursday after uni I bumped into Winston, the Chinese
school friend I was fond of, on the train. He was now a medical
student at Sydney Uni, not really enjoying it, but hoping things
would smooth out in the coming years.

As his life was pretty flat, he asked me out. We took a train to
North Sydney by 10pm because that was where the under 20s
flocked to dance on Thursday nights. But we both knew we
could never be more than friends. You could not choose whom
to fall in love with. For me, it just had to be Pete.

Dreary days rolled by.

Lonely, I would scan fellow commuters and chat inside my
head,

*"Hello guys. I have spoken with thousands and thousands of
you. And you've pushed me, and jostled me about. I'm with you
at the City2Surf and Mini Marathon. Among you at many
concerts and sporting events. Right now, next to you on the train.
Do you know that I'm sad? You know, I have Sinead O'Connor's
'Nothing Compares 2U' stuck in my head. So talk to me, train
buddies. Crack a joke. Let's discuss what caused that macho guy
over there to ink his arm with X-rated designs. Do you suppose
he really can't get by without them? Or did he gag when he
discovered these tattoos after a night in booze-land?*

*See the nice middle-aged couple by the back row? Every
morning they chat quietly while eating a fruit breakfast. Baffles
me how they cut the pieces in perfect cubes of exactly the same
size—2.54mm? And why would that girl with a pierced lip hog
the seat next to her with her bags while the lot of you have to
stand? You, charcoal suit glaring from the aisle, breathing fire.
Dare to yank her headset? Ask whether she's bought a valid
train ticket for her bags."*

I had no mental strength to listen to classical music. At home I shoved Pete's violin up high in the cupboard, too distraught to see it.

But his thoughtful gifts were all around. The perfect laughing-banksia man. The shells. The dried leaves, the pretty ones he had picked up from my home streets as we walked Bronson. I had framed them too. His violin CDs. The tape of him whistling beautifully. And the cool jade ring around my finger—*safety, peace of mind, kindness, and eternity...*

Deep inside I knew, I just knew, Pete would do nothing to hurt me. Something was terribly wrong.

Every night I worried about this as I brushed Bronson's fur. This was a way of bonding with Bronson. It showed him who was the boss, too. A few times he had knots and matting which had to be cut out because they couldn't be brushed out.

"Rah-rah-rah-rah-raaah rah-rah"

"Woof-woof!"

"What do you think, Bronson?" I asked miserably. "You know Pete's the loveliest guy alive. So what's wrong? Should I just sit home and let things happen? Me, the little fighter?"

What could I do? Gosh, what could I do?

I could send him a person-to-person registered express letter. That was what I did.

A few days later I flew outside when a FedEx van stopped beneath my room. At last! Smiling broadly I could have kissed the delivery man. But he handed my own letter back to me. Bewildered I looked at it. *Failed delivery.*

Pain sliced through my chest as I staggered inside. I closed the door. Leaned on it. Then slid boneless to the floor with my sinking spirit. There, in the foyer where my love first kissed me, I broke down.

That night I had a nightmare.

In the dream I attended an evening party, where, swathed in happiness, I came to realise it was to be my wedding ball. Tulips were everywhere as if people were walking in a field of them and overhead brilliant chandeliers glittered merrily. But—but the groom never showed up! I waited and waited. I saw wisps of snow floating down silently from the now open ceiling. Slowly... So slowly... Cold and quiet. Into the grand ballroom that was now vacant of people or flowers. Except for a solitary girl in a pretty wedding gown...

I was caught in that dream, cold and helpless, trying to break free but I could not. Tied... I had to endure the dream for a very long time even after I realised I was dreaming.

The first thing I saw when I could finally open my eyes was a photo of Pete on my night table. I had one whole wall of my photos of him in my room. In one, I remembered how the sun had slanted in the kitchen and played on his shiny blue-black hair. In another, he was happily laughing. In this one on the night table he was maintaining strong eye contact, silently conveying his deep love.

With a trembling hand I reached for it and touched his beloved face. His eyes looked back at me and I felt a meeting of our souls. In my mind I heard his voice. *Sydney... there's no way I can live without you.*

I jumped out of the bed and hauled his duffel bag from my wardrobe, the one he left because he was to come back soon. Earlier I had laundered the clothes he had worn to swimming and skating. I dug out his T-shirt, stared at it, and changed into it. The moment it wrapped my body I felt some kind of relief. There was his subtle scent that I relished. But more, I felt as if he was with me and I *could* feel his love.

There was a land out there. In a parallel world. In that land, we were one. Nobody could take this away from us. 'Cause nobody else knew this place. In this land of ours, nobody else existed.

After many days of near insomnia, I finally fell asleep.

Waking up, I drove to Freshwater and surfed by myself, needing the adrenalin. There I made the discovery that although it did not conjure Pete, shouting to the waves deadened my frustration a bit. And hey, I lived in Sydney—why would I mope in a dark corner when I could have endless, magnificent views?

From then on I went surfing by myself *every day*. Even in the coldest autumn, and when I could only afford to be there a short time. On chilly mornings there was hardly anybody about. The beach was all mine. I watched the glorious sun, rising golden from the glittering Pacific, casting orangey-yellow hues of dawn on the intriguing patterns of cirrus clouds above.

Alone I screamed my heart out loud to the roaring waves. "My love, where are you?"

*I drove to Freshwater and surfed by myself,
needing the adrenalin.*

The Taxis Refuse To Take Us

"C'mon. We'll pay for your parking. The taxis always refuse to take us home," Petra, Monica's very beautiful doll-like girlfriend, whined.

"I know all about taxi complaints, girls. Either drivers refuse drunks, or they take advantage by taking you the long way home."

"So you'll drive us?" Monica tried to make me feel guilty, "It's not safe for young girls to be stranded in the City you know."

Duh. 'Young girls'? Only in my taxi complaints girls referred to themselves as young. Who again wanted to go out in the first place?

"Catch the NightRide," I advised. It was okay if friends happened to drink around me, but why should I go out of my way to watch them drink? It was plain unintelligent (no-brainer, Pete would say) to force myself to do so just to gain their acceptance.

"We'll ask the boys too," hazel-eyed Chantelle offered, trying to entice me. "Seven can fit in your big car, right? Whom do you prefer? The regulars? I'll text Stefan and Trevor. "

"No thank you."

"You want someone new? Good idea! Can't stand a man for more than a few weeks. I love the anticipation of going to bed with a new body." Chantelle smiled eagerly. "Shall we pick up some cute boys tonight?"

"Just you. Hope you have a good time." And be safe.

"You have to try it Sydney... Sex will loosen you up a bit."

"Sydney has a guy overseas," Monica interjected.

"Fantastic. That means this is her chance to go out bonking others! Check out if she's got the best deal. And Sydney, who knows you'll meet Mr Right tonight?!"

"Yeah right. Are you suggesting I wait for Mr Right by bonking every Mr Right Now?" I shook my head. "Think again."

"Sydney..." Chantelle whined. "Think of the fun."

"You know I work twenty hours on weekends." My excuse. True anyway. "I just want to be lazy in the evenings."

"Must you work every frigging weekend?" Petra whinged. "Chuck a sickie for once!"

But Monica managed a kind smile. "Well, it's not fair of us to expect you to play chauffeur on a regular basis."

"Regular basis?" her miffed girlfriend continued bitching in stage whispers, "She's only driven us home three times!"

Three times were way too many as I had not enjoyed the experience. With my current frame of mind, I was especially not in the right shape. I didn't want to be a cranky wet blanket. And I was not for the after-drinking sex. There was no way I could participate just-for-the-fun-of-it. What if in their soused oblivion they forgot protection? What if some freaky sleaze took advantage of their vulnerability? Ask pregnant teens out there, Auntie Kate once admonished, how many would remember it fondly as youthful foibles? Call me chicken, but it truly scared the hell out of me.

Outside the last class Trevor hounded me. This senior student was not one to leave me alone.

"Come join us," he urged, walking beside me. "It's Friday evening."

"No, thank you. Have to take calls tomorrow at 6am."

"Sydney, missing out on grog is a social death," he lectured, coming to stop in front of me, blocking my way. "Folks will think you're abnormal. There's no need to be so strict at our age. All of us drink all the time, and do our study and our projects and our exams and we'll all get our degree. No one is harmed. Don't waste your youth being a prude when you're only young once. How can you even relate to friends?"

"Well, news flash. I'm a nonconformist." I smiled at him to lessen the sting of my words. "Trevor, I refuse any pre-cast mould 'cause I want to be accepted for who I am. But in case you're curious, my friends and I rub well enough together. Hey, they all claimed to be my best friends when I arrived with homemade baking at last week's group assignment. Go, enjoy yourselves."

"What about a movie?" he switched. He threw in a cajoling smile, too. Too suave for my taste. I did not like the calculating gleam in his blue eyes. "Anything you want to see?"

"Not at the moment. Thanks. Good night."

I rang Craig/Bridget, hoping they had heard from Pete or his family.

"I'll chase them again," Craig offered. "Come over this evening, bring Bronson. We'll have dinner and walk the dogs."

I heartily accepted. When I arrived home I quickly packed Bronson into Dad's car—which I layered with a doggie hammock because he shed a lot of hair—and drove to Roseville.

"I've called the family's home and left a message on their answering machine again," Craig reported.

"And I texted every member of the household," Bridget added. "Hopefully this time one of them will reply."

It was at Killara cricket oval, as we were running and laughing with the dogs under the oval's bright lights, that the bad news arrived.

"Pete met with an awful accident in March," Lance replied to Bridget's SMS. *"He's off the life support. But still in a terrible condition."*

My stomach dropped. My legs lost all their power to support me.

"He's okay," Bridget took me in her arms. "He's off the life support. He'll be alright."

"He was put on life support!" I cried. "That meant it was very serious!"

We hurried home to call Lance using the landline, sitting in Craig's living room with the speaker on.

"Why didn't anybody let us know?" Craig asked as my tummy knotted in fear.

"We've been frantic here," explained Lance in a voice eerily similar to Pete's. "You wouldn't believe how hysterical and difficult Mom's been. Favourite son and all that. In the beginning she even needed to be given sedatives. Now she's kinda very angry all the time, you don't wanna cross her. Anyway, we've been to the hospital every time when we don't have to be somewhere else. And Pete—God... Pete's gone!"

I gasped.

"What do you mean he's gone?" Craig asked.

"He doesn't recognize us anymore. He's been out of the coma for a few days now. His eyes are open. But that's about it."

"What happened to him? What injuries?"

"A bicycle accident. A hit and run. Pete regularly went cycling after dinner. Even in the coldest spring evening. But he wasn't wearing a helmet when the car hit him."

"That doesn't sound like Pete!"

"I know. Everybody's saying Pete's always been careful. But the fact is, he didn't wear a helmet that night. Suffered a closed brain injury. Many broken bones. Nearly bled to death too. Luckily another car found him soon enough."

"So what's his condition now?"

"Looks like a mummy. Doesn't recognize anyone. Can't talk at all. Screams very loudly in pain—usually when he tries to move, but of course he can't move at all."

"No..." I sobbed. My poor Pete!

"Who's that?" Lance asked curiously.

"We have Sydney here," Craig informed him. "She's Pete's dear friend."

"Yes," Lance responded. "Pete had her pictures everywhere in his room. I've packed up all his belongings in the apartment, though. Brought them back here. His condition looks to be a long-term thing, Dad says to pack up." Then he addressed me, "I'm sorry Sydney..."

"Hi," I managed. "What does his doctor say?"

"They can't tell. They can't tell whether his brain injury will completely heal. Whether his broken arm and leg will ever regain their full use. It's just wait and see."

He was very blunt about it. Perhaps because he was only 17, he did not try to gloss up the facts as he knew them. He gave only honest answers.

"What about his ex?" I asked, remembering.

"She's out of the picture. The divorce was through just before the accident. She's in an alcohol-rehab centre somewhere in New York."

"Which hospital is Pete in?" Craig asked.

"Mass General. It's one of the best."

"Super. You hear that, Sydney? Massachusetts General. Pete's getting the best care. He'll be alright in no time," Craig tried to ease my anxiety. "Hey Lance, Pete does have medical insurance, doesn't he? Or do we need to chip in?"

"He does have one. Forever careful, old Pete. He's all covered. Thank you."

"Lance," I asked, my mind clicking at something else, "When exactly did this happen?"

"Monday, March the 20th. He was found at nine-oh-five pm." Boston time.

The hair on my neck stood up. *11:05am, Tuesday, 21 March 2000*, Sydney time.

I was frantic. The thought of my love in a critical condition and the tremendous fear of never again seeing his beloved face ate at me. I desperately needed to get over there.

But I didn't have any money. All my savings had gone to pay for uni. I had lived frugally day to day, my dismal salary going to my books and food. Damn if I asked my parents' help for anything. I was too proud.

Eventually, my worries exceeding my pride, I phoned Dad, hoping to borrow some funds.

But as it turned out he had just been sacked. My wonderful Dad tried to help his employees and paid for it. As the company's new Chief Geophysicist, he was petitioned by the local employees to increase their meagre pay. Dad heartily approved, thinking these people deserved it because the company was making HUGE profits.

"You wouldn't believe it!" he confided. "My drafter was only paid a pathetic 75 dollars a month! I visited. They could only afford to live in appalling condition." It so went against his conscience, because his pay was over a half-million dollars a year.

But the American oil company objected to the pay rise and Dad lost his job.

"What about—Geraldine?" I asked.

"She still has her job. At the moment I'm staying here with her while she makes up her mind whether to follow me home."

"What's there to decide? She wants to build a family with you! She can't possibly want to stay there."

"But she loves it here."

"Living in woop-woop?" I asked in disbelief.

"Honey, this part of Balikpapan where the oil people live is a very posh one. Very upper class. Country-club life and such. She's made friends. Expats' wives and highly-educated locals."

"But she loves you, Dad. Doesn't she?" My Dad was a great bloke. And very handsome too. "You should come first!"

"I'll wait a bit for her decision."

So Dad was in hot water. No way would I burden him with my own problems. I was too tongue-tied to mention anything, let alone borrow money.

Still I must see Pete urgently. Swallowing my pride, quelling my fear, I called on Mum at her partner's opulent home for help.

She objected fiercely and we had a big fight.

"You're putting too much importance on this relationship," she protested, ranting and raving. "And at an age when you haven't the maturity to know better. Well, I'll have you know. A man isn't a woman's destiny in life! He is *not* the purpose of a woman's existence. Not a woman's raison d'être. To live happily you first have to discover your own self. Make something of yourself for yourself that satisfies your intelligence and self respect. Know your worth. Find your own purpose in life. And I repeat, your purpose in life isn't the man you're in love with!"

"Of course not," I retorted. "I totally agree with you. I believe the man we're in love with is our friend along the journey to those goals. But without him to share our life, the journey will be lonely and those achievements will be hollow.

"I may be young but I know firsthand—through *my parents'* abandonment," I threw her a dirty look, "that as social beings we all need genuine companionship to feel complete. After you left me alone, I found it with Pete. I'm not giving him up for any reason. No, no, no! I wanna grow up with him! Grow old with him! But he's sick, so please... I *need* your help to visit him now."

"No way! You're only 18! You can't leave your study, give up your future, to go halfway across the world."

"I'm not giving up my study... Only deferring it. And it's not like I'm going away for fun."

"Still irresponsible! Even if it's not for fun. A complete waste of time because there's absolutely nothing—nothing!—you can do over there. You're too young to understand, but teenage love will soon fade."

"No! Our love will last forever."

"Spoken exactly like a teenager. But sorry Miss, I'm not paying for you to waste your time and resources on your silly, immature love."

"Mum?" I begged. "Please..."

"No way! Do you hear me? No. Way."

"What do you want me to do? Ditch my boyfriend because he's become an invalid?" I stomped my foot, working myself into a rage. "You're *so mean!* So heartless!"—my volume escalated. "I'm *never* going to visit you again!"

Angry and crying, I left. Hating her. Hating the clash. But as I was running to the door someone snatched at my arm.

Ettoré had appeared from nowhere, looking at me with fury.

"Don't do this to your mother," he protested sternly, looking like he would love to give me a sound trashing. He whirled me around and dragged me back to Mum in purposeful steps. His grip on my arm hurt. I couldn't believe how strong he was, sophisticated Mr Beautiful of the slender, delicate frame. Fiercely he instructed me, eyes flashing, "Now hug your Mum!"

And somehow I ended up in Mum's arms, both of us crying. We were two different individuals who could not relate with each other. What had life done to us? We used to be a happy family, what felt like a million lifetimes ago. I used to adore her, even when she was bossy and strict and hogged the internet and bought me grownup shoes that I wouldn't be seen dead wearing.

In the aftermath Mum went to freshen up. Ettoré took me to the kitchen and sat me at his table, a contemporary glass-and-steel affair.

"Be good to everyone." He shoved a glass of cold water at me. His unsmiling jaw tight. "Say only kind words. Soft words. Because you never know one day you may have to eat them."

"But she wants me to get over Pete!" I railed in full despair. "How could I go on my merry way when Pete's in this condition?" Could you do that to someone dear to your heart? When the going gets very, very tough, would you walk away from him who has taught you the meaning of the word 'euphoria' and has promised to love you until he dies? "It hurts me to know he's in pain."

"I could help you, you know."

My eyes widened.

"I could find you sponsors for a visa," he continued.

For the first time, a glimmer of hope flickered in my heart.

"I have connections. Everywhere." He took the seat across from me. "My business takes me all over the world. Hey, I can even attend a meeting in New York this week, instead of my deputy. I can easily fly to Boston from there."

I gaped.

"Yes, I'll do it," he came to a swift decision. "Your Mum and I will go. But we're not taking you with us. Stay home and study. We'll check on Pete and report everything to you. Alright? We'll assess whether it'll be a good thing for you to go to him then. And if so, what you may need."

"But I'm going to die if I don't see him *now*!"

"Use your head, Sydney. He's been in the hospital for several weeks, you say. It won't make much difference to wait a week longer."

"What if—"

"No what ifs! And what other options do you have anyway?"

Oh. I stared at him like a halfwit. What other options? Contritely I reined in my temper.

"But—, but you and Mum are key executives... Very important and very busy. You'd really do this? Drop everything and go thousands of miles to check Pete out for me?"

"Time for parental leave," he reasoned. "Annette loves you. I'll talk her into agreeing to this. And with the phone and internet, I can still do most of my work throughout the trip."

"Please tell Pete," I asked with pent-up emotion, "Tell Pete I love him."

"Be strong," he ordered strictly. "You're useless to Pete broken."

It was extremely hard to cope with the interminable wait.

Missing my school friends, I perused their emails.

Lucy was in the Army and "so not writing about it" because she had had enough "after the whole day living it". She wrote she was awfully tired every night and could not manage to jot down more than a few lines each time.

In stark contrast, Brenna who was studying music in Melbourne waxed rhapsodies about the pianist she had fallen madly in love with. She went on and on about him, positively head over heels.

Meanwhile Alex in India grimly recounted the world's many miseries he witnessed. Appalling living conditions. Child slavery. Underage prostitution. Poverty beyond imagination. Contaminated water and diseases. Deforestation. I asked him if it was so disturbing, why didn't he move on? "*The lovely people*", he replied. "On my first day, I wondered why the hell had people come here. At the end of the third day, I was already making plans to extend my stay. And I'll definitely come back here in the future."

How could I mention my woes to these friends? Lucy, struggling to be the future hero of our country. Brenna—I would not dent her joy. And Alex. Wouldn't it be shallow of me to compete with hefty world issues?

In silence I grieved for my Pete.

Then one morning, during my break at campus, I had a phone call from Nina.

"Sydney. You okay?" she enquired in a concerned tone.

For a moment I could not answer.

"Why shouldn't I be?" I replied after a pause.

"Well—I had a dream about you. In the dream, you looked sad."

Somehow this made me burst into tears.

"Pete's injured!" I wailed. "He had an accident, Nina. A despicable hit-and-run! It's been weeks! And still he's hardly conscious!"

"No... So sorry to hear that. Where is he?"

"In Boston! So far away I can't see him!"

"Pray for him to get better."

"But he's in America!"

"Sydney? Your prayer for him will reach God, no matter the location. It's the same one God, darl, wherever you are."

"If there was a God, he wouldn't be so cruel! If there was a God, he wouldn't have let this happen to Pete! He's the most wonderful person, Nina. He doesn't deserve this. Not at all! No, I don't believe there's a God!"

Then I realised a few people were watching me. In fact, Trevor was looking at me strangely. Did I look deranged? I whirled around and stormed off.

"May I visit?" Pete knew her from his stint at the call centre and I needed to pour my heart out to someone who had met my love. "Can't talk right now."

I arrived as her kids were leaving for a kung-fu practice, all in their white uniform.

"You don't take your mum along?" I asked.

"She already knows how to throw you. Easy."

"Really?" I turned to Nina. "Then why don't you go to their practice and throw all the smart-assed guys?"

"Um—I don't touch strangers. You know, it's hard to throw a man without touching him."

I laughed.

Nina had baked some pastries for me, making me miss Pete even more. My love—a champ in the kitchen.

"Pete needs your prayers," she advised. "God does exist and He is there for your benefit."

"What God? There's no God. If God did exist, why so much mess? If he was one, then why did he create so many confusing religions?"

"Because our ancestors had not developed the internet. Or TV. Or jet planes. One civilisation didn't have the means to communicate with another. So the limit was with the people—not God."

"Oh?"

"Religion is God's grace, His way to show people how to live easier. God loves *all* people. So He chose a messenger from among each people as a guide. Confucius for the Chinese. Zoroaster for the Persians. There haven't been any people to whom a messenger of God has not been sent."

"But how come God picked unintelligent guides? Take how Moses preached 'creation'. That was plain uninformed!"

"That was in parables, though, don't take them literally. Three thousand years ago Moses' followers weren't exactly attending the likes of Oxford or Harvard there in Egypt, were they? God could hardly sprout quantum physics then, could he? He taught creation in metaphors people could understand then. The limit was with the people *then*—not God."

"But why are there such enormous discords among religions? How come they differ so much from one another?"

"Sydney... in the beginning they varied depending on the level of intellectual and psychological evolution of the different peoples. Later, certain followers altered them to suit their ego or politics. Handed down through generations, they've suffered the Chinese-whisper effect, changing them from the original teachings. Safe to say, all abhorrent beliefs or practices you see in any religion are later additions, instead of from God. But the basics of all religions are the same. Love for all. Be accountable for your actions."

I mulled this over. Supposedly there were rational answers to humanity's infinite questions. If you hadn't stumbled upon these answers yet, the limit was with you—not with God. The Perfect, All-Knowing God loves you and provides for you. Like, God has started to create petroleum in the earth's subsurface 400 million years ago, knowing you would need it for cars and planes today.

"Give Pete the gift of prayers, Sydney. You'll find that God does listen to those in anguish."

"What if there's no God? I'll be praying in vain."

"What's there to lose?" she countered. "Praying is free."

"How do you even expect me to pray when I have no flaming idea which religion to follow?"

"How do you visit your Mum when you don't have her building pass?"

"I phone her, of course."

"That's it. You contact her directly and she'll let you in. So speak directly to God. Pray in your own way for Pete's recovery."

Did I believe there was a God? Perhaps I did. Pete said he had seen and read about several very spiritual people. Did I believe in God? Well... I still had to find out more about this.

"So Nina," I stood up. "You really think an old guy with a white beard in the sky will listen?"

She laughed. "Stop it. God is invisible. We know He's here through His works."

When I came home I cried to God—whoever God was—

because with distance and money as hindrance, praying was my only option. I needed to believe there was a Being who had the power to help my Pete.

"God, if you exist, please help Pete and me."

I prayed while walking around watering my garden. I prayed as I stood slicing tomatoes for my dinner. I prayed hugging a cushion, staring at my empty fireplace. I prayed kneeling down in front of my bed. I prayed lying on my pillow, a picture of Pete looking on from the night table.

I fervently prayed he would get better.

One late afternoon, as I left to walk Bronson, I saw Trevor waiting in front of my house with his little dog. Vaguely I wondered why Trevor, who lived in Wollstonecraft, would come this far just to walk his dog. Indulging his pet?

His little shih-tzu was more exuberant than my long-haired collie. Bronson had grown very long fur and he looked magnificent and very dignified. He looked at Li'l Shiht with interest but refused to be drawn to play. And both the dogs were too lazy to run.

"I can't tell whether it's because Bronson is downright lazy or highly intelligent," I had once written to Pete, *"but his haughty demeanour is so endearing, and I fall in love with him more because he makes me laugh. Pete, you should see us running.*

When I run around the oval, at first he'll just stand still in that majestic posturing of his, watching me in a condescending stare, his now long mane looking so beautiful. After I've run three sides of the oval, he'll sprint towards me and run the last side of the oval with me, joyously barking and biting at the side of my shirt.

When we reach the starting point, he'll stand still again and watch, his haughty expression saying: 'Why are you stupidly running all around the oval, when you can just traverse it quickly?'

He will join me again when I've run the three sides of the oval."

To that Pete had replied,

"Give Bronson a hug from me. Tell the little baggage I love him 'cause he makes you happy. I talked to my flatmate about him and Mario gave me a recipe for dog toothpaste:

2 Tablesp bicarbonate soda

Add olive oil just enough to make it into paste

Add 2 teasp aniseed essence.

Try this, 'cause I think his $26 toothpaste from your vet is a rip off."

"It works?" Trevor asked me now when I told him about this cheap recipe. We were talking about dog habits and dog breeds and everything dog. And he had never brushed his dog's teeth.

"Sure does. Bronson's breath isn't smelly at all."

When we returned in the diminishing light to my house, where Trevor had parked his car, he asked, "Can Li'l Shiht please have some water?"

I took them to the backyard. As it was getting dark early at this time of the year, I switched on the lights. At that moment I heard a car coming. By the sound of it, Ettoré's Maserati.

My heart pounded so hard. News at last!

Honey, He Will Always Be A Vegetable!

"I'm sorry honey, but he'll always be a vegetable."

"No! I won't have it. Not my Pete, no! Not my love. My life. No!"

"Darling..." Mum took me into her arms. "We questioned his doctors all about it. The orthopaedic surgeon. The neurosurgeon. I know you're shocked. But hush now, keep your cool."

"Let her cry," Ettoré suggested. "Time enough to talk later."

I pulled away from Mum at this. Fresh tears kept spilling out, but I faced them.

"I want to talk. Please... Don't leave anything out."

Ettoré took me to the couch. I tried hard to suppress the sobs jerking my body and he wrapped a consoling arm around my shoulders.

"He has regained consciousness, but not awareness," Mum explained. "When we visited, his eyes were open, but he just stared, unseeing, oblivious of everything. There was no response whatsoever to any sound or sight. He didn't show recognition to anybody—even his mum. He didn't know what was going on. He didn't talk, or couldn't.

"It was a month after his accident. He had been like that since coming out of the coma. The first three weeks, he was totally out. The doctor said *severe* brain injury occurred when the patient was in a prolonged coma. As in days, weeks, or longer. Well, Pete was out for three weeks, and based on the doctor's experience this type of patient would stay in a vegetative state, which is exactly Pete's current unresponsive state. So honey, he's not there.

"His body is broken. Bandages and plasters everywhere. Closed right brain injury. Broken right shin. Broken right arm. Jarred shoulder. And there's nobody inhabiting this broken shell. He's simply not there."

"He *is* there," I declared fiercely, swiping at my tears. *There was a parallel land out there...* "I still *feel* him. We have this connection. *I* know."

"Darling... We've seen how close you two were. But we're telling you the truth. Generally, patients with moderate traumatic brain injury can recover with treatment. They can successfully learn to overcome their deficits. But Pete's case is a severe one, honey. How will he *learn* to get better when he doesn't even know what's going on and can't respond to stimulation? His doctors say not to expect much."

"No! They're so wrong! He'll get better." I stood up and paced and paced furiously. I was extremely angry with whoever had hit my Pete. Why, oh why, had he not been wearing his helmet that night?

"So Pete's injured. So the injury is extensive. He can't even talk. That means he needs me now more than ever! I have to be there. Oh God, I have to be there." I hugged myself. "Help me, *please help me*, I have to be there."

Mum ordered, "Be reasonable," and Ettoré asked, "What about your study?" at the same time.

They looked at each other and silently they agreed Ettoré was the one to talk.

"Annette and I will have to discuss this," Ettoré offered. "With your Dad, too."

"Dad?" Ettoré and Dad *knew* each other?

"Of course he should know. You want to go overseas. You're

in the middle of your study. You're wearing your heart on your sleeve. You aren't thinking straight. You're only 18 and you love Pete too much. There's definitely a streak of emotional fanaticism in you. What can you do? What can you do for him?"

"I can care for him."

"There are doctors and highly trained nurses doing that already."

"But they're only doing their duty! They don't love him."

Ettoré took a deep breath.

"Honey, even if he gets better—which at the moment is a very big ask—he won't be the same as before. Before this accident Pete sure could string more words together than your teen friends. He was interesting and we liked him. But he's changed. He'll never be your original flame again.

"How will you cope with a disabled person who'll forever be dependent on you for pretty much everything? How are you going to finance your life? That is, if you can even do that. How will you get him to marry you when he can't even recognise you, let alone talk and go through a marriage ceremony?

"Yes Sydney, we're talking marriage here. Big-eyed, are you? You can't possibly stay in the US. What work can you do there to support yourself? Flipping burgers or waiting tables? You have to bring him down here. And how do you think you can do this if you aren't married to him? You don't even have a decent income to support his expenses. You think our Immigration will grant a burdensome foreigner entry and get free hospital and medical support like the rest of us Aussies?

"Do you understand that? A disabled person will need looking after *all day*. It's a gruelling task. How will you do that by yourself? You can't afford to be a dropout because your study is something to fall back on. Your future kids will require expenses. They won't appreciate parents who are Centrelink parasites—one on disability pension, the other an underpaid worker. Where will your self-esteem be when you depend on tax payers' handout? So you need a good job for your family's survival. For your own dignity. For your sanity. Do you see all that?

"And what about fun? You're only 18. 18! You want to throw away your youth just like that? For an injured man? How long can you cope? How long before you cave in under the burden? And what about sex? Yes, Sydney. You won't be young and innocent for always. One day you'll grow up and you *will* need sex. Suppose he remains a vegetable. There wouldn't be any sex. There wouldn't be kids either. What then? You'd be chained to him. Would you grow to hate him? Would you cheat on him?

"And your parents love you so much! Neither of them will allow you to throw your life away just because you can't get over this enormous feeling of love. Yes he was great, before the accident. But are you prepared to accept him if it turned out to be the worst?

"So think this through. Evaluate all possible consequences. Think calmly. Take your time. If you think you could cope with all that, if you think you could come up with the solution to every single question that I've just mentioned, bring your proposal to us tomorrow. Or whenever you're ready. Explain why your parents should allow you to go to the US. Why it is the only sensible thing to do. Rationally like an adult, not emotionally. And don't give me smart-assed juvenile answers. I want you to use your brain.

"Think long term. If we lend you money to finance this trip— and give you connections to gain the necessary visa—outline how you'll pay us back. For your mother, the greatest payback will be your safety and happiness. But don't take advantage of her. An adult acts like an adult—meaning they pay their own way. They make money to support their decisions and their lifestyle. They have the dignity not to whine and beg!"

I stared at him in amazement. Ettoré, the pretty boy, saying all this? He must have thought of every possible deterrent on the flight home. I turned to Mum. She was big-eyed too. Ettoré, the pretty boy, saying all this?

"We still have jet lag," he stood up. "So come late if you want to see us tomorrow. Ciao for now."

"Will you be alright by yourself?" Mum asked. Her hair was untidy and she was still wearing her rumpled clothes from the plane. For once, my usually elegant mother did not bother about her appearance. "I could stay."

"I'll be alright," I assured her. "I have to be. For Pete."

I waved them off with a heavy heart and returned to pacing the living room. Thinking hard and missing Pete. Missing his warm hugs and the twinkle in his eyes. Ettoré's warnings had awoken me. I could not afford to crumple or be volatile emotionally. Had to work out a plan. Somebody, help me...

"I'm here. For you."

I whirled around, startled. Trevor! I had forgotten about him completely. He hovered near the French doors, a scowl marring his normally cheerful face. Trevor was a looker with nice cheek bones, well-proportioned nose and sculpted lips. Couldn't like his eyes, though. There was something cunning and untrustworthy there. At least that was how he came across.

"No need to chase a dying man."

"Eavesdropping?" I asked resentfully. "He's not dying. He just needs time to recover from an accident."

Trevor advanced towards me and touched my cheek. I stepped back. Again he advanced. I swatted at his hand, finding his persistence and his touch repulsive.

"A vegetable for life, I heard." He stood too close, his face bending over mine, crowding my personal space. I could see the flecks of colour in his blue eyes and I could see his blond eyelashes. "Sounds like he's too much trouble to stick with. Get over him. Try your chances with me instead."

"Whaat?" I stepped away again. "You can't be interested in me that way."

"Yes I am. Very interested." He looked at me up and down. "I'd love to do interesting things with you."

Oh no. I didn't think I had done anything to give him hope or inspire unholy thoughts. He was a proficient tutor, attentive and helpful, brilliant and extremely handsome. But Trevor had an inflated ego. I had listened to him talking and at times found him in love with himself—instead of with me.

"Cut it out Trevor," I grumbled, unamused and devoid of amorous interest. "I'm very much into an intimate one-on-one, deep, meaningful relationship. I'm very selfish that way. I won't waste time with casual—"

"You don't get it, baby. When you're mine, I'll have no need for others. Just you. Well, Monica says she wants to be invited, but if you're into one-on-one..." he shrugged, "then we won't include her."

"What's that supposed to mean?" I knitted my brows.

"Monica doesn't like men. She was only with me a few times to show me what she could do, gunning for an invitation to play when I'd have you. Actually, she's only been anticipating having sex with you."

"Eww!"

"You aren't racist, are you? East Asians have the smoothest skin—their grownups are naturally hairless like Western babies."

"It's not that!" I was shaking my head in horror and disbelief. We were totally on different planets here. "But I had no notion her kindness was motivated by—well, an ulterior motive."

"She *is* kind. This is uni life, but. You're not that naïve, are you? But perhaps you are. That's what I like best about you, Sydney. Adoringly innocent. But surely you can understand a guy's needs?"

"Trevor... We're really different! For me, my love has to be what I am to him. I expect the same kind of unwavering, undying loyalty that I give him. Meaning, it'd be demeaning if my guy had a backup. As you *do*. Trust me, you'll be happier to stick with your own kind."

"Now you're being self righteous again. Do you know how offensive that is? We're intellectually equal."

"I don't intend to offend you. But I *can't* connect with you. My Pete is more than my intellectual equal. He's capable of a mental relationship as well as a physical and emotional one. He's thoughtful. Considerate. He treats our friendship as an art. He invests time, attention, and creative effort into it. I'm very much in love with him and we're indispensable to each other. We're perfect soul mates."

"But he's now incapable of all that!" he spat. "He has become a witless vegetable! It would've been better for him if he'd just died."

And somehow my hand flew to his cheek.

"Ow f(*bleep*)!" he yelled, "B(*bleep*)!"

"How dare you say Pete would be better off dead! Or to even think it." I was aghast that somebody wanted Pete dead, and horrified that for the first time I had just hit somebody.

"Sheesh! You prefer a vegetable when you can do better?" he snarled in derision. "You going to chase a dying man? Give me a break!"

Gosh. How I wanted to howl.

"Get out!" I said, cross and shaken. "Don't you dare speak to me again."

He looked contemptuously at me, one hand cradling his cheek. I looked back in defiance.

"One last chance," he offered with stiff jaw. I blinked. Still trying for me? After swearing at me? How thick!

"I don't need another boyfriend." A shallow and conceited one at that. What I needed was to convince my parents to let me go to the US—and fund it.

"You'll be sorry," he warned, unrepentant. "You'll have to fend off the boys on your own from now on! They've let you be because of me, d'you know that? Now they'll all descend on you like vultures, asking to touch you and crawl all over you."

"Only if I let them," I retorted, chin up… while inwardly I cringed.

"They'll get angry when you reject them 'cause boys have their pride too! They'll refuse to stay your friends 'cause there are so many obliging chicks out there at uni."

"They're welcome to their own fun." Then I would know who my real friends were.

"And I'm very good at what I do and I'll be famous. When I make my millions, babes will jump me from everywhere. And with that kind of money, who needs to be tied to one woman anyway? I'll have as many chicks as I want."

"Tell that to your mother, will you." I looked to the backyard and called Li'l Shiht. "Trevor... you may want to be chosen for what you are as a person instead of your millions. But I wish you the best in your career."

"Well, good riddance!"

I opened the door and let a very offended Trevor pass.

I was at the McMahons Point penthouse late the next day in a state of fear and hope, my pride and arrogance fully discarded.

"First of all, assuming the worst," I offered calmly, so terrified of floundering. "In case he never recovered. You ask how I'd get him to marry me, get our Immigration's approval, and support him. You ask about missing fun and sex and kids and cheating on him. Well, the answer to all that is zilch. You're bluffing. If he couldn't even recognise me, of course there'd be none of that. Easy. But I don't want the worst to happen.

"Please give me one year. I'll face whatever happens then when we cross that bridge. But I need to go to him now. I don't want to live my life with regrets. I don't want—somewhere in the future—to look back wishing I had done things differently. I don't want should've-could've-didn't.

"Pete has given me the happiness and emotional fulfilment I've been constantly seeking. And he's given me a purpose in life with our plan to someday dedicate our life to helping others. When I was a hideous anorexic—I scared even myself—Pete cared for me. He's told me that he loves me no matter what. He told me that I'll always be number one to him. He told me that he will love me until he dies. So why can't I do the same for him? Why should I abandon him just because he's insensible and doesn't know what I'm doing? Pete doesn't deserve that. He's a very fine man and he's very important to me. I wouldn't be able to live with myself or forgive myself should I walk away now. I'd hate myself.

"But I'm also reasonable, realistic and practical. I set goals for myself that are modest enough for me to actually achieve. So I ask you to give Pete this one year—instead of forever as I wish it to be—because I want to be responsible for my debt. I'll pay you back every single dollar I borrow with my future earnings. I'm very conscientious in fulfilling my obligations. I promise to complete my studies and get a respectable career. Only then, if still needed, will I become Pete's carer again.

"*Please*. Help me."

My pleas worked and so I organised my trip to the US as soon as possible.

The flight to New York felt endless.

A single mother with a hyperactive three-year old sat next to me. The boy refused to wear the seatbelt when the plane took off. He knew how to unbuckle himself and escaped, passing in front of my knees, laughing merrily down the aisle.

"He's too quick," the mother fretted. "I can't control him."

"Don't worry," consoled the single man sitting on her other side. "Close your eyes, and pretend that he's not your son."

The mother proceeded to do just that and embarked on a mile-high fling. She found this single man—at least, single above the clouds—irresistibly charming. And for most of the flight they engaged in lots of slobbery kissing and touching. Eww!

Kate's ex, Brent, an extremely good looking black man who was now an instructor at an American dance academy, joined me on the flight from New York to Boston because my parents had asked him to make sure I was safe.

"It's only a three-hour drive to Boston," he explained when we waited for the call to our flight. "But you must be exhausted after your long trip."

I told him about his daughter Frances who was only twelve but already a better cook than me, just like her mum; and a better dancer than me, just like her dad. Brent's very dark eyes shone with love and pride.

"She holidays here every second summer," he said with longing. "But it's never enough."

He suggested that I learn massage for a bed-ridden patient as it would benefit Pete. Right away I liked him. He was extraordinarily charismatic, and the kind of person I could relate to from the first meeting. We chatted left and right that the time flew so fast. I wondered how he and Kate drifted apart. Work commitment? He must have had to follow his employer touring the world, while she had to chase other singers as a music journalist. And sure enough, eventually he asked,

"How's Kate?"

With those few words he put a whole world of love, pain, and regrets in his voice and in his eyes.

"Kate?" I repeated.

He shrugged and smiled in embarrassment.

"Girl," he said. "People have a crush all the time. When years and years have passed, you gotta know which of those was your true love, 'cause remembering, sometimes you wish you'd never been born."

"Ouch."

"She's very special," he said defensively, his forlorn smile heartbreaking. My heart went out to him. There and then I promised myself that I would never look back someday, haunted by the loss of precious someone.

"She's terrific," I touched his arm. "She's great. She's lovely. I love Kate very much."

In Boston he took me to a studio at a suburb called Beacon Hill. It was an old part of downtown Boston similar to Sydney's The Rocks, with narrow colonial streets, brick *sidewalks*, and old buildings that shouted history. The apartment Brent had found for me was in a beautiful building, sparkling clean, tastefully furnished, with a modern kitchenette. It looked so stylish that I was sure it was going to be very expensive. If I had had any previous knowledge of Boston, I would have chosen a cheaper place to live.

"Ettoré specified the location to be near the hospital," Brent explained. "When I found this, he said, take it."

I phoned Ettoré in frantic protest, "How am I ever going to pay this back? It's an expensive studio!"

"Your Mum will roast me if you get mugged. So put up with it. It's only a studio anyway. Not a posh penthouse."

"Not posh? It's far from dilapidated! How am I going to pay for it?"

"So aim high. Grow up to be successful. We've found you this place so you can easily commute to the hospital. Knowing your penchant for walking, we selected a place with a humongous park nearby. It's also close to shops and hip restaurants. Stay safe for your Mum, or she'll have my neck."

"Ettoré, I'm not paying for more than the medium price of a Boston studio. I'll find out how much that is. And that's the amount I'll pay you back."

"Smart girl. Deal. Keep well. And keep us informed."

Next Brent took me to MGH.
To the shell of my beloved.

I Miss the Rosellas outside My Window

To Pete in his Secret Land

Hello Gorgeous. In whatever world you may be, you'd better come back. For a couple of months now we've been together in your hometown. Every day I hold your beloved face in my hands and looking into your clear eyes I tell you a million things. They say you aren't in there Pete. But I feel you. Though you don't respond physically, your presence is as strong as ever.

So why on earth did you come back only once?

You greeted me the first time we were reunited.

"Pete," I had called. You were sitting up with your right arm and leg secured to the bed to prevent you from making sudden movements, but you swivelled your head to face me and something flickered in your eyes. Everybody else gasped aloud. I rushed towards you. "Darling."

But just like that your eyes became blank. The flare of recognition was gone.

I called and called you, panicking. You didn't respond. You didn't know what was going on.

"That was very good already." Someone wearing a 'Nurse

213

Wilmot' name-tag tapped my arm gently, "He's never done that before."

"Brief. But it was something," commented a Dr Rushworth, the neurosurgeon who'd expressed pessimism about your recovery. "He's never shown the slightest response to anyone before. Can you visit again?"

"I'll stay all day," I agreed. "Every day."

I was overjoyed at seeing you again. Anguished at seeing you so. With fear and uncertainty I hugged you. How your warmth and familiar scent soothed my frayed nerves at once. I loved feeling you reassuringly solid. Your steady heartbeat soothed me to calmness. It felt like relief... Like the serenity that came when watering my backyard garden after a very hectic day. I savoured the wonderful peace of holding you again in my arms gratefully. I so didn't regret coming all the way here to be with you.

Gradually I became aware of an unsmiling, well-dressed woman sitting on the other side of the bed. She was slender and beautiful, had your colouring, a narrow face, and high cheekbones. Immediately I recognised her as your Mom from the pictures.

"Hi," I nodded to her, my chin on your shoulder. "I'm Sydney."

She didn't respond at all. Her cold, cold eyes shot me with potent dislike before turning away.

Aw Pete, how it hurt!

Dearest, even though you've been out of the coma since mid-April, you're still living-in-a-secret-land. You've regained consciousness, but not awareness. Your eyes are open but you don't know me. You don't respond to stimulation. Because you don't seem to know what's been happening, I'm typing things for you here on my lap-top—a last-minute gift from Ettoré.

The morning after my arrival, a Sister Fleming greeted me kindly. She was motherly, had golden hair and golden eyes, and I was to find out later that she also had a golden heart.

"Came all the way from Australia, did you?" she shook her

head in wonder. "He's had his wash. All yours now, sweetie. We haven't shaved him. Wanna do that?"

"Um—how do you shave a man?"

"Not rocket science. Just be creative. He can't protest any which way, even if you nick him."

"Oh."

"There'll be breakfast. He was put on high-protein drip until recently. Now he's able to take food, as long as he can just swallow without chewing. And for yourself, do you know here you can pre-order all your meals to be taken with the patient?"

And Pete, when I kissed you good morning... instead of becoming electrified you gave me an unaffected expression, devoid of amorous interest or any previous attraction. A blank stare! Imagine how demeaning that would be if this was your normal self.

I pray to God, whoever God is, to return you me. Perhaps there's no God to heed me. But praying is free, right? I have nothing to lose.

That day the scab on your temple had healed. The one on your jaw had even peeled away, revealing pinkish new skin. There was a raw scar at the back of your right ear where they had made an opening and stitched you up again. They told me that in a closed head injury, the inside volume of the skull was constant while the brain swelled, so they had to make incision to lessen the pressure. Shaved your head around it too.

"So Pete, how do we do this?" I squirted some foam from a disposable shaving kit on your brittle cheek. "Well, if you won't talk, you'll have to put up with whatever I do. Never done this in my life. Promise not to cut you though. Stay still."

Working your jaw a section at a time, I shaved around your scabs with care. Your blank eyes didn't flicker.

"Lovely," your chiselled jaw was now smooth. "I'll be an expert in no time."

Breakfast was hard. Had to spoon-feed you. After only half of the cereal you clenched your mouth shut like a child's.

"Alright. What now Pete? Juice?" Once again I had to spoon-feed you. Once again you clenched your lips tight.

"*Coffee?*" *I waved my coffee cup under your nose. No reaction. I opened the lid. No reaction.* "*Stop being particular, Pete. You want your favourite Sumatran coffee? Chippendale is far away in Sydney. As far away as Sumatra itself. Where on earth do you get one in Boston anyway? Any idea?*"

And then I smelled it.

"*Nurse!*" *I rang the bell and jumped far, far away in fear. Gosh, I had seen the catheter's cable snaking from under the sheets going down to a catchment—but I hadn't anticipated any other bodily function!*

A Sister Allen came and shook her head. I was to discover later that there were two Sister Allens. This one was a very big, tall woman, with an angular no-nonsense face.

"*What kind of a girlfriend are you?*" *She placed her hands on her ample hips.* "*Didn't you ask to look after him?*"

"*Um—everything else but this!*" *I said, horrified.*

"*Wanna learn?*"

"*No! Please. No.*"

Her chuckle was full of mirth, "*Okay, okay, I get it. You're his girlfriend, except in technicality. 'S that it? Good for you. Many girls these days would've given in easily to such a gorgeous hunk. I'll take over here. Five minutes to change his diaper. Scares you, does it?*"

I ran from the room very, very fast.

A sobering thought came to me, Pete. What if you continued to be disabled forever? At home I wouldn't be able to summon any nurse.

So I started my vigil.

First of all I enrolled myself in several patient massage courses near the hospital. One after another. First was the massage to stimulate the muscles and blood circulation of a bedridden patient. Next, foot reflexology. Then general head and body massage to relax and calm you down. All of these massages supposedly have other benefits too such as general wellbeing and prevention of headaches and bed sores, and to stimulate appetite.

Jonathan, the staff member at the course, was very sympathetic when I described your condition.

"Let me ring MGH for the specifics," he suggested. "We'll tailor a patient-customised program for you."

So my love, for a few hours daily I've been attending therapeutic massage lessons. They teach me different massage strokes. To extend muscles, to knead, to release deep-muscle knots, to minimise tension, to stimulate and excite. The slow steady strokes increase your flow of blood which helps to effectively remove toxins. Vigorous and pressure techniques are used to soothe, reduce swelling and pain level, and clear your lungs to improve respiration. At no time at all should I touch your injured bones or put pressure on your badly jarred right shoulder.

Back at the hospital they showed me how to prise your jaw open so I could brush your teeth. To prevent bed sores, they taught me how to carefully roll you to a different side every few hours when you sleep or to sit you up when awake. And to prevent bed sores, a few times a day your shoulders, hips, knees and heels also need washing, wiping and lotion.

They taught me how to crank your bed with you correctly positioned. Aw Pete, heaving you isn't easy. Your lithe build is deceptive! You are heavy because of your muscles. Have to heed your jarred shoulder and broken limbs, too. Your right arm, your violin arm... oh love!

Your Mom comes after teaching, her nose up in the air. I greet her, and as always she walks to the other side of the bed, imperiously ordering the catering staff to pass your food tray to her. She claims the honour of feeding you dinner. Darling, other people may think us weird, competing for the privilege of who gets to look after a —, a —, well... an injured beloved, but I'll shoot anyone who dares look down on you!

Your Mom fusses over you and completely refuses to acknowledge my presence.

I visited Mario at your shared apartment near MIT in the first week, taking the red line of Boston's very cheap subway from Charles/MGH. The old building was a far cry from mine at Beacon Hill. As I waited at your third-floor door, a grumpy-looking black guy wearing a green sweat appeared down the corridor and eyed me with menace. I gave him a polite nod. At that, his features softened. He nodded back with a slight smile before disappearing down the stairwell. There. If you were polite, people should be nice to you... I hoped.

The lock rattled and the door in front of me opened an inch. "Sydney???" I heard an exclamation. The person opened the door wide—revealing a Latino dude with wavy, longish hair. "Sydney!"

"Er... yes..."

"Pete," a pleasing smile adorned his face. "He had your pictures. Come in, come in. I'm Mario." He had an olive complexion and was easy on the eye. "Have a seat. What brought you here? Have you seen Pete? How's he doing? What can I do for you Sydney?"

Slowly I sat down. "Tell me. Tell me everything you remember of that last day."

My thoughts whirling from my conversation with Mario, I took the subway back across the river. Pete, he said you hadn't been wearing a helmet because the clasp was broken. He said that was suspicious and he couldn't stop thinking about it, but had no idea about what really happened. At the hospital I asked your Mom if she knew more. No response. When your sister turned up, she nodded to me once before dismissing me for the entire visit.

I sent Lance a text, "What's the progress on Pete's accident investigation?"

He answered, "What investigation? It was an accident. No witness came forward. No investigation."

THAT'S IT? My frustrated mind screamed at the injustice. But I knew nothing...

Your brother turned up the next afternoon and greeted me cheerfully. "I'm having final high-school exams so I can't come *to the hospital every day."*

Then he looked at you and his throat moved. His eyes glazed. "Thank you for caring for him, Sydney..."

Pete, I've taken pictures of you to record the changes in your appearance. Your facial scars have gone, your hair is longer that it covers the ugly scar behind your ear, and you're losing weight. I know how much weight you've lost from massaging you. As I progress with my massage lessons, they allow me to give you massages. I put on your soothing violin music and give you a full massage in the afternoon before your nap. At night I do your feet, shoulders and head to help you sleep well. Massaging makes me sleepy too, you know. Returning to my apartment, I fall asleep quickly.

I bring my laptop to the hospital. But I can't concentrate on studying. Not inspired to start any animation project either. Mostly all I want is to talk to you quietly. Oh Pete, perhaps the feminists of the world will frown at a girl who can only focus on her guy. Or perhaps they'll understand my agony.

Late afternoons bring your family from across the river.

They regard me with unfavourable reservation and they don't bother to pretend to like me. Your Mom reeks with contempt and disapproval. She still sees me as a home-wrecker and Australians as uncultured and uncouth. Your Dad comes late from MIT, greeting me kindly before being steered away in conversation.

Imagine me in the same room with these haughty people and being ignored? I'm a quiet girl, darling, but I don't think you can call me haughty. I'm reserved, not arrogant. I might shyly withdraw, but I don't snub anyone. Your family chat among themselves on topics I know nothing about.

Hopefully no-one else will ever be subjected to a similar situation, nightly or otherwise.

Disheartened by a few days of unsuccessful attempts at small talk, I've become silent. Really Pete, the Aussie in me baulks at breathing the same air as someone else without being friendly.

Sometimes I toy with the idea of doing or saying outrageous things just to drive your Mom up the wall a bit. Like giving you a very sexy kiss in front of her, say. But I consider the consequences. Since she's your mother, it's highly probable we'll come into contact now and then in the years to come. I'm already in her black book.

After weeks of torture, I emailed Nina, hoping for some ground-breaking revelation.

"Where is God?"

She wrote, "He's closer to you than your internal jugular vein."

I wrote, "I don't know whether God really exists. I've prayed and I've prayed, just in case. All I want is Pete's return. Why isn't there any result?"

"Patience."

"How long?"

"It varies. Joseph was wrongly imprisoned for nine years. Jonah was in the whale only for three days. Pete will get better when the time is right."

"Nine years?!?" *Talk about a revelation.* "What am I going to do with my life? What if he never gets better? How do you know? What if God doesn't answer my prayers or grant me my request?"

"God loves you and He will grant your request when what you ask is good for you. He knows things better. It's like this: When a baby cries for milk, his mum will hurry to give it to him. Because it's good for him. But when this baby wants a piece of beautiful, fascinating red coal from the fireplace to play with, his mum—who has superior knowledge—refuses to give it to him. The baby begs and cries until he throws up, still there's no way on earth the mum will ever grant him his wish. The baby—out of his limited knowledge—thinks his mum cruel, but we all know his mum loves him very much. Now Sydney, as far as Pete is concerned, we aren't asking for a dangerous hot coal here. Perhaps his body needs more healing first."

"Waiting is torture."

"Do not despair of God's grace. Persevere. Even when the last ray of hope departs, keep your trust in God. He will not abandon you.

Do you know the McLaughlin's song? When tomorrow comes, today will be gone."

Love, one soothing aspect about you is the fact that you're always serene. Your calm face radiates constant peace and tranquillity. Perhaps you've become used to the pain. It relieves my concern that I've never heard you scream or cry or whine. At the most you'd only wince, and only rarely. When you become tired you just slip away to sleep.

Every morning I speak to you as if you understand. I tell you about my new acquisitions, from the thrift store that Barbie-doll-like Nurse Clifton told me about.

I bought the coolest lightweight bicycle—at only $20. You wouldn't believe it Pete, it actually looks brand new! I have so much fun riding it. It feels like—freedom! I love the cycleway here, only in some parts we still have to compete with other road users.

I also bought a horror paperback at only a quarter from that shop. Could you imagine buying a book so cheaply? And I read it last night, feeling scared all by myself, as if the fiend was waiting for me behind the bathroom door...

And I saw a rough collie this morning! Poking his head out from the back window of a car, lolling his tongue at me. Same colours as Bronson. I've left the handsome baggage with Angus and Lauren. Missing him, I tailed the car for quite a distance.

Do you know how much I miss home, Pete? I miss my backyard and the pretty rosellas and lorikeets outside my window. And the surfs and the walks. I miss them badly. But more... I miss the twinkle in your eyes.

Where are you, dearest? Are you alright? How are you feeling?

With you but without you, the days and weeks creep slowly away.

I live frugally, afraid to use Mum's credit card apart from necessities. Hey Pete, don't you think everything in Sydney is actually more expensive? Or overpriced?

As long as I don't compare it to your scrumptious cooking, the hospital food is okayish. (I know, I know, you don't like your yucky no-chewing, swallow-only food). Outside, the food outlets are just as atrocious as I remember them from my previous visit to the US. They're cheap but hopeless. Unless you cook, healthy food is only available at expensive restaurants. And Pete, why is it compulsory to pay tips here? Back home we only tip when we want to.

Also here there are an amazing number of TV commercials advertising medicines for constipation and other digestive ailments. Doesn't anyone here eat fresh fruit and vegies?

MGH itself is great—NSW hospitals could learn a few things or two.

Many staff and students are curious about me and Australia— asking me direct questions. Not nosily or rudely, but in a very open and friendly way, showing interest and sympathy. So Pete, where are the bozos? I won't believe in any stereotyping now.

"How's the prince today?" Rowe, a Harvard resident with pretty grey eyes who loves to chat with me, asks every morning. Rowe studied medicine after her failed CPR attempt to revive her dying little brother.

"Looks fine, thank you. But you better make sure."

"Isn't he gorgeous," she always says. "I fall in love with him more and more each day. Imagine if he could talk!"

This morning my love, after all her teasing talk while checking on you, she looked into my eyes for a very long time.

"Imagine if he could talk... I think I understand... I think I can see just how it was between you two." And she patted my arm as tears brimmed up my eyes.

Come back Pete. Oh come back my love...

Sister Fleming had golden hair and golden eyes, and I was to find out later that she also had a golden heart.

"How's the prince today?" Rowe, a Harvard resident with pretty grey eyes, asks every morning

You Can't Generalise Aussie Girls Are All Easy

Nobody would honour me except the honourable, I told myself. During the time when my love needed me, I was there for him.

Yet being in the same room with Pete's condescending family was heartbreaking. One evening I could not bear it and silently left. I walked on the hospital streets, around massive hospital buildings, hugging my pain to myself.

God how I love Pete!

I walked and walked. Spending most of my time in Pete's sick room, I did not get to know Boston much. The *feel* of Boston was oddly different from the feel of Sydney. Vegetation— different trees. People—different racial composition. Same layout, though. It sprawled from the water's edge on the east to the lands beyond. They had this Charles River with several bridges just as we had the Parramatta River. Sometimes I sat by the water's edge, endlessly drawing. I took pictures of lots of things too. I always had my camera with me.

Their parks were much like ours, except we had more. Their historic parts had elegant colonial-style buildings much like early Sydney, except they had more. The modern parts of the city were like ours, complete with ugly peak-hour traffic just like ours.

They whinged about politicians and local issues just as we did.

Their public transport was much better though. Their subways, trains, and endless buses were very reliable, frequent and way cheaper. Except ours were cleaner.

A car stopped nearby. Pete's tall sister came out, still wearing her smart business suit from work. Her big, luxurious brown hair shone in the street light. And how the shape of her eyes resembled Pete's! Except the expression. Pete had never ever looked at me with disdain.

"Go back home," she ordered without preamble. "You're wastin' your time."

I stood where I was on the *footpath*, shaking my head in silence.

"Pete doesn't need you. It isn't even Pete. That body there is only a shell!"

It hurt like hell when people gave up on my beloved. (*"Don't tell me it's not worth fighting for..."*) What if *you* were the one who became disabled? How would you like it if your love turned their back on you? How would you feel? Think it will never happen to you? You have a guarantee? My love had been a perfectly strong man before all this.

"Pete will return."

"The doctors say he's *not* gonna come back. *They* should know. They've dealt with hundreds of cases. They're very familiar with the outcome." She spoke in exasperation. "What're you gonna do with your life? You're young. Get over it. Get over him. Go home where you've come from. Don't waste your life."

Get over him? Instead of going downhill, my affection for Pete had grown heaps stronger. In fact, earlier I had not even known that a love this profound could exist. That anyone *could* love so deeply. Or that I had it in me. But now I knew.

Love was not only a feeling. It was also an intense drive to act! When I cared for someone a great deal, I could not just claim that I felt so while I did nothing. There was no way I could just stand watching, let alone watch from far, far away.

"Pete was always there for me when I needed him. I'm not about to abandon him now."

"You don't get it," she declared snidely. "He doesn't need you. What has your visit done for him? See any improvement?"

I looked down at my shoes. My shoe laces were fascinating indeed.

"Your stay is pointless! For over two months you've wasted your time and money. Isn't that enough? He doesn't know what's going on. And it's not about to improve! Sooner or later." She desperately tried to drum her point home. "It's true his wounds will heal. But that's all. You aren't gonna spend your days minding someone who doesn't even recognize you, are you?"

"But he does! He looked at me once. He'll do it again."

"Do you know how pathetic that sounds?" she asked pityingly. "No? Go back home. Get over it! You're too young to cope with all this mess. Frankly, you look so wrung-out and miserable. Because you *are*. Go do somethin' for yourself for once."

But the thought of going home was absolutely horrendous. To some day look back, haunted. Remembering Pete as my doomed love. No! *Nooo!*

Pete was my life. Without him I would never be whole.

Eve stomped back to her car shaking her head. At the last moment she whirled around and opened the door,

"Get in. I'll give you a lift home."

"No, thank you. I mean to return to the hospital. Pete needs a massage before his sleep."

"He's not gonna die missing one massage. You look awful. Go home and rest. I'll take you. Do you know Boston isn't safe to walk alone at night? No? The way you walk, you aren't tuned in to what's going on. You were oblivious of those kids up there catcalling you. Did you even hear them?"

I blinked.

"Do you even follow the local news?" she insisted. "Get in."

I had taken a bus instead of riding my bike in the rain this morning. I thought of how Pete used to worry about my safety even when he agreed that Sydney was a very safe city. Apparently I was not supposed to feel safe here. Reluctantly, I complied.

"How long have you known Pete?" she asked, turning to face

me. Her husband was driving. On the *wrong* side of the road, like everyone else.

"Since November."

"'S that all? And did you fall into bed straight away?"

"No!"

"Since when have you been together?"

"The new year."

"And you'll throw your life away for someone you hardly know?"

"I know Pete very well. We know each other *deeply*."

She shook her head in disbelief.

"Did you know that he loved his wife? Did you know that he was mad about her? He chased her for three years! He loved her *deeply*," she mocked me. "Did you know that if *you* had stayed away, chances were they'd get back together? A marriage is sacred, you know. I don't have a problem with you but you upset Mom so much, and I don't like seeing her upset.

"And did you know that Pete had gone out with his wife for three years before they married? And you—you've gone out with him only for a little more than a month and you want to devote your whole life to him? A sick, nonsensical him, at that.

"Get real.

"You're young so you think your love is the world. It'll fade, you know. Especially with the added burden of his medical condition. He *will* be a vegetable for life. Can't you get that?"

"Please... I've heard all that before. But I wouldn't be able to live with myself should I leave him. I'll stay."

I hated being 18. I hated it that people associated being young with being dumb. Why was I blamed for staunchly looking after the man I loved? Would we have to be married first before people believed that he was important to me? Yeah, I suspected married couples got more respect.

"How do you finance this?" Eve looked up when the car pulled to a stop near my building. "You have this kind of money?"

I sealed my lips tight.

Eve plopped down by my side one evening and taunted, "Pete worshipped his wife, you know."

I had sauntered to the visitor lounge after my dinner companions, Nurse Bingham and Sister McNeil, returned to duty. Now, Eve liked to antagonise me for no reason and I was so determined not to let her have the upper hand.

"Don't you sound like a broken record," I dismissed her jibe. Sipping my drink, I leaned back comfortably.

"He was so in love with her. He used to buy her exotic flowers... expensive perfumes... sexy lingerie... " She persisted in trying to rub salt into the wound. "He showered her with gifts *all* the time."

"This was all in the forgotten past." The new Pete gave me *heartfelt* and *thoughtful* gifts. I would not trade my jade ring for anything, and not because it was his only non budget-conscious present. *Safety, kindness, eternity...* It was true the jade itself did not have the power to keep me safe, but that he cared was a sentiment I appreciated. "Pete says he's never experienced a connection as deep as ours with anyone before."

She laughed out loud.

"How naïve you are! Guys would say anything to get into your panties."

"No. You're so wrong. Pete's never tried to—, to—, well, we haven't—you know. He says he'll wait for me to grow up and be ready to jump to the abyss. He wants me to marry him one day."

"Really? You haven't slept together?"

"That's right. He doesn't want me to make an important decision until I'm truly comfortable with it."

"And you an Australian?"

"*So?*" I bristled. "What's being an Australian got to do with this?"

"But your schools give you condoms in your first week in high school. They openly teach tweens on how not to get knocked up. Girls over there are quietly immunized against herpes and other contagious sexual diseases, at school, at 12-years old. I know all of this for a fact, you know."

"They're just our government's methods to minimise the risks;

to lower the health costs for those who choose to be sexually active. 'Cause in Australia the government has the obligation to provide free health care."

"But it drives very young kids to experience sex early! That means you Aussie girls are worldly!"

"Not worldly. You can have knowledge about things that you aren't involved in." Man, was she successful in drawing me into a skirmish after all? "But not all kids—or grownups—want to be, well, worldly. Unlike in some other countries, Aussie mums have yet to consider birth-control pills as necessary breakfast items for their tweens. Just like here. People there are the same as the people here."

I was heaps annoyed. I didn't like anyone bashing my dear countrymen and women. But I came from a land where, according to the prevailing opinion among our young generation, religion was a repulsive word. My friends gave pressies at Christmas, but hardly any were churchie and many were atheists. While many adult atheists were thinkers of impeccable morals, my young friends only wanted freedom. To most of them abstinence was for the uncool and narrow-minded.

So how was I to defend the rampant underage sex at home now? They were facts, for God's sake.

It rankled. I was not overjoyed. Friends with liberated lifestyles at home always demanded acceptance of their unbridled, liberated ways while they themselves were so judgemental. Refusing to be open minded about those who weren't like them, they branded me backward for living my life the way I felt comfortable with. I remembered the snickering. Sydney, the weird, outdated girl who did not drink or smoke or sleep with boys. Or with girls for that matter.

At home I had shrugged it off as a trifling annoyance. Nobody would think badly of me except the low people, right? Why would I lose sleep over this. Whatever floated your boat. No worries.

But here—here was Eve bagging *my* people. Thoroughly irked, I hit back, "You can't generalise that Aussie girls are all easy. Look around. You have more underage pregnancies here because kids aren't taught to be careful."

"Ouch. I asked for it, didn't I?" she conceded. But she wasn't done goading me. Her active mind promptly thought up another taunt, "Now, what if Pete will never recognize you again? Who'll be there for you?"

"My dog?"

"You're a smart ass."

"How else do you expect me to answer that?"

"Obstinate!" But she was smiling broadly. "Sydney, I think I like you. I mean it. But I can't get it. What's so special about a sick man who can't even respond to you? Considering your short time with Pete, how come you have this stubborn devotion? You haven't even known that level of intimacy. Was he really that wonderful?"

"He *is*. Please don't refer to him in the past tense. It annoys me big time. And don't refer to his ex as his wife—he doesn't like it. His ex is an ex for a reason, he said. Why do you and your Mom keep placing her on a pedestal?"

"Because it was Pete who left her to travel the world! Mom had wanted him to stay home with his wife."

"Stay home? What was he supposed to do? Join her in a threesome or group sex?"

"Whaat?"

"Yes! You really don't know, Pete. I'm afraid that wasn't his style. He's very decent and romantic. And very philosophical about these things."

She slumped on the sofa, her very beautiful green eyes round, jaw hanging.

"Didn't your husband look after Pete's divorce?" I asked.

"His law firm did. Callum is family, and couldn't get involved. And it was all confidential."

"There you go. Alright, Eve. She was making out with another guy in front of Pete. Do you blame him for leaving?"

"What?! God..." her hands flew to frame her face. "How sad. Poor Pete. He was so young then. Oh God... I didn't know..."

"He threw his wedding ring into a beggar's bowl *two years* before we met! So I had nothing to do with his marriage break-up, alright? That was a totally separate phase of his life. And it's useless trying to make me feel guilty for accepting a divorcing man, because I don't! Pete is lovely. I could rave all night about his morals."

It took her some time to come to terms with this revelation.

"So you must be a virgin then," she concluded after a while. "How old fashioned. Tell me, now that Pete is in his current shape, do you regret not falling into bed while you could?"

"I wouldn't trade a single moment of what we had to do it differently. I'll never forget the indescribable euphoria of those fantastic six weeks of my life. I could tell, he valued me as a person."

"Oh?" she pondered this. "I don't think you know what you're missing, really. So, how did you two become involved?"

And I told her about our very precious friendship. About Pete's intuitiveness. I told Eve about the sports we played and the places we visited, while all the time my mind was wandering down the avenue of many, many affectionate moments. I remembered vividly Pete's warm hugs when he arrived at my door. The twinkle in his eyes. Him feeding me breakfast. Us holding hands everywhere we went. Cuddling up watching TV. His exquisite kisses. His wonderful voice sending me to sleep. His vibrant morning calls. The intimacy and exuberance of his enchanting romantic-violin concerto.

Eve snatched a serviette, quietly drying my cheeks that somehow had become wet.

From that evening Eve's mean stance towards me changed. She chatted about Pete the child and brought me photographs of a young Pete growing up. She was still of the opinion that he would remain a shell for good, but she kind of approved that I looked after him.

"Even when it's beyond me why you'd want to," she chirped. "Perhaps everyone should be wonderful, so they aren't dumped when problems arise. By the way, Lance has finished his exams and he's not allowed to travel far while Pete's sick. Go out with him and his friends."

You Don't Have To Be Strong All The Time

"Hi Sydney." Rowe came in with old Dr Rushworth when I was massaging Pete one afternoon. "I heard you've completed your patient-massage course. Congratulations for being a certified masseuse!"

"Thank you. I've memorised the complete maps of nerve ends and muscles. The better to help Pete." I nodded to Dr Rushworth.

"He's lost quite a bit of weight," the doctor commented.

"He'll return to normal when all his wounds heal," I ran a loving hand through Pete's now longish hair before moving back to allow them access to him.

The tall, silver-haired doctor faced me. "It may not be wise to be so optimistic," he said in a stiff, cold voice.

He took me on a one-flew-over-the-cuckoos'-nest tour to observe his other patients. All of them were in a very sorry state.

"I have dealt with too many accident victims. As you can see for yourself, there's no guarantee my patients can ever overcome the trauma."

Politely I suppressed my objections.

I woke up the next day with renewed determination to help Pete recover. Caring for him was the only thing I had. It kind of

232

gave me strength, because I had some purpose. A reason to get out of bed every morning. Looking out my window to a beautiful late June day, I said my prayers, asking for Pete's complete and speedy recovery. Hopefully there really was a God listening somewhere.

As I brushed my hair absently I noticed so many grey strands that had made their appearance among my chestnut locks. I dismissed them. This was not the time to worry about myself. I had somebody to look after.

But I did not count that my resolve would be put to the test immediately.

When Pete needed help, with both the number one and two by the smell of them, I pressed the bell for a nurse. But no one came. I knew there have been several emergencies in other rooms. All the meds were extremely busy. I rang again. Still no answer. I looked at my beloved, feeling terrible. If I were sick and senseless, I would not want to be left stinky and messy.

I walked to and fro in the small green room, its usual clean scent now contaminated. My eyes caught the stack of clean nappies and new catheters. I stopped, fidgeted, threw Pete a look over my shoulder. He did not know what was going on. He did not what was happening to him. His clear eyes stayed emotionless. He was helpless. *My love!* I whirled around, my chest ripped apart.

With shaking hands I pulled down his sheet. I closed my eyes tightly to strengthen my resolve. Oh Lord. *Help...* I had been praying quite a bit lately, but never for this. This was totally out of my imagination. I opened my eyes. Lifted his hospital garment. And looked.

With a broken heart I set to work. Which girl ever had to *see* her beloved this way? Don't ask me. Oh don't ask me! No words could ever describe the anguish I was going through. Pete didn't have any awareness. He did not know I was cleaning him up. Angrily I swiped at my eyes with my forearm. Fresh tears kept rushing out. I reached for a nappy and a new condom catheter. A condom catheter is an external catheter. When the patient is a male it is easier to put on. It has a lower risk of infection compared to the type that you have to insert into the bladder via his urethra. I would not look at his face as I put it on.

"Oh Sydney..." Sister Fleming arrived at that moment, looking worried to find me in tears.

"I'm changing him," one sob escaped. "It's okay."

"Are you sure?" she asked in sympathy.

"This is just a simple procedure, right? No big deal. I've come to reason that if any nurse has to do it, it may as well be me," another sob. "While I'm here."

Pete was mine. Mine to love. Mine to look after.

She opened her arms and I stared at her, my chest and throat tight with emotion. Hesitating.

"'S okay darlin'. All these months you've stood firm and braved it all. Come, you don't have to be strong all the time."

And I collapsed in her motherly arms and cried a river.

My maiden, missish reservation vanished out the window. As I cut Pete's nails after lunch, I decided to care for my beloved in *every* possible way whenever necessary. Unless it was something beyond my strength or requiring medical expertise.

I buffed his nails with my manicure sponge to a perfect gloss. He actually would not fuss over his nails to this degree—I did this just to fill the time. We were listening in quiet to Mendelssohn's enchanting romantic-violin concerto which Pete himself had played with carefully placed striking moments. I hoped to trigger his conscious mind through his love of violin.

Then I heard firm footsteps behind me.

I first thought it was the catering staff coming to collect the plates, but the steps sounded too solid instead of the usual shuffling. I turned around. To my surprise a hulking blond man with glittering silver eyes was standing there.

"Dad?"

He opened his arms and I flew into them, tears rushing to my eyes. "Dad, oh Dad..."

"How's he today?" he asked in a hush tone after I controlled myself.

"He—he doesn't react to anything," I said dejectedly. "Look. His stare is very blank."

"No," Dad objected. "His eyes flickered with interest just now. When you were crying."

"Really?"

"Positive. Once. I saw it."

"Dad... do you know that was only the second time?"

We rushed to tell Dr Rushworth.

"It's possible he will improve," the doctor conceded, looking harried. "But we don't know when it will eventuate. Or how significantly. The comatose duration, as well as how much is recovered within the first month, are good indicators of long-term recovery. Pete was in a coma for three weeks, and that was rather long. And although he's regained consciousness after that, he hasn't shown any awareness of his surroundings. He first responded to stimulation at six weeks when Sydney arrived. And nothing more has happened until today."

"That's a great improvement," Dad beamed. One thing about Dad, he believed in positive thinking. Dad was sunshine. He forever radiated vitality and optimism.

When Pete fell asleep, Dad pulled me out to his rental car and took me sailing on a small rented daysailer.

"So what's happening with Geraldine, Dad?" I turned my face to the beautiful sunshine as we headed out to the estuary. Pretty colours were sprouting along the riverbank.

"She's just had a hefty pay rise. Did a brilliant well-log analysis and found a new oil closure off the Mahakam Delta. Everybody else was against her but she insisted it was oil—movable oil. Geraldine convinced the company to drill it, and, bingo! She was right. So she's bringing in a whole lot of money to the company. They, of course, tripled her beginner salary."

"Good on her. But what's happening between you, Dad?"

"Well, I'm here, aren't I?" Dad smiled with unconcern. "She's not keen on leaving her burgeoning career. I respect that."

"But what about love? Loyalty? Companionship?"

"'Fraid not her immediate priority. Don't worry, hon. The world is big."

© Ia Uaro

He took me sailing on a small rented daysailer

"So you aren't going back there?"

"Nope." And he smiled with genuine pleasure. "But I did manage to increase the locals' pay before the hubbub. They're really grateful. Gave me presents when I left."

"Dad... I'm so proud of you."

He stayed with me, admiring the sophisticated decor of my spacious studio as he folded out the sofa bed at night. I offered to sleep there because Dad was so tall his legs would hang out of the edge. He agreed to use my longer bed because it wasn't pink.

"Although it smells girlie," he complained as he carried Pete's photo from my bedside table to the TV stand next to me. "And you just want to claim the best seat to watch TV, don't you?"

"Hah! The TV watches *me* every night."

"What?! Are you saying you've been wasting all these wonderful, eleventy-nine American channels? How could you do such a grave injustice!" He started flicking the channels happily.

I confiscated the remote control and poked my tongue at him. "I need to be at the hospital early."

"Iyiyiyi! Heartless! Spoilsport!" He threw a pillow at me, hard! "And you'll drag me to jog in that big park near here first thing too, I suppose?"

We fought. He made me laugh. We chatted, reminiscing about our old adventures, until sleep claimed us.

One morning Dad convinced me to leave Pete's bedside all day, saying that Pete would have wanted me to do something I liked. He took me canoeing and horse riding over an hour's drive north, at the enchanting Harold Parker State Forest.

"I love this so much, Dad." We navigated the canoe around the peaceful lake. This park was a vast area of beautiful serenity rather like Hornsby's Crosslands but with different vegetation, and they had organised facilities for horse-riding, mountain-biking, skiing and such. "I feel guilty for enjoying myself. I must come back here again with Pete, someday."

"Yes," Dad agreed, brashly optimistic. "You will."

We reached Boston late after an ugly traffic. They still allowed us in at the hospital because I was allowed in at all hours. I needed to check on Pete for a few minutes, or I would suffer a major worry all night. "See? He's fine," Dad smiled. "No harm done."

Dad stayed the whole week, and, sunny Aussie bloke that he was, he managed to charm Pete's family. Afterwards he left for a North Sea exploration site off Scotland's Aberdeen. He was starting his own consultant company in exploration geophysics, assisting oil companies around the globe. For the rest of the year he was also booked to lecture in several world universities.

A few afternoons later Mum and Ettoré turned up too.

After all the hugs and kisses she took me to a hair salon and told the stylist, "Please dye her hair like this," she pointed to her own hair. "Exactly the same colour as this."

"Why?" I asked, dumbfounded.

"Look at you," Mum whirled me to face the mirror, pointing to the grey strands I had been ignoring. "You wouldn't want Pete to regain awareness and find an old hag," she coaxed. "Would you now?"

"*Well...*"

"And please cut it in layers around her face like this," Mum pointed a picture of a model on the wall to the stylist.

"No," I objected. "Pete doesn't want me to cut my hair."

"Keep the length," my bossy Mum ordered. "But cut the sides fashionably stylish."

Through the mirrors I watched Mum and Ettoré sitting behind me while the stylist worked on my hair. They spoke quietly, heads together conspiring, and I had the feeling that they were truly close.

I observed that when Mum was talking with Ettoré, she was not all mighty and bossy. She was not in her here-I-come-all-capable-and-I'll-solve-all-your-problems mode. She was— feminine, sort of. Sweet, even. I could see it in her expression and body language.

Maybe Ettoré was just who she needed, since during her marriage to Dad everybody relied on her to be the family's problem solver and law enforcer. She had not been given the chance to express her femininity. Looking back, I wondered whether Mum had resented being married to Dad for this reason. Dad was kind of a happy big boy who never grew up to become a mature man, forever playful and going on adventures, taking her for granted at home.

And savvy Ettoré was good for her. He was good to her.

They had taken rooms at a posh hotel next to MGH and I was to stay with them for the week. We had fancy dinner at a hip restaurant nearby, and they escorted me back to the hospital afterwards. Pete's family was still there on their evening visit and I made the introduction. To my surprise, Eve extended a dinner invitation to all of us.

When we dined at her apartment the next evening, her mom was not present but her dad and brother were there. Lance shared Pete's height and lithe built, but with ruddy complexion and brown hair. Their dad Clive was an older, brown-haired version of Pete. He usually came to look at Pete near the end of the visiting hours and greeted me on arrival, but then his wife would steer him away to chat about... exam papers!

"I want to thank Sydney for being so caring to Pete. And Sydney's family for being supportive," Eve told the table after civilised getting-acquainted conversation. "Now, where's it going from here?"

For a long time everybody was quiet. Then Ettoré—linking hands with Mum, I noticed—spoke, "We've given Sydney one year to defer uni. The evaluation will hinge on Pete's condition." He stopped and looked at me. "For now, for what it's worth, how can we help you, Sydney?"

I was speechless.

Mum was watching me with glazed eyes. At that moment her love for me hit me with full force. And tears welled up in my own eyes.

"How can we help you, Sydney?" Lance asked with an affable smile.

"How can we help you, Sydney?" everybody else took their cue.

Some of the weight that I had not even realised burdening me was immediately lifted from my shoulders. I could breathe easier. Their sympathy would not help bringing Pete back to me, but nonetheless I was overwhelmed by their sincerity.

So far I had discovered that I had an aptitude for mental work. I had enough courage to tackle long, difficult hardships and see things through. Yet no matter how you relied on your own competence and fortitude, kindness from others lifted your mood. Waiting was the hardest thing to do, especially without a guarantee of the outcome. As you fight to show the world a convincing bravado, the affection of others eased your inner sorrow.

"Go out more," Mum looked into my eyes that night. She shifted my newly dyed hair and let the long strands slide between her fingers. "Do shopping, and whatever other girls usually do. Don't worry about using the credit card".

But I was not inspired to shop.

She took me to a concert at NEC. There, immersed in magical music, I imagined Pete when he had been among the performers, but soon the memories of my birthday flooded in. My eyes closed. I could hear my love's recital. The thrilling strains of his violin. The exuberance. Searching. Intimate. *Sydney, I'll love until I die...* As pain pierced me like hell, I prayed an earnest plea for my love's recovery.

Mum placed her chin on my shoulder when she hugged me goodbye and confessed, "We let you come here to find closure between you and Pete, so you could move on with your life. We hoped you'd see Pete's condition firsthand, come to your senses, and give up on your own. But after Harry told me how miserable you were, we came here to reprimand you and bring you back home with us. Yet looking at your grey hair, there was no way I could do it. I don't have the heart to separate you from your love."

"I *love* him, Mum..." my voice trembled. "Thank you. I feel so much closer to you than ever. Thanks for everything."

"So you'll wear the Manolo Blahniks now?"

"No! No way!"

Summer wave replaced the cold spring of Boston. I jogged along the park's lakeside, wondering whether Bronson missed me. He was with his siblings at Lauren's and Angus'. I missed him. But teeming with life and vivacity, the world was cheerier. There were children escaping the heat by fountains. Tourists shopping. Locals playing. I noticed fascinating objects for photography.

My grandparents came down from Vancouver. They visited for a fortnight, during which Nanna tried her best to spoil me with Canadian dishes. And no, not just with pancakes and maple syrup.

I took many photos of her and her cooking. I did not know how she did it in my limited kitchenette, but she could make even the simplest food special. Yup. *Poutine* it was, Canadian fries and gravy, but with the world's best gravy and roast beef. One day she knocked on my neighbour's door with a plate of butter tarts ("I caught him looking our way, his nose must be curious."). I took some to the hospital and the nurses swore I was an angel. Another day we had a picnic of *tourtière* among the weeping willows in the nearby Public Garden. Nanna regaled me with stories of Mum growing up. I asked her about herself and Grandpa—the love story.

We Like Your Accent

Eve took me girlie shopping at Macy's and Filene's in Downtown Crossing, where she shopped and complained about my disinterest in shopping. She took me to watch comedy flicks at "Loew's Theatres across from Boston Common, which was walking distance from my studio. She had a membership to a gym and once a week she took me there too, complaining that her Jewish hubby jogged in the street because it saved him $600 a year. After the gym she regularly took me to restaurants in the North End.

"At least I have the good sense to exercise first," she said, savouring a fiery Spanish dish. Restaurants in the North End were amazing, no wonder they contributed to make Boston famous. Very expensive, but just wonderful to eat at. "I *love* eating."

"Pete says we should learn to cook the food we love. Wouldn't you economise when you cook instead of eating out? Callum would love you more."

She laughed. As she sipped her iced tea, she asked, "Hey, do you know what they call a male tea bag when you put it in hot water?"

I shook my head, puzzled.

"Hebrews!"

I laughed. Eve told me some more jokes about her mixed-faith marriage. I hoped they would be forever happy and promote interfaith tolerance. This world of ours sure needs it.

"You're very special, Sydney," she told me one night as we came out of AMC cinema at Harvard Square with her husband after watching a horror movie. This time, instead of watching a comedy, we had been screaming ourselves happy. Scared to death and loving it. Callum was complaining that his ears were nearly deaf and he had our nail marks on his arms. "You're the sister I never had. I've always wanted to have a sister."

"Same here."

"When I was little, I was disappointed each time a baby brother was born."

As we walked among the bustling tourists and academics I asked Callum, "Don't you have a sister?"

He shook his curly head.

"He has brothers," his wife complained. "I already have brothers."

Thus Eve and I embarked on what we called a 'sistership'. Light-hearted and friendly sisterhood minus sibling fights. She was fun and entertainingly clever.

Sunny Lance had taken me roaming the many museums of this highly cultural city. I told him I had visited The Museum of Science only—as it was very close to the hospital. So he took me to the fascinating Museum of Fine Arts, Isabella Stewart Gardner Museum, and the Harvard Art Museum. Lance was an amazing guy who could fall asleep any time he set himself to. He wouldn't waste even five minutes waiting for something without falling into a micro sleep. In the bus. In the subway. On the hospital couch. He was obsessed with sleeping and did so every chance he could.

"How can you do that, Lance? Falling asleep anytime you will it?"

"Just sit in front of the computer all night," he said helpfully. Go figure.

Fortunately he was attentive when awake. One Saturday morning he showed up at my studio early while I was still in "pyjamas". His eyes glazed when he recognised Pete's T-shirt. Quietly he left and came back with a whole stack more of Pete's shirts for me. I looked up at the ceiling... some dirt bothering my eyes.

That day he took me to watch the Red Sox in action at Fenway Park and introduced me to his many friends, kids from various racial backgrounds.

"We've heard much about you from Pete," a golden-eyed cutie declared.

"Miguel," I took a shot. "You play bass."

"Wow. Or—yeay! I'm known in Australia," he crowed with a pleased smile. "He told you about us?"

A black kid with friendly eyes interjected, "Did he also tell you Miguel is a Spanish don who loves many girls?" Miguel only grinned at this teasing. "And who am I, Sydney?"

"Ashleigh. Guitarist."

"Derek here," a machoish boy joined in. "Think The Sox will win?"

They were so fanatical about baseball, just like us and cricket. Eagerly they taught me the rules so I could join them cheering and jeering. In this festive atmosphere, among the loud crowd, the enthusiasm was infectious. And I swear, to win people's hearts here all I had to do was wish The Sox to win.

After the game Gilang, with the G as in 'grass', invited us to his house. He was an international student who lived alone, and his "house" made me blink. An ornate mansion overlooking the water, it had a music room filled with musical instruments for a modern band.

"Mom doesn't approve of kids' music," Lance said. "She kinda looks down on my pals 'cause we play rock 'n roll. Come, Sydney, which instrument do you play?"

"Nothing."

"Don't be shy. We're all amateurs here. No symphony player

among us."

"Honestly. I don't play at all."

He stared at me with comic disbelief before throwing his head back, laughing merrily.

"Super!" he whooped. "Mom can't stand anyone who doesn't play the classics. You can't imagine what I've had to suffer, having my talented brother flaunted in front of my nose all my life. But you don't play even a bit? How brave of Pete to choose you. I like you, Sydney!"

"Don't be annoyed with Pete for what he is," I defended Pete. "He never brags. I've never known anyone who knows Pete to dislike him."

"Agreed," he said easily. "It's Mom who always compares us."

The friends, six of them, played like a professional rock band. I enjoyed their feel-good music. Lance, son of a piano teacher that he was, played the piano well but he preferred the drum. Gilang himself was rather good on saxophone. The main singers were Ashleigh and Irish Sean who played the keyboard. These two delighted us with their very different voices and lovely duet, but basically everyone in the "band" loved to join in the singing as well. And me? I was the water girl. Of course.

"Sing, Sydney," urged Ashleigh.

"Nope. You guys are too good. I won't humiliate myself with my off-key singing."

The boys were enjoying their pre-uni vacation. Gilang, a happy, unassuming boy with dark-chocolate eyes wanted to study biotechnology. His parents said it would help him to make friends quickly if he had something to share. Since his hobby was music, they suggested it. Thus the fun-filled US mansion.

"Pete said my country's gross national income per capita was way less than three bucks a day," Gilang confided to me. "He sorta opened my eyes to giving something back after my studies."

"Sounds very Pete, huh?" Lance joined in.

"That's him," I shook my head, my mind somewhere in the happy past.

Lance tilted his head to look at me, a gesture so much like Pete's.

On the Red Line train to MGH he said, "Sydney, Pete would've liked it if you hang out with us. He often joined us too." Then he leaned back, closed his eyes, and fell promptly asleep. It amazed me no end how he could wake up when he was supposed to. So far we had never missed a stop.

Throughout the summer Lance regularly took me to their "band practice" while Pete was napping. Once, Gilang gifted himself with tattoos on his left arm for his 18th birthday present. But his dad, who disapproved of tattoos, unexpectedly showed up and hauled Gilang to the hospital. His dad ordered all the tattoos to be surgically removed. When it healed after his dad's departure back home, Gilang promptly had the same arm inked again. It costed him $600 for the first designs. The following week he added $600 worth of colours. The week after $600 worth more details. All in one forearm.

Several of these friends had girls they dated.

"Tell me Sydney," Miguel, a Hispanic-lover-in-the-making who preferred romantic dates to sport, and who talked really a lot, approached me one Friday afternoon. "Where should I take my date? What sort of first outing do you girls prefer?"

"Just ask her what she likes. If you don't like it, be prepared to suggest your preference."

"Hey Sydney," Derek, a Matt-Damon-wannabe, struck a posture in front of me, sleeves tightly rolled up to show off impressive gym-honed biceps. He was always very conscious about muscle building. "Do you think my date will like my new shirt?"

"*Me*? Advising you? I'm hopeless about fashion! I pretty much think it's your personality that counts. She won't ditch you if you're very interesting," I told him. Derek made a mock crestfallen expression that made me laugh. "Nice biceps, though."

"Honestly?" he dropped to the big chair in front of me, hands clasped, elbows on knees. "Where'd you want to go when a guy asks you out? What do you like? In other words, how did Pete impress you? Apart from his pretty face?"

Shy Sean came near us. He was very tall, but because of his very youthful face people did not normally realise this until he loomed before you. He sat down next to me, hazel eyes showing interest in our chat.

"But Pete doesn't have to do anything," I replied. "He just has to exist. Breathe. I like that best. Him. Just—being there, courteously unobtrusive. A constant presence. Never pushy. Being polite is free, you know. Yeah, I like a guy being himself, never pretending to be what he's not. You can do that."

"So I can be a schlub from gym?" Derek asked.

"Only if you shower first. Common sense, man. Personal hygiene is big. And... I believe I do notice people's toenails."

They all burst out laughing.

"Choose me, choose me," smiley Ashleigh came over with his guitar. "I don't give a damn how I look but I'll keep you entertained." The black kid with the golden tonsils, he proceeded to sing Blink 182's *She left me roses by the stairs…*"

That very evening my phone rang when I was in Pete's sick room. It was Derek.

"Don't have your dinner tonight," he ordered. "We're taking you to eat out."

"We?"

"The band. You have a date with all of us. You should learn something about Boston's famous jaunts."

"Oh? Where are we going?"

"Back Bay. Not too far from your place. There's this billiards-and-bowling alley with great food."

"Billiards and bowling? But I'm exhausted already."

"You won't be. Not when you hear the music."

"But why'd you want to go out with me?"

"'Cause your voice is *hot*, even when you don't know how to sing."

"Whaat?"

He laughed out loud. "Just pulling your leg. Okay Sydney, 'cause you're fun to hang out with. And, 'cause we like your accent!"

When I looked up, Pete's Mom was eyeing me wrathfully and my heart lurched. My spirit plummeted. Alright, alright, 'fess up. She had the power to rob me of any light.

Pete's Mom revelled in staying bitter. She loved her arrogance and did her best to be unpleasant. And she was successful.

"Sydney?" Derek prompted.

Time to do something about my bruised spirit.

"Good-o," I deliberately chose the Australian expression. "I'll give it a go."

"Super! We'll pick you up."

Pete's Mom threw me another of her hostile looks when the boys arrived. I supposed that was okay, since she even glared at Lance, her own son. They greeted me happily and noisily ("We've all cleaned our toenails, Sydney!"), kissing my cheeks with loud smacks, but lost all their vocabulary when greeting Pete's Mom. Typical teens, my parents would say.

"Save me from your Mom, darling," I whispered into Pete's neck. "Get better."

We had Boston's famous seafood, which tasted so good after continuous hospital fare.

"Glad you like it!" Ashleigh shouted when I ate with gusto. The friends had been drumming and belting out songs following the loud music in this very noisy restaurant, with onlookers throwing indulgent smiles at them.

"Pity legal drinking age here is 21!" Miguel shouted.

"A relief no one's pressuring me into drinking!" I shouted back.

"But I wish I were 18 living Down Under!" Derek, beside me, commented wistfully. *Well...* I wasn't about to mention Dad's abandoned cellar. I told him about our exorbitant food and drink prices instead, and asked him to come when loaded.

After their music practices I went on a few more outings with them. We had scrumptious lobsters at the Legal Sea Foods on the waterfront, and very close from there was the New England Aquarium—a gorgeous facility similar to our Manly Aquarium with its tall five-storey central aquarium tank filled with sharks and sea turtles, moray eels and plenty of other large fish. Of course, it had yet to beat Sydney Aquarium's Great Barrier Reef with its *real* Nemo's world.

The boys sang everywhere. They sang by the river and in the car during Boston's ugly traffic jam. Their light mood was contagious. Carefree and full of high energy, they made me laugh. For a while their joy revived me and eased my worries.

But nothing—nothing!—could make my love get better.

What's Your Weight Today?

Pete's condition remained the same when September rolled in. Lance's gang were about to start uni. They had admission to Harvard, MIT and Boston University, with cheerful Lance going for Biomedical Forensic Sciences. His Mom, of course, lamented the fact that he was not good enough for NEC. Tough. He didn't even want to study music.

Back home, Sydney Olympics were about to start. One afternoon I watched the frenzy of preparation for the Opening Ceremony on TV while massaging Pete. Once I had a picture of me taken at the 1300500 office, holding one of the Olympic torches. Seeing it now with its design of boomerang and Opera House made me homesick. Poignant longings clawed at my heart.

Inhaling the lovely citrus scent of the massage oil, I continued massaging Pete. I was now an experienced masseuse, specifically for long-term bed-ridden patients. And how these months had changed me... I now did with love the things I had been squeamish about at the start.

I washed the massage oil away and applied lotion. All the

while Pete's face was very calm, but his stare was blank. He didn't know me. He did not know what was going on.

"Do not despair of God's grace," I chanted to myself as I put on his clean hospital shirt, expertly wrangling his arm's cast through.

"Do not despair of God's grace," I repeated like a mantra, standing by his hospital window. The view wasn't much here. The picturesque riverbank was blocked by the tops of other buildings.

I took stock of my situation, Pete's stagnant condition, and the hospital's efforts.

Recently Dr McGlynn, the orthopaedic surgeon, had opened Pete's casts, taken more X-rays, and decided to put new casts on to allow more time for more healing.

"His bones should completely heal," he explained. "But he will need to go through extensive physiotherapy to recoup the complete use of his arm and leg. That can only be done if he can follow the instructions. Meaning, he needs to be able to understand his physiotherapist." He looked at me with compassion, his kind eyes complementing the unspoken words.

My beloved would have to understand, and respond, before he could learn to walk again.

"The same applies to his brain," the doctor continued. "New scientific research shows that the health and function of a patient's brain can be improved with the right mental workout. But he needs to have the capability to follow these workouts."

Oh God, when would Pete come back?

His family loved him but he would remain a burden in their lives.

And because Pete was a patient you couldn't chat with, the hospital staff could not view him as a person. They did not know his dreams, his ideas and interests. His feelings and wishes. His ambitions and anxieties. They did not know his rich life stories. They had no idea how lovely he was as a person or what he could give others. (I had Bread's *"If"* playing in my head, *"If a picture paints a thousand words, then why can't I paint you? The words will never show, the you I've come to know..."*) To them he was an endless chore. No more.

I dreaded the inevitable end of my one year. The day when I would have to pack up and really leave. (*"If a man could be two places at one time I'd be with you..."*) It was unavoidable. Creeping slowly but surely.

There was no way I could go back on my words regarding the one-year-only promise. Just wasn't me. I had to meet their terms and keep my end of the agreement or my heart would twist with heavy guilt. No begging for prolonged help. I must complete my studies first before consigning the rest of my life to caring for Pete.

Anxiety crept up on me, getting a grip on my heart and mind. How, just how, would I ever have the strength to leave Pete alone in his present condition? In helplessness I prayed, "I have no one else to ask, Lord, please, oh please return my love to normal-land."

Patience. My love would recover. *Keep your trust in God even after the last ray of hope has departed...* I hugged myself, standing there by the hospital window, silent tears running unchecked.

"Sydney," asked Pete from behind me in a very clear voice. "What's your weight today?"

I whirled around.
"What's your weight today?"

Pete, his hair so long now, was looking at me intently. After his wash, I had left him sitting at a slight recline on his bed. He had been awake, but as usual oblivious to his surroundings. But now—now his eyes were wide and clear. Very, very alert.

"Honey, you're crying," he said. "What's wrong?"

Honey. I *knew* that tone! That word.

And he opened his left arm. Actually he must have tried to open both his arms, because now he looked at his plastered right arm with a puzzled expression. He turned to me again.

"Come here," he motioned with his left arm once more. "Sweetheart. Are you okay?"

I flew to him. My heart in my throat, with trembling fingers I touched his face. Frowning, he looked back at me with full attention and concern.

"Pete," my tears were unstoppable as I hugged him. "Darling..."

He wrapped me to his chest with one arm, "Honey, what's wrong?"

Honey. My memory rushed back to the past. There was something about Pete's voice that was very calming. The way he said the word "honey", I could sense that he really meant it. That it wasn't just a term. When he said it, I felt I was very dear to him.

"How come you're crying? And you've lost weight again. What's bothering you? Love?" Surpassing all expectation, there was nothing wrong or unusual about his speech whatsoever.

Overwhelmed, I wailed out loud.

"Had an accident, did I? Where are we? Is this Hornsby Hospital? Or St. Leonard's North Shore?"

Running footsteps were rushing in. I looked up. Pete was highly alert. His clear eyes the colour of Dorrigo's freshest grass in spring checked the newcomers curiously. His left arm tightened around me, as if trying to protect me from these intruders.

"You're back," Nurse Graham stated the obvious.

I tried to suppress my sobs, unsuccessfully.

"Shh darling, I'm here." Pete whispered, tapping my back, trying to comfort me. "It's okay. It's gonna be okay. Shh. Love?"

A few more meds swept in.

"Why's Sydney crying?" Pete demanded the audience.

"Because I'm so happy!" I wailed.

"She's happy," someone told Pete. "Because you're talking. You're aware of your surroundings. Welcome back to the land of the living."

It was Dr Elektra.

"You're an American," Pete stated with wonder.

There was a quiet moment.

"Of course," the doctor replied smoothly after a short lull. "I'm Dr Elektra, your ward doctor. And very good. You're aware of my accent. We need to play twenty questions here. Tell me, what's your name?"

Pete knew his full name but could not answer where he was. The doctor silently showed him a hospital logo on the patient chart.

"MGH?" Pete's eyes widened. "I was born here." He tried to sit upright. Couldn't. I straightened up from his chest, but his arm tightened as he looked at me. "Sydney? Are we really in Boston? How come? Why are we in the US? What's going on?"

He did not remember anything about his accident. He had no recollection whatsoever about these past six months either, even when his eyes had been open.

But now he was very alert. His speech was normal, defying the prediction that he would need speech therapy if he ever "returned". He answered the doctor's questions lucidly and posed his own with amazing rational clarity. His voice and expression were calm and well controlled. His eyes clear. There was no sign at all that he was suffering from a grievous brain injury.

The relief I felt was tremendous. Forever in my life I would thank God each time I remembered this moment. The moment God granted me my two big wishes.

I would be lying if I said that I had been utterly confident Pete would ever *return*, even while telling everybody else so. I had to confess too, after seeing several of Dr Rushworth's other patients, I had the morbid fear that Pete might end up with speech difficulties and stay mentally disabled forever.

These issues had always been foremost in my mind when I prayed. And how I prayed day and night! I asked God for Pete's return. And I asked that he return in his normal respectable self, his wit intact. Before today, they had seemed like enormous requests, but I asked God anyway. And He had granted me my prayers.

How blessed I felt.

Pete had spent three weeks in a coma and nothing much had

been recovered in the first month. All these months he had been awake but completely oblivious. Since the coma duration and the first-month recovery were the indicators of a patient's long-term recovery, Pete's chance of returning to normal had been close to nil. His sudden awareness and normal speech were nothing short of a miracle.

Whoever God was, He had restored Pete to me. So yes, other people could be godless as they pleased. For myself, from that afternoon I became a believer. I had no more fear about the future because, after the recent ordeal, I *knew* God had the power to help me.

Patiently Dr McGlynn detailed his condition and progress while Pete listened in astonishment. He had no idea at all how he had come to be there.

We held hands tightly while the doctors and nurses checked on him. His grip was hard as if he was afraid I would leave him to face these strangers alone. It touched me that he clung to me when scared, or at least, wary. Dr Elektra and Dr McGlynn pretended that they did not notice this and continued to talk reassuringly. Dr Elektra turned the TV on to Sydney Olympics Opening Ceremony broadcast, showing Pete that it was really September 2000.

"Almost six months..." Pete wondered aloud. "My leg and arm must be okay now. So can we get rid of the casts?"

"Not yet," Dr McGlynn answered. "Yours weren't minor fractures. Your shin was fully broken in two. The bones protruded haphazardly from your skin. We use metal plates to hold it together. We saved your leg, yes, but it takes time for the bones to fully heal and grow. The same applies for your arm. But eventually, you may reclaim the full use of your arm and leg."

"They're itchy under the casts. Stink, too."

"Unfortunately that's unavoidable. We'll give you something to ease the itch. Won't eliminate it completely, though."

"All the more reason to get rid of the casts."

"Can't grant you that wish. You want to heal properly without side effects. Later, I'm confident sessions of extensive physiotherapy will give you a complete recovery. Yes, I'm very pleased with this development." The doctor beamed at me, "As Sydney surely is."

Happy tears still ran silently down my cheeks. When Pete looked at me again, he smiled his first smile in ages. How it banished all the blues! *My love, my sunshine.*

He pulled me towards him for a long-overdue kiss. I wasn't aware of the others leaving us, too lost kissing him back for all I was worth. How good, oh how good, to be held close to his heart again.

"Alone at last," Pete said later, "For a while there, I thought they'd never leave. Now honey, how are you?"

I phoned and texted everyone when he slipped into a peaceful nap.

"He's back Eve! He's back!"

"That's because of you, Sydney! God hears you. We'll be forever indebted to you," Eve wept with me over the phone. "I love you Sydney..."

Lance came immediately. He was hugging and kissing me in a blaze of joy when Pete shouted at him to let me go.

"Great to have you back and grumpy," Lance hugged and thumped him. "Welcome back!"

"Thank you. And find your own girl! Don't touch Sydney."

"Hey, not even a brotherly hug and kiss?" Eyes dancing with mischief, Lance grabbed my waist and planted a smacking kiss on my cheek. "You can't stop me, can you now?"

Pete attempted to sit up and winced in pain. I rushed to help him. He wiped my cheek with the end of his bed sheet and kissed me there himself. Lance fell over laughing.

Then Pete asked, "Sydney? Did I have an accident? Where are we? Why is Lance here?"

Confused, I pulled back and looked at him. He quickly grabbed my hand and laced our fingers as if afraid I would leave him.

"Pete, don't you remember? Dr McGlynn was here explaining

everything to you."

"Dr McGlynn? Who's he?"

"Dark hair? Brown eyes? You spoke with him before you slept."

"I don't remember."

"But Pete, you talked with him for a very long time. He explained everything in details. How can you forget meeting him?"

"Honey, all I know is seeing you skinny. What's your weight today?"

"You're skinny too at the moment. But think darling, what else do you remember?"

He was quiet. He looked at me. Looked at Lance longer, trying hard to figure out how he came to be with us. His gaze travelled around the room. He fixed his eyes on the hospital logo. And something dawned.

"MGH," he wondered in a hushed tone. "But why are we in Boston, darling? Why aren't we home in Sydney? What are we doing here?" Worry was written in his eyes. "And I don't remember any doctor. Will he open my casts? They're annoying."

"You still need the casts." Patiently I repeated the doctor's explanation about his condition. I explained why he was in Boston and how his accident happened.

"But I always wore my helmet," he protested in complete astonishment, his eyes bewildered.

It was sad that he didn't have any memory of the incident.

He did not have any memory of these last months in hospital.

And he had totally forgotten the entire waking-up episode before his recent nap.

"Honey, why don't I remember?" he asked with apprehension.

"Chill out bro," Lance hitched his hip onto the bed beside Pete. "You have Sydney here to remind you of everything. She's your excellent nurse. She loves you to distraction. Even when I couldn't see what was so awesome about a sick man who couldn't even respond to her. They thought you'd be a vegetable, Pete, and for a while there you really were. But Sydney still loves you, regardless. Lucky guy."

Just then we heard certain footsteps click-clicking on the floor outside and my heart fell. Lance looked at me knowingly and lifted his brows.

"Pete? Guess I better leave you to visit with your Mom, okay? I'll just grab myself some dinner."

Pete clutched my fingers tighter.

"I need my dinner, okay?" I implored.

"Oh. Okay," he pulled me down for a quick kiss. I hugged him, my heart overflowing with gratitude that he was now aware of me.

When I straightened, his Mom stood inside the door glaring at me. I walked out in composed dignity, nodding politely at her. As usual she ignored me. And as usual, it made me sad.

"Bye for now," Lance told Pete behind me. "I'll just keep Sydney happy."

"I know why you're following me," I elbowed Lance. "Well, tough. Your crush Nurse Eigenheusen is rostered off this evening."

"*No...*" he made a crestfallen face. Nurse Eigenheusen was the prettiest creature in the entire hospital. Some naughty patients called her "Nurse Egg" because of her mouthful name, but it did not stop her from being very tall and very beautiful.

Lance chatted with me while I was having my dinner. I had only eaten some when Eve rushed in to say that Pete demanded my company. I made an immediate move to stand up, eager to rush back to Pete, but Lance held my elbow to stop me.

"Tell old Pete Sydney has to eat," he told Eve. "She has to look after herself too."

My newly acquired sister and brother threw a look at each other, agreeing, and Eve left again.

"What was that look?" I questioned. "Why did Eve and you exchange such a look?"

Lance looked left and right.

"Out with it," I prompted.

"Um. Your parents..." he looked up at the ceiling.

I put my fork down.

"*Well...* I guess it's okay if you know now. Your parents were concerned about you. They felt very bad for making you sad after their divorce. For making you dependent on Pete. So they sorta asked Eve and me to look after you. They didn't want you, um, thinking of suicide."

"Suicide?" I gaped. Unbelievable! "Why would I want to die when my love needed me? All I wanted was to care for him until he healed. It never crossed my mind to be anywhere away from him. And I'd still love Pete whether my parents had divorced or not."

Lance had the grace to look sheepish. I thought of my parents. *They loved me...* And I laughed.

"Honey, where've you been?" Pete phoned me close to 2am a fortnight later. "I'm so worried. Nobody's visited for days."

At this stage, the hospital was still subjecting him to a set of brain scans and tests. His sudden return to awareness intrigued the meds. Unfortunate for Pete, he was going to have a lot of problems. He forgot many things. Especially immediate things. Stuff that happened recently. Words spoken not long ago. He had to finish reading a book in one sitting, or he would struggle to remember the threads from a previous day's reading. The long and short of it was—Pete suffered permanent short-term memory loss.

"Darling," I yawned, very sleepy. "I was there last night past the visiting hours, giving you a massage."

"That's what Nurse Fleming said, but I don't remember at all." Pete sounded agitated. Nurse Fleming was the son of Sister Fleming. He was a very entertaining bloke with a great sense of humour. If he could not calm Pete down, then Pete must be in an exceptionally bad shape. "Feels like I haven't seen you for days—it's unbearable. I'm so lonely. You can't believe how quiet it is here."

"That's because it's only two in the morning. Most patients must be sleeping."

"Really?" he was really confused. "Were you asleep?"

"Mmm."

"I'm sorry, darling. I didn't mean to disturb you. The nurse programmed your number on the speed dial and I felt I'd go mad if I didn't hear your voice. Sorry to wake you."

"Pete. Don't feel bad. Ever." I sat upright in my bed. "Call me any time. How are you feeling?"

"Pretty good. Apart from my plaguey arm and leg, of course. It's just too lonely here," he paused. "Honey, why aren't we married yet?"

"Is this a real question or are you being whimsical?"

"A real question. For the life of me I don't remember why. They say you've looked after me in every possible way—"

"Pete!" I had ceased helping him with intimate matters as soon as he regained awareness. "That was when you were sick! I was only nursing you."

"Well I'm still sick—"

"Your wits are back now."

"But you still have to massage me a few times a day. You wash me and you know my body. Now how come I still have to keep my hands to myself?"

"Pete!"

"Darling, explain that."

"Pete... Do you remember how old I am?"

"'Course I do. You're 18. Your birthday is February the fourth. It was raining all day on your birthday, and we spent it roaming The Art Gallery and The Museum of Contemporary Art. You love walking in the rain so much. Since it was only misty rain from the one gallery to the next, I obliged you. You were laughing so happily Sydney. I'll never forget how happy you looked, playing in the rain. And that evening we saw a play at the Glen Street Theatre in Belrose."

"Really Pete, you remember all that?" I asked eagerly, my hopes soaring high. "What happened on your birthday?"

"We drove to Hawks Nest. We were crazy about surfing."

"Yeay! You *do* remember!"

He was very pleased too to retain older memories. We chatted joyfully and I was struck by the realisation that this felt very good. To be up all night. Talking and laughing with him. In the quiet early hours. I could live like this. The peace and solitude felt so beautiful and sweet.

We talked about the events while he was "away". I told him I had never had a brother or a sister before. Now because of him, Eve and Lance had become my very dear sister and brother.

"Super," he approved. "As long as your feelings towards me aren't brotherly."

I laughed.

"I love that laughter. Can't get enough of listening to you. How's the elephant today?"

And I laughed louder.

"Sydney, I'm talking romance here, and you find it hilarious?"

When I arrived at the hospital at the usual time, Pete's eyes lit up with so much happiness. Yup. No more blank stares. And his one good arm could hug me back.

"You smell so good," he kissed my cheek affectionately. "Honey, what's your weight today?"

"And good morning to you too." I hugged him tighter, loving his scent and his comforting warmth. Nurse Fleming from the night shift had earlier wheeled him to the shower and washed his hair clean. "How are you feeling?"

"Miserable," he waved his good hand at his casts.

"You have *one* good leg."

He burst out laughing.

I brushed his very beautiful hair and secured it in a ponytail. When I was shaving him, he traced a line with his finger down the side of my cheek to my jaw, watching me closely with smouldering intensity. I used to shave his face effortlessly. But now the exquisite feelings that I had only known with him made me clumsy. My hands were unsteady. My breathing at times was suspended, my heartbeat erratic.

"You're tired," he said. "Didn't you sleep well?"

I considered him for a moment. With his short-term memory loss, Pete freaked out when asked about things he forgot or about hazy memories. He hated it when people asked, *"Do you remember?"* or *"Don't you remember?"* He also said the most useless instructions were *"Don't forget"* and *"Please remember"*.

"Darling, will you get offended if my question starts with *'Do you remember?'"*

"You can ask me anything. It's your privilege."

"Okay Pete. Question is, do you remember that you phoned me this morning?"

I Refuse To Wallow in Misery

One October afternoon Pete beat me easily at chess.

"Sydney isn't much of a challenge at chess," he teased me.

"She did very well!" Nurse Dalziel loyally defended me. "She just didn't anticipate that unprecedented attack on her queen."

We burst out laughing.

Seeing Pete's smile, I felt relief. I had no intention of reminding him of how sad he had been yesterday.

Pete's short-term memory loss meant big chunks of recent events—events between his accident and now—could be deleted from his memory. The time range of "recent" varied. These "blanks" could happen after five minutes, several hours, the next day, or more.

The size of the "blanks" varied too. At times he forgot an entire "episode". At times he only forgot parts of the scene, with some hazy recollection. But there were also moments he remembered an event with total clarity.

Now and then he lost his sense of time, feeling that days had passed when actually it had only been one day—or the opposite. Often he woke up blurting out strange questions for seemingly no reason. At times, they were questions he had previously asked and had been answered.

With brain exercises, *sometimes* he could retrieve *deleted items*. I had to remind him about things again and again until he eventually remembered them. I usually took notes to help remind him of what was being discussed or done during his appointments. In a notebook I jotted down his questions and people's answers to help him recall them later. Not always successfully.

Today, seeing his smile, I was glad he had forgotten yesterday.

Yesterday, they opened the cast on his leg for a whole day of freedom, leaving it unplastered. This gave me high hopes that his leg had healed. They told us not to move it until they were done checking the scans. But at the end of the day they decided the plaster had to go back on. Pete and I had howled simultaneously. We then looked at each other in surprise, never seeing each other *this* upset. Pete had angry, disappointed tears in his eyes, just like I did. But as he looked at me, his eyes softened. We ended up laughing at the whole situation.

"Look on the bright side," I hugged him. "Your arm is out of cast."

His right hand was limp though. It flopped uselessly at the wrist. And his shoulder pain made it difficult for him to lift his arm.

Streams of friends cheered us up. When they heard of Pete's "return", many showed up, while those overseas sent emails and phoned. I discovered Pete was everybody's best friend. No surprise there. He could be calm, he could be vivacious. At times playful, at times serious. With his balanced temper and personality, in happy or troubled times Pete was simply great to spend time with. What special was, he kept in touch with each one of these friends.

In a happy turn of events, my friend Alex reached the US and visited us. Right away the guys chatted animatedly about travels. Oh, the travellers, they had met! They reminisced about particular places both had visited, exchanging experiences and information in full enthusiasm. And you know, how disgustingly world weary they could sound at times.

"Sweetheart," Pete caught my amused smile, "Are you laughing at us?"

"Yes Sydney," Alex turned to me. "What have you learnt, away from home? What do you think about Americans?"

"Well boys," I obliged and put in my two cents, "to say all Americans are obnoxious is like saying all Aussies are bogans."

Boston in fall was gloriously colourful. Pity Pete could not go outside. To alleviate his boredom I offered to take him to an outer corridor.

"Pete, I hate it that you have to go through all this torture," I helped him painstakingly move to his wheelchair.

"Don't worry, honey. Trials and afflictions are there for some reason. They make you a better person. When you pass an exam, you go to the next level, don't you?"

"What an insight. But why? Why Pete? Ever stop to reflect why all this has happened? Why you? When you've always been such a good person! So undeserving of injury."

"Darling, so loyal you are. But look around. Some babies are born blind. Some with Down syndrome. Who says they deserve that?" Trust Pete to say something profound. "But have compassion for everyone. The people who are perfectly normal, who's to say that they don't have their own trials? Some suffer more than people with disabilities, you know."

"But you're in pain!"

"Lighten up, love. Nobody should whine. I refuse to wallow in misery. Why should our limitations give us an excuse to brood in gloom? I sure don't enjoy brooding! You believe in God, don't you? In the next life, there'll be no more suffering. That's why life is easier when we have God to explain the things beyond human understanding. When we're all given new bodies in the next world, all disabilities will be gone."

He smiled his most soothing, relaxed smile that immediately calmed me. How sensitive he was of my feelings. How astute. How well he knew me. I couldn't help falling in love all over again. Right there and then, looking into his *very* peaceful eyes, I knew I was home.

"How do you know that?" I wheeled him outside. With one arm, he could hardly push the wheelchair himself in a straight line. "Let's look at it more deeply during tonight's phone call."

Pete and I sometimes discussed philosophy during the night. At times we ended up talking for hours. He didn't define faith as something that could not be proven, or was logically inexplicable. For example, he said angels don't have wings, because you only need wings to travel through the air. When angels come from a parallel world to ours, they don't pass through air as the medium. That's right. Don't get me started on the many topics we discussed.

Pete's analytical powers were not affected by his brain injury.

He said we weren't meant to stay dumb. He said there are three stages of human development. First is the physical state, when we all act on basic instincts. Later on we are meant to progress to the moral state, where our reason and conscience start to guide our actions. And lastly, reaching the spiritual state, we will attain full control of our faculties, body and mind. Here is the-soul-at-ease, we rule our desires instead of being their slaves.

I loved how he stimulated my mind. I loved getting lost in a discussion until we lost track of time. To me, Pete never ceased to be interesting.

"Honey," he called now as I stood facing the afternoon sunshine. "What's your weight today?"

Amused by this repeated question, my lips twitched with a smile as I glanced back at him. Now that he was better, his real personality returned in full force. Calm. Selfless. He stopped worrying about himself and started worrying about me.

"I'll tell you next year."

"Darling, why aren't we married yet?"

I searched his face. Now when Pete had an idea or question, he latched on to it. When his mind found the answer unacceptable, he would not veer away from it. One thing had changed for sure. Unlike he often did in Sydney—perhaps subconsciously—Pete did not view me as a little girl anymore.

"I want to look after you so much," he said with a yearning

look.

"Say again?"

"You heard me. I wanna care for you."

"This from a man in cast?" I laughed. "Just how are you going to accomplish that?" I looked at his still useless arm and leg pointedly.

"At least I'm good to order you about," he grinned up from his wheelchair. "I plan to make sure you look after yourself."

"You're so wonderful, d'you know that?" I bent to give him a big hug. "Now cut that out. Sounds like a proposal, you know. You'll be in hot water if I say yes."

"Is that a yes?" Seriously. Very seriously. "I want you to say yes."

A shiver ran through me. I lost my smile and went still. My heart stopped. Then slowly thumped with fear. And... elation?

"Is this—for real?" I asked haltingly, shaking in my shoes. "Are you really—asking me?"

"Yes. For real. All I am, all I want is to be with you. Marry me and be happy!"

Getting married had crossed my mind a couple of times, but each time I dismissed it, thinking we were too young. In my mind, it would not happen for another ten years. Still, I *had* thought about it because I wanted it. The freedom to be with Pete night and day and call him my own. To love Pete with everything I was and had. To give without fear. And above all, *to belong*.

"*Please...*" he pleaded. "I'm not talking about the big elephant here—we've always been together and I know how committed you are to me. Sure the getting-physical part will be my great joy. But getting married is so much more than that. This is about something closer and more intimate to me, something I deeply care about. And I *care* for you... I want to *love* you... Do I make sense?" He forked desperate fingers through his hair.

"It's *not* about convenience, though it'll be a bonus. It's *not* about other people's recognition either, though I do want to shout my love for you to the world. *Please...*" Oh... those earnest eyes! "I feel—I feel it's necessary that we completely *belong* with each other. I've been thinking a lot about this. All this time I've been recuperating. I understand many people don't value marriage, and it doesn't seem fair asking you to get married so young. While I'm sick, as well. But you aren't going to look after a sick man forever. I'll get better, and we'll do loads of fun stuff. Staying young for always. I—"

"Pete?"

"Yes?"

"Shut up."

"Er..."

"Just stop babbling. Shut up."

He looked at me in trepidation.

And I launched myself at him. I hugged him. Kissed him.

"The months when you were 'gone' Pete, I wanted *so* much for us to completely belong to each other. I was terrified of losing you again. So yes." Joyous tears spilled over. "Yes Pete. Yes!"

"Sydney I can't live without you," he said excitedly, his speech accelerated by a rush of emotion. "You won't regret this, I promise! If you're ever disappointed in me or in something, let me know and we'll work on it together."

"Cool. I'll hold you to that."

"Oops, on that note..." He stopped to look down at his wheelchair and shook his head. "Oh, heck, shouldn't I have kneeled down for this?" He smiled sheepishly. "Or at least I should've had roses. And a ring."

"I know... You're forgiven 'cause I'm the happiest of all girls."

"And about to be happier," his hand shot to muss up my hair. "A-s-a-p?" He asked eagerly, eyes sparkling.

I straightened and scrunched my nose at him.

"No way. Darling, agreeing doesn't mean a-s-a-p. We have a horde of things to think through."

"But you've just agreed to marry me."

"As I've said, I'm only agreeing *now* because we've been through so much and I've known the very real terror of almost losing you. But being madly in love and getting married so young doesn't entitle us to be careless."

"Darling, what are you saying?"

"I'm certain we're meant to be together. But to go ahead we must think everything through, Pete. Carefully. What are the consequences? Where are we going to live? How are we going to support ourselves? What arrangements are we going to make for tackling our problems? What else may turn up that we should be prepared for? Lots of stuff to work out. So yeah, let's have a very long engagement."

"No!"

"Yes!"

"Honey, we can't even stand a separation for longer than several hours. Our greatest hardship is saying goodbye at the end of the day because we can't bear to be apart. So we may as well be married."

"I know, I know. But love, look at you. Still in a cast and *you* dream about looking after *me*? Life isn't going to be a rose garden for a while, Pete. Get well first," I ordered.

"Gosh..." he whined. "You're bossy. Sounds like we're married already."

He watched me intently. Now, I so didn't want him to be sick. But with his return to awareness, he again had the power to make my heart go pitter-patter. Physically he was still weak and pale. He had lost a significant amount of weight. He had lost his glorious tan from Sydney summer too. But his potent gaze was far from lifeless. His intense masculinity overwhelmed me. I felt disconcerted, all nervous and tingly. And trust Pete to sense it. Sometimes he was amused by my loss of composure. Sometimes smug.

"Right. If you're so adamant in taking life seriously—," he flashed me a teasing smirk, "then let's work things out while I'm in here. Shall we make it as soon as I'm discharged? It'll give me the incentive to get well quickly." A wink.

"That'll depend on what comes up when we talk things over."

"Sydney..." he groaned. "You're very strict. Hey, you don't even sound 18, you know." At that moment he realised he had made a discovery. "You—you sound mature, sweetheart... You've grown up." He tilted his head, now looking at me with an assessing stare. "You look self-assured... I've seen how competent you are in handling things around here. The way you talk with the staff is very charming. So charming they'd do things happily for you."

"Hang on. You've just described my Mum!"

"And what's wrong with that? You're kind to them. You smile. And Sydney, at night, even as I worry about your being alone, you confidently go home. Very independent. It's in your steps. The way you move. I suspect you don't need me that much anymore. But darling, you're still the girl I fell in love with and I wanna be with you every chance I can."

I contemplated him for a while. This was the man I had agreed to spend the rest of my life with. So... Time for total honesty.

"Um—perhaps I should show you something. Look. Look at my hair, Pete." I bent so he could check my hair near the scalp. Half a centimetre of it had more grey strands. I told him how Mum made me dye it back to the original chestnut.

Pete was watching me closely now, his smile gone. Unnerved, I played with my hair self-consciously.

"Didn't function well in a crisis, did I? You wouldn't believe how kind everybody was, those dark months alone with you but *without* you. I feel frightened remembering it now. I know God was here. He saw me standing by your side. He saw me walking alone. He sent Lance's gang and the hospital staff to be my friends. But I know I don't want to live that life again! Pete, don't ever, ever go away again..."

He kept eyeing me as I tensed. Suddenly he pulled at my waist in a fierce hug and buried his face on my stomach. His shoulders were racked by sobs he couldn't suppress.

For a moment I was stunned. Then I wrapped my arms around his head. My legs against his wheelchair hurt.

"I'm sorry," he anguished. "What you must have been through because of me. I'll make it up to you. Sydney, I've never been so much loved!"

Every Time I See Roses, I Think of You

"Every time I see roses, I think of you," Pete scribbled in his untidy left-hand writing. His left-hand drawing looked better though, he'd managed a decent picture of his water jug. Desmond and Christine, his physiotherapists, had shown him an exercise to fix his floppy, limp right hand. They taught him to push with his arm flat and his hand up at a square angle. In a few days this exercise had straightened the hand and we were hopeful he could use it fully soon. Pity his shoulder was still in pain.

"What are you doing Pete?" I asked as he handed me a single fragrant rose.

"I'm starting an ardent campaign to get an immediate wedding date," he grinned.

Every morning after that my fiancé greeted me with a single rose. He knew well how to express his love. And not only with the uniquely designed diamond ring he ordered online. It was in the looks he threw at me. In his affectionate tone when we chatted face to face or on the phone. Really. We did not need to talk about a risqué topic or mention anything bawdy to have a very intimate conversation.

But in case you are wondering, during these weeks Pete

adamantly refused to talk about the big elephant.

I had asked him about it one Saturday afternoon after my outing with Eve. It was massage time. We put on some calming music and I started from his feet, going up. He was decently covered and only exposed where I was massaging him, one part each time.

But massage moments were such electrical moments. I did not dare look into his eyes when he was on his back. But he still made me nervous even face-down on his tummy. I talked incessantly about nothings to lighten the charged air. The movie I just saw with Eve. The crunchy leaves outside my apartment. The plan to move him to physio-rehab—when his arms could hold crutches—so he could learn to walk.

Touching him now when he was alert was such a Herculean task. When I couldn't help dropping a kiss on the back of his shoulder, which had such an intriguing pattern of fine hair, he whirled around so fast and caught me.

We ended up in a most dizzying kiss. It was only a kiss. Hands off. Honestly. Nevertheless, we lost control, and flew somewhere I had never been. As in, I ended up keening into his mouth as fireworks exploded, clinging to him for dear life. My arms, desperately wrapped around his neck with all my might, were close to strangling him. My nails dug deep into my palms.

"What was that?" I asked in a barely audible voice when I could speak.

One beautiful eyebrow cocked, but he did not say anything.

"Pete?" I asked, wide-eyed. Questioning.

He shook his head.

"But—how? We only kissed!"

He stubbornly refused to comment.

"Um, when people mentioned sex, I thought I sort of knew what it was all about. But obviously I had no idea!"

Still silent.

I looked at him with a high level of physical curiosity. If he could create fireworks with just a kiss, what else could he do?

"Pete? Open Book Management?"

He gave me a pained expression and laughed.

"I'll take a raincheck, okay? When it's action time, we can explore and have intimate talk all you want. Or not. We'll have terrific silences too. But now I can't talk to *you* about it. I'm sorry, but no. I can't be indifferent with you."

"And that's a bad thing why?" A pity he was a badly injured boy, I did not have the heart to put his discipline to the test.

"Don't spoil our wedding night. Make it special. Romantic. Magical. You want it to be most memorable, not just another night. Hey, you won't even let Eve spoil the movies you want to watch."

"But she *is* a spoiler. She reads movie reviews!"

"Exactly my point!"

November came and went. Pete's injured leg was out of its cast and he had been with the physio-rehab learning to walk again. He could not use a crutch because the brain damage gave him very poor balance. But he did okay with the walking frame, despite persistent shoulder pain.

The hospital's plastic surgeon said all Pete needed now was a skin graft to cover the large scar exposing his shin. This surgery was needed to prevent it from opening again, just in case he banged his leg.

But a week after Thanksgiving a ghastly, tiny boil had popped up on the scar of his right arm. It was caused by a severe bone infection erupting around the screws of the metal plate holding his bone together. Acute osteomyelitis, they called it. So the rehab sent him back to the main hospital.

At first they inserted drainage and flushed the wound with soluble antibiotics. After days without improvement, the hospital scheduled a bone-graft surgery for this arm next week.

It was *so* unfair. He had progressed so well, but this setback made this arm useless and painful again. He could not lift it to hold his walking frame. And he still suffered shoulder pain too. All this, just when he was getting ready to apply for a job as a violinist in Sydney. He could not even use this arm.

This evening, he was suffering terrible pain and had a high

fever. It was snowing outside, but in here he had a raging temperature.

"Yes, yes, I'll marry you. *Now*. Immediately. Just get better!" I cried on his chest. "Pete, don't leave me alone... I'll die if you go away again."

"Sydney," he managed a thin smile. While his face contained his fever, his eyes underneath the cold compress radiated peace and delight. "Things can only get better, now that you've agreed to marry me a-s-a-p." And he winced in pain, "Gosh, it takes going through this torture to secure it!"

They eventually carried out an emergency surgery. The infection had spread so quickly and so badly that Pete nearly lost his arm.

Next was the surgery on his shin.

In Sydney Mum had a fit, panicking about how to produce a wedding gown at such short notice. Well... I had a good idea.

"Mum, you're on speaker. We'll discuss the dress when the groom isn't listening."

"Of course," she agreed. "Now... Birth control?"

"*Muum!*"

"You and Pete want a baby while things are still unsettled? If not, start taking the pill now."

"*Muum...* I can hear Ettoré laughing behind you!"

"You're on speaker too," piped Ettoré. "And Sydney? Pete? We're engaged too."

"Whaat? Ohmygod... I'm so happy. Congratulations!"

"We'll get married in my hometown in June, when Pete will be well enough to take you there."

"Super," Pete joined in. "Thanks for considering me. Congratulations."

"And Sydney?" Mum again, "*I'll* be off the pill."

"Great! Mum, I'm *so* happy..."

Pete's Mom went ballistic when she found us plotting, heads

bent together over my laptop, working on a list titled "<u>How to Get Married</u>". Since we told her in October, she had dismissed our engagement. Now she was affronted by our audacity in making plans to get married.

After his recent surgeries, Pete's right arm bone-graft and his shin skin-graft were still healing. At this stage he could not use his right arm to hold the walking frame, but his physiotherapist had given him some leg exercises while sitting down. Hence we were all sitting in the hospital lounge.

"We would love your blessing, Mom," Pete asserted. "But we're going ahead regardless."

"But you're not even whole! You'll be disabled for life. How do you hope she'll be faithful to you and stay married to you for life? You have one broken marriage behind you when you had all your faculties intact!"

"Sydney has been faithful, loyal, and steadfast even when I was a total vegetable."

"And you want to chain her to you for life?" she derided. "With your handicap? When she can find a normal man who's better than you? One who can make her happier?"

"I'll have only Pete." I clenched my fists. She must know how hurtful her words were. "No other."

Pete squeezed my hand. Both in gratitude and to calm me down.

"It'll be February the fourth?" his Mom verified, still wearing anger.

"Yes. Hopefully I'll be out of here, or I'll insist on being released, come what may. Eve's organizing it." And he threw Eve, who had joined us, a happy smile.

"Yes," Eve confirmed. "Callum is looking into the legalities. And Sydney, your parents won't hear of a no-frills wedding for their only child. They insist on paying. We've been lucky to secure a venue, because a couple moved their reservation to spring."

Eve of the big heart threw herself into the preparations. In the following weeks she kept consulting us to make sure we approved of the details even though we weren't fussy. Cake. Flowers. Everything.

"As long as the wedding car is discreet, Eve," Pete put in, eyes dancing. "I don't want the driver to see us necking."

Eve and I gaped. And he laughed. "Don't worry about every little thing, Eve... Thanks so much for all your hard work."

Pete and I managed the invitations from his sick room. He personally phoned our friends and relatives, and I sent the specifics via emails. Every one heartily accepted. Probably because of Pete's suffering, they were delighted his healing would culminate in a joyous celebration.

Apart from his grouchy Mom, nobody had voiced objection. Many did curiously question whether I knew what I was doing marrying a handicapped man. And to get married so young, at that. But nobody interfered or tried to change my mind.

"Think of how low the telephone bill is going to be!" Callum had even teased. "Pete will be just by your side as you fall asleep or wake up."

I screamed when I opened my apartment door the morning of my wedding day. With joy.

"WOW! LUCY! BRENNA! What the?! How?"

And the girls—who had written saying they could not afford the airfare—were all over me, laughing, shrieking "SYDNEEY!"

Down the hallway my neighbours opened the doors and popped their heads out, unaccustomed to early Sunday noise.

"Morning Lee, Simon, sorry! Too excited. Big surprise." I waved at them, hauled my big surprises inside, and closed my door.

All at once it became a very noisy morning. "We're here courtesy of your mum as a surprise to complete your happiness"... "Arrived yesterday morning..." "Staying at Gilang's with your cousins..." "Spent the whole of yesterday with Lance's gang..." "Last night ate clam chowder, watched people, and bought cheap souvenirs at Faneuil Hall's Quincy

Market..."

"And you didn't think to see me first?" I yelled in a royal snit. "Whose friends are you?"

"Chill out, you twit, it's called a surprise!" Lucy shrugged off her stylish winter coat.

"I'm hungry and we can catch up—or better yet tell me about your cute neighbour, the one in the red tracksuit—while eating breakfast," Brenna marched to the table. "We've bought doughnuts. Lots of 'em. Which one do you want first?"

"Hey, backtrack a bit. My neighbour? What happened to your darling pianist?"

"Who? The selfish, control freak? I'm single again. Close your jaw, Sydney. Yup. That's more becoming a bride. You heard it right. The world's still turning too. Aren't these doughnuts sinful? Welcome to America!"

Sing With Me, Darling

My beloved was released after ten-month convalescence at the hospital.

It was a freezing-cold winter day. The Sydneysider in me had cringed at the thought of getting married in a closed room, but Dad had thoughtfully asked Eve for a venue within walls of glass to bring in the outdoors. It was warm inside. And it showcased the spectacular view of the river, the city's skyline, and the clear blue sky.

But nothing! Nothing of that mattered when I saw my handsome groom, his arm in a sling, his ponytail replaced by a stylish haircut, his magnificent shoulders encased in wedding finery. Because his eyes lit up *so* happily when he looked at me.

"Happy birthday Sydney," he whispered as I came to his side. "I love you *so* much!"

"Love you too."

"You look amazing! I love it that you wear your hair down, so long and beautiful. And it's so clever to have this wreath of tiny fragrant roses for your veil. This is very you."

"Thanks. Kirsten created this Maid Marion style." My cousin

278

had flown to Boston from her cruise ship which was currently docked in New York. "She said I shouldn't try to look older and be somebody else."

He laughed, the beautiful sound of it filling my ears and my heart with so much warmth.

"She cut my hair this morning. And then she said she was running late for you and would need to wave her magic wand. Love the result, though."

We chatted happily and had a bit of a laugh. We were missing each other so much because we had been banned from talking on the phone last night ("The bride has to sleep!" Mum's austere command).

"Have I told you I like your cute little jacket? You look classy." Then his eyes widened and he did a double take. Now Pete might forget recent events, but he remembered the past in minute detail. The moment he realised what I had done, he shook his head at me, eyes gleaming dangerously. "Do I see what I see?"

"You'll have to make sure a bit later," I smiled.

"I can't believe you're pulling this on me," he put his forehead on mine, laughing.

"It's Mum's fault. She couldn't think of what to get me. Well I remembered the favourite LBD. So I said, 'Get the dressmaker to copy that one, Mum, just pretty it up a bit for a wedding.' So they made it full length in the whitest chiffon, with matching bridal jacket 'cause it's winter. Thought you'd appreciate the joke."

"Love your sense of humour, but gosh... it's gonna be torture waiting. But I'll get my revenge!"

Lance the best man nudged him. "Can private jokes wait for later? The whole room is waiting. You two want to get married or not?"

Everybody was smiling, my instant bridesmaids grinning ear to ear. Our family and close friends were there. His cousins. Musician friends. Grandpa Stuart and Nanna Véronique. Grandad Geoff. Aunt Olivia and her husband. Cousin Kirsten and her cruise-ship engineer husband. Cousin Stephen the pilot and his Pommy fiancée. Kate, Craig, Brent and their families. Lots of the hospital staff who, after so many months, now felt like family.

Pete's loving eyes smiled into mine. But when I said my vow his gaze changed, overcome by deep emotions. *This is it*... Overwhelming feelings swamped us. As soon as we had said the vows we flew into a tight, wordless embrace, oblivious to the world.

The following few hours flowed with tremendous peace, joy, and—nervousness. At any given moment I was acutely aware of my dashing husband.

"You can buy our Sydney home," Dad told Pete as I linked arms with Grandad Geoff and Aunt Olivia.

"Son-in-law discount?" Pete bargained.

"Sure. I'll throw in the car and the Harley too. But I warn you I'll visit very often."

"You're most welcome. Stay anytime."

And oh, even though several world-class musicians were in attendance, it was Lance's gang—*my* pals—who brightened the day with the instruments from Gilang's sophisticated music room.

When Ashleigh crooned a heartfelt "It Had to Be You", Pete and I turned to each other.

"I'm thinking of our last dance on board the Valentine-dinner cruise," he laced our fingers together.

"I know."

"So glad we've come through the last year unscathed."

"Me too." Then I looked pointedly at his arm.

"*Well*, sort of," he conceded.

I laughed. "Pete, after surviving 2000, I'm up for whatever comes next."

"On to the next challenge? Super. It's called putting up with me." He smiled. Endless challenges and exquisite promises were swimming in his eyes. I didn't know how long I was lost in them.

Beaming guests, and teary-eyed Mum, shooed us into the wedding car which took us to a romantic honeymoon resort outside Boston.

Now, you respect our privacy, don't you? Pete and I sure didn't invite anyone to our amorous moments.

And no, I'm not about to tell you how to do it if you don't know.

Suffice to say, the beauty of this level of intimacy was a revelation. Nobody—nobody!—could be more wonderful than Pete.

"Pete, will you ever forget tonight?" I asked my memory-problem husband as we drifted to sleep in each other's arms for the very first time. He had been humming a beautiful melody softly, but faltered sleepily.

"Mmm, better remind me again and again my love..."

It snowed the whole week. Who cared? We lived in each other's heart, where storm or sunshine was always welcomed. We were not bystanders, and we weren't miserably standing on the porch.

The glorious physical blended our hearts and souls indescribably closer. We lived in the clouds, where Pete, not angels, sang to me. The intoxicating bliss sure dispelled all the grief and suffering of the past year. And we found a home in each other.

One fine morning I stood sipping my tea by the window, gazing at the resort's white fairy landscape outside.

"Darling," Pete came up behind me and pulled me to him. "You had a dream last night."

"Did I? *You remember?*"

"Oh yes! This one I'm not gonna forget, ever, in my life. Made a note to remind me."

The smile in his voice aroused suspicion in me. I tried to twist around but his arms held me in place and he buried his face on my neck. He *was* laughing. Or trying hard not to.

"What is it? Did I talk in my sleep?"

"Better than that!" He took away my teacup and produced his phone with a cheeky grin. Abruptly I felt my heart beat in suspense. He chose the "recording" option and pressed "play". And there was my voice... *I was singing in my sleep!*

"Ohmygod!" I shrieked, "Gimme that!"

"No way! You can't delete it. It's the first time I've heard you sing!"

"Pete, I'm going to die!" I fought to wrestle it from him.

"Careful my arm!" he turned and twisted.

"Then stop being cruel!"

"Cruel? But I love your voice. I'll treasure this always. Besides, nobody sings properly in sleep anyway." He held me again. Too mortified to look at him, I buried my face in his shoulder. "Sydney, darling, you should keep singing. I always think people who sing while they work are people who appreciate life."

"You call that—*that*—singing? I'm tone-deaf!" I broke free and ran away to hide in embarrassment.

A moment later he opened the wardrobe... where I was hugging my knees on the floor.

"Nobody's tone-deaf, baby," he crouched in front of me. "I love your singing. But if *you* wanna sing better, I can teach you, you know." He lifted my chin, "Sing with me, darling."

Slowly I looked at him.

"Promise not to laugh?"

His beautiful eyes gleamed with a naughty glint, "That depends..."

I Was There

"So how's married life, sparkling new bride?" teased a smiling Sister Orton, who was normally very strict and businesslike, when I visited the nurse's station.

After Pete's birthday we returned to Boston and lived in my nearby studio to complete his physiotherapy and tests. This morning they were doing some tests that I didn't need to attend. Time to catch up with my hospital friends.

"Managed to get some sleep yet?" Nurse Eigenheusen nudged me.

"And how are you today?" I asked back with a straight face.

"Sydney..." Sister Fleming hugged me. "You're blushing!"

"I've been so in love with Pete for months, yet he never came home to my place!" complained Rowe. "But then, I haven't guarded him tenaciously like a mother tiger." And she lifted her pretty brow teasingly, "How's Pete at home?"

"He's fine, thank you," I skirted around their insinuation. "As long as he remembers to walk properly, he can walk without a limp. Premeditative walk, we call it. He does limp when he runs spontaneously, like when we play ball games in the park. Only his arm—the pain shooting through his arm has been persistent. He can only play his violin ten to fifteen minutes at the most. If he persists, the pain becomes so severe that he loses control over his hand movements. So yeah, since he's right-handed he can't play his violin well."

My phone rang as we chatted.

"Darling, how much, how much do you love me?" Pete asked in an agitated voice which was so unlike him. At once my whole attention reverted to him.

"Darling," I asked very slowly, very calmly, though my heart thudded with terror. "What's happened?"

"Disaster. Big one. Join us at Dr Rushworth's?"

He was pacing the room, his expression devastated, when I rushed in. I went to him and he took my hands in a tight grip.

"I swear to you I didn't know about this when I wanted us to get married quickly," he pleaded fearfully. Talking fast. Not his calm self at all. "Honestly, I didn't mean to trap you."

I looked at his tormented eyes. His usually unruffled demeanour had taken leave. Calm down, I told myself, you were useless panicked. I pulled him down next to me on the sofa and wrapped my arms around his waist.

"The right brain controls our creative aptitude," old doctor Dr Rushworth explained in his deep baritone. "We've found Pete's can't cope with new music. It seems he retains his previous music skills and large repertoire. But the injury has altered his brain function. He can't learn the latest elaborate works of new composers. Not easily. That means he won't be able to play in a symphony orchestra except for his earlier music.

"Unfortunately because of his right-arm pain, so far he can only play very short violin pieces. Will they hire him if he can only play—at maximum—ten minutes in an hour? And we don't know yet how significantly or when this right arm will heal. Or whether it will ever heal.

"Furthermore, the right-brain injury plays havoc with Pete's left hand motor skills. This is because the right brain controls the functions on our left. This condition will make it extremely difficult for him to train his left hand to play the violin.

"I have to send the full report of these findings to the job Pete is applying for in Australia." He gestured to the sheaf of papers strewn on the table in front of him and announced coldly, "For the time being, any chance of him playing in an orchestra again is cut short."

Oh no... What my love must be feeling! Classics and violin had been his lifelong passion.

"Let me see," my arms tightened around him. "Pete has difficulties with motor skills on both hands. The right one due to his right-arm injury. The left one due to the right-brain injury. He's very fortunate to keep his previous music repertoire, but can't really learn the elaborate works of new composers?"

"Yes. That's right."

"Can he do some other job? Like, teaching classics?"

"Of course he can. But don't aim for higher college or schools. His occupational therapist says kids will take advantage of his forgetfulness. If you can help him to organize private tuition for children who are serious in wanting to learn the classics, Pete will certainly manage. That way, he won't be taxing his arm too much."

My beloved was very quiet and pensive when we left the hospital. My heart reached out to him, knowing what he had lost, knowing how great a musician he could have been. What a waste of a brilliant talent. If he had been able to work in his previous field, he would be making a lot of money. He would have professional satisfaction and worldwide recognition. And he would not have to go through so much agony.

Sorrow filled my soul. I wished I could take away his pain but knew I couldn't. And tomorrow—tomorrow, if he forgot, I would have to remind him the details of Dr Rushworth's explanation, reliving the pain again.

"Pete, I feel for you. I'm sorry. So sorry this happened to you." We walked with our gloved fingers laced together, boots crunching and sloshing through last night's fall of thin snow. I stopped, stood on my tiptoe to kiss his dear cheek, and walked again. "How do you feel, love?"

"I feel bad because you've married a broken man," he managed in a very low voice.

"Whaat? Aren't you supposed to feel bad because your career as a great violinist is in jeopardy?"

"I won't miss it that much 'cause I can still play the violin ten minutes each time." He squeezed my hand tighter. "You see, I can still play parts of the elaborate movements. A sequence each time. Or play short pieces. Violin fills me with joy. Problem is, playing for myself won't bring in money. This is an absolute disaster."

I nodded in sympathy.

"Sydney," he talked haltingly, wariness marring his voice. "I love you *so* much I'll understand if you want out. But I really don't want you to. I'm so in love with you I'm selfish enough to want us together for always."

"Of course we will be. Why would I want out?"

"Because I won't be a great musician."

"That's not why I married you." The thought that he was afraid I would leave crushed me. I felt deeply for him. Well, I was not his Mom and I was not his ex! He did not have to be a great star to be worthy of my affection. "Darling, I didn't even know you were a musician, remember? We used to take calls together."

"That's another thing. I may have to end up with a low-paying job, if I can even hold a job. So honey, I won't make much money," he reasoned in distress. He was deeply troubled for losing all that he used to have, all that he used to be. "Are you sure you'll still be happy with me?"

"Of course. We'll manage. If you can't work yet, then I will. There's always a job in Australia as long as we aren't lazy. At the very worst, I can do gardening or patient massage. Also, do you remember the share certificates that Mum and Ettoré have given us for our wedding present? Would you like to consult them about the best way to invest your property money?"

"Sure. But honey, for myself, I'm not fussy. After my travels, I see little point in amassing wealth, except to share it with those in need. When the doctor told me, my only concern was you. I wanted you to be comfortable. I was terrified you'd blame me for marrying you before I could even stand on my own feet. Don't you mind what I am now?"

"'Course not. I myself have many shortcomings—some I don't even realise. Pete, you don't mean to suggest that because you suffer from brain damage you're then unworthy of love, do you?"

He was silent.

"Wrong, Pete. Your injury is heart wrenching. But you're still the same fine man I fell in love with. You have a high degree of sensitivity and compassion. You have a strong drive to do good. You're unwilling to hurt anyone. You're unique. You shine and stand out from the crowd. And anyway, although forgetful, you're still brilliant. Your analytical mind is sharp and you're very witty."

"Wow. Thank you. You're not saying that just because we're newly married—loved-up pair and all that—are you?"

The insecurities in his voice stopped me in my tracks. I held his gaze and told him resolutely, "You forget, darling, so I'll have to remind you. To me, being with you has always been better than being without you. I was there Pete, all the time when your condition was so bad and so uncertain. It was a whole lot worse than today. I was there, Pete, when you didn't even know how to smile. Or how to brush your teeth. And had to have a catheter.

"They thought you'd be a vegetable, Pete, and for a while there you really were.

"I did cry praying for you, but never once was I dispirited because I wasn't loved. Never once did I feel all alone in the big wide world. Never once did I have any suicidal thoughts. You know I went through all that after my parents' divorce. But simply being near you gave me courage and strength.

"Now you're heaps better, thank God!

"Yes I was there Pete, the first time you smiled again. D'you know how much that first smile meant to me? You can't imagine my happiness! I was positively euphoric. Waiting was the hardest thing to do, Pete... but you're worth it.

"I love you. I'll love you until I die.

"So yeah, you're stuck with me 'cause I'm never, never going away from you! I'm in love with you and I *need* you. And I love you *so much* that I need to know you're okay every minute of the day.

"Looks like our life will be an interesting long journey. But we'll be together each step of the way, right? I *need* you. Please trust me, darling... I'm not whole without you."

"Honey... don't cry," he reached for me and wrapped me to his chest.

"I'm not crying," I swiped angrily at my stupid tears. "I'm a strong woman! I'm brave and I'll face whatever comes next. Alone, I'd be broken but I'd manage alright 'cause God would help me. But I wanna be with you!"

"I know, I know. Sweetheart, I'm sorry I made you cry." He helped dab my eyes and looked at me with a tentative smile. "I believe you. I've always sensed this goodness in you. You're the best of the blessings God has given me, Sydney. But the problems needed to be aired and dissected 'cause they could become big issues, okay? We need to verbalize all of the hurdles to clearly understand each other. To ensure no regrets. And it seems we have no problems." His smile became more relaxed. "Not between us at any rate."

"True," I was able to smile back now. "We do have real problems concerning the practicalities. But we'll solve them. During the last year I've learnt more about the real me, Pete. The person I am inside. I've found I'm not a person who lives lightly or superficially. I enjoy living at full capacity. Passionately. Intensely. And I'm not averse to challenge or struggle. So yes, Pete, we'll work out whatever may come."

"I don't have much, darling, but I give you my all." He kissed my nose, looking happier. "So we're a team?"

"A team?" I smiled into his clear, gorgeous eyes and stepped back. We had been stopping near the sculpture of Make Way For Ducklings, with thin snow all around. "Not right now, darling, 'cause right now we're going to be enemies." I scooped up some snow and threw it at him. "There! Take life seriously, husband!"

"Not fair!" he protested, dodging my missile. But he bent down and scooped up some snow, ready to retaliate. "I only have one good arm!"

So we arrived home laughing after the snow fight, both of us very wet and very cold. Fine reasons to share a nice hot shower, right?

Make Way For Ducklings

Epilogue

In Australia, Darling

In Sydney, ten years later

"Aaarck!" the baby cries.

I nudge sleepily at Pete, "It's your turn, darling."

"Funny," he mumbles. "It feels like your turn, wifey."

"Honestly, it's yours."

"How do I know you aren't taking advantage of my forgetfulness?"

"Well you can't. Just take my word for it."

"Aaarck!" the baby calls imperiously.

"She needs cleaning," I tickle him. "I can tell by the way she calls".

"Ecstatic," he grumbles as he disentangles our limbs, "How fortunate for me..." Walking to the baby's room he throws a dangerous smile over his shoulder, "Just wait for my compensation."

Since my graduation, we have become foster carers for displaced babies. These are transient babies. They come and go, arriving from abusive homes—often in the middle of the night—to go to hopefully loving ones. We are their refuge until the government finds them permanent new homes, which can take from a few days to several weeks.

We used to travel the world during uni holidays. Once we volunteered in a disaster relief program, where Aussies are famous for being very helpful. Next, purely for fun, we became volunteer-mentors with Children International Summer Vacation, which is great for character building and world peace. Another time, we played tourists just because, climbing the Alps with Pete's Dutch friend Ietje.

Seeing my enthusiasm, Pete wanted to postpone kids until I hit 30.

"I don't want you to feel that your wings have been clipped early 'cause we can't travel easily with very young kids. But since you've finished your studies, how about we care for others' babies before having our own? That way we can help others, and still have a few months every year just for each other—the two of us travelling and doing fun stuff."

"You're so good, Pete. You don't just dream and talk." I remembered him saying that to glorify God means to have a good relationship with all of His creations. "You actively takes actions whenever possible, doing something *real* for the less fortunate."

"We're actually on the same page, honey. You sacrifice your creature comforts and you don't get frustrated with me. You're the one who has to *remind* me of a hundred details every day."

"Rightio... you're the boss, Pete. And I'm the manager of the boss."

Pete often hugs me out of the blue and says, "Thank you for putting up with me. I know it can't be easy for you. I'm very lucky." But he is worth it. Although forgetful, my playful and quick-witted husband likes to make me laugh. Our marriage has given me a wonderful home and peace of mind, along with sizzling romance and immense physical bliss. Without real issues between the two of us, we can focus on work and on helping others. In our book, marriage means freedom to soar as free as a bird.

I listen to Pete cooing to Tessa now and she replies with adorable gurgling sounds. She is actually the last transient baby we will care. The good news is... in several months we will have our very own baby!

How exciting. Pete is thrilled. Often we can't stop smiling...

dreaming...

The phone rings.

"Sydney, where are you and Pete?" Sinead, who now has a degree in Early Childhood Education under her belt, asks anxiously.

She returned to Aussieland and married Jack a few years back. They had that dream wedding at Lisgar Gardens—with me as the bridesmaid. Now she works as a manager of a childcare centre in Gosford, while Jack still stays at the same call centre but as a manager.

Once Pete and I visited the old call centre before 1300500 moved away. Some friends of the original lot had slimmed down. Some were lost to cancer. Some gave birth. Some married. Some changed partners. Some changed gender.

Jack, Pete and Kevin regularly meet for "male bonding"—whatever that is. They go fishing and watching games. Handsome Kevin, who still parties hard and changes girlfriends at whim, recently received a promotion to head a research centre in medical physics. Now, the "boys" actually meet more often. But with work, babies and what-nots, it has been quite a few months since Pete and I last caught up with Sinead.

"You and Pete are supposed to be here for dinner," Sinead whines. "The roast is ready."

"Really?" I yawn, like parents of brand-new babies very often yawn. Pete and I have planned to remain lazy this evening. "I didn't know that."

"But I phoned and talked with Pete to invite you guys and he said 'Sure'." She imitates Pete's accent. "I said to come early, and he said 'Sure'."

"Sinead... You know Pete's short-term memory. Looks like it slipped off his mind completely."

My husband has been giving me proper singing lessons for years and years now. He has also given me piano lessons. He keeps encouraging me, saying my progress isn't hopeless. Well, so far I can hit the keys a bit to accompany him on short violin pieces. Of course, he plays breathtaking, soulful violin while my piano attempt is still... Well, let's just say Pete's sound-proof music room prevents me from offending our neighbours' ears. And... well, this afternoon we got a bit carried away in there.

Speaking of music, twice now the neurosurgeons at a prominent private hospital in Sydney have put him under the knife. They opened the back of his neck. They said fixing the nerves in his spinal cord would alleviate the severe pain and return the function of his right arm. Yet not much changed after two long and very painful spinal surgeries. That's right, the first one "failed", so they did it again. "Failed" again, unfortunately. I knew they had tried, but I couldn't help feeling angry with them for inflicting these elaborate tortures on Pete. Now he can use his arm, but with constant lingering pain.

With his arm's condition and the permanent short-term memory loss, Pete can only teach. He has been giving private music tuition for kids interested in the classics.

"Sorry Sinead," I say now. "Is it still on? Mind if we arrive an hour from now?"

That is how we go to dinner in Gosford. Baby in the capsule in tow, because we don't have the time to arrange for a baby sitter.

"So, how's life exactly," Sinead asks me during dinner, "with a man who has a short-term memory?"

Pete and I shoot each other a look. The gleam in his eyes says he remembers our afternoon in his sound-proof music room, and my cheeks burn. He winks.

"Apart from the fact that if it rained every day of the week, he'd lose seven umbrellas?" I answered Sinead. "The plus side is that he's still fascinated anew in you even after ten years of marriage. Just like in 50 First Dates."

And she laughs and laughs when I throw in the woes:

"Pete rang me twice to wish me a happy birthday," Craig told me.

"Pete sent me gift vouchers twice for my birthday," Lance said.

"Pete phoned me twice to wish me a happy Mother's Day," Mum said.

"Pete called me twice to talk about the game's score," Kevin said.

"Pete brought Bronson to me twice regarding his eyes," the vet said.

"Pete thanked me twice for minding the baby while you went surfing," Kate said.

"Darling," I said, "these stack of seasons greeting cards, you were meant to drop them in the mail box four months ago. How come they're still in the glove box?"

Also, "Pete, you need to stop buying printer's ink. We have too many spare cartridges already."

Or, "Pete, aren't we supposed to volunteer in Africa this summer? How come the confirmation says you've booked it for Nepal? It'll be freezing cold in the northern hemisphere, darling."

And, "Pete, where are you?"

"In Australia, darling."

"Seriously?"

"Prowling the car parks in Chatswood. I can't remember where I parked the Harley. Didn't I call you, honey? Thought I did. Sorry. Now I've looked on every level. Can't find it. I kinda thought I parked in Chatswood Chase but it's not there. I've just finished checking Westfield's car park. Not here either. I've been searching for over two hours now. But it's still somewhere in the southern hemisphere!"

And recently, "Hello," greeted a bunch of Pete's musician friends—members of a visiting international symphony—when I answered the doorbell one Friday evening. And they came in and kissed my cheek and handed me lots of flowers and chocolates. "Thanks for inviting us over for dinner."

Whaat? Bewildered, I whirled around. My gorgeous hubby came out from the baby's room, an eight-month-old boy on his hip. He looked surprised, then remorse and bashful.

"I'm sorry honey. I must have completely forgotten to tell you that I'd invited friends over for dinner. Please, could you mind Roger?" A most charming, apologetic smile lifted the corner of his beautiful lips. "I'll whip up something quickly."

I looked at the guests apologetically, but despite this

embarrassing blunder they had a hearty good laugh. Gathering in Pete's huge, comfortable kitchen, we chatted merrily as he delivered his magic. Of course, when Pete cooks, you don't allow him to leave the kitchen or he will easily get sidetracked and you end up with a burnt dinner.

Pete usually forgets things after sleep and after a change of room or location. I have come to suspect that when an item has been deleted from Pete's memory, it is gone. Brain exercise or no, there is no way he can retrieve it. If he has any knowledge about the deleted item, it is because others *tell* him later, and not because they are successful in *reminding* him. It is a second-chance knowledge, yet fresh and new to Pete.

What a relief mobile phones have been invented. Pete sets many alarms in his to remind him of his duties and appointments. And to take many pictures for the moments he wants to remember. Like the fiery autumn leaves of our romantic getaway, Dorrigo, or fallen rose petals covering our backyard, or the beautiful little fish he caught before kissing it and throwing it back to the ocean.

Pete remembers the names of all his teachers since kindergarten and everyone at NEC. He remembers everything he played as a child prodigy of eleven years old in a San Francisco concert. But he has difficulty remembering what his students were up to last week. So yeah, lately he has one phone with massive memory so he can record their progress easily.

Trouble is, often he forgets to take the phone with him and has to call home from a public phone, "Darling, I'm in the shops. What is it again that I have to buy?"

"Mmm, let me think... A diamond?"

The End

Ia Uaro

Ia was born in the beautiful and remote, world's widest tea plantation by Mount Kerinci in Sumatra where her dad was the plantation's accountant, her mum a teacher. Her dad died when Ia was 13, and Ia moved across the ocean. She proceeded to become the busiest teen ever: playing in a drum band, tutoring maths, learning languages including English as the fifth language, and, at 17, a teen magazine published Ia's first fiction as a serial. Inundated by her fans' letters, the publisher printed it as a book, which was subsequently bought by the Indonesian Department of Education for high-school libraries.

Ia used the proceeds to help fund her university studies, during which time she was active in aero-modelling, martial arts, mountaineering, speleology... and studied petroleum seismology among her music-playing friends. After her graduation Ia worked with French, Norwegian and American geophysical companies, besides being a volunteer translator.

In Sydney since 1995, Ia is a mum who does several kinds of volunteer work for the community, assesses manuscripts, and writes real-life socio-fiction. Her husband, who suffers permanent partial brain damage, says Ia now sleep-talks in English.

Part of SYDNEY'S SONG's proceeds will be donated to the Brain Foundation.

Ia's website: http://sydneyssong.net
Twitter: @sydneyssong
Blog: Chapters of Life http://sydneyssong.net/blog
Guestbook: http://sydneyssong.net/gbook
Facebook: www.facebook.com./SydneysSong.IaUaro